Jane Fallon is the multi-awardwinning television producer behind shows such as *This Life*, *Teachers* and *20 Things to Do before You're 30*. This is her first novel.

Getting Rid of Matthew

JANE FALLON

PENGUIN BOOKS

PENGUIN BOOKS

Published by the Penguin Group
Penguin Books Ltd, 80 Strand, London WC2R ORL, England
Penguin Group (USA), Inc., 375 Hudson Street, New York, New York 10014, USA
Penguin Group (Canada), 90 Eglinton Avenue East, Suite 700, Toronto, Ontario, Canada
M4P 2Y3 (a division of Pearson Penguin Canada Inc.)
Penguin Ireland, 25 St Stephen's Green, Dublin 2, Ireland
(a division of Penguin Books Ltd)
Penguin Group (Australia), 250 Camberwell Road, Camberwell,
Victoria 3124, Australia (a division of Pearson Australia Group Pty Ltd)
Penguin Books India Pvt Ltd, 11 Community Centre,
Panchsheel Park, New Delhi – 110 017, India
Penguin Group (NZ), 67 Apollo Drive, Mairangi Bay, Auckland 1310, New Zealand
(a division of Pearson New Zealand Ltd)
Penguin Books (South Africa) (Pty) Ltd, 24 Sturdee Avenue,
Rosebank, Johannesburg 2196, South Africa

Penguin Books Ltd, Registered Offices: 80 Strand, London WC2R ORL, England

www.penguin.com

First published by Penguin Books 2007

9

Copyright © Jane Fallon, 2007
All rights reserved

The moral right of the author has been asserted

Set in 12.5/14.75pt Monotype Garamond
by Palimpsest Book Production Limited, Grangemouth, Stirlingshire
Printed in England by Clays Ltd, St Ives plc

ISBN-13: 978-0-141-02529-2

I

The bedroom was dark, lit only by a sliver of brightness from the wall light in the basement well outside edging its way round the sides of the blind. Helen could just make out the clock as it clicked over to eight fifteen. She knew she should wake Matthew, but she also knew that he would be in a foul temper because she had forgotten to set the alarm. And the longer she left it, the worse his mood would be. She had no choice. She poked a finger gently in his ribs, and then once more when he didn't respond, and he turned over irritably and picked up his watch from the low table beside the bed.

'Fuck, I'm late.'

Helen watched sleepily as he jolted out from under the duvet, smoothing down his charcoal-grey hair at the sides, and started to pull on his clothes – his work uniform of a dark, tasteful, beautifully fitted bespoke suit, well-cut shirt and soft black calf-leather shoes – not bothering to take a shower. He bent down to kiss her brusquely good-bye and pulled the bedroom door shut behind him. She lay back on the pillow, which smelt faintly of the Armani Black Code she had given him on their anniversary, and stared at the crack in the ceiling. It was definitely getting bigger, and she wondered if she should speak to her upstairs neighbours about it. Not that she knew them. She'd seen them only three or four times in the two years she'd lived here. A couple in their thirties: he was a bit stringy-looking, pale, as if he never went outside; she wore a fleece and had a mousy bob. They had an unexpectedly rampaging sex life though, which Helen could hear through the ceiling about five nights a week and sometimes in the afternoons. It was all very shouty and theatrical. Lots of 'Oh, baby's and 'Yes, yes'es and banging on the headboard. Once, they had been at it at the same time as Matthew and Helen, and it had become a bit of a competition, a sort of groan-off. Helen had always had a competitive streak.

Now she heard the click of the front door closing and Matthew's heavy footsteps going up the stairs to the street and thought about getting up. Deciding against it, she pulled the covers over her head and settled back down, then stuck one arm out into the cold room, fumbled for the remote and flicked on the TV. After all, what was the point of getting up – it was only a couple of hours before she'd be going back to bed again anyway. Because Matthew wasn't heading off for work. It wasn't eight fifteen in the morning, it was eight fifteen in the evening, and he was heading home to dinner in his own house. With his wife. Oh, and his two beautiful children. Because Matthew was married, and not to Helen – to a woman called Sophie. And Helen had spent every Monday night like this for the past four years. And most Wednesday and Thursday evenings, too.

And every Monday and every Wednesday and every Thursday when Matthew went home at eight o'clock, Helen was left alone to choose one of two exciting options: watch TV in bed on her own or get up and watch TV in the living room on her own.

Now, she lay under the dark of the duvet and listened as another scene of marital discord played out on *EastEnders*. Somebody's husband accusing his wife of playing around. Lots of shouting, everything out in the open; they'd either stay together or they wouldn't. That was the way it worked in soaps, but Helen knew the reality was far more complicated. The reality would make for terrible TV because nothing ever really got resolved. The reality was a man coming over three nights a week for a couple of hours and then going home to his wife as if nothing had happened. Over and over again. For years on end.

Helen had never expected to be someone's mistress. She had wanted three things in life: a highly paid job in public relations, a flat of her own and a man, also belonging to her exclusively. Somehow she'd ended up as a personal assistant, which was a secretary in anyone else's vocabulary. She didn't earn enough to buy, so she rented a one-bedroom flat off Camden High Street with a small, dark basement courtyard out the back, a crack in the bedroom ceiling and a large damp patch on the bathroom wall. And as for the man – well, she believed in true love and commitment and till death do us part, it had just never happened to her.

She had grown up watching her parents' dogged devotion to one another, their 'us against the world' united front which often excluded even her, their only child, and she'd been trying to locate that perfect partner for herself ever since, to find her own gang of two. She'd just never imagined she would find it with someone who was already another woman's husband.

Somewhere, way back in her previous life, Helen had been engaged to another man, the most recent in a series of long-term boyfriends. Looking back now, she couldn't remember exactly what she'd seen in Simon. Well, she could, because he was young and good-looking and he had a reasonable job and just the right amount of ambition, but she now found it impossible to fathom why she had stayed with him for five years, except that that was how she was. The one legacy of her parents she couldn't shake off was the idea that relationships were for life. Once she decided that a relationship was worth having, she hung in there determinedly in spite of any warning signs trying to tell her otherwise. So, she ignored the fact that she was the one making all the future plans and she tried not to notice how his eyes glazed over when she talked about saving up for a deposit on a flat. She had invested years in this man, it had to pay off, there was no way she was going to admit defeat. She had all her eggs in one basket and she had no intention of moving them. That is, until Simon threw them out and jumped up and down on them one evening. They'd been cooking dinner together, their nightly ritual, which, Helen thought, was a sure indicator that their relationship was mature and serious.

'I'm being transferred,' Simon had muttered into a colander full of the potatoes he was peeling.

Helen had flung her arms round him. 'You got the promotion? Regional manager, wow. So we're moving to Manchester?'

He'd kept his head down, seemingly engrossed in digging out a particularly stubborn eye. 'Erm . . . not exactly, no.'

4

'Where then?' He was making her nervous, standing there stiffly while she attempted to hug him. He'd put down the potato peeler and turned to look at her, taking a deep breath like a ham actor about to have his big soap-opera moment.

'*I'm* moving to Manchester. On my own.'

He'd gone on to say that of course it wasn't Helen's fault. It was all him, he was afraid of the commitment. He felt too young, he said, to be settling down with one woman. It was all a matter of timing – if he'd met Helen a few years later when he felt ready for such a big step . . .

'I love you so much, it's just me, I'm such a fuck-up. I know I'll regret this but it's something I have to do,' he'd whined, wallowing in his role. He'd insisted there was no one else involved, and Helen had believed him – had, in fact, felt sorry for him, he seemed so pained by the choice he was having to make.

Two months later the news had filtered back to her that he was getting married to another woman.

Helen had been thirty-five. Bruised and battered by the failure of the relationship more than the loss of Simon himself, she had taken the separation hard. She'd made a promise to herself that she would have some fun, take opportunities when they arose without stopping endlessly to analyse their potential. And, right on cue, Matthew had come along – her boss, of course, and twenty years older than she was – but why avoid a perfectly good cliché when it's staring you in the face? He was handsome in the way that men in their fifties are allowed to be considered handsome despite (or maybe even because of) the grey hair and the paunch. Tall and confident, he gave off the impression that he revelled in his alpha status. His hair was thinning but he still wore it collar length and swept back, disguising the round hairless spot fairly successfully. When the time came for him to shave it all off and just be bald and proud, he would get away with that as he seemed to get away with everything, because he had a way of striding around the world as if he owned it, that absolute self-belief that public schoolboys have, a way of challenging anyone to dispute their place high up in the social order. He had the ability to make anyone feel as if they were the centre of his world at any given moment. Physically, his most striking assets – his only striking asset – were his pale icy-blue eyes, which stood out in a face that was fairly ordinary, but he carried himself as if he were the most attractive man in the room and somehow that seemed to make it so. His success at work seemed to work as an aphrodisiac, too, on a certain type of woman of which Helen was a prime example. Mainly though, he was good company – funny, a storyteller, a good listener. He was loyal. Unless you were his wife, of course.

Helen had started to work at Global PR at the age of thirty-four, a bit of a late starter, having spent the best part of her twenties travelling and partying, and trying to ignore the irritating voice in her head telling her to get on the career ladder before it was too late. She'd spent the time since she'd got back from her world trip drifting from job to job: accountant's assistant, shop manager, theatre administrator. Periodically, she'd applied for the post of account manager at one of the bigger, showier public relations companies, but she'd always got knocked back. Finally, she'd decided that a foot on the bottom rung was better than no foothold at all and she'd accepted a job as assistant to Matthew Shallcross, Managing Director of Global PR, a middling-sized but flourishing company.

Global was a slightly overblown name for a company whose clients were exclusively British, but they had cornered the market in a certain type of up-and-coming tabloid favourite. It wasn't large enough to attract the rich and famous but, over the years, it had become adept at forming relationships with those at the beginning of their fifteen minutes and blasting them into the papers with cleverly thought up stunts. It was easy when you had clients who would do anything if it would put them in the nationals. Every now and again one of these wannabes would fuck up – drink-driving, getting someone who wasn't their wife pregnant, going into rehab – and the Global account managers would be out fighting fires and raking in the money. These occasional high-profile blips, if handled correctly, guaranteed an interest in the client, which could be very lucrative. In truth, it was a little tacky, encouraging young and not very bright people to lay their whole lives out for public examination, but Helen considered it the sharp end of PR, and she loved it. And, after a while, when she overcame the irritation of correcting her friends every time they called her a secretary . . .

–'I'm his personal assistant.'

–'But, what do you do?'

–'I look after him . . . make his appointments, organize meetings.'

–'Filing?'

–'A bit'

–'Typing?'

–'So?'

–'That's exactly what I do – typing, filing, fixing meetings. You're a secretary, get over it.'

... she'd started to get off on the vicarious power that being the boss's assistant afforded her. She was the one who could say yes or no to meetings or telephone calls and, after a while, to requests for press statements. Then, once he started to trust her, Matthew had her read and later write all the releases that were sent out to the papers for several of his less high-profile clients. He'd encouraged her ambitions to have clients of her own and, the more he encouraged, the more those ambitions grew.

Helen believed that several of the other girls in the office envied her for her proximity to the man generally considered the most powerful of the company directors, but she'd kept focused on her work until a fateful lunch had changed everything. If you'd have asked her at the time what she thought about women who had affairs with married men, she would have said they were sad, desperate, unfeeling betrayers of other women. Told you they were top of her list of offenders. People to be looked down on and reviled ...

Helen had considered whether Matthew was attractive during the time she'd been working for him, of course she had, and she'd thought that, yes, he was, in an older man sort of a way, but that was it. So, when he'd reached across the table at Quo Vadis and taken hold of her hand, she'd surprised herself by not pulling away.

'I've been wanting to do this for ages,' he'd said and Helen had felt her heart leap up to the back of her throat. She had no idea how to respond, so she'd just sat there and let him take charge.

Matthew had carried on, 'The thing is, I think you're beautiful. And I've been trying not to acknowledge that that's what I think for months.'

Helen had blushed. Not prettily like the delicate heroine of a romantic novel but a deep, slightly clammy, crimson.

'You know I'm married, of course.'

She'd managed to grunt a 'yes'.

'We have young children. If it wasn't for them . . . I'm not going to give you that line – you know, that my wife no longer understands me but . . . it is true we've drifted apart. We share the care of the kids; that's pretty much it.' He'd laughed. 'Can you see where this is going yet?'

Helen was still incapable of speech. Her free hand fiddled with the stem of her glass.

'No pressure. I don't want you to think that if you say you're not interested, then I'll make life hard for you at work or anything like that. Just think about it and, if you decide that, maybe, we could take things a bit further, then you know where I am. That's all I wanted to say.'

And, in that moment, she'd realized that she wanted to sleep with him. It was something about his self-assurance, something about the way his fingers stroked the back of her hand while he talked to her, the way his eyes never left her face while she'd stammered and begun to sweat.

She'd gone back to the office in a haze and could barely look at him for the rest of the afternoon.

That night she'd bored her best friend, Rachel, stupid in the pub.

'Should I?'

'No,' said Rachel.

'Maybe . . .'

'No,' said Rachel.

'What if . . .'

'Are you even listening to me?' Rachel eventually snapped. 'He's married. Don't do it. Don't become one of those women we hate.'

'Women we hate' were a big part of the bond between Rachel and Helen. They had started a mental list soon after they'd met, backpacking in India, and when they got back to London and Helen was staying in Rachel's West Brompton flat while she looked for her own place, they had started to write it down. They kept a copy each and, regularly, when they were drunk and at each other's flats, they would check them through and update each other with the newest entries. 'Women who steal other women's husbands' had been there from the beginning but, in Helen's mind, her case was different. For a start, she had never encouraged Matthew; he had done all the pursuing.

'You're right. But . . . I think he really likes me.'

'Oh, for fuck's sake. Of course he likes you, you're twenty years younger than him and about to fall into his bed just because he's asked you to. Plus, you do his typing and make him cups of tea. You're a middle-aged man's fantasy. What's not to like?'

'I knew I shouldn't have told you about it,' said Helen sulkily. 'I knew you wouldn't understand.'

The next morning she'd waited till Matthew was alone in his office and gone in, shutting the door behind her.

'OK,' she'd said.

'OK what?' He'd looked up from his paperwork and smiled at her. She'd blushed.

'If you want to . . . you know . . . then it's OK, we can . . . you know . . . if you like. I'd like to.'

Matthew had laughed. 'Are you talking in code?'

He'd pretended to look round the office. 'Are we being bugged?'

Helen was scarlet. 'You know what I mean.'

'I do. And I'm very happy. Are you free on Wednesday evening?'

Helen had gulped so hard it made a noise.

'Yes.'

Next thing she knew, he was in her bed and all her commonsense and ambition and everything she recognized about herself had gone out of the window. And Helen had kept saying to herself and Helen's friends had kept saying to her, 'Get out now. This can't have a happy ending', and she'd ignored everyone because, inevitably, after a few weeks, she'd decided that she loved him and he had finally confessed that he loved her, too. And, of course, after a few months, Matthew had told her he wanted to leave his wife, Sophie, when the time was right. And, of course, that had been four years ago and he'd never left her for even a weekend, as far as Helen could remember.

They had been fantastic, though, those first few months with Matthew. He was so much older than any man she'd been with before, it was like a whole different world. He knew how to make her feel special. Despite the fact that they rarely went out anywhere for fear of being seen together, he'd introduced her to all kinds of new experiences – food and music and wines that had simply never been on her radar before. And being newly in love and eager to please, she had pretended to love all sorts of things which, later, once the relationship had settled down, she was able to admit to herself she hated. Like Miles Davis and foie gras and sickly sweet Château d'Yquem.

On their fourth 'date' he'd brought over a copy of Baudelaire's *The Flowers of Evil* and presented it to her, telling her that she would find it unlike anything she'd ever read before. Helen, who had a passable 2:2 in French Literature, had missed her moment to tell him this and, not wanting him to think his gift was unwelcome, had gushed her thanks. No one had ever bought her a book of poems before. Later, lying in bed in a postcoital flush, he'd asked her for her life history.

'Start from the beginning,' he'd said, seeming genuinely interested in the tiny details of her past. When she'd reached the part about leaving home and moving to London, she'd skipped forward rapidly through her university days, but he'd stopped her mid flow.

'What did you study?'

Helen could feel herself colouring up. 'Er . . . French,' she mumbled.

Matthew propped himself up on his elbows and looked down at her. 'French?'

'Mmm.'

He was starting to smile. 'Literature?'

'Kind of.'

'Kind of?'

'I mean, yes. Literature.' She was blushing furiously now. Why hadn't she just said, when he'd given her the book?

'So . . . Baudelaire . . . ?'

'My dissertation.'

Matthew laughed noisily. 'Why didn't you say?'

'Because I didn't want to spoil your present.'

He'd kissed her forehead. 'Well, in that case, you can explain them to me, because I'm clueless. I just liked the look of the cover.'

She knew he was patronizing her and she didn't know why she didn't mind. It was just that no one had ever been this *interested* in her before. It took the pressure off, being the one who was there to be pleased rather than the one who always had to do the pleasing. It was so liberating not always to have to be the adult.

Matthew had lived, too. He'd been through stuff – not just in a 'got married and had kids' kind of way – but he'd been alive for twenty years longer than she had. He'd been through the sixties and experienced it first-hand. She didn't know why this impressed her – she couldn't have been less interested in the endless bangings on of the previous generation about the sixties – but somehow it set him apart, made him interesting by proxy, by virtue of just having been alive.

In the early days of their relationship Helen had made sure she wore her best underwear on Matthew days, rushing home from the office where they both worked to give herself ten minutes to shower and change ready to be undressed again. Their evenings were all about sex, their excitement only heightened by their restricted access to one another and the extended foreplay of a day spent pretending to be no more than colleagues. Gradually, sleep crept in, signalling to Helen a more mature phase in the relationship – they were bonding on a deeper level, it seemed to her, able to relax in each other's company. She stopped worrying whether she was in Rigby and Peller or M&S, she no longer felt the need to retouch her make-up every time his back was turned. She looked back fondly on this time as the nirvana period, that perfect stage when physical desire was joined by companionship and profound respect. It didn't last long. These days, sleep often won out entirely, exhausted as Matthew always was by his high-powered working day. And, more and more, Helen was finding that she didn't really mind. There was something coupley about it, something more real than the frantic nature of the early days. And if it was less exciting, then so what? Excitement couldn't last for ever.

After a few months, Matthew had felt uncomfortable asking Helen to take dictation or pick up his dry cleaning, so he'd requested she be found a new boss. This, of course, was interpreted by Human Resources as meaning that she was difficult to get on with, or incompetent or both, and so the promotion which had been looming drifted away and Helen missed her moment. That had been three and a half years ago. Of course, she could have left and gone to work somewhere else where she might have been more appreciated, but she'd somehow never got around to it, and she was now officially 'secretary material,' with little reason for anyone to look at her for anything more exciting. Besides which, if she left, she'd miss those stolen moments throughout the day with Matthew and, deep down, she knew that if she wasn't right there under his nose, someone else would probably catch his eye.

So, now Helen took dictation and arranged meetings and drew up proposals for Laura, a high-flying thirty-nine-year-old director of the company, who'd also started off as a personal assistant but had steadily climbed the ladder over the years. Laura was good at her job, she was a considerate boss, she encouraged and supported Helen, always gave her credit where it was due (which was often, because Helen was clever, although she seemed to have forgotten this, and she had a lot of good ideas, for which Laura was very grateful), and indulged her occasional mood swings. She would never for a moment consider asking Helen to fetch her dry cleaning. Helen hated her.

When she and Matthew had first got together, Helen had suppressed her guilt by pushing all thoughts of his wife from her mind – this was a short-term thing to help her get over being fucked about by Simon, an exercise in building self-esteem. It was wrong, but it would be short-lived and no one would be any the wiser. After a while, when she'd realized that things had got a little more complicated than that, the guilt had begun to set in. Tiny stabs at first, and then huge waves that had made it hard for her to look at her reflection in the mirror in the mornings. How would she feel if that were her blithely saying goodbye to her husband as he went off to work, with no idea about the double life he was leading? It was an irrefutable truth that if no woman ever went with a married man, then no wife would ever have to endure the heartbreak of finding out that her life as she understood it was a sham. As long as one woman was prepared to do it, then all women were in danger. And, currently, she was that one woman.

So she knew she should call time on her and Matthew's relationship now, before any real harm was done, but suddenly it didn't seem so straightforward. She had feelings for him. She would miss him. 'Why should I be the one to give him up,' she caught herself thinking one day, 'when it's me he's in love with?' She began to feel little stings of jealousy whenever Matthew mentioned his wife's name. And, almost overnight, she began to want to fight to keep her man and, in order to do that, she had to demonize Sophie and make her the enemy. You couldn't fight a woman you felt sorry for. You'd lose.

2

Sophie Shallcross was sitting in her large raised-ground-floor kitchen-diner in her beautiful five-bedroom, two-reception semi-detached townhouse in an up-and-coming street in Kentish Town, watching Matthew tuck into his pasta putanesca and listening indulgently to the details of his stressful day, including the game of squash with colleague Alan which he had apparently just won. She loved hearing the minutiae of his working life, the characters and gossip and the interoffice dramas that she herself never had time for, cramming, as she did, a full day's work into the hours between nine and three, so that she could get home in time for the children's noisy and demanding return from school. She rested her chin in her hand, elbow on the table, and laughed when he told her how Alan had skidded and banged into the wall, then thrown his racquet across the court as if it were to blame. After the kids went to bed – nine-thirty, no later, no exceptions except for birthdays and Christmas and the odd trip to the theatre – they would curl up on the sofa and have a glass of wine, her favourite time of the day.

Matthew was able to keep his life with Sophie and the children – Suzanne, twelve, and ten-year-old Claudia – separated in his head from his affair with Helen. He felt no guilt. Indeed, when he was at home, he barely thought about Helen at all, which he thought made him a good husband and father. In fact, Matthew was pretty incapable of ever thinking about two things at once, as most men are, so he tended to go with whatever he was presented with – if Sophie was in front of him, he'd think about Sophie; if Helen was in front of him, he'd think about Helen; if it was an egg sandwich . . . well, you get the picture. Helen could distinctly remember the day when she'd told him she was pregnant just as she handed him a plate of stir-fried chicken. It was as though his brain was split down the middle; she could see him struggling to focus – Ooh, noodles/my life's ruined – like a dog with schizophrenia. She'd had an abortion, of course. She was the mistress.

'Why are you always home so late?' Suzanne now asked inconveniently. 'You're never here in time to help Mum cook dinner, and she's been at work all day, too.'

Suzanne had been learning about the suffragettes in Year 8 history, and she took her studies very seriously.

'Don't talk shit,' said blissfully unemancipated Claudia – who by the way had also just learned about swearing in the playground of Kentish Town Juniors and liked to practice at every opportunity. 'Mummies do the cooking.'

'Don't say "shit", Claudia,' Matthew jumped in.

Sophie picked up her cue. 'You know I get home at three-thirty and Dad's never here till after eight, he works much longer hours than me.'

'That's my point, exactly,' triumphed Suzanne.

This was a pretty representative dinner-table conversation at the Shallcross household. Like most families, they could play their roles on autopilot.

Although Sophie had assumed the traditional role of

care-giver to her family, she was anything but an average housewife. She'd got a first from Durham, for a start. In maths. She had a career in the city doing something un-explainable and earning a small fortune – more than Matthew, as it happened – and was so indispensable that she was able to arrange her hours to suit herself. If truth be told, it was because she wanted to, not because she felt she had to. However hard she'd worked or however high she'd gone, Sophie had always put family life first. Never mind that she got up at six, dressed in a suit, over-saw Suzanne and Claudia's preparations for school, made their packed lunches, walked them to the end of the road, got on the tube, rarely took a proper lunch break, got back on the tube, helped the girls with their homework, made dinner from scratch (no ready meals in this house-hold), loaded the dishwasher, sorted out everyone's clothes for the next day and tried to stay awake long enough to offer Matthew some adult chat and a sympa-thetic ear for his problems at the office. There'd been little or no time for anything else for the past twelve years – no exercise classes or drinks with the girls. And it was true that she had been passed over for promotion recently because she was never in the office when the West Coast kicked in. But she had an absolute faith in the love and stability of her family and, for Sophie, that was worth a few sacrifices. Oh dear.

This evening panned out just like any other evening. It was two weeks to Christmas, and Matthew and Sophie had to decide what to get the girls while avoiding all the things they knew they wanted the most – make-up, high-heeled shoes, dogs, mini-skirts. Then there was the question of who was arriving when and who was sleeping where. Christmas at the Shallcross house was always a full-blown family affair with Matthew's mother and sisters and the sisters' husbands and children.

'Gerbil for Claudia?' Sophie asked, knowing what the answer would be.

'No.'

'Hamster? Guinea pig? Rat?'

'No, no and no. No pets, we agreed.'

'OK. I'll think of something else. Oh, and we need to get the box of decorations down.'

'I'll do it at the weekend.'

'And a tree.'

'Weekend.'

'And order the turkey.'

At about ten-thirty and a bottle of Sancerre down, Matthew felt an uncharacteristic twinge of sentiment about Helen and what, through the hue of his third glass, seemed to him to be the uncomplicated nature of his other life with her, uncluttered by family and duty. He sneaked off to the study – doubling up as a children's bedroom for the Christmas period – and dialled her number. Helen, who was tucked up in bed asleep, feigned indifference, although a late-evening phone call was a real event. Matthew found himself promising to come over on Tuesday in lieu of Thursday, which was the day of Claudia's nativity play. Helen tried to give the impression that she might not be free but couldn't keep it up. It was all over in less than three minutes and everybody was happy.

In the tastefully deep-red living room with original

coving and architraves at 155 Bartholomew Road, Sophie yawned and stretched and started to tidy away the lists she had made. She slipped her arms round Matthew's broad back and kissed the base of his neck, her favourite place, where the grey wispy hairs curled flat against it like a baby's.

'Amanda and Edwin have invited us over for a pre-Christmas drink on Tuesday. Can you bear it?' Amanda was the elder and slightly more annoying of Matthew's two younger sisters.

'If I must.' Matthew turned round and kissed her back.

'I've said we'll be there at seven. Can you get away early?'

'No problem,' he said, entirely forgetting the promise he'd made to Helen only forty minutes ago. 'I'll come home first and pick you up.'

3

Lying in bed now, Helen replayed the phone conversation in her mind, looking for hidden clues. There had been only a handful of occasions over the years when Matthew had agreed to see her outside the appointed times. She wondered what had prompted it. Maybe a row with Sophie, she thought hopefully. She tried to picture Matthew arriving back at the family home, briefcase in hand, fresh from a hard day's work (and a lot more besides), kissing his children hello, his wife edgy about the fact he was home so late, the dinner ruined, the recriminations culminating in a shouting match. But, although she'd never met her, Helen wasn't stupid – she knew that Sophie couldn't really be the unattractive, grey-haired, past-her-sell-by-date harridan she liked to imagine on lonely Monday, Wednesday and Thursday nights after Matthew had left to go home. Why would he have married her if so? More to the point, why would he still be married to her all these years later and rushing anxiously home so that Sophie wouldn't suspect that he hadn't in fact been working late at the office or playing squash with one of his colleagues? If he'd rather be with Helen, as he always said he would, then why wouldn't he just stay the night and fuck what Sophie thought. That was . . . unless . . .

Stop! Helen pulled herself back from drifting off along

a well-trodden but pointless thought process and dragged herself out of bed in an effort to think about something else. She pulled on a pair of baggy pyjama bottoms and a T-shirt, walked through to the living room and picked up the phone to call Rachel for the usual debrief. Helen could always rely on Rachel to help her get things into perspective – even if she was in the pub or on a date, Rachel would drop everything to indulge Helen's whinging. That's what friends were for. What Rachel didn't know, though, is that her friendship made Helen feel better in more ways than one. Rachel was more successful than Helen, more beautiful, better off, but – and it's a big but – she was single. She had no man of her own – not even a time share in one like Helen had, and that, Helen couldn't help but think – and it was a thought she wasn't proud of and would never dream of voicing out loud – put her lower down in the female pecking order. And every woman needs a friend she can feel superior to.

Their conversations usually went something like this:

'Do you think he still sleeps with her?'

'No, of course he doesn't.'

'How can you be so sure?'

'He hasn't found her attractive in years, hasn't he told you that loads of times?'

'Yeah, but do you think he means it? Why's he still with her then?'

Then Rachel would run through her repertoire of stock answers:

'Maybe she's threatened to kill herself if he ever leaves her. Or she's got a terminal illness and he figures he should just wait it out. Or she's loaded and he needs to find a way to get her money before he can go. Or she's psychotic and he's afraid of what she might do.'

They never reached any conclusions. And, of course, Rachel never said what she really thought, which was 'What is wrong with you? Obviously, he still loves her – what are you wasting your time for?', so Helen always came away from their chats having somehow convinced herself that Matthew really was trapped in a loveless marriage just waiting for the right moment to end it all and move in with her.

Helen had often fantasized about somehow letting Sophie know what exactly her husband did with his evenings. In her favourite fantasy, a distraught (and, frankly, ugly) Sophie threw Matthew out into the street without even a hope of a reconciliation, but Matthew, far from being upset, was relieved that he could finally live the life he'd wanted for the past four years. It tended to go on that he bought a big and beautiful home in the country and set Helen up as the boss of a small company making hand-turned pots (in her fantasies, Helen was always proficient in skills she had, in reality, never even tried). Conveniently, Matthew forgot all about his already existing offspring.

Helen had guessed, wrongly, it turned out, that Sophie was in her early fifties. She knew she worked and liked to think that, like herself, Sophie had a job rather than a career. Something homely, she imagined. Maybe volunteering in the Oxfam shop, sorting through other people's old pants for a living,

Sophie, as it happened, was forty-five. Dark-haired and

dark-eyed, she actually looked a lot like Helen but had committed the cardinal sin of being a few years older. It wouldn't be hard to imagine them as friends if it weren't for one small detail . . .

Over the years, Helen's real friends had begun to drift away one by one. They'd replaced the pub with quiet nights in and dinners for two, and vodka shots with bottles of Pinot Grigio. Once a year, maybe, Helen would throw a dinner party and invite four or six of her girlfriends (well, two or three of her girlfriends and their partners because, whether she liked it or not, they came in pairs now). She'd listen to the conversations about children and kitchen-appliance buying and try to pretend she was interested ('He can use the toilet on his own now. How amazing! Wearing pull-ups already? Wow!'), but usually she was quietly suffocating with boredom. She'd try to deflect the questions about Matthew and Sophie and whether or not it was time she cut him loose with good grace. Lately she'd begun to feel that her friends were starting to judge her, looking at their (mostly hideously unattractive) husbands and worrying that they might be thinking of getting a Helen on the side.

She rarely got invited back – a single woman, unlike a single man, was a bit of an embarrassment, even with friends. Invite that new couple you've met on holiday and the wife will be upset if he spends all evening chatting to an unattached woman. If she finds out that that woman is actually the mistress of someone else's husband, then suddenly the whole evening goes tits up. So, on the nights when Helen did go out these days, she went out with

Rachel and they drank and danced and bitched about men just as they had when they were in their twenties. Only they were both about to be forty and it was starting to look a little like desperation.

Now, Helen settled down with a glass of wine in one hand, looking forward to sharing her good news with Rachel. She hit the number three shortcut button on the cordless phone (number one: Matthew's mobile; number two: Mum and Dad; number three: Rachel; number four: Rachel's mobile; number five: Mum's mobile; number six: work. Jesus she was sad). Rachel's phone rang. And rang. Eventually, just as Helen was about to give up, Rachel answered. She sounded distracted.

'Hi.'

'Rach, it's me. Guess what . . .'

'Helen. Hi. It's . . erm . . . can I call you back tomorrow? It's not a very good time right now. Neil's here.'

OK. Neil was the man Rachel had met at a club a couple of weeks ago. Nice enough, worked in IT. Good-looking. Helen knew they'd seen each other a few times since, she'd heard most of the details. Dinner once. Few drinks in the pub. Sex on date three. He'd stayed over on date four. Rachel's usual pattern. In a week she'd be bored of him. In two he'd be history.

Since Helen had known Rachel, there'd been many Neils, or so she thought. While Helen held out hopelessly for Simon and then Matthew, Rachel's relationships rarely lasted more than a couple of weeks. In the last few months alone, there'd been Martin the fireman (too unreconstructed), Ian the bookshop owner (dull) and Nick the twenty-three-year-old hairdresser who had left her for a nineteen-year-old boy. There had been nothing to indicate that Neil would be any different.

She pressed Rachel further. 'He won't mind if you chat for a bit.'

'I can't. I'll call you tomorrow, OK?'

'But Matthew just called me. At half-ten at night. He's putting in a Tuesday. Tell Neil to go and put the kettle on or make a cocktail or something and you can help me decide what's happened to him at home to make him want to do that.'

'I told you, I can't. Look, we're having a really good time and I don't want to break the mood, OK? I'm not going to leave him twiddling his thumbs while I chat to you. If it was life or death, then maybe, but it's not. It can wait till the morning. Love you. Bye.'

Rachel clicked the phone down. Helen sat, handset in one hand, glass of wine in the other, confused. In their ten-year friendship, never once had Rachel not had time for her. Never once had a man taken precedence over indulging Helen in the traumas of her personal life. It could only mean one thing. Neil was special. Neil was going to be the man to rescue Rachel from the stigma of being single. Helen would no longer be able to pity her friend for her lack of success in relationships. Her one area of smug superiority was gone. Rachel was prettier, more successful, earned more than Helen did, and now she had a man of her own – her very own, because Neil, to Helen's knowledge, didn't have a wife and kids tucked away anywhere. Rachel had won.

It was the end of an era and Helen knew it.

She looked at the clock and decided to go to bed. After all, it was ten forty-five already, there was fuck-all on the TV and she had to be up for work in the morning.

When Helen and Matthew saw each other briefly at work the next day, she was feeling warm and indulgent towards him because he'd changed his plans in order to see her, while he felt loving towards her because he'd forgotten all about next week's clash of dates and she was being nice to him for, it seemed to him, no particular reason, which is always a vote-winner. They both went off for the weekend happy.

Helen managed to prise Rachel away from Neil for a bit of Saturday-afternoon shopping and, despite the fact that she had to listen to a blow-by-blow account of true love blossoming, they had a laugh and she managed to talk about herself and her own relationship just enough to make it worth while. Saturday night and Sunday she had to spend on her own, but she filled her time browsing the shops and the internet to find the perfect Christmas gift for the man who had everything, including a wife who might wonder where he got a new cashmere jumper from anyway. It was a skill finding something that he plausibly might have bought for himself but which you were fairly confident he wouldn't actually buy for himself between now and Christmas, if you get my drift. She'd settled on a Paul Smith briefcase.

On Monday Matthew was out at meetings all day, but so was Laura, so Helen had a good day of interspersing typing the odd document with reading magazines and listening to the radio. She considered calling Rachel for a gossip but decided against it.

Six thirty on the dot, her front doorbell rang, and there was Matthew as usual. Bottle of wine and a tub of ice cream in hand. They went through their usual routine – quick catch-up about the goings-on at work, drink then bed, half-hearted fumble then both gratefully drifting off to sleep.

At five to eight Matthew looked at his watch on the bedside table and started to get up.

'See you in the morning,' she said, switching off the alarm before it rang.

He leant down to kiss her and she circled his neck with her arms, holding him there.

'Maybe you can get away a bit early tomorrow night? I could cook you dinner. Or will you have to eat at home?'

A momentary look of puzzlement crossed Matthew's face and then, as he said . . . 'Tomorrow?' . . . there was a slowly dawning realization.

'. . . Did we say tomorrow?' he asked, clutching at straws. 'I can't tomorrow, something's come up.'

And then all hell broke loose.

'What do you mean, "Something's come up"?'

'Just . . . family stuff. You know.'

'You forgot about me, didn't you? You forgot you'd promised to see me and you made some fucking arrangement with your wife.'

'Calm down,' he said patronizingly.

'Calm down? You never think about me sat on my own here night after night.'

'Go out, then. I'm not stopping you.'

'I can't. I have no one to go out with any more. No

one wants to be friends with someone who's screwing a married man.'

'Oh, so that's my fault, is it? I have to lie constantly to be with you. Have you any idea how hard that is?'

'I'm not asking you to lie.'

'Yes, you are. Continually. You ask me to come over, you want to see me for lunch. Christ, I've lost count of the times you've tried to persuade me to tell Sophie I'm going on a conference so that I can take you away for a weekend.'

'You'd never do it though, would you?'

'Because I don't want to get caught. We both agreed . . .'

'Fuck what we agreed. I'm sick of being second best, of always having to be the one who gets let down . . .'

'I'm sorry about tomorrow. Really. But you've always known this was how it had to be.'

'Well, not any more,' Helen said defiantly. 'I mean it.'

'So, what, you think I should just tell my wife and children that I'm hardly ever home early because I'm with my girlfriend?'

'Why not?'

'Are you fucking mad?'

'No, I'm not fucking mad. I just don't see what would be so fucking awful about telling the truth to your perfect fucking wife after all these years.'

Silence.

There was a subject Helen and Matthew always avoided except when they were having a blazing row. The subject of 'Why won't you leave your wife for me?' Now it was out there and it couldn't be taken back.

'Leave Sophie out of this. This has fuck-all to do with her.'

'Why are you always defending her?'

'Because she's my wife, and none of this is her fault. And you knew I was married when we got into this.' Matthew put on his coat. 'I'm late. I have to go or she'll wonder where I've been.'

Helen couldn't back down this time. 'Then tell her, for god's sake. I've had enough, honestly. Just tell Sophie about me, or that's it. I mean it this time. It's over.'

'Fine.'

Matthew closed the front door behind him.

4

Sophie would never have admitted it but she dreaded Christmas.

She couldn't quite remember how the tradition had started that everyone came to them and she became everyone's slave for a few days. She had a dim recollection that they had all discussed an arrangement once whereby she and Matthew would do Christmas at their house one year, then his two sisters would take a turn each, thereby sharing the burden evenly.

Sophie and Matthew had happily offered to play hosts the first year and really went to town with food and decorations, made up games and devised quizzes. Suzanne and Claudia were eight and six at the time, so full of the joys of Christmas. Matthew's sisters Amanda and Louisa sighed disingenuously over the domestic bliss and Sophie's organizational skills. Matthew's sisters' husbands, Edwin and Jason, cooed over her gravy and homemade orange-shortcrust-with-Grand-Marnier mince pies and muttered about their own wives' shortcomings in the kitchen, and Amanda's children, Jocasta and Benji, ran riot and wrecked the place safe in the knowledge that no one was going to tell them not to, as their parents had clearly abdicated any kind of grown-up responsibility for a few days. Sophie and Matthew fetched drinks and nibbles and cleaned up spills and washed towels and nearly killed themselves in the process, but at least they were confident that this would only happen once every three years.

Wrong.

The following year, Amanda, whose turn it was meant to be, announced in October that she was pregnant and that she couldn't possibly cope with the arrangements. Louisa declared that her house was in disarray because of the new extension currently under construction and then everything just went very quiet until Sophie stepped in and offered that she and Matthew would willingly repeat the previous year's invitation, and even extend it to Matthew's now widowed mother, Sheila. This time round, Sophie's parents Bill and Alice came for the day as well. Luckily, her older brother, her only sibling, had the sense to spend Christmas in Spain every year with his own children and, recently, grandchildren. It never would have occurred to him to invite Sophie and Matthew along, or for them to go if he did, Sophie's relationship with her brother being perfectly amicable but increasingly distant. That Christmas, things were only marred by Amanda's constant throwing-up, which seemed to get worse whenever there were potatoes that needed peeling.

The year after, Amanda's young baby and Louisa's own pregnancy provided the excuses. Expectations were higher and tempers shorter.

Last year, no one had even bothered to keep up the pretence, they just asked when they should turn up and put in their requests for en suite bathrooms (essential when you have a toddler) and downstairs rooms (vital when pregnant, Amanda again), followed, after their arrival, by demands for cups of tea and rounds of sandwiches. A fight broke out over the remote control and Suzanne declared it the worst Christmas ever.

So that was five adults and four children in addition to the two adults and two children who actually lived in the house and the two additional guests for Christmas Day. One vegan, two vegetarians, a dairy allergy, a gluten intolerant, a drunk and a recovering alcoholic. Fifteen people in all.

Oh, and Amanda's six-month-old baby, so that would make sixteen. But it was odds on that Louisa and Jason's marriage might not last till Christmas, so maybe it'd be fifteen after all.

'Perhaps we should just tell them all we're going away,' Matthew had said a couple of days earlier, feeling especially constrained by the inevitability of it all, the arguments, the drinking, the tears. 'Do something spontaneous for once, go to a hotel and leave them all to fend for themselves.'

Sophie had laughed, wishing they could do exactly that. 'You know we can't,' she'd said.

Following their argument, Helen and Matthew had pretty much avoided each other, except when their paths had crossed at work. The day after, Tuesday, Matthew had gone to the drinks at Amanda and Edwin's and made slightly strained conversation about the hunting ban (Matthew and Sophie pro, Edwin and Amanda against) and golfing holidays in Portugal (Edwin pro, Matthew, Sophie and Amanda against). Edwin drank too much as usual and tried to pick a fight with Amanda about her decision to get Jocasta – aged nine – a Prada handbag. Three-year-old India drew a felt-tip-pen scribble on Matthew's Ted Baker coat and was sent to her room, and baby Molly knocked over a glass of Merlot on the white couch. Helen, meanwhile, sat at home, convinced that Matthew would turn up repentant, flowers in hand, at any second. He didn't obviously.

On Wednesday Matthew was away visiting one of Global's more important clients all day, his phone switched off. Helen went home from work as usual, watched the clock move past seven and then eight o'clock, took off her make-up, got into her pyjamas and cried herself to sleep.

Thursday night was, of course, Claudia's nativity. Helen thought about sending Matthew an email to see if he had changed his mind and was coming over as usual, but she knew that his bitch of a twenty-six-year-old assistant, Jenny, opened all his emails as a matter of course. Jenny also answered all of his telephone calls and, anyway, Helen and Matthew had long ago agreed to phone each other at work only in an emergency. She tried hanging about outside the conference room when she knew his weekly strategy meeting would be over, but there were too many people around and all she could do was try a half-hearted smile on him. That evening she waited and waited again, candles burning, white wine chilling, but he didn't show. She decided that he was sulking and just wanted to make her feel bad.

Claudia was playing a Wise Man, wearing a beard and long striped outfit with open-toed sandals. When she went to present the Virgin Mary with her gift of myrrh, she stubbed her toe on the baby's crib and said, 'Bollocks', very loudly.

Friday was the last day in the office before the two-week Christmas shutdown. Helen had convinced herself that Matthew would be happy that he'd taught her a lesson and would, any moment now, make an excuse to pop into her office in order to make it up to her. She had been intending to give him the briefcase the night before, but now it sat, wrapped up in silver paper and ribbon, under her desk. She knew she shouldn't really risk giving it to him in the office, but he'd left her no choice.

She went to the secretaries' annual Christmas lunch and got a bit drunk and tearful. For a split second she considered getting off with Jamie, the company's only male assistant, but he was barely twenty-seven and not even good-looking, so she decided against it. She tried to bring the conversation around to Matthew as much as she could without giving herself away but only managed to find out that he'd bought Sophie a pair of Tiffany earrings for Christmas, that he'd once asked Jenny to buy him some new underwear when he was going on a conference and had forgotten to pack any (Calvin Klein, black, large) and that Laura often rang up to invite him out to lunch and he sometimes went. None of this made Helen very happy.

At about four o'clock she decided to use an emergency phone call and got an out-of-office message: 'Matthew Shallcross has left for the Christmas break and will be back at work on 4 January.' She tried his mobile; switched off.

That night, Helen, Rachel and Neil went to the pub together, and Helen had to concede that Neil was actually really nice and funny and clearly adored Rachel.

What's more, when Rachel talked to him about a band or a cool club, he didn't think it was hilarious and cute to say, 'Is that a new brand of cereal?' When Rachel told a story involving breakdancing and a rara skirt he didn't say, 'I had a mortgage and a child to support by then, so I missed out on all that eighties stuff.' (Sophie was Matthew's second wife, by the way, and he already had a son when he met her, Leo, who was now thirty-eight, by his first wife, Hannah. Confusingly, Leo was old enough to be father to Suzanne and Claudia, just as Matthew could have been Helen's parent, though she didn't like to think about that, inviting as it did comparisons with her own reliable and entirely sexless father, who was just five years older.)

What's more, Rachel's evening didn't end abruptly at eight o'clock because her boyfriend had a wife to get home to.

Helen stayed out far too late and had far too much to drink, went home and cried a lot and didn't go out for two whole days.

For the past few years Helen had spent Christmas Day alone in her flat. She could have gone home to her parents, but it was too shaming at nearly forty years old to be turning up single. So, she told them she was spending the day with her boyfriend – not Matthew, her parents would have practically disowned her if they'd thought she was seeing another woman's husband – oh no, this was imaginary boyfriend, Carlo, who Helen had been telling them about for as long as she could remember. It was a tricky call but, on balance, it was worth having to deal with the offence her mother had taken because Carlo had never deigned to visit with Helen rather than face her pity and disappointment that her only daughter was a middle-aged spinster. One year, dreading the miserable day of bad TV and turkey nuggets, she'd decided to go home anyway, telling her mum and dad that Carlo had gone to his own parents in Spain for a change. She couldn't remember why or when he'd become Spanish, but over the years she'd found that she had a tendency to elaborate the lie to fill in silences, and he was now not only foreign but wealthy and, she thought she could remember once saying, famous in his own country, for what she couldn't recall. By lunchtime, her mum was making sad eyes at her about the fact that he hadn't yet called to wish Helen happy Christmas. By mid afternoon it had progressed to 'Have you had a fight?', and by early evening Helen had been forced to have a one-way conversation on her mobile within earshot of the living room, laughing at unheard jokes and declaring her love into the void. She'd chosen never to repeat the experience again.

Christmas for Helen had been a bit of a trauma for as long as she could remember. She had always loved the build-up – the shop-window displays and the fairy lights and the schmaltzy films on TV – but the actual day itself had always been a let-down. Having no brothers or sisters, it had always been a staid affair, none of the games and laughing and hysteria that her friends had told her about. The day seemed endless, with a long, dull, formal lunch and no TV allowed until Mum and Dad woke up from their afternoon nap and they had turkey sandwiches in front of the game shows. As she got older, the prospect of the long, dark, dreary day began to eclipse any enjoyment she experienced in the run-up. She began to dread the whole holiday season.

Usually, these days, Helen got through it by going out with Rachel for a raucous Christmas Eve and then sleeping through most of the next day. This year, she couldn't quite face the joy that was Rachel and Neil together, so she lied to Rachel, too, and told her she was going to a club with yet more imaginary friends, and then she took to her bed with a bottle of vodka.

To Sophie's dismay, Christmas Eve with the Shallcrosses was following its usual pattern. Amanda and Edwin and their family had arrived along with Matthew's mother, Sheila, and were busy criticizing anything they could find to criticize, from the year of the wine they'd been offered to the make of the glasses it was given to them in. Louisa and Jason were late, probably arguing. Louisa would be having a gin and tonic and rubbing it in the face of newly teetotal Jason. These days, when she really wanted to get at him, she told him he was no fun now he didn't drink, which, for someone who once woke up in a police cell after slapping her in the face during a drunken row, was tough to hear.

'Do you remember when Louisa bought her first boyfriend, that Wilson boy, home to dinner and he brought a bottle of *Cava*?' Sheila was saying now to Amanda, who laughed heartily at Sophie didn't know what.

'Yes, and he said, "It must be good because it cost £6."' Amanda dabbed at her eyes helplessly.

Sophie made a mental note to hide the six bottles of Cava she had bought from Oddbins earlier to bulk up her supplies behind the crate of Laurent Perrier in the kitchen. In all the years she'd been with Matthew, she had never managed to anticipate what the next gem of condescension to come out of his mother's or sisters' mouths would be.

She was under no illusions. She knew that both Amanda and her mother thought that Matthew had sold himself short when he'd married her and found her very middle class to their *faux* upper. Amanda liked to think she bore a striking similarity to Princess Michael of Kent, the refined woman's pin-up – which, in fact, she did – and affected a cut-glass accent to match which could slice bread. Sheila, who in no small part resembled Lady Thatcher, wore white gloves to church on Sundays and was the only person Sophie had ever met who actually read *Horse and Hound*, even though she hated animals of all kinds. They were ridiculous women, and Sophie often found herself pitying them despite their, at times, open hostility. Louisa had never been overly fond of Sophie either, come to that, but in her case it was because no woman would ever be good enough for her older brother no matter what. Sophie often marvelled at how someone as charming and laidback and *fun* as Matthew could be related to three such disagreeable people.

By nine o'clock Louisa and Jason had turned up and everyone was settled in. Sophie was already exhausted, fixing drinks, offering around mince pies and sausage rolls and washing glasses. Louisa and Jason were making a big show of not speaking to each other, and she was doing her best to drive both him and Amanda insane by flirting with Edwin, who was lapping up the attention, along with Matthew's twenty-five-year-old malt whisky. Sheila had already told Sophie that she thought she had put on weight and was now in the utility room trying to explain to her why Filipinas were untrustworthy in the kitchen. Suzanne was sulking in her room because she couldn't watch TV. Benji and India were fighting over a GameBoy. The baby was crying, although no one seemed to be doing anything about it. Claudia had managed to spill Coke down Jocasta's Juicy Couture top after several attempts, so at least she was happy. Matthew felt a sharp pang of longing for the cool, uncluttered quiet of Helen's flat. For a split second he thought about calling her, but he poured himself another drink and pushed that thought to the back of his mind.

By eleven, Louisa was sitting on the sofa with Edwin, listening intently to his every word and 'accidentally' brushing his leg with her hand whenever she thought Jason might be watching. Edwin, half a bottle down, had started to slur in a way that would have been comical had the whole scene not been so gruesome. He placed his hand on Louisa's leg and began patting it like she was a well-behaved Labrador. She giggled like a teenager and looked to check she had her husband's attention.

'Edwin, really, you shouldn't be doing that,' she said in a stage whisper, making no effort to stop him. 'Jason'll get jealous.' In fact, Louisa's leg was getting a bit sore from all the patting. She could feel a patch of her thigh reddening up under her grey wool trousers. She wished he would do something a bit more . . . well . . . playful. She decided to force the issue.

'I never knew you were such a terrible flirt, Edwin,' she purred, placing her hand over his and holding it there.

'Maybe we should all have an early night,' cut in Matthew, who had no idea how to handle the situation. He stood up. 'What do you say, Jason?'

Jason's eyes were glued to his wife and brother-in-law. Matthew sat back down again, unsure what to do next. Edwin, who was still resolutely working his way through the drinks cabinet, looked oblivious to the tension all around him.

'OK, kids, I think that's bedtime.' Matthew waved his arms in an attempt to herd the girls towards the hall. The younger children had already been sent upstairs, but Claudia, who had persuaded Suzanne out of her room with promises of adults misbehaving, was trying to decide how best to use the new word she'd just learnt – it sounded like 'runt' – and was hoping that Jason might use it again so that she could make sure she'd got the pronunciation and context right. Jocasta had gone very quiet, occasionally wiping her eyes with the sleeve of her Paul Frank pyjamas. None of them moved.

Checking that she still had Jason's full attention, Louisa leaned in and whispered loudly in Edwin's ear, 'I know you've always fancied me.'

Jason, having manfully resisted this far, poured himself a large glass of Merlot.

Finally, Matthew had had enough. He took the phone and shut himself in his and Sophie's French Renaissance bedroom and dialled Helen's number. He heard three rings, and then the answerphone clicked in, Helen's voice sounding chirpy and youthful and inviting. He hung up without leaving a message, then a stabbing pain hit him – where was she? Despite the fact that Matthew had a wife that he still, occasionally, had sex with, he went into paroxysms of jealousy if another man went within a few feet of Helen. Now he started to imagine her in a variety of excruciating scenarios with unlikely looking younger men, sharing a cosy drink in a pub, sharing a drunken kiss in the street, sharing a bed. He couldn't believe he'd been stupid enough not to try to make up with her before the Christmas break. Who knows what she was – at this very moment – doing to get back at him? Well, we do, of course, and that was sleeping off a drink-induced near-coma, her mouth open, with just a hint of dribble coming out and very unattractive noises rattling around her nasal passages – but in Matthew's mind, she'd already met, seduced and all but married someone new.

He tried her mobile, poised to hang up when he heard her answer. Turned off. Matthew sat on the bed staring at the duvet. Fuck. He was still sat like this when Sophie came in spoiling for a fight. This'd be a similar fight to the one Matthew and Sophie had had last Christmas and the Christmas before. It went along these lines:

'Your fucking family are out of control.'

'I didn't invite them.'

'Oh, and I did? They invited themselves and, what, you expect me to say no, then never hear the last of it all year?'

'No! I'd rather you told them we'd love them all to stay and have them ruin our Christmas. Again.'

Somehow Matthew always managed to gain the high ground in this argument despite the fact that it was his family who were running riot downstairs.

Matthew and Sophie got into bed, turned their backs on each other and tried to sleep. It was the perfect end to a perfect day. Happy Christmas.

On Christmas Day, Helen killed time by making a list of everything she hated about Matthew:

His lack of commitment
His spinelessness
The way he actually said the word 'atchoo' whenever he sneezed
His nose hair
The crinkly skin on his stomach
The ring tone on his mobile
The teddy bear he bought her for her birthday once
His taste in music
His taste in films
His taste full stop
His assistant, Jenny
His ears (there was nothing really wrong with his ears but she was on a roll)
His Prada shoes, which she was convinced his wife had bought for him (right)
His Tag watch, which she was convinced his wife had bought for him (wrong)
His wife

When she'd finished, it was a quite impressive two pages long. She called her parents to say 'Happy

Christmas' and then lay down on the sofa to watch TV and wait for her hangover to shift.

The sound of Alka-Seltzer fizzing in water had punctuated the morning at Matthew and Sophie's house, too, where things had gone from bad to worse. The kids had opened their presents and, now that was over, the adults were free to drop the pretence of happy families and go back to their singular pursuits. Sophie and Matthew had prepared lunch in strained silence, fending off offers of help from Bill and Alice, who were trying unsuccessfully to jolly up the atmosphere by repeating their favourite 'when Sophie was little' stories to an utterly disinterested audience. Edwin was avoiding eye contact with Louisa, who, in turn, could not look at Amanda.

Halfway through the trendily retro first course of prawn cocktail, Matthew excused himself from the table, went out into the back garden and phoned Helen's mobile, believing she was at her parents', because she'd never let on about her sad little Christmas meals for one.

Recognizing the number, Helen answered with practised nonchalance.

'I just called to say "Happy Christmas."'

'Mmm-hmm.'

'And I'm sorry I've been such an arse. I know it's hard for you and I really . . . well, I really just wanted to say sorry.'

'OK.' (She was loving herself for pulling off such a virtuoso performance.)

'Am I forgiven, Helly?'

'Sure.' (Matthew was sweating now, this wasn't the gushing make-up he was picturing.)

'Are you OK?'

'Yup.'

'Having a good time?'

'Fantastic.'

Silence. Then . . . 'Where were you last night?'

She'd won.

'Actually, Matthew, I've got to go. Mum needs some help. Bye.'

She put the phone down as Matthew was still trying to get the words 'I love you' out.

Ordinarily, Helen would have been beside herself that not only had she handled the call so well but that he had called her in the first place, but today she felt strangely unbothered. She rummaged around and found her list and added, 'The way he calls me Helly.'

Matthew replaced the receiver, heart beating fast. Something was going on. Usually at Christmas, she leaped at his phone calls, answering after only one ring as if she had been waiting all day to hear from him, which, of course, she had been. He was always the one to break off because his children were calling him, or there was a meal on the table, or they were all being summoned to play charades. She would get tearful and clingy and ask when he would be able to call again, tell him she was miserable, that she missed him. Today, she hadn't been able to get off the phone quickly enough. For the first time in his life, he felt like he wasn't the one in control.

*

By ten, everyone at Bartholomew Road had sloped off to bed after a strained evening politely working their way through the quizzes Sophie had prepared. Matthew and Sophie were left alone to have the fight Matthew had been looking for all day, ever since his conversation with Helen had somehow made him feel irrationally angry with Sophie for . . . well, he wasn't quite sure what for.

She gave him the opener he'd been waiting for: 'What happened to you at lunch?'

And somehow – Sophie didn't have the faintest idea why – this led them into the biggest shouting match they'd had in years. Sophie struggled to keep track of the accusations Matthew was hurling at her, which seemed to encompass everything from her not appreciating how much stress he was under at work, through their social life having diminished to near non-existence, to the fact that her mother had asked him how he could stand getting home from work so late so often. 'She was having a go,' he ranted, 'trying to say I don't pull my weight or I don't spend enough time with the kids or something.' 'No, she wasn't,' Sophie almost shouted back. 'She was trying to make conversation, she's just not very good at it, sorry.' Somewhere in there he threw in their dwindling sex life, the pressure on him to succeed and, bizarrely, her taste in work clothes. 'Frumpy,' he'd shouted. 'What the fuck's it got to do with you what I wear to work?' she'd screamed back. 'You hardly look like you've stepped off the cover of *GQ*.'

Sophie had only ever seen him like this once before, and that was when she'd first told him she was pregnant with Suzanne, just under thirteen years ago. Conveniently forgetting that he was responsible, he'd spluttered and raged about never wanting to go through fatherhood again. He'd been there, done it, fucked it up. How dare she get pregnant without consulting him? How dare he get her pregnant without consulting her? she'd countered. He'd told her it made him feel constrained and suffocated and how he'd just got out of a relationship that had made him feel like that and he wasn't happy to find himself in another. He'd told her he didn't want to feel tied down by children and obligations and nappies and parents' evenings. The highlight of the whole episode was when he'd added that he didn't want to have to go through another pregnancy watching the woman he loved expand like a hot-air balloon and seeing the varicose veins and the red raw stripes across her Spacehopper stomach. He loved her body, he'd said, as if that was going to endear him to her now, he didn't want to watch it disintegrate.

'Why did you marry me then?' Sophie had asked.

'Because I love you,' he'd said, in such a pathetic, self-centred way that Sophie had hated him in that moment. She'd lain awake through the night plotting ways to leave him and bring up her baby on her own. By the morning she had a comprehensive plan of crèches and new houses and part-time work, but Matthew had apologized – as he always did, after the event, when he knew his point had been made and noted – and so she gave him another chance. In truth, she was tired and hormonal and scared and she couldn't face going through the next eight months alone. A few weeks later, completely out of nowhere, he'd suddenly started to throw himself into the pregnancy (a bit too much, to be honest; sometimes he had got on her nerves, wanting to discuss what was going on inside of her with anyone who'd listen). He'd helped her plan the birth ('No, Matthew, I don't want to lie naked in a paddling pool with you and the midwife in there in your swimming costumes, I want to go into a hospital and be given lots of drugs') and he'd held her hand throughout the event itself and breathed with her and timed her contractions and, to be honest, generally got in the way. Two years later, when she'd told him she was expecting again, he'd whooped and hollered and picked her up and swung her round the kitchen.

This time, though, there were no cups of tea and tearful regrets in the morning. Just a silence which remained intact despite Sophie's best efforts to puncture it, and the odd, unsettling guilty looks he kept throwing her way when he thought she wasn't watching.

Helen passed the next few days ignoring her phone (missed calls from Matthew: eight; messages left: three) and making more lists. 'Reasons to leave Matthew' stretched to three and a half pages. 'Reasons to stay with Matthew' was pitifully short, containing, as it did, just three entries:

He says he loves me
He can be funny
Who else am I going to go out with?

After she'd written number three, she'd burst into tears, because it was truly one of the most pathetic things she had ever seen.

She had another night out with Rachel and Neil and surprised herself by having a really good time. Neil's mate James chatted her up and she flirted back even though she didn't fancy him in the slightest. But, she was flattered and they had a laugh. He was a single man, her age, and he didn't have a club foot or a disfiguring skin condition, which was in itself a revelation to her. The evening passed too quickly, and she didn't think about Matthew once. Her answerphone blinked two messages. She couldn't be bothered to listen to them.

The next night, when another of Neil's friends, Chris (newly divorced, three children), asked her if she was single, she'd said yes. He asked her if she fancied a drink, just with him and, although she said no – anyone could see from a mile off the fresh baggage he was carrying around with him – it made her think. She went home. Two messages. She listened to them: Matthew going, 'I'm miserable without hearing your voice, call me.' She didn't.

She went to bed and woke up listening to her upstairs neighbours having very noisy sex again. The woman (Helen didn't even know her name, this being London) was putting on a particularly spectacular performance. Not many words today, it was all 'ooh's and 'aah's, like an appreciative audience at a pantomime. 'He's behind you!' Helen wanted to shout. She lay there for a while trying to decide whether she thought it was genuine or not and came down on the side of not. It was too depressing to think otherwise. She dragged herself out of bed and decided to walk down the high street to the local newsagent for a paper.

Camden was always a shock to the system in the early

morning, too loud and brash and obscenely awake – that was what she loved about it, its relentlessness, its refusal to give up and come quietly. She pushed through the crowds milling around the market in Inverness Street and shuffled around the corner shop avoiding eye contact with the other shoppers. She was just opening her front door, juggling the newspaper, a litre of milk and a packet of instant noodles, when the door to the upstairs opened, and there they were, the couple from the flat above. They smiled half-heartedly at her, and the woman said, 'Hello' in a quiet flat little voice. She was dressed in her usual shapeless fleece and baggy trousers. Helen scanned them for giveaway signs that they had finished shagging each other senseless less than fifteen minutes ago but, as ever, they were exuding dreary, lifeless timidity. They were the kind of people who would suck the life out of a room at a party but, clearly, when they were alone, it was a different story.

'Happy Christmas,' the ratty-looking man said as they passed.

'Thanks,' said Helen, as she pushed her way into her flat, desperate to avoid further conversation. 'You, too.' She didn't know why their double life unsettled her, but it did. It made her feel like they knew a secret she would never be party to.

The following night, Helen stayed in, had a large glass of wine and thought about her situation. It was the longest time she had gone without speaking to Matthew for the whole of their relationship and, with a bit of distance, the entire thing was starting to look like a bit of a farce. Years of his rigid schedule, her fitting in with him, him cancelling, her acquiescing, him panicking, her backing down.

By her second glass, she was thinking about James and Chris and the fact that, despite her not being interested in either of them, they were living proof that single, reasonable-looking men of her own age did exist. Plus, there was no denying that spending time with men who weren't already adults by the time the Beatles were past their best was fun. She tried to remember what it was she used to pity about Rachel's single life, but she was struggling.

As she poured glass three, she was wondering what the point of the last four and a bit years had been. Four years ago she had been thirty-five – young, she now realized – she could have met someone, married them and had two children by now if she hadn't taken herself out of the running. (Not that she wanted children, although they somehow always crept into her perfect life fantasy with Matthew, more as a means of ensuring his full attention and devotion than anything else. In that fantasy there was definitely a full-time nanny – old and haggard and unthreatening, of course – on hand at all times so she never had to see the children let alone look after them.) As it was, all she had to show for those last few years were some grey hairs she had to keep covering up by having her roots done every six weeks and some lines around her eyes and mouth. Oh, and the loss of her career, her independence and her self-esteem. Well, fuck it, she thought, topping up her glass again. Fuck it, fuck him, fuck everything.

The doorbell rang.

Helen caught sight of herself in the hall mirror as she went to answer it. No make-up, unwashed hair, pyjamas on. She opened the door and there, on her doorstep, was Matthew. It took her a minute to notice the two large suitcases at his feet because she was distracted by his eyes, which were red and puffy, as if he'd been crying.

'Hello,' she said.

He held his arms out wide. 'I've done it. I've left Sophie. I've told her everything and I've brought all my stuff. Well, not all my stuff but all the essentials. There's some more in the car, but I'll have to go back and get the rest once she's calmed down a bit. Sorry, I'm rambling. What I'm trying to say is I'm moving in with you.'

5

While Matthew tearfully told Helen that he'd spent the whole of the previous day and night thinking about her and figuring out for himself what it was he truly wanted, she found she was thinking about the frozen lasagne she'd left in the oven and how much she had been looking forward to it, which wasn't a good sign. She was aware that she was tuning in and out of his monologue, catching bits here and there.

'. . . Once they'd all gone she made me sit down and talk . . . tried to pretend it was all OK . . . asked me point blank if there was someone else . . . told her that I love you . . . blah blah something something . . .'

Eh?

'What did you say?' She forced her brain to focus.

'I said she didn't have any idea. She'd never even suspected all these years.'

'Oh.'

Come on, she thought, concentrate, this is serious. But she looked at Matthew sobbing his heart out on the couch and found herself struggling to equate this rather broken-down grey-haired man, who was only a few years away from his bus pass, with the man she had yearned for and fretted over and lusted after for the past four years.

'I've given up everything. A fifteen-year marriage. My house. Oh god, maybe my children', he was saying. 'I was so awful to her, I said things I never should have said. But it's worth it for you, I've realized that now. I have done the right thing, haven't I? Because there's no turning back.'

She peeled him off her and stood up. 'I just need to turn the oven off.'

Out in the kitchen, Helen leaned her head against the cool of the fridge door and tried to make sense of what was going on. This was everything she'd been asking him for, it was an overwhelming statement of the strength of his feeling for her, but she herself felt disconnected. She should be throwing herself into his arms, crying with happiness and gratitude, laughing at the prospect of a shared future, so why wasn't she? Why couldn't she give him the affirmation he so obviously needed? And why was this happening now? Why not any other time in the past four years, when she'd been asking and cajoling and, sometimes, she thought shamefully, begging? Why hadn't he rung her beforehand and said, 'I'm about to leave Sophie, just checking you're still up for it'? Oh yes, she thought, because she hadn't been answering his phone calls – that was why. She shut the kitchen door and called Rachel, running the tap loudly so that Matthew couldn't hear.

'Matthew's left Sophie. He's told her everything and walked out on her and the kids. He's here.'

'What? I can't hear you.'

'Oh, fuck it,' Helen said, turning the tap off again. She repeated in a stage whisper what she had just told her friend.

'That's fantastic.' Rachel sounded postcoitally sleepy.

'I don't know if it is. Is it?' Helen was irritated. 'Haven't you been listening to anything I've been saying for the past couple of weeks? Things have changed. I've changed. I'm not sure what I want any more.'

In actual fact, Rachel had spent so many years listening to Helen go on and on about the complications of her relationship that it now washed over her and she rarely took in the details.

'Oh, shit, yeah. Shit. Well, you'll just have to tell him to go again.'

'Rachel, are you listening to me? He's told Sophie and the children. I can't just say, "Actually, I know I've been asking you to do this for the past four years but what if it's not the right decision?" I can't just say, "I know you've done exactly what I've always told you I wanted, what I more or less gave you an ultimatum about less than two weeks ago, but maybe you should think about whether it would be better to go back to your suicidal wife and your two devastated children and tell them it was all a wind-up?"'

'Why not?'

'Because he's only done it because of me. It's all my fault. What the fuck should I do?'

'I don't know, tell him you need some time. Tell him you've got a terminal illness and you're going to be dead soon, so he might as well stay with his family.'

Helen could tell Rachel's heart just wasn't in this conversation and she could hear Neil in the background, cajoling her to come back to bed.

'Oh, forget it.'

She put the phone down. OK, she thought, the facts

are these: I've already potentially ruined three people's lives – Sophie's and the two girls'. She realized with a wave of guilt that she could only remember the name of one of Matthew's daughters – Claudia.

What I can't now do is add Matthew to that list. I have to make sure this is really what we want. Both of us.

She fixed a smile on her face and forced herself back out into the living room. Matthew was looking at her like an abandoned puppy hidden behind a skip on an RSPCA advert. She noticed that he was wearing a rather comfy pullover, a bit like something her dad might like, and realized that she'd never seen him in anything other than his office uniform of a variety of well-fitting suits and hand-finished shirts. Or naked. Naked or suited, the two faces of Matthew Shallcross – anything else seemed faintly ludicrous. He had jeans on – jeans, the young person's uniform, which aged him a good ten years and, god, were those trainers? His usually immaculately combed hair was standing up in places like a baby bird's, and she could see his bald spot peeking pink and vulnerable, like a long-forgotten fontanelle, through the strands. He was pitiful. She sat on the sofa next to him and put her arms round him.

The next morning, Helen got up early because there was a stranger in her bed – or that's how it seemed. She'd spent most of the night trying to work out how she'd got to the stage where yesterday evening wasn't the happiest of her life and why, in fact, she now felt like crying, while Matthew slept like a baby. Well, a baby with sinus trouble, because Helen had discovered that he snored, a fact which thus far she'd been blissfully unaware of, having never had the pleasure of his company for a whole night before.

The sight of her tiny living room overcome with boxes and suitcases brought her mood down further. For a man who'd upped and left in a hurry, he'd managed to do a lot of packing. She could see things which resembled skis and, God forbid, a guitar. She poked about a bit and came across a shoe-cleaning kit. Surely not? What kind of man owned a shoe-cleaning kit, for fuck's sake, let alone remembered to pack it when he was in the midst of the biggest crisis of his life? She dug a bit deeper and found herself opening a small photo album – always a mistake. Photos of a happy, smiling family looked back at her. Clearly, in the rush to find the vital shoe brushes, Matthew hadn't had time to edit out the pictures of Sophie and there she was – well, Helen could only assume it was her, although the real Sophie didn't come close to any of the pictures Helen had been carrying around in her head. Helen didn't know if she was more shocked by Sophie being so much younger than she'd thought, so much more beautiful, so happy-looking or just by the fact that she was real. She sank down into an armchair and began to leaf through the book from the beginning.

In a previous life, Helen would have scanned these photographs with the precision of a laser looking for details to torture herself with. Once she'd got over the shock of Sophie's looks, she would have fixated on her and Matthew's body language, looking for tell-tale signs of affection. Today, all she could see was two children who clearly loved their dad and a woman who looked open and friendly and confident and who blatantly had no idea that her life was about to fall apart. A woman caught in a perfect, happy moment, arms round her children, leaning against her husband. Who took it? Helen wondered. Who else was there at such an intimate, uncomplicated second, or maybe this was how Matthew and Sophie always were when they were together. She had to talk to Matthew. If this wasn't what she truly wanted, then she had no right to take him away from his family.

She sneaked into the bedroom and looked down at him fast asleep, trying to rationalize how she felt. The nervous energy she had always experienced when she was around him before seemed to have entirely disappeared and been replaced by – what?

Pity?

Embarrassment?

Matthew slid a finger into his nostril in his sleep and rooted around a bit.

Distaste?

He looked as if he didn't quite know where he was when she woke him up. Then a brief look of panic crossed his face. She decided to tackle it head on and sat down on the bed beside him, stroking his shoulder.

'You can still go home, you know, if you think you've done the wrong thing. I'll understand. Tell Sophie you were drunk and you made it all up or something.'

'Don't say that. What are you saying? I did this for you. I can never go back now, not after what I've done to them in the last couple of days.'

'I'm just saying, if you think you've made a mistake,

then it's OK. I'll support you whatever you want to do. I mean, maybe we've rushed into it a bit.'

'Rushed into it? You've been telling me that this was what you wanted for years. I did this for you,' he said, for the first but – believe me – not for the last time. 'Tell me I've done the right thing.'

Then he said the saddest sentence known to mankind: 'Don't you want me?'

She couldn't push him any further. He was so desperate and so pathetic, she had to put him out of his misery.

'God . . . Matthew . . . you know I do. This is all I've ever wanted. I just want you to be sure it's what you want, too, and you're not just doing it because I've pressurized you.'

'I want us to be a proper couple,' he said. 'I want us to live together. I want to meet your friends and you to meet mine. I want to wake up next to you every morning and go to sleep next to you every night.'

Helen would have sworn she could feel the walls of her already tiny flat moving in to suffocate her.

'Me, too.'

He leaned in to kiss her, and they had awkward and slightly self-conscious sex. She noticed that his unfreshened morning breath was a little offputting.

6

In Bartholomew Road, Sophie was struggling to understand what the last twenty-four hours had been about. She was waiting for Matthew to breeze through the front door and tell her it was all a joke. After their row she had known there was something seriously up with him, but she'd assumed it was work. Matthew had a way of hitting out at those around him when he was wounded, and she had convinced herself that he had messed up a campaign or been voted off the board or asked to take early retirement. Maybe he had developed a gambling habit and had blown all their savings, or he was just feeling his age and kicking out against it as he sometimes did. She knew he took ageing very badly, as if it were a personal slight happening only to him. But there was nothing that had happened in the last fifteen years that had prepared her for the truth. She knew that when he'd finally broken down and told her what had been going on, the natural reaction would have been to shout and cry and even throw things, but she'd sat in a stiff and unmoving shocked silence. It just wasn't real. It had flitted through her mind that they'd get through this. It could take years and hard work, maybe counselling. No one need know about it; they'd present a happy front while they repaired their marriage from the inside out and, one day, eventually, it'd be forgotten. She'd even heard people say that their relationships ended up stronger after they'd gone through something like this, although, at the moment, it was hard to see how. Then she'd heard him talking about arranging visits to see the girls and coming back to get the rest of his possessions, and she'd realized he was going. This was it. After all these years it had come to a straight choice between her and another woman, and the other woman had won. History counted for nothing.

She knew that she had to put on a brave face for the children, but she also knew that they'd silently witnessed the shouting match that had gone on last night but were pretending they hadn't. Despite Sophie's best efforts, Claudia caught her crying in the bathroom.

'Where's Dad?'

'I'm not sure, darling. He's gone away for a bit.'

'Is he ever coming back?'

'He's coming back to see you and Suzanne, of course he is,' Sophie said, hugging her daughter. 'He'd never not want to see you.'

Suzanne stomped in, aggravated at being left out.

'What's going on?'

'Apparently Daddy's being a bit of a cunt,' said Claudia, who'd been practising and had a feeling she might be allowed to get away with it at that moment. 'Isn't he, Mum?'

Sophie laughed despite herself.

'Yes, sweetheart, he is a bit. And don't say that word.'

There was still a day to go before it was time to go back to work. Matthew set about unpacking his bags and boxes, mainly to put his things in piles on the living-room floor, although Helen had managed to clear out one drawer in the bedroom. Among other things, he seemed to have brought a pile of washing, Helen noticed. She forced herself to offer to put it into the machine.

'No, no,' he protested. 'I can do it myself.'

They were being very polite and on their best behaviour as if they were two strangers who had found each other through a 'room mate wanted' ad. Helen realized she couldn't remember how they'd ever used to have fun together, if indeed they had.

Matthew's mobile phone rang. Amanda. He took it into the bedroom, and Helen could hear his muttered, defensive conversation. When he came out, he looked drawn, and she felt genuinely sorry for him, because she guessed he'd had a sisterly dressing-down. Fuck, thought Helen, how am I ever going to explain this to Mum and Dad. When the ringing started again at about six o'clock, Matthew made a joke about throwing the phone out of the window, then went white when he looked at the caller ID.

'It's Suzanne.'

Helen knew a reaction was expected, but she was struggling to place quite who Suzanne was in Matthew's overstuffed family so she settled on an expression which she thought said, 'Really! How interesting,' but which in fact read as blank.

'My daughter.'

He sounded hurt that he had to remind her.

'I know! Answer it.'

More shuffling off into the bedroom, more low voices. Despite herself, Helen couldn't resist listening in. She heard Matthew comforting and reassuring Suzanne, who was obviously in pieces. He was trying to convince her things'd be no different between them.

'You and Claudia can come over here whenever you like. You can meet Helen and hang out with us at the weekends.'

Ignoring the slightly disturbing fact that Matthew had just used the expression 'hang out', Helen went straight for the big scary thought at the heart of what she'd just heard. Never in any of her fantasies about life with Matthew post-Sophie did she factor in his children, and now they were about to start coming over whenever they felt like it. Don't get me wrong – she felt bad for them in a way she'd never imagined she could. She didn't want them to lose touch with their father, but couldn't he go and visit them somewhere? Take them to the zoo and then McDonald's for lunch like part-time fathers always did in films?

Move back in with them and pretend nothing had happened?

It had never been a decision for Helen not to have children, it was something she had always known. The responsibility was too much, the potential for fucking it up too great. Besides, she wanted to make something of her life, be ambitious, carefree, spontaneous – everything her parents weren't. It had occurred to her in the past that maybe that was one of the reasons she had allowed herself to be suckered into a relationship with a married man – because the last thing he was ever going to do was put pressure on her to have a child.

It was strange, then, that the one time in her life she

had been pregnant, early on in her affair with Matthew, when they were both still capable of getting so carried away by lust that they took risks, she hadn't taken the decision to have an abortion lightly. For a couple of days before she broke the good news to her boyfriend, she had indulged herself in a fantasy in which the prospect of a baby was just the impetus Matthew needed to leave home and move in with her and their perfect child. Hormones raging, she had made lists of the pros and cons:

Pros

Matthew will have to tell Sophie
Matthew and me = happy ever after
Six months off work

Cons

Stretch marks
Never look good in a bikini again

She knew there were more cons, but she just couldn't think of them and, when she looked at her lists, she was shocked by how self-obsessed and superficial they made her seem compared to the tiny life that was now growing inside her. She made herself cry with the deep spiritual meaning of it all. She convinced herself that Matthew would be as moved, as delighted, as overwhelmed as she was.

When she finally got through to him that it *was* true, they were soon to be parents, he went insane. Angry – how could she, why hadn't she used protection (he glossed over the fact that clearly neither had he). Frightened – oh my god, Sophie, my poor children. Accusatory – are you sure it's mine? He had shouted and pleaded and finally begged Helen to get rid of it, eventually resorting to telling her he would have nothing to do with either her or the baby if she didn't. Finally, beaten down by his constant nagging and his threats to leave her, she had agreed. Matthew had paid, of course, in traditional cad fashion, but had not accompanied her to the private clinic. That duty had been left to Rachel, who was equally convinced that she was doing the right thing, but for different reasons (why would you want to have a kid with that two-timing loser?). For about three weeks after it was all over, Helen had cried pretty much all the time. She knew it was just her hormones going into overdrive, but she was convinced she would never stop. She told Matthew she hated him and, then, panicked that he might take her seriously, called him back and apologized. She took time off work and lolled around the flat in her dressing-gown watching TV and eating.

Then, suddenly, one morning, her mood had shifted as fast as it had come on. She opened her eyes and thought, 'Fucking hell, that was a lucky escape.' She was horrified that her body had nearly conned her into doing something she so fundamentally didn't want. She even thanked Matthew for his bombastic approach to making her make the right decision. She got out her lists and revised them as a reference for the future, in case she ever nearly lost her mind again. They now read:

Pros

Six months off work

Cons

Stretch marks
Never look good in a bikini again
Career prospects over (this was in the days before it became
    apparent that they were all over anyway)
Matthew will leave me
Single parent
Life over because I have to look after a baby and can never
    go out again, no other man will want me and my body will
    have fallen to bits

She had underlined the last several times.

Matthew's youngest daughter, Claudia, would have been six at the time, and if Helen's original fantasy had all gone to plan, would have spent most of her life without a father.

7

On her first day back at work, Helen went to meet Rachel in a café on Berwick Street for lunch, having kept out of Matthew's way pretty successfully all morning. They'd decided last night that it wouldn't be a good idea to let the office in on their little secret at this stage, something Helen felt grateful for – how would she ever have explained to her colleagues that she had been shagging the boss for the past god knows how many years but just somehow failed to mention it. They'd travelled into work separately, Matthew in his large impractical car and Helen on the overcrowded underground, and had only passed in the corridor once so far, where they'd carried off a pretty convincing friendly-but-business-like 'Hello.'

'I feel guilty about his family.'

Rachel snorted. 'Since when? You hate Sophie.'

Sophie had been on the 'Women we hate' list for some years now, even though Rachel had protested that she had no feelings about her either way. Helen had countered that she herself had no problem with women who'd had therapy but that she had allowed Rachel to keep them on for all this time.

'I don't know Sophie,' she replied now.

'Never stopped you hating her.'

'Which is why I feel guilty. Stop trying to make me feel worse.'

'Well, send him back to her then.'

So Helen explained how she'd tried to broach the subject of him going back and how clingy Matthew had become and how, because he'd burnt all his bridges because of her, she had to try to make it work.

Rachel wasn't convinced. 'How flattering to have a man want to spend the rest of his life with you because he doesn't think his wife'll take him back if you throw him out.'

'It's not like that.' Helen knew it pretty much was.

'Well, it sounds like it.'

They sat in grumpy silence for a minute or so, then Helen softened.

'I think he really loves me. And, like you said, it's what I've always wanted. I just need to get used to the idea, that's all.'

What Helen loved most about Rachel is that she never once said, 'I told you it'd all end in tears.'

In forty-eight hours Sophie had gone through crying, anger, disbelief, hatred and ended up back at crying again. She'd dealt with endless calls from Matthew's endless family all phoning to say how dreadfully he'd behaved but without exception leaving her feeling as if it must somehow have been her fault. Suzanne had more or less said this outright to her. Claudia, slightly more touchingly, had taken her mother's side – not that Sophie was encouraging either of them to choose – and had declared she'd never speak to her father again.

What the girls knew was that Daddy had moved out, that he had a new friend and that he was living with her now. Sophie was trying to spare them the gorier details while trawling through them herself to try and make some sense of what'd gone on.

If the truth be told, Sophie shouldn't have been surprised by what had happened to her, having, as she had, stolen Matthew herself from the first Mrs Shallcross all those years ago under very similar circumstances. Because, oh yes, Sophie had been a mistress too, once, before a wedding and children and a bit of history had blurred this fact from people's memories – even her own, sometimes, because she had tried hard to blank the fact from her mind over the years. Sophie had been thirty, Matthew forty-five, the same age as his wife. It hadn't passed Sophie by that Mrs Shallcross the first was exactly the same age that she was now when Matthew had moved on.

Matthew had told her that his marriage to Hannah was dead and had been for a long time. He'd stayed with her, he'd said, at first, until his son Leo left home, in an effort to do the right thing and, since then, from habit. Hannah knew, he'd added, that their relationship was over and, in fact, she wanted that just as much as he did. There hadn't been anyone else in all that time, but then he hadn't met anyone like Sophie. He couldn't pass up this chance for happiness just because – on paper – he had a wife. Hannah would be the first to say as much. He'd made it sound so plausible.

Sophie had often wondered since what it was that had made her give in to him. There was something about the fact that he was married that made the relationship less real, less scary. She had known from the off that she couldn't have the whole of him, and so it wasn't an issue. She'd had no expectations that he would turn out to be the love of her life, and so she'd put no pressure on him to prove that he was. By the time he asked her to marry him six months later, she was hooked. Hannah, he'd said, understood and was delighted for him.

It was only after he'd moved his stuff into her two-bedroom flat in Muswell Hill and the wedding plans were well underway that she'd realized that this was a bit of an exaggeration. In fact, it was an out-and-out lie. Hannah was not delighted for him, she didn't understand. Indeed, when Sophie had opened her front door one day and faced a hysterical, abusive, crying middle-aged woman, she'd realized that Hannah hadn't even known until a few days ago, when Matthew had walked out. She had tried to persuade Hannah to at least come inside and talk but, understandably, Hannah had preferred to stand on the front doorstep calling her a whore and a slut in front of all the neighbours. Matthew was conveniently out at the time, playing golf with a friend, oblivious to the havoc he had caused.

For some reason – she could no longer remember why – Sophie had forgiven him. It had taken a while, but he'd somehow proved he was serious by filing for divorce and throwing himself into his new life, in that way that Matthew had of making whatever he was doing at the time seem like the most exciting thing in the world. The wedding had had to be postponed, of course, until he was officially a free man, but when it happened, it was moving and beautiful and everything she'd ever dreamed of. She'd forced herself to forget all about his alleged womanizing and Hannah's near-breakdown on her doorstep. She'd succeeded.

Now, she was the one watching him walk away.

Matthew wouldn't tell her exactly how old Helen was. When she asked, as all women would, 'Is she younger than me?', he'd blustered and wouldn't give her a straight answer. In fact, the only details she'd managed to wring out of him were these:

Her name was Helen
He'd met her through work
She had a flat in London
She wasn't married
They'd never had sex in Matthew and Sophie's house (for some reason this had seemed of prime importance to her)
She was younger than Sophie – the blustering had given that away
He'd been seeing her for 'a while', although, when pressed, he wouldn't elaborate on what exactly 'a while' meant

Matthew and Sophie's courtship had been a whirlwind affair. She had been the accountant in the office where he was then working – clearly, Matthew could only look for a mistress within a ten-metre radius. Six months of clandestine meetings in the conference room, then a proposal. Looking back, she could see now that this was his mid-life crisis. His only child had – finally – left home, and he was now alone with his wife, to face up to getting older, just the two of them for probably another forty years, and he panicked. He looked at his wife of twenty-four years and saw a woman with lines round her eyes and stray grey hairs, and bits that were sagging where before they'd been pert, and thought that she was getting old. Which meant that so was he. Far better to look at a young face staring back at you every morning than someone who's a living reminder of your own mortality. With an insight that comes only after the event, much like Helen's, Sophie now realized that it was timing as much as anything that had made Matthew choose her.

Sophie had never believed in karma or fate. She was far too sensible to buy into anything so New Age. But even she had to admit that there was a certain poetic justice in what had just happened to her. She was paying for what she had done to Hannah. She wondered what Hannah would think when she heard, whether, all these years on, it would still feel like a small victory. Whether she'd have stopped caring by the time Matthew – inevitably – did the same thing to Helen.

8

Every day, Helen was discovering things about Matthew she never knew before, and most of them weren't good.

He dyed his hair. To be honest, she'd worked this out already, but seeing the bottle of Just For Men in the bathroom cabinet meant he had given up all pretence – at least to her.

He wore slippers. Not flip-flops, not an old pair of moccasins. Slippers. With a fur lining.

He made a roaring noise when he yawned. How had she not known this before? Had he never yawned in front of her in over four years, or was he just keeping a lid on the sound, knowing how mind-numbingly irritating it was?

He laid his clothes out for the next day at work before he went to sleep at night. Helen didn't know why this was so annoying. In fact, it was probably quite sensible, but it just felt so . . . comfy . . . like something his wife used to do for him or something they taught him at boarding school. Helen had to resist the urge to rumple them or to swap them with something different to confuse him. Once he'd picked out his outfit, he wore it no matter what, so if he went to bed on a wintry night but woke up in the sunshine, he'd still put on the sweater that was hanging there waiting.

His car had a name. A name. His. Car. Had. A. Name.

Helen knew this was probably down to his kids, the kind of cutesy thing that families did, but when one day he forgot where he was and said to her, 'Let's go in Delia,' she stared at him open-mouthed for so long that it crossed his mind she might be having a stroke. She finally pulled herself together enough to ask him not to anthropomorphize inanimate objects in front of her ever again. Ever. Again.

'Sorry, Helly,' he'd said, slightly sheepishly.

'And don't call me Helly. I hate it when you call me that.'

'I always call you Helly,' he'd replied petulantly.

'Exactly.'

It wasn't going unnoticed that Matthew was a little distracted at work. His shirts looked a bit, well, crumpled, for starters. And, at Wednesday's morning catch-up meeting, he'd looked panic-stricken when he'd realized that he had left a client's strategy, which he had drawn up over the Christmas break, on his computer at home.

'I'll ring Sophie and get her to email it over,' offered Jenny helpfully.

'NO! No . . . she's not there. No one's there at the moment. I can remember the key points.'

His years of experience meant that he sailed through the meeting with the client without giving away that he was making it up as he went along, but he knew Jenny had noticed that something was up, and his efforts to overcompensate by being extra nice to her for the rest of the day simply convinced her that she was right.

That night, Helen looked round at the mess that used to be her living room.

'You forgot your laptop?'

She dug around in the nearest box. 'You remembered a . . . toy car . . . but you forgot your computer?'

'It's vintage. A collectible.'

She rummaged about some more. 'There's hundreds of them in here. Are you eight years old?'

'They're worth a fortune.'

'What are you going to do, open a shop? Jesus, Matthew.'

He looked hurt and she felt bad, but irritation got the better of her and she turned on her heels and left the room. She had a long bath and when she came back into the living room, Matthew's stuff was tidied away neatly into a corner and he was in the kitchen rustling up something unspeakable-looking in a wok. He waved a spatula at her proudly when he saw her come in as if to say, 'Look how clever I am.'

'It's nearly ready. Chinese, how does that sound?'

'Fantastic.'

He had only been there a few days, but Helen was longing to be left on her own with a microwave curry. She wanted to loll about in her pyjamas with no make-up on, eating and watching the TV. She wanted to neck back glasses of wine at her own pace, not go through the tortured niceties of, 'Do you want another glass?', 'I don't know, do you?', 'Well, I will if you will.' Her parents used to waste whole evenings that way. Politeness, that great substitute for passion.

She sat down to eat. The conversation was stilted. What did they ever used to talk about, for fuck's sake? Helen was reduced to making appreciative noises about the (disgusting) food while Matthew valiantly tried to fill the silence with the kind of talk about work they had always successfully avoided.

Helen had had enough.

'Why don't I put the TV on?'

'While we're eating?' he said, as if she'd just suggested having a dump on the table.

'Just to help us unwind a bit. Something mindless so we can forget about work. But we don't have to.'

'No, if you want to, then put it on.'

'No, no, it's fine. Not if you don't want it on.' Oh, fuck, she thought, here we go: 'You first' – 'No, you' – 'No, you' – 'No, really, you' – for the next forty years.

'You're right,' he said. 'What's wrong with putting the TV on? It's just Sophie and I never liked the kids watching . . .' He trailed off, as if he'd said too much, then got up and switched on the television in the corner. They finished their meal in front of *Emmerdale*, in silence. Helen hadn't got the heart to say, 'Turn over – there'll be something better on the other side.'

Over the next couple of days, Helen realized that however uneasy she was, Matthew was simply going to refuse to admit that he'd made the wrong decision. The only way for him to cope with the momentousness of what he'd done, not to mention the guilt, was for him to believe totally that it had all been for the sake of a great love he was powerless to ignore.

So, when she served up undercooked pink chicken with burnt fries for dinner, he smiled and said, 'I'm going to have to teach you to cook,' like she was eight years old.

When she told him she quite fancied the eighteen-year-old boy who served in the deli down the road, he laughed so much she was afraid she'd need to resuscitate him.

When she shaved her legs in the bath and left the tiny hairs clinging round the rim, she caught him whistling to himself as he cleaned it out.

And the more he worked to show how much he loved her, the more she found herself perversely trying to put him off. Maybe it was a test – like an adolescent pushing the boundaries to straining point, waiting to be rejected, waiting for the proof of what they've long suspected, that their parents have hated them all along – maybe she was subconsciously trying to make herself as unattractive as possible to test the limits of his devotion. Or maybe, she wondered, was she really just trying to push him away because she didn't want him any more. It was a thought too harsh to indulge, she thought of herself as enough of a bitch already – this would push her over the edge even in her own eyes: to lure a man away from his loving family and then kick him back out again, as if the competition was all and the prize irrelevant. You love me the most, I win, now fuck off.

So she tried to play nice, but the stubborn child in her wasn't having any of it.

She stopped shaving her armpits altogether. And her bikini line.

She told him she'd once caught Chlamydia from a man whose name she never got round to asking.

She told him she had a moustache she had to have waxed off every six weeks.

She told him she didn't feel like sex and he just said, 'Fine.'

She picked holes in the way he dressed.

She stopped brushing her teeth.

And combing her hair.

And plucking the stray hag-whisker that grew out of her chin.

She bought a packet of Tena incontinence pads for women and left them lying about in the bathroom.

And all the time Matthew just kept telling her he loved her and said, 'Isn't it great that we're finally together?' and 'This is it now, you and me, for ever,' and other such Mills and Boon classics.

9

It was Friday morning and Helen was typing up a press release for Laura and trying to stop herself altering the occasional word where she thought things could be improved. It concerned the rumours that ex-*Northampton Park* soap-opera 'babe' (just been sacked, in dire need of some column inches) Jennifer Spearman had just got engaged to reality-show singer Paulo (gay, terrified of losing his fan base of eleven-year-old girls). There had, of course, been no rumours, but this release, which denied the relationship vehemently, along with a few well-placed 'unauthorized' pictures of the couple seemingly caught unawares in a variety of intimate situations, was designed to ensure there soon would be.

As a personal assistant, Helen didn't qualify for an office of her own, instead she shared a large open-plan space with two other PAs, black-haired, thin-lipped Jenny and Jamie, who was harmless enough if a bit too easily influenced. It was the modern-day equivalent of the secretaries' typing pool, although, as with models and supermodels, no one was called a secretary any more, there were only PAs and, when they reached stellar status, Executive PAs.

Jenny was poison. Only twenty-six, she considered herself the most senior among the PAs because she looked after Matthew. She spoke in a baby voice – a cartoon helium whine with her 'r's pronounced as soft 'w's

– which belied her fierce power-hungry streak. She fought tooth and nail to make sure that her name was the first on any general memo, that her chair cost £5 more than Helen's or Jamie's, that she had control of the stationery catalogue. Rumour had it that she had once been caught measuring the length of the desks to make sure hers was the largest. She had a bully's mentality and, because Jamie was weak and Helen could not be bothered to fight, she was able to reign as the self-appointed queen of the office.

The open-plan area led directly off the company's main foyer and, at around eleven o'clock, just as she was beginning to wonder how to fill the long hours before lunchtime, Helen's eye was drawn to the reception desk, where a woman was waiting for Annie, Global's podgy-faced receptionist, to get off the phone. She was holding something that looked like a computer bag. Helen let her gaze move up to the woman's face, and her heart nearly stopped beating. It was Sophie.

Helen ducked down behind her monitor, then peeped over the top of it again like a private eye with a newspaper. What the fuck was she doing here? Panic made her thought processes cloudy, and she was convinced that Sophie had come for a showdown with her, husband-stealing, child-orphaning bitch that she was. It played out in her mind like a scene from *Trisha*, the whole office looking on as the wronged wife shouted and cried and threatened and maybe even hit out, Helen having to defend herself both morally and physically, trying to put a spin on the situation that made taking a man away from his wife and young children seem like the acceptable thing to do. Matthew coming in and seeing his wife and girlfriend going at it like teenagers. Her colleagues alternately open-mouthed or smirking behind their hands. Embarrassment, shame, ridicule. She'd got as far as having to resign from her job without a hope of a reference, when she looked again at the bag over Sophie's shoulder. The computer, of course – she'd brought Matthew his computer. Calmer now, her brain allowed back in the memory of Matthew saying that he hadn't told Sophie the identity of the woman he was leaving her for. Helen breathed again. She was off the hook. For now.

Having got fear out of her system, curiosity took over. Picking up a file from her desk, she walked over to a filing cabinet close to the reception area just as Annie put down the phone and greeted Sophie. Pretending to riffle through random papers, she listened as Annie said she'd let Matthew know that Sophie was there. Sophie jumped in.

'No. I'm in a rush. I'll just leave the computer.'

She had a nice voice. Friendly. Helen had a surreptitious look. Sophie looked like her photo, unsurprisingly enough, but slighter, with a not bad figure. Helen waited for the long-held feelings of loathing to overwhelm her. Here she was in the flesh, the enemy, the focus of so much negative energy over the last four years that you could plug light bulbs into her. She'd dreamt and fantasized about this moment for so long – seeing Sophie in the flesh, getting a good look at her – that it felt almost a let-down that Sophie was just a woman. A woman who was shaking slightly with the strain of trying to hold it together. It was obvious she'd made an effort today, in case she bumped into her husband, but no amount of make-up could disguise the dark circles round her eyes. Where was Matthew anyway? thought Helen. She considered ringing him to warn him to steer clear of reception, but Sophie was turning to leave, exchanging banal pleasantries with Annie. She'd nearly made it through the door when Matthew strode out of the conference room opposite and all but collided with her.

There was a toe-curling moment which probably only lasted ten seconds but seemed like a minute, when neither one spoke, followed by an awkward stuttered 'hello'. Though she tried to pretend it wasn't happening, a tear sprung out of the corner of Sophie's eye and trickled down her cheek. Annie, who had a preternatural sense for identifying a potential source of gossip, didn't even try to pretend she wasn't listening in.

Sophie gave Matthew his laptop. 'I thought you might need this.'

He lowered his voice, but not enough that he couldn't be heard by Annie. 'How are the girls?'

For fuck's sake, Matthew, thought Helen, take her into your office, don't make her have this conversation in public.

Sophie's voice was shaky and barely audible. 'Missing you, of course.'

'Tell them I miss them too,' he was saying, and Helen was practically blushing at the humiliation Sophie must be feeling.

'Phone them and tell them yourself.'

And Sophie left him standing there, her dignity (almost) intact.

*

It was all round the office in minutes. Helen kept her head down at her computer but could practically feel a Mexican wave of whispering travelling round the room.

Eventually Jenny came and sat on her desk. 'Have you heard?'

For a moment, Helen considered standing up and shouting, 'Yes and it's all because of me. I'm the reason his wife was crying and his shirts aren't ironed and his kids are going to grow up without a father.' But she settled on, 'Heard what?'

'Matthew and his wife have split up. He's moved out – no one knows where.'

She took a dramatic pause for a reaction. Helen contorted her face into something she hoped would pass off as surprise.

'How sad.'

'I knew there was something up with him. Oh my god!' Jenny's stage whisper reached a squeakier pitch. 'You don't think he's gone off with someone else, do you?'

'How the fuck would I know?' said Helen, a touch too defensively.

'Imagine. How gross. I mean he's so . . . old. Hey,' she shouted across at reception, 'what if Matthew's been shagging around?'

Annie gave a visceral shudder of revulsion. 'Grim, I bet he's all . . . saggy.'

'With grey pubes,' added another girl, Liza, who Helen had always hated anyway, walking through the lobby on her way to the IT department, 'and droopy man-tits.'

Great, thought Helen, who for some reason had always

believed that her female colleagues found Matthew rather attractive. Absolutely fucking great.

'They can never find out it's me.'

Helen and Matthew were eating dinner at the kitchen table again. This time, she'd cooked – fish fingers, oven chips and frozen peas, a meal she was secretly hoping might make him yearn for Sophie's grown-up dinners.

'I mean it, Matthew, we can't ever tell anyone at work.'

He'd got his puppy-dog look back. The one which made Helen want to kick him.

'Are you ashamed of me?'

'Of course I'm not, I just don't think it'll do either of us any good.'

'But I want to show you off. I want everyone to know how much in love we are.'

She felt sick.

'Tell you what, why don't we just wait a bit and then we can tell them we got together after you left Sophie. It'll be cleaner like that. Otherwise, everyone's going to think I'm a rampaging bitch.'

'OK,' he agreed reluctantly. 'I suppose we could wait a month.'

'Let's make it two.' She put her hand over his and smiled at him, thinking 'OK, I have two months to work out what I'm going to do.'

It had been nearly two weeks since Matthew had moved in, and Sophie's only contact with him had been the excruciating laptop moment. She knew enough about Annie to know that the news would be all round Global now, if it wasn't already, and her stomach turned over as she imagined the pseudo sympathy and mock concern for her that would be peppering Matthew's colleagues' conversations. She was in an angry phase – how dare he allow her to be humiliated like that and, more to the point, why had she bothered worrying about whether he needed his computer, it was none of her concern now – so when he called to say he needed to get more of his stuff, she thought about telling him where to shove it. But that wasn't her. As usual, she would accommodate and try and make things as painless and easy as possible for everyone other than herself. He asked if he could come when the girls were going to be there, and Sophie gave him a time on Sunday afternoon when she could go off to the supermarket and they need only have the bare minimum of contact. She couldn't face either a row or an attempt at conversation.

He arrived promptly at two and hesitated on the doorstep, unsure whether to ring the bell or just let himself in. Sophie could see him through the Venetian blinds on the kitchen window, hands in his coat pockets, the slight stoop he always affected when he was feeling uneasy. He looked tired. She called Suzanne to let him in and take him up to the living room, and then she slipped out of the front door. She didn't even want to say hello.

To Helen it felt as if, for a couple of hours, she had got her old life back. She lay on the sofa reading a book, revelling in the silence. She knew she should be trying to clear more space to make room for Matthew's things, but she couldn't be bothered to move. She wondered idly how he was getting on, then dismissed the thought as quickly as it had come.

At about five o'clock, she heard his car pulling up outside and started to drag herself up towards the front door. She stopped as she heard Matthew's voice talking to . . . who? She pulled back the curtain a fraction and drew it again when she saw Matthew flanked by two small pre-teenage girls, each carrying a box. Fuck! He'd brought Claudia and what's-her-name. Helen rushed to the mirror and started tweaking at her frizzy Sunday-afternoon hair and wiping away at yesterday's smudged mascara, which was encrusted beneath her eyes.

How could he do this to me? she thought. Without so much as a phone call? Had he no idea that adolescent girls valued appearances above all else? She had already planned what she would wear on their first meeting – FCUK jeans, high brown boots from Aldo and the baby-blue Paul Frank hoodie which, she knew, was way too young for her but which she was hoping would make her look 'cool'. Labels that adolescent girls had heard of and would admire. She had decided to go for the big-sister approach. Admittedly a scarily old big sister – it was all a bit *Whatever Happened to Baby Jane?*', but anyway. Now the only clean item of clothing to hand was an age-appropriate fitted light-grey jumper which she wore to work, but it would have to do. She was pulling the clean top on over her head when she heard his key turning in the front door. Affecting an air of what she thought looked like sophisticated nonchalance, she managed to arrive in the hall seemingly unruffled, as he led the girls in.

Matthew was in overcompensatingly jolly-father mode.

'Look who I've brought to meet you,' he said.

'What a lovely surprise,' said Helen, almost convincingly.

'They've been dying to see you for themselves, haven't you, girls?' From the looks on his daughters' faces, any idiot could tell that this was a lie.

'This is Suzanne.' He indicated the taller, slightly less sullen-looking of the two. 'And this is Claudia.'

Claudia looked Helen up and down like she was sizing up a rival.

Helen smiled in what she believed was a youthful, pally manner. 'It's so great to meet you. Your dad talks about you both all the time so I feel like I, kind of, know you already. And I'm really hoping we can be, like, friends.'

The girls looked at her blankly.

'Do you know you've got your jumper on inside out?' Claudia said, and then immediately turned back to her father. 'Can we go home now?'

'No, Claudia. Don't be rude, say "hello" to Helen.'

Suzanne muttered an almost inaudible hello, while Claudia fixed Helen with a blank stare.

'It'll take them a bit of time to get used to you,' said Matthew apologetically. 'Come into the living room, girls, and you can chat to Helen while I get you a drink.'

'This is a dump,' Helen thought she heard Claudia say, as he ushered them on through.

When Sophie had brought Suzanne home from the hospital, Matthew had told her that he saw it as his second chance to prove himself as a father. His relationship with his son, then twenty-six, had always been fairly formal –

Matthew had not taken easily to parenthood first time round and had always been slightly afraid of the judgemental gaze of his eldest child – but it become almost non-existent following Matthew's abandonment of Leo's mother. Bizarrely, Leo had always got on well with Sophie, who he saw – quite rightly, it now seemed – as another potential victim of his father's selfishness. He placed the blame for the break-up squarely on Matthew's shoulders and, although he never mentioned it, it sat between them like a glass partition preventing them from ever getting too close. So Matthew mostly kept in touch with his only son via his second wife, a situation he knew was flawed at the best of times but about to become impossible.

Suzanne, therefore, had only ever known Matthew as a dedicated, devoted, doting father. Forced into the role of 'the clever one' by the arrival of much prettier sister Claudia, she'd been struggling to live up to this reputation ever since, but the amount of praise and attention she received from Matthew when she did well in an exam made the hours of secret studying she did, in an effort to make it look like she wasn't even trying, worth it. She was a placid, easy-going child on the surface, but she was hiding some frantic paddling underneath.

Claudia, on the other hand, seethed with resentment at her pigeon-holing as 'the pretty one', because she believed, quite rightly, as it happened, that the reality was that she was also the cleverest. She knew all about Suzanne's clandestine cramming, but she never let on, and the harder Suzanne worked, the more Claudia assumed an attitude that said she couldn't care less about school. Her bad behaviour, optimistically described by her teachers as 'a phase', was so clearly a reaction to her bore-dom in a class full of children who she had overtaken academically a couple of years before that any amateur psychologist could have spotted it, but sadly there was never an amateur psychologist around when you needed one.

For someone who wanted to get it right this time, Matthew had managed to bring up two rather fucked-up daughters.

While Matthew was fetching tea and Diet Cokes, Helen decided to try talking to the less scary-looking of the two, Suzanne.

'This must be really hard for you. I'm sorry.'

Claudia made a noise that was a cross between a snort and a sigh and rolled her eyes all at the same time, which, thought Helen, must take some doing. Suzanne was teary-eyed. She twirled her fingers round and round in her sandy-blond curly hair, and Helen could see the effort it was taking to hold back from crying.

'I want him to come home.'

'I know. Perhaps he will' – Helen laughed in what she thought was an endearingly self-effacing manner – 'once he gets fed up of me.' Oh, great, she thought, now I'm making bad jokes. Not only that, bad jokes about their father being an unreliable old philanderer.

'What I mean is, when he realizes how much he misses you all.'

'Do you mean that?' Suzanne's naïve straw-clutching was actually making Helen feel even more like shit, if that was possible, but before she could step in with something else equally comforting, Claudia jumped in, all bravado.

'Don't be so stupid. Of course she doesn't. And, anyway, I wouldn't want him to come home now.'

Suzanne started all-out crying just as Matthew, cheery Dad smile plastered across his face, came in with the drinks. His expression dropped, and he looked accusingly at Helen as if she'd been hitting his kids with a ruler the minute he'd left the room. She shrugged at him.

'Can we go yet, Dad?' asked Claudia.

'Yes,' said Matthew. 'I think we'd better.'

Helen could've sworn Claudia muttered 'bitch' at her under her breath as they left.

The following weekend, Matthew wanted to invite Suzanne and Claudia over again, but Helen was having none of it. She could see that befriending his daughters wasn't going to be an easy ride and, at the moment, it all felt a bit like hard work. She persuaded Matthew that it was too soon for the girls but failed to convince him that he should take them out instead thus leaving her with a blissfully empty flat.

'The whole point is that I want them to feel they have a second home here,' he whined. 'Not that they have a part-time father who has to take them places they don't want to go every time they see him.' They agreed on the subsequent Sunday and settled down for an uneventful couple of days.

At four o'clock on Saturday, the doorbell rang. Helen opened it to find an elderly, well-groomed woman who looked vaguely familiar on the doorstep.

'Is Matthew in?' the woman asked.

'He's not. He'll be back in about an hour.'

Matthew had, in fact, gone to the local supermarket to do the weekly shop in an effort to be useful, something he'd never in his life done before. At this moment, he was paralysed with fear in front of the vegetable counter, trying to work out what the difference was between a cherry and a plum tomato and whether or not it mattered.

'Good. It's you I came to see. I'm Sheila.' She had a voice that could grate cheese, and Helen took an instant dislike to her, 'posh women' having been one of the first to feature on Helen and Rachel's list of 'Women we hate'.

The woman swept past Helen into the hall and through to the living room. She was incredibly well dressed for a Sunday, thought Helen, who was in sweatpants and T-shirt, which might as well have been pyjamas. Sheila, on the other hand, was wearing a neat white blouse under a pale-blue cashmere sweater, tan trousers and heels. Women like that had the ability to make Helen feel like one of the Beverly Hillbillies, and Sheila was no exception. She even smelt expensive. She clicked across the wooden floor and, with a flick of her blow-dried-to-within-an-inch-of-its-life hair, she looked round, taking in the dirty plates with toast crusts still left on them, the piles of magazines and newspapers lying on every surface and Matthew's boxes still in the corner. Helen dredged her memory for 'Sheila'. Wasn't wife number one called something like that? she was wondering, when Sheila put her out of her misery.

'I'm Matthew's mother.'

Of course. He might be old, but he had surely never been married to a woman who was now in her eighties.

'Right. Nice to meet you,' said Helen unconvincingly. 'Shall I make some tea?'

'It's completely unforgivable what you've done, breaking up a family, leaving those girls without a father. I hope you're ashamed of yourself.'

'Milk and sugar?' Helen stormed off to the kitchen to

try and compose herself. No such luck – Sheila followed her.

'I suppose it's his money, is it?'

Helen took a deep breath. 'I don't know. Does he have any?'

Sheila ignored her. 'I bet you never even gave his family a second thought, did you?'

Helen resisted the urge to say, 'What, and Sophie did when she stole him away from his first wife?' and said instead, 'I've told him he should go back to them if that's what he wants to do.'

'It's too late for that, though, isn't it? Sophie would never take him back.'

'Then why are you here?' asked Helen, all pretence of making tea having been forgotten.

'My daughters and I are very concerned about the effect that this will have on the girls.'

'Is that the daughter who came on to the other daughter's husband at Christmas? Or the one who's married to an alcoholic? Or is that the same one? I can never remember,' said Helen, who had decided to give up on politeness.

Sheila ignored her again. 'If you're going to become part of this family – and I don't see what I can do to prevent that happening – then we would like to know that you're intending to take your responsibilities as a stepmother seriously.'

'Or what?' Helen was gradually reverting to being four-teen years of age.

'Or I'd ask you not to try and ingratiate yourself into their lives. They were very upset after their visit here last weekend.'

Oh, go fuck yourself, thought Helen, but what she said was, 'Shall I show you out?'

'She's a fucking stupid interfering fucking bitch,' Helen was shouting at Matthew later that afternoon.

'She's my mother.'

'Well, she's a fucking stupid interfering fucking bitch of a mother. And tell her not to come round here again.'

Sunday evening was looming. Somehow, when Helen had been feeling at a particularly low ebb, she'd found herself agreeing to a night out to introduce her boyfriend to her best friend. At the time it had been over a week away and had felt like she'd have all the time in the world to get out of it. Now, it was tomorrow night, and she had to take desperate measures. She called Rachel.

'OK, so I'm just going to tell him you've cried off. I'll say you're busy at work.'

'No way! You've been whining on about this man for four years. I am not going to miss my chance to get a look at him.'

'I'll say I'm ill – then we'll have to stay home. You can sit in the pub all night waiting for us if you want, but we won't be there.'

'If you don't show up, I'm coming round to your flat,' said Rachel laughing. 'There's no getting out of it.'

Matthew was irritatingly twittery as they got ready, changing his outfit twice – suit versus jeans and a shirt: the jeans won, to Helen's dismay – and primping about in front of the mirror like an adolescent girl. He looked more rumpled these days, Helen thought, older. It was as if he left his confident, powerful self on the bedroom floor every evening, along with his suit, and slipped into slightly shambolic Dad mode. Even his walk was different – more apologetic, less authoritative. Helen resisted the urge to tell him to trim his nose hairs and suck his stomach in. But as they got into the cab, she could practically smell his nervousness, and it brought out all her worst and most selfish qualities.

'Just don't say anything to embarrass me,' she said supportively.

In the pub, Rachel was all smiles as she said hello to Matthew and introduced him to Neil, but Helen knew that what she really wanted to say was, 'God, you really are old.' They filled a few minutes hanging up coats and ordering drinks, and everyone struggled for a way to start the conversation. Rachel was first:

'So, Matthew, any more wives we should know about, or is it just the two?'

Matthew started to stammer out an answer. Helen stopped him. 'She's joking, Matthew.' She glared at Rachel. 'That's Rachel's idea of a joke.'

'I knew that,' he said, in a quite endearingly self-deprecating way.

'Actually, I was just curious,' persisted Rachel. 'Were you married to your first wife when you started going out with Sophie? I mean, is that something you do?'

'Rachel!' This time it was Neil who came to Matthew's aid. 'I'm sorry, Matthew.'

'It's fine. Rachel, I can understand your concern for

Helen. You wouldn't be a good friend if you didn't want to make sure that she was making the right choices. And, yes, I'm afraid I was still married to Hannah when I met Sophie and, no, it's not something I'm proud of. But I want to reassure you that I love Helen and I intend to make her truly happy for the rest of her life.'

He was trying his best, but he sounded like a vicar giving a sermon. Helen was mortified.

'Can we talk about something else?'

But Rachel wasn't giving up: 'You've got kids, haven't you? You must be missing them terribly.'

'I am,' said Matthew, looking to see where the next poisoned dart was coming from.

'It's awful for them really, losing their dad at such a young age. Who knows what the psychological effects might be . . .'

Neil stood up, cutting her off. 'Pool, Matthew? I'm a bit shit but it's got to be better than sitting here getting interrogated.'

Helen touched his arm. 'That's a great idea. Go and play. Rachel and I have got lots to catch up on.'

'What the fuck are you doing?' Helen hissed at Rachel as soon as Matthew and Neil were out of earshot.

'Trying to help you out. I figured that even if he still thinks he wants you, he'll decide he can't stand the thought of having to deal with your best friend for the rest of his life.'

'Well, stop. He loves me. I'm obviously irresistible.'

'He's an old man, Helen. He'd find the fact you still have all your own teeth irresistible.'

97

'We're going to make it work,' Helen said, not entirely convincingly, 'so you need to get used to the idea.'

'Just as well, because he's never going to leave – at least not until he's got somewhere else to go. I've worked it out, he's a relayer, he never ends one relationship until he's got another one on the go. He's terrified of being alone.'

Rachel had a lot of theories about relationships which, considering none of her own liaisons had ever lasted more than a few weeks, was a bit of a joke. Men, she broke down into:

Serial monogamists
Mummy-replacers
Commitmentphobes
Darren Days
Nice boys
New men (possibly the most loathsome group of all)
Too-lazy-to-moves
Bit-on-the-siders
Normal, grown-up, well-balanced men (few and far between)
Relayers

Women, she tended to be slightly less generous with, putting them into one of only three categories:

Women like me (i.e. nice, loyal, faithful, reliable)
Husband-stealers
Bunny-boilers

Up to now, she had had Matthew down as a bit-on-the-sider, a man with a wife who has affairs but has no intention of going anywhere because he has it too good at home. Helen, of course, had moved from being a woman-like-me to a husband-stealer many years ago.

'I have to try and make it work,' Helen was saying, beginning to sound like a looped sample on a rap record.

'Well, I guess you'd better because, I'm telling you, he's there to stay unless you find some other woman willing to take him on,' Rachel insisted again.

'Just be nice to him when they come back,' Helen pleaded.

So, when Matthew and Neil returned from their game, Rachel made a real effort to be friendly, which left Matthew wondering whether she might be schizophrenic.

'I like him,' said Neil to Rachel on their way home.

'Don't get too attached,' said Rachel.

Unaware that her husband was the subject of such intense speculation, Sophie was redecorating the bedroom in an effort to remove any trace of him. The house next door had a skip outside, and she was filling it with golf clubs and boxes of books and tennis racquets, all things which she assumed he would at some point want to come back and collect. Looking out of the window, she could see a couple of the students who lived in the hall of residence up the road rummaging through and helping themselves, and she smiled for the first time that day. His clothes she donated to a charity, because she liked the idea of seeing one of the local homeless men asleep in a doorway wearing Matthew's favourite Armani sweater.

When Suzanne and Claudia had returned from their visit to Matthew's new home Sophie had stuck to the promise she had made herself and didn't ask them any probing questions, but over the last week or so, things had slipped out and she now knew that:

Helen lived in a basement
It was about a ten-minute drive away (but she didn't know in which direction)
It had a wooden floor
Helen had long dark hair
She was very pretty

This last was forced out of Suzanne by Sophie, whose curiosity had finally got the better of her. Suzanne then tried to soften the blow by adding, 'But nowhere near as pretty as you, Mum,' but it was too late.

'Looks aren't important, you know,' Sophie had said, not managing to sound even half-convincing.

Knowing that Helen was 'very pretty' of course made Sophie feel worse, although there is a case for thinking it should have made her feel better. If your husband leaves you for someone who looks like a gorgon, that's when you should really get depressed, because it obviously means that he's now so out of love with you that looks don't even enter the equation. That his new love's personality is so stunning compared to yours that he's willing to overlook the fact that she's an utter munter. That he's prepared to have sex with the lights off for the rest of his life because at least he'll be having it with someone who's not you. At least if he leaves you for someone better looking, you can tell yourself he's just having a mid-life crisis – or, in Matthew's case, another mid-life crisis.

Anyway, since that conversation, Sophie had tried to avoid the subject of Helen with the girls, in case she heard something else equally as depressing. But she'd taken to going to the gym and got her nails painted and had her lowlights done in the fear that all her friends would gang up behind her back when they – inevitably – met Helen to say things like, 'It was only a matter of time – Sophie's lovely, but Helen's so . . . pretty.' She thought about asking Suzanne how old she thought Helen was but, knowing how children saw adults, she knew the answer she'd get would be either seventeen or sixty and she'd be none the wiser, so she talked herself out of it.

She wondered if he was going to file for divorce or if that was something she was meant to do, and she made a mental note to get a solicitor.

She came across a photo of the two of them on their wedding day and drew glasses and a moustache and a large hairy wart on Matthew, then felt bad about it and tried to rub it off, but she couldn't.

She cleared out the drawer in his desk in the study and found a drawing Claudia had done for him when she was four years old. It was of a family: mother, father and two small girls and a dog they had never had. They stood in a row next to a tree and the sun beamed with a big smiling face above them. Under the people, she'd labelled them, and she'd underlined the word 'Daddy' three times, as if to imply that he was really important. Matthew must have kept hold of it through four different houses and at least three changes of desk. Sophie refused to cry again. She smoothed out the sheet of paper and put it back in the drawer.

II

Most days, Helen found herself flicking through the photo album that Matthew had hastily thrown in with his cricket pads and his Homer Simpson hip flask when he moved in. The pictures, she had discovered, had notes written on the back in hand-writing she didn't recognize which could only be Sophie's. 'Matt and the girls. Braunton, 2003,' said one, which showed the three of them windswept on a rainy beach. Did Sophie call him Matt? That seemed so wrong – he was a Matthew through and through. Did he call her 'Soph', she wondered? Another, a picture of a smiling couple, arms around each other, Sophie's dark head resting on Matthew's shoulder, had 'Second Honeymoon!!!!' scrawled on the reverse. Had they gone on a second honeymoon? When? She turned the picture over again, looking for clues. Sophie's dark nut-brown eyes were screwed up against the sun. Her hair was longer than it was now, curling past her shoulders, sunglasses pushing it back off her face, freckles still visible through the tan. Matthew's arm rested proprietorially around her shoulders. Helen knew they went away every year, usually to Italy – a villa in Tuscany, in fact, in a stroke of great originality among the English upper middle classes – but what year had they deemed the break deserved to be called a second honeymoon, with all the sex and rediscovery and renewed commitment that implied? She hid the album back in its box again before Matthew could catch her looking.

Claudia and Suzanne were due over at three. In an effort to win them round to a point of at least civility, Helen had bought cakes and sausage rolls and made sandwiches. Matthew, touched that she was trying so hard to get along with his children, hugged her with tears in his eyes.

'I'm a vegan.'

Claudia turned her nose up at the table full of food and threw herself into the armchair.

'Since when?' asked Matthew, trying to hide the exasperation in his voice.

'I just am, that's all.'

Suzanne was making an effort in order to please her father. She'd piled her plate high with food and was slowly working her way through it while eyeing Helen warily.

'Don't eat too much,' said her father. 'You'll make yourself sick.'

'So, how's school?' Helen asked, stunned by her own lack of imagination.

'OK,' said Suzanne. Claudia said nothing. That was that then.

'Tell Helen what you were telling me in the car on the way over,' said Matthew to Claudia. 'About the play.'

'No.' Claudia turned her face to look out of the window at the small backyard.

'Claudia's playing the main part,' offered up Suzanne helpfully. 'She's going to be a princess.'

Helen passed up the chance to say, 'She'd better be a

good actress then.' At least one of them's speaking to me, she thought. I'll just concentrate on her.

'How about you?' she said to Suzanne. 'Are you an actress, too?'

'No, I'm no good,' Suzanne said, betraying more than a bit of envy, and Helen felt a moment of pity for her. How awful to be the plainer, less talented older sister and to know without a doubt that that's what you are.

'Well, everyone's good at different things. Your dad told me you did really well in your exams last term.' (Please let it be the right sister. In truth, she couldn't remember which one of the girls Matthew had been banging on about at the time because she hadn't been listening.)

'Did he?' Suzanne came to life all at once and beamed at her father.

'I did,' said Matthew indulgently. 'She did brilliantly. In fact, they both did brilliantly, didn't you, girls?'

Nice one, Matthew, thought Helen, way to go to deny Suzanne her moment.

By four o'clock, Helen was exhausted and desperate for the girls to go home, bored with the sullen one-way street that was substituting for a conversation. Matthew, sensing the atmosphere deteriorating, took Claudia out the back so they could plant a few bulbs together in the tiny dark patio that passed for a garden. Once out from under her sister's disapproving gaze, Suzanne had become quite chatty and, being without guile herself, had not been suspicious when Helen's curiosity got the better of her and she found herself firing off a series of Sophie-related questions. Helen now knew that Sophie:

Worked in the City

Travelled to work by tube

Used her maiden name, Marcombe, at work

Sometimes went to the gym in her lunch hour

Never went out in the evenings (never??)

Didn't seem to have any friends, at least none Suzanne knew
the names of

Currently spent quite a lot of time crying

Fucking hell, thought Helen, what a life.

Once she was safely at her desk on Monday morning, Helen looked up Sophie Marcombe on Yahoo and found what she was looking for. Sophie was Senior Accounts Director at May and Co. Financial Services in Finsbury Square. Curious, she looked her up on Friends Reunited and found three Sophie Marcombes of various ages. One at a school in Iver in Buckinghamshire had notes which read, 'I'm married to Matthew and have two daughters. Work in the City.' She checked the year – Sophie was forty-five or forty-six depending on when her birthday was. She looked up Finsbury Square in the *A to Z*, Iver Heath Junior School, May and Co. and Bartholomew Road, the street where she knew Matthew and Sophie's family home was, on Up My Street. She looked at her watch.

Helen, in fact, didn't just know where Sophie lived, she had seen the house. Once, early on in her relationship with Matthew and overwhelmed with curiosity about her rival, she had checked through Matthew's personal records at work – a favour granted her by a friend who worked in Human Resources – and found his address. She had taken the tube to Kentish Town instead of Camden after work on a non-Matthew night and walked round the corner to Bartholomew Road, a street of majestic houses mostly divided into flats but gradually being reclaimed as family homes by wealthy owners. She had followed the street as it doubled back on itself, and she'd found number 155, four storeys plus a basement of sandy-coloured brick with a small, tidy front garden containing a couple of rose-bushes and space for two cars. Matthew's car was absent – she had obviously beaten him to it – but another, a small Peugeot, presumably Sophie's, was parked up neatly.

It was winter and the lights were on in the raised ground and first floors but from her vantage point across and slightly up the street, there was precious little to see. She'd paced up and down a little, feeling rather foolish. She'd thought about ringing the doorbell – 'Hello, madam, I'm just doing a survey' – but she knew Matthew would be home any minute and, anyway, could she really pull it off? And even if she did, to what end? She'd decided to call it a day and maybe to come back on a weekend, when she might stand a chance of seeing Sophie getting in or out of her car or walking round the corner to the shops, and was traipsing back towards the tube station when a familiar car drove past her, then stopped and reversed, and Matthew got out and started shouting. He was beside himself with rage and, she could see, panic. What did she think she was doing? What if Sophie had seen her? How dare she play games with his life like this? She had felt embarrassed and stupid and angry all at the same time but, mostly, she had been afraid that she would lose him, that he'd feel he could never trust her to be discreet again. It had been days before he'd calmed down, and she'd had to do some serious pleading. She'd never attempted anything like it again.

Now, years later, the same compulsion had engulfed her once more. Today, luckily for Helen, Laura was having a long lunch with a client so wasn't there to notice that Helen slipped out herself at twelve thirty. By ten to one she was sitting on a bench in the square opposite the entrance to May and Co., watching as people left and walked to local cafés and restaurants. She didn't know why, but she just wanted to get another look at Sophie, in a relaxed and familiar environment this time, one where she wasn't on the back foot. She felt like Steve Irwin camped out by a crocodile's watery home. She just wanted to study the subject in her own habitat.

Every woman knows that this is a familiar impulse – the anonymous look, the urge to check out the ex or the perceived rival or the girl from the IT department he just happened to drop into the conversation once. It's easy to take a small detour on the way home to go past her office. It's only another tiny step to walk by her house en route to the shops. Might as well go the whole hog and sit in a car outside for four straight hours in the hope of seeing – what? A woman you've seen before entering or leaving. Maybe a glimpse of her current boyfriend or her mother or her sister or her dog. Or even her sister's dog. There was no denying it – a twelve-foot-long reptile with big teeth is a twelve-foot-long reptile with big teeth wherever you spot it – but so much more satisfying to watch it swimming in a lake than in a zoo.

Helen was getting bored and starting to freeze when, at four minutes past one, she saw Sophie coming out of the front door of May and Co. White coat, brown boots, umbrella. She stood up, then sat down again, then stood and followed from a distance. She could see that Sophie had gone into Eat, so she went in, too, and poked around half-heartedly in the sandwich section. Sophie was already at the counter ordering soup, so Helen grabbed a chicken wrap and got into the queue behind her. She suddenly saw what it must be like to be a bloke, always expected to make the first move on a girl. She had an overwhelming urge to speak to Sophie and tried to think of an opening line.

'Nice day.' Too banal.

'Is the soup here good?' Only required a one-word answer and, anyway, what kind of a freak had never tried the soup at Eat before?

'Do you work round here?' Too creepy, lesbian stalker not being the image she was going for.

'Do you know the way to the nearest tube station?' Perfect. Not exactly a conversation launcher, but it'd have to do.

Sophie was collecting her change, turning round to go towards the door.

'Excuse me, do you know the way to the nearest tube station?' Helen was saying, but Sophie had already moved out of earshot and was heading into the street. Helen thought of running after her and tapping her on the shoulder, but the man behind the counter had started to answer her question and she was obliged to stay and listen to directions that she had no need of in order not to be rude. When she finally got outside, Sophie had long gone.

Thank god.

What had she been thinking of? Now the moment was

over, she went pale thinking of what might have happened. 'Where's the underground?' – and then what? 'Oh, by the way, I thought I'd just mention it, I'm the woman your husband has left you for. Must rush. Nice to meet you. Bye.' What was the best that could have happened? Sophie giving her directions she didn't want? She made her way back to the office dejected, trying to figure out what was going on in her head. She was trying to decide whether to call Rachel and confess her weird stalking trip, when she was intercepted by Annie.

'Guess what?' she was saying, eyes blazing with the excitement of having a hot piece of gossip to impart. 'Amelia from Human Resources spoke to Matthew's wife this morning, and she told her that Matthew *has* gone off with someone else and, not only that – it's someone he met through work. And . . .' There was a big dramatic pause while Helen held her breath and waited for the worst '. . . her name's Helen.'

Annie lived to be the imparter of stories. That wasn't to say she was a wit who loved to entertain. There was no art in her tale-telling, she just wanted to be the centre of attention, and revelled in her position as Global's scandal oracle. It was a miracle that she had never even caught the scent of Helen and Matthew, but she was one of those blonde big-breasted women who – despite having a face that looked like Play-Doh, a squashy baby's face that probably looked cute when she was twenty but now was more puffy Pound Puppy – believed she possessed the only two qualities of interest to a man. It had never occurred to her that anybody could find a brunette or a redhead attractive and, if they were smaller than a 36C, then forget it.

It was a defence mechanism, of course. When she looked in the mirror at night, she could be brought to tears by the loss of her youthful puppy-fatty beauty, but she thought that if she shouted loudly and often enough about poor old so and so with her 34As and how sorry she felt for her sister, who hadn't inherited their mother's honey tones as she had, then everyone would start to agree with her. She knew that Helen was pretty – way prettier now, even as she was approaching forty, than she herself had ever been – but she comforted herself that it was a prettiness no man would ever be excited by. She simply refused to see Helen as sexually attractive.

Helen decided the best defence was to laugh in a 'What a ludicrous coincidence' sort of a way. But Annie wasn't finished.

'So, we all know it's not you. It's not, is it?' she said, laughing. 'You're not that desperate. And you've got Carlo.' (Oh, yes, fictitious Carlo existed in Helen's life story to her work colleagues, too.) 'That leaves Helen from Accounts, but I think she's married – not that that counts for much – she's pig ugly, though, but then I suppose he's old, he'd be grateful for whatever he could get . . . Then there's Helen from Simpson's – Matthew handled that account – do you remember? – and he did spend an awful lot of time on it. Plus, she's blonde. Jenny says she remembers them working late quite a bit. There's a Helen who works at Barker and Co., and they went out to dinner once when we first got the account. Oh, and then that woman at the travel agent's who organizes all his trips, she's called Helen or Helena or something like that. God, who knew there were so many Helens?'

For our Helen, the relief that she'd not yet been rumbled was slightly dwarfed by her annoyance that her colleagues couldn't even contemplate that she'd be in the running as far as Matthew was concerned. Half of her wanted to say, 'Why is it a foregone conclusion that it's not me?' but she decided to quit while she was ahead. Attack them before they attacked her.

'I bet it is Helen from Accounts,' Helen found herself saying. 'She's always moaning on about her husband, and she went on that company retreat that Matthew went on, remember? Also, I'm sure I remember her saying she fancied him once.'

Oh god, she thought, I'm going to hell.

The rest of the day went by in a bit of a blur, but the Helen-from-Accounts rumour had taken on its own momentum, with considerable help from Annie, and by late afternoon it might as well have been gospel. Helen rang Rachel just before she left the office.

'You have to meet me for a drink. Now. And don't bring Neil.'

Then she rang and left a message on Matthew's mobile saying that she needed some girly time with her friend and she'd see him at home later.

On the way to the lift, she bumped into Jenny, coming back from a coffee run.

'Have you heard about Matthew and Helen-from-Accounts?' Jenny'd got the gossip glow.

'I know,' Helen called back over her shoulder. 'Gross, isn't it?'

*

Rachel could barely contain her laughter, even though Helen was clearly stressed out and in need of a bit of moral support.

'So tell me, what she's like, Helen-from-Accounts?'

'Mousy, married, probably loves her husband. Certainly doesn't deserve to have everyone gossiping about her behind her back.'

'It's genius. And did she really ever say she fancied Matthew?'

'No, of course not, I added that bit.'

'Nice touch.'

'All I've done is put off the inevitable. And make it even worse for myself once they do find out.'

'I wouldn't worry about that,' Rachel said helpfully. 'Your life's pretty much over anyway once they realize.'

Back at home, Helen thought of telling Matthew about Helen-from-Accounts but decided against it. It would only have worried him, thinking that everyone in the office was talking about him and watching his every move. Besides, he might have made a big deal of going into work and denying it for the other Helen's sake, and it suited this Helen to have people believing it was the truth.

On Tuesday, despite her best instincts screaming at her to stay in the office and eat a sandwich at her desk, Helen was back at her lunchtime post again, having told Laura she needed an extra-long lunch break to go to the dentist. It was a beautifully sunny January day and the square was peppered with people venturing out for the first time that year, faces turned up to the sky like penguins watching an overhead airplane, sleeves rolled up defiantly even though they were shivering. Once again, Helen followed Sophie to Eat, lurked about behind her, then followed her back again towards the front door of May and Co., then past it when Sophie walked on and turned into the square. She sat on a bench in the cool winter sun, took a newspaper out of her bag and read while she ate her sandwich (crayfish and rocket – she had dithered between that and ham, brie and honey mustard while Helen looked on, wondering what she was doing there and pretending to be interested in the writing on the side of a tuna and cucumber baguette).

Helen didn't know what to do other than go and sit on the next bench along and keep an eye on her prey. To what end, she had no idea, but it felt defeatist to turn around and go back to work. Sophie was flicking through her *Metro*, and Helen took the opportunity to have a good stare at her as she walked past, trying again to imagine that this woman was the same woman she had been obsessing about for years, the woman she had quizzed Matthew about so many times. It seemed so bizarre that she had a whole life of her own, a whole independent way of being that existed outside of Helen's head. It was almost like seeing Harry Potter walking up Camden High Street or Shrek in the corner shop buying tea bags. She looks pale, Helen thought, forgetting that this was January and everyone looked pale. She knew she shouldn't stare in case Sophie glanced up and caught her gawping, but she couldn't drag her eyes away. Consequently, she didn't notice the overgrown tree root poking out of the pathway in front of her or the fact that her left foot was heading straight for it.

'Aaagh.'

Helen lay sprawled on the frozen ground clutching her ankle, which was throbbing and swelling up all at the same time. In her memory afterwards, she was all Kate Winslet in *Sense and Sensibility* but, in reality, she was red in the face and slightly snotty and tearful, as much from the embarrassment as from the pain. She was trying to see if she could haul herself up without drawing any more attention to herself, when she noticed that Sophie had lowered her paper, and was looking at her, concerned.

'Are you OK?'

Oh god, she's talking to me. 'My ankle. I think I've sprained it. Aaagh.'

'Here, see if you can walk.' Sophie helped to pull her to her feet, and Helen winced as she put the weight on to her foot.

'No . . . it hurts. Sorry, I'm sure you've got things to do. I'll be OK. I just need to rest it for a bit, I think.'

'Well, you can't do that out here,' said kindhearted Sophie. 'My office is just over there. You can sit in there for a bit and, then, if it doesn't get any better, we can get you a taxi to Casualty.'

Oh my god, oh my god, oh my god.

All Helen's impulses were telling her to run away, that this surely couldn't lead to anything good, but she really had twisted her ankle, she really couldn't walk, it really would be foolish to sit out in the cold waiting for it to feel better and, besides, how could she resist a look inside Sophie's office?

'Ouch,' she said, as she hobbled towards the red-stuccoed front of the May and Co. building. Sophie gave her her arm, and Helen leant on her for support.

Helen was lying on the sofa in Sophie's office, taking it all in. It was disconcertingly tidy and well organized, with neat piles of paper in labelled trays and books graded according to height on the dark wood shelves.

There was no *personality* in the room, Helen thought, no pictures on the wall or photos on the desk – not that Helen was a fan of those women who plastered their offices with pictures of their children as if they were advertising them for sale, but there ought to be something, even if it was just a lipstick, lying on the desk top.

'I know. I'm a control freak.' Sophie had clocked her looking round. 'It's the only way I'm able to keep on top of everything. I can't afford the time to indulge myself in any distractions. Plus, I work in finance, so I'm probably autistic.'

Sophie's assistant had made Helen a mug of tea, and Sophie had propped her foot up on a cushion. Helen had a sneaky look at her watch, twenty-eight minutes past one. She ought to leave now to get back to the office by two.

'I'm Sophie, by the way.' Sophie extended her hand to shake.

'Helen . . . a . . . Eleanor . . .' stuttered Helen.

'Do you work round here?'

Oh god. Think.

'I'm a publicist. Freelance. I work from home. I live

just round the corner. In . . . erm . . .' She hesitated, because she barely knew where she was, let alone the names of any local streets. '. . . Well, just round the corner anyway.'

'My husband's in PR. Well, my ex-husband, I suppose. Ex-husband to be, actually.'

'Oh, I'm sorry.'

'Don't be. He turned out to be a shit.'

'Right.'

There was an awkward moment in which Helen, momentarily blindsided by this unprovoked mention of Matthew, couldn't think of anything to say and Sophie absorbed herself in moving papers in and out of her in-tray. Thankfully, the silence was punctured by the phone ringing.

'Sorry.' Sophie half-looked up at her. 'Do you mind if I get that?'

Helen gestured, go ahead, don't mind me. She listened in as Sophie took the call in the hope of gleaning another helpful piece of inside-Sophie information, but the conversation turned out to be about capital gains tax and other equally dull but far more complicated monetary things. Helen watched out of the corner of her eye as Sophie chatted, oblivious. She noticed how Sophie wound the telephone cord round and round in her free hand as she talked. I do that, she thought. In fact, it occurred to her as she studied Sophie's face, physically, we could be sisters, although Helen was sallow-skinned to Sophie's porcelain. She wondered what Hannah looked like. Matthew obviously only had one type, and once they got to forty-five, he moved on to a younger version of the same woman. How deeply flattering, she thought. If I'd had exactly the same personality but had blond hair, he probably wouldn't have been interested. She made up her mind to search for pictures of his first wife to see if her theory was true. By the time Sophie's call had finished, it was clear that she needed to get on with her work, and Helen was all too aware that she ought to get back to the office herself, so she gingerly tried her ankle and, although it was agony, declared that she felt OK to walk home. She felt reluctant to end the moment, though, and frustrated that she hadn't used the opportunity to learn more about Sophie to better effect. Fuck it, she thought. What have I got to lose? Well, actually, pretty much everything, her conscience's alter ego was saying, but she ignored her own voice of reason, not for the first time. It was now or never, so she tried her best shot.

'Is there a good gym round here? I haven't lived here very long, and I haven't had a chance to have a good look round.'

Sophie bought it.

'I've just joined Fit For Life in City Road. It's not bad. Gets a bit crowded at lunchtime.'

'Great. I'll have a look.'

'Tell you what, they gave me a load of guest passes – you can come with me one day if you want. Once your ankle's better.'

Hallelujah. Helen could hear the crowds roaring.

'That'd be brilliant.'

So they exchanged numbers, and Helen thanked Sophie for looking after her and promised to call. Sophie picked up a file from her desk and absorbed herself in it and, within a couple of minutes, had more or less forgotten all about her lunchtime encounter.

'So, what was she like?'

Helen had told Rachel an edited version of the story, which somehow had her down in Finsbury Square on legitimate business and the meeting with Sophie a completely million-to-one-shot random encounter. She wasn't sure that Rachel believed her.

'She's . . . OK. Just . . . normal, you know,' Helen said noncommittally.

'For fuck's sake, you've been obsessed with this woman for years. You must have more of an opinion on her than, "She's OK."'

'Quite nice, I suppose, actually . . . I don't know.'

'Mumsy?'

'No, actually.'

'Frumpy?'

'No.'

'Funny? Clever? New-best-friend material?'

'No. Of course not. She's just . . . ordinary. A bit dull, you know.'

'Any deformities, scars, bits missing?'

'Not that I could see.'

'God, how disappointing.'

Helen-from-Accounts had never been so popular. People were practically queuing to have lunch with her and were showing a real interest in her as a person, asking all about her home life and her husband. She had no idea what had brought on this sudden surge in status, but she was grateful for it, having always up to this point eaten her lunch alone, sitting at her desk with a magazine. Today, she was sitting in Prêt with Annie and Jenny, eating a mozzarella and avocado salad and answering their questions about who she liked and didn't like at Global.

'How about Matthew?' Annie was saying. 'What do you think of him?'

Helen-from-Accounts had always found Matthew to be charming – friendly, polite, patient when his expenses weren't paid on time.

'Oh, I like him,' she said, not realizing the trap she was allowing herself to fall into.

Jenny made a small, strangled noise which turned into a cough.

'How about Anthony?' said Helen-from-Accounts, mentioning one of the other directors. 'I'm not sure about him.'

'Oh, he's OK,' said Jenny, 'but do you think Matthew's good-looking?'

'I think he's attractive,' said Helen-from-Accounts, and there was an almost audible thump as she dug her own grave and fell into it. And to make things worse for herself, she blushed, because she wasn't used to making girly chat and the excitement of making new friends was giving her a hot flush.

Matthew and Helen were going through their usual evening routine. Dinner in front of *Emmerdale* (both now hooked), few glasses of wine, on the sofa, feet up, watch TV till bedtime. They almost never went out, except to have a meal at a local restaurant where they knew they'd never bump into anyone who would recognize them. They hadn't yet repeated the dismal evening with Rachel and Neil, and Helen had put a ban on Matthew meeting any of her other friends. His friends all seemed to be of the married-couples-with-children variety, and none of them seemed keen to befriend Helen at this point, which suited her down to the ground. Helen had got used to the sight of Matthew flopping round the flat in his pyjama bottoms and T-shirt and she'd long since stopped making any effort to look good at home. They made pleasant if rather anodyne conversation and they had sex much less frequently than when they'd only seen each other for a few hours a week. Helen couldn't believe that Matthew was happy, but he kept saying that he was, so who was she to argue. She, of course, wasn't happy, but we know that already.

Tonight, though, Matthew had come home with a big bunch of lilies and arranged them in a green glass vase which he'd placed on the coffee table in the living room. Helen had never been one for flowers – not that she didn't like them, she loved having a tiny aromatic piece of nature in her home – rather, she had never been one for receiving flowers from men. They were like chocolates or perfume, gifts that required no imagination, no inside knowledge of the recipient. Autistic men's gifts: 'She woman, must give flowers.' It seemed to her that there was nothing more insulting than being given a bouquet or a box of Ferrero Rocher on your birthday by someone who purported to know your inner soul better than anyone. But the random nature of Matthew's gift – it wasn't a special day, they weren't make-up flowers to compensate for a missed date or a drunken argument – the fact that he had just tried to do something nice for her, touched her and, despite the fact that they were now blocking out part of the TV screen, she snuggled up next to him affectionately with her head on his chest, and he stroked her hair gratefully. She wished she could feel for him like she used to, or at least like she used to believe she did.

'Did you and Sophie ever have a second honeymoon?' she asked, genuinely wanting to know the answer.

Matthew looked cornered, like she'd shown him CCTV footage of himself with his hand in the till.

'Erm . . . no, no . . . of course not,' he stammered, protesting way too much.

'Lots of couples do, you know, when they've been together a while.'

'You know what our relationship was like the past few years. I could barely stand to spend time with her.'

Helen felt guilty that she'd forced him into this position where he felt he wasn't allowed to admit to even the tiniest glimmer of affection for his wife.

'You can tell me, you know. I won't mind.'

But, of course, Matthew wasn't going to be caught out again. He'd fallen for this line of Helen's once before, when she'd got him to admit that he and Sophie still had occasional sex, and then she'd forgotten that she'd promised she wouldn't mind and she'd got angry and irrational. He wasn't going down that path a second time.

'I told you, no,' he said, standing up. 'Let's not talk about Sophie.'

*

Later that evening, Matthew's mobile rang, and he moved through to the other room so as not to disturb Helen's TV-watching. He came back looking anxious.

'That was Louisa. Jason's left her and moved in with another woman. Apparently, it's been going on since before Christmas.'

'Fucking hell, it runs in the family!'

'Louisa wants to know if she can come and stay here for a few days while he moves his stuff out.'

'No. Matthew, no. This flat's too small for us two, let alone one of your sisters.'

'And the baby.'

'And the baby. Christ. Ring her and tell her we're really sorry but no. I feel really bad for her, I really do, but she'll have to go and stay with Amanda or something.'

'I've already told her yes. She's driving up now, she'll be here in about an hour.'

'Fucking hell, Matthew. I mean . . . fucking hell. This is my flat. You can't randomly invite people to stay.'

'Thank you for reminding me that this isn't my home. But I left my wife and my own beautiful house for you, if you remember' – oh, here we go – 'and I think the least you can do is let me put up a member of my family who's in trouble.'

'Looks like I have fuck-all say in the matter if you've already told her it's OK.'

They stomped around for the next hour or so, tidying in silence and making up a bed on the sofa. Helen wasn't sure she'd ever met a two-year-old baby in the flesh before and wanted to ask Matthew what it'd need to sleep on – but that would have meant speaking to him, so she didn't bother. At nine o'clock, the doorbell rang and a tearful woman carrying a crying child was let in. Helen didn't think she'd ever seen so much snot and tears. Louisa's nose – prominent at the best of times – glowed red and shiny, and her mousy brown hair curled flat and damp against her head. Helen knew that Matthew's sisters were a good few years younger than him – the product of his father's return to the family after a sojourn with his secretary – and she guessed that Louisa, as the youngest, must be around forty-six, but she was the kind of woman it was impossible to age, she was so conventional, from her paisley neckscarf to her matching gloves, shoes and handbag. The baby – it was wearing a dress, so it must be a girl although, otherwise, there was precious little to go on – was put on the floor, where she toddled around sticking her covered-in-god-knows-what fingers into Helen's things.

Helen got some wine while Louisa cried all over Matthew and told him what had been going on in a series of incoherent, sobby sentences. Louisa had scarcely acknowledged Helen's existence, except for a quick onceover when she first came in. Now, she was so wrapped up in her own misery that she was ignoring little snotty's attempts to electrocute herself by poking her fingers in the back of the TV, so Helen had to step in.

'Erm . . . should she be doing that?'

Louisa gave the baby a cursory glance.

'Jemima.'

Jemima? What sort of a fucking name was that?

Jemima, of course, being two years old, took no notice, and Louisa was already back to snivelling all over her older brother, so Helen had no choice other than to hoick the baby away from the television herself. She held her at arm's length, then placed her down next to her mother. No way, she thought, am I going to be babysitter to this child.

'I'm going to bed,' she announced to the room. 'Louisa, the sofa's all made up. Jemima'll have to sleep in with you, I'm afraid. Help yourself to anything. I'm sure Matthew will show you where stuff is.'

Louisa didn't even look up from her crying.

'OK, night then.' Helen backed out of the room.

Between Matthew tripping over a chair as he made his way to bed at midnight, Jemima crying and Louisa getting up and making herself tea at six, Helen had maybe three hours' sleep. So, she wasn't in the best of moods when she came into the kitchen and found Louisa sitting feeding Jemima at the table.

'Morning.' She tried to inject a bubbliness into her voice that was alien to her.

Louisa looked at her coolly, gazing out from red, swollen eyes. 'So now you know what effect your actions will have had.'

Oh, great.

'Excuse me?'

'You're seeing it from the other side. How a woman feels when her husband's gone off with someone else, left her alone with her children. It's not pleasant, is it?'

Why did all of Matthew's family speak like Barbara Cartland had written their script for them?

'Matthew's the one who left Sophie, not me.'

'But if women like you weren't out there beckoning, men wouldn't be tempted.'

'"Women like me" meaning what, exactly?' Helen was considering how it would feel to punch Louisa square in one of her red pig's eyes.

'Women who think that marriage means nothing, women who think that their bit of fun is worth more than another woman's years of commitment and emotional investment, women who think it's OK for children to grow up without a father, women who don't have a man of their own.'

'Well, thank you for that succinct and scarily accurate assessment of my character. Just one thing – have you ever considered that some women push their men away? Drive them into the arms of other people by bitching and nagging and . . . boring them to death? By being sanctimonious and superior and . . . self-righteous?'

And, with that, Helen flounced out of the front door and off to work without saying goodbye to Matthew. She knew he'd be furious when Louisa reported back – indeed, she knew she'd be furious with herself when she calmed down a bit – but Louisa had started it, for fuck's sake.

Geoff Sweeney, or Mr-Helen-from-Accounts, to give him his full name, had noticed that his wife was wearing a striking new pink hooded top instead of her usual navy suit for work this morning. At thirty-four, she had adopted a style that would best suit someone twice her age. Knee-length skirts with tights – tan in summer, navy in winter – and low-heeled court shoes. Under the tailored M&S jacket which had acquired a slight sheen with age, she wore one of her many button-up shirts. Her jewellery was always gold in colour and consisted of a plain link chain around her neck with the word 'Helen' spelt out in slanty handwriting in the middle, and a matching gold link bracelet. The necklace was just a link or two too tight, and the 'Helen', resting too snugly on the front of her throat, flapped up and down when she spoke. Helen-from-Accounts' hair was short and manageable, cut in a flick, crying out for some product to control the slight frizz that crept in when the days were too warm, too wet or too stressful. All she needed was a name badge to complete the impression that she had just stepped out from behind the counter of the NatWest.

Beneath the flick was a face that resembled that of a small, timid shrew. She was neither pretty nor ugly, just nondescript, having a face that was forgotten instantly because of its absolute ordinariness. If her nose had been larger or her chin more pronounced, then her face might have had the distinctiveness to make an impression. As it was, she washed over people unremembered. Her voice wavered nervously and, listening to her, people felt an overwhelming urge to speed things up and finish off her sentences themselves. In fact, they often did so, so she frequently found herself squeezed out of conversations and consequently became increasingly uneasy in social situations.

'The girls in the office all wear stuff like this to work,' she told Geoff, and he was pleased that she seemed to be making some new friends at last. He kissed her good-bye as she got into the car.

'Love you, bunny,' he said.

'Love you, too,' Helen-from-Accounts waved at him over her shoulder as she drove off.

'Look at her. What the fuck is she wearing?' Annie laughed as she watched Helen-from-Accounts through the glass window in the accounts office. 'She as much as admitted it to us at lunch yesterday, you know. Well, she said she thought Matthew was attractive and, let's face it, there can't be many people who'd admit to that.'

Helen looked up from the pile of mail she was sorting through in reception just as Helen-from-Accounts waved a cheery greeting to Annie.

'Sad,' said Helen, nodding, 'she's really sad.'

That's something else I can add to my personal profile, she thought, as she walked through to her desk:

Husband-thief
Child-orphaner
Liar
Massive bitch

She sat down and turned her computer on.

When she got home that night, Louisa was still there, cooking for Matthew in the kitchen, snotty toddler running riot, looking at Helen as though *she* were the interloper.

13

Matthew's girls now came over every Sunday afternoon. History had been made because Claudia had spoken without being prompted and without saying anything insulting. The landmark exchange had gone something like this:

Helen: 'Hi, how are you?'

Claudia: 'OK.'

Helen: 'Do want to have a look outside and see how your bulbs are coming up?'

Silence. An eye roll followed, and Claudia turned her attention to her dad. But, a voluntary OK was still better than nothing, and Helen felt like she'd won a victory. She hadn't been able to get Suzanne on her own to continue her fact-finding mission about Sophie, but she'd learnt a few interesting facts from things Claudia accusingly let slip to her father:

Sophie had called a solicitor to talk about filing for divorce
She had drunk most of a bottle of wine on her own on Wednesday evening and then thrown up on the living-room carpet
Louisa had called her to tell her that the woman Matthew had gone off with was a stupid bitch and that it would never last

Claudia smiled at Helen for the first time ever while she relayed this last gem.

'Claudia! Apologize to Helen. Now.'

'It's OK, Matthew, she's only repeating what someone else said. And I probably deserve it. Don't tell her off.'

Claudia had looked at Helen for a moment as if she were thinking, 'OK, she's got me out of trouble. Interesting.' And she discovered that she felt a bit bad for having told the story in the first place. But not so bad that she wouldn't do it again.

Helen had an assignation. Monday, twelve forty-five, at the entrance to Fit For Life in City Road. She had thought about cancelling it all morning, all weekend, in fact, and had even half-dialled Sophie's number a couple of times. But, at quarter past twelve she got up from her desk and walked to Tottenham Court Road tube station as if going to see your boyfriend's estranged wife for an exercise session was the most natural thing in the world. She was approaching it as she would a first date, fussing about what she was wearing, how much make-up to put on, whether to be fashionably late or politely early. Would Sophie prefer a friend who was trendy and girly or sophisticated and womanly? Or even sporty and boyish. Just remember your name is Eleanor, she said to herself, as she got off the underground at Old Street.

The remainder of the week had passed fairly uneventfully. Louisa had finally left on Friday morning. In front of Matthew, she'd acted civil although a bit cold, and Helen had managed to avoid being alone with her for a second time, hiding in the bedroom in the mornings till Matthew was out of the bathroom and chatting with his sister. The subject of Helen's marriage-wrecking ways hadn't come up again and Jemima's attention-grabbing tantrums had provided the perfect diversion whenever conversation had run low. Each evening, Louisa had borrowed the phone to call both Jason and his new girl-friend in turn and shout abuse. On the second night, when Jason didn't answer his mobile, Louisa left a message telling him that Jemima was gravely ill and that he must call her back as a matter of urgency. He did, of course, and Louisa answered like a demented fishwife, telling him that he'd never see his fucking daughter again and that if she ever was, in fact, seriously unwell, he'd never even get to hear about it till it was too late. Helen knew she should feel sorry for Louisa, but she just couldn't find it in herself.

Before she left work on Friday, Helen had called Sophie to say that her ankle was better and to make a plan. Truthfully, Sophie had forgotten all about her, having, let's be fair, more important things on her mind, like the break-up of her marriage. But when Helen had reminded her of her offer, Sophie had been gracious and even, Helen thought, friendly. Sophie, in fact, was irritated by this imposition on her time. True, she would have been going to the gym at lunchtime anyway as part of her new regime, but the thought of having to make polite conver-sation with a total stranger – even one who seemed perfectly normal and amiable – weighed on her all week-end. She was a loner by nature anyway – a state which had been solidified by her devotion to her work and family, meaning as it did that she had no time for friends – and her split from Matthew had made her feel even more isolated and awkward around people she didn't know well – as if she might as well have been wearing a badge that said 'failure' or 'loser' or 'reject'. Still, she had agreed with this woman, this Eleanor, that she would show her round; she had to go through with it. She'd just make it as quick as possible, be polite and get out.

Sophie had never been good at making friends. At school she was always the third girl in a gang of three. The one who knew that, after a while, the other two were meeting up behind her back in the evenings. The one who lived under threat of being dropped at any moment. If she had been asked who her best childhood friend was, she wouldn't have been able to come up with an answer. It would be Kelly and Michelle when she was seven, Charlotte and Catherine when she was nine, Ella and Nadia at twelve and Olivia and Emma at fifteen. Asked the same question, none of these girls, she knew, would even remember her, let alone pick her. She wasn't unpopular, that wasn't the problem, but she'd never been able to understand how those singular bonds worked, how to sustain an intimacy with someone which involved phoning them two or three times a day and seeing them whenever you could persuade your parents to let you.

It was inevitable, then, that when she married Matthew she would quickly let all her girlfriends slide. She'd blamed it on her work schedule, but it was just easier to do the couples thing, part-time relationships with the wives and girlfriends of Matthew's friends. Amicable enough but nothing intimate. There was no question of them ever meeting up independently of their husbands, and none of them had any idea what they would talk about if they did.

Sometimes, inside the cosy safety of her tight-knit family life, Sophie felt heavy with loneliness. But only sometimes.

Helen got to Fit For Life with two minutes to spare. It was one of those grey and windy early February days which turn London from a vibrant city into a drearily oppressive and claustrophobic tangle of grey stone and angry people, and Helen suddenly felt crushingly depressed. What was she doing here? Why couldn't she just accept that Matthew had chosen her and be happy? She found herself wondering where her old life had gone. OK, so she hadn't liked it very much at the time, but now it seemed idyllic. It used to be that she lived for the Matthew days, the Mondays, Wednesdays and Thursdays when he came over. Now she couldn't understand why she never used to revel in the other four nights of the week, when she would be left alone to suit herself.

'Eleanor. Hi.'

Helen paused just a fraction too long before she realized that that was her, and looked up.

'You look like you're having a bad day.'

She gave Sophie her best 'Look how friendly I am' smile.

'No! I'm fine. Raring to go.'

They went through the formalities of signing Helen in (Eleanor Pitt in honour of Brad, who happened to be on the cover of a copy of *Heat* in reception) and chatted about the dismal weather on the way to the changing rooms. Once inside, Helen realized with alarm that the space was communal with no cubicles, so she and Sophie would have to change side by side.

'You've been to a gym before, presumably,' Sophie was

saying as she took off her coat and then pulled her cream sweater over her head, revealing a white lacy bra underneath.

Helen forced herself not to look and then felt like the school-gates pervert when she couldn't resist giving Sophie a quick onceover as she stepped out of her brown trousers.

OK, nice figure. Bigger tits than me, bit of a crinkly stomach, few stretchmarks, touch of cellulite around her thighs but, frankly, not bad. Nothing that Matthew could ever have complained about anyway. He'd seen this woman, this stranger, naked every day for the past fifteen years, how odd was that?

'Yes, it's just 'cos I've moved . . .'

I really should have written myself a biography, she thought, terrified that she was going to give herself away somehow. Had she told Sophie she'd only just moved in when she met her the other day? She couldn't remember.

Apparently she had.

'Oh, yes, how are you finding it?'

'Good, good. Yes, good.'

Great, Helen thought. If she could just keep up this scintillating level of conversation, they'd be best friends in no time.

They started off on the cross-trainers, subconsciously keeping an eye on each other so as not to be outdone. Sophie kept up a bit of a commentary about how the machine worked, and Helen, who had been to the gym twice a week every week for the past five years, pretended to be interested. Helen could sense that Sophie just wanted to get the session over with, not in a hostile way but in an I-wish-I'd-never-offered-but-seeing-as-I-did-I'd-better-be-polite way. She knew exactly how she'd be feeling if it were her in Sophie's position. Bored and fractious. Trying to make conversation, she asked Sophie if she had any children, but Sophie just replied, 'Yes, two,' and left it at that. She tried asking her questions about her work and that killed about a minute and a half, then Sophie asked about hers and she made a few more things up and tried to file them somewhere in her memory where she'd be able to find them again if she needed to. More small talk as they moved across to the rowing machines, the merits of the blood-group diet over Atkins (Helen couldn't care less and she was pretty sure Sophie couldn't either), *Big Brother*, Harvey Nichols versus Selfridges. They'd reached the all-time low of the state of the transport system in London, and Helen was about to call it quits, cut the session short and retreat back to the relative comfort of her office, when a miracle happened. A man fell over on one of the running machines. And not just any man. A big fat man with a bad comb-over. And when he fell, he didn't just fall, he stumbled for a while first, wildly grasping about to steady himself like an obese Fred Astaire in mid tap routine, and then he seemed to give up and landed face first, sliding backwards to end up on the gym floor.

It was number one on the list of things you shouldn't laugh at. Well, numbers one to four really:

A fat man
With a comb-over
Falling over
And hurting himself

It might have been relief at the distraction, but Helen couldn't stop her smile and could feel herself starting to laugh. She heard a snort and looked over at Sophie, who had gone red in the face and was shaking. This was ludicrous, two grown women who really should know better in hysterics over someone else's misfortune. The man was sitting up now and being attended to by a couple of more compassionate samaritans, who were throwing the odd disapproving look in Helen and Sophie's direction, but his comb-over was standing up on top of his head and he looked like a chicken. Helen had tears appearing in the corners of her eyes and Sophie was trying hard to cover her rudeness by pretending to cough. Both of them had pretty much given up all pretence of rowing.

'Sauna,' Sophie just about managed to say.

'Mmm,' was all Helen could get out in reply.

It was a breakthrough.

Suddenly, conversation seemed easy. Helen pretty much managed to forget that Sophie was Sophie and Sophie got over her lack of practice at making girlfriends and they found that they chatted away effortlessly about pretty much nothing and made each other laugh a bit. By the time Helen had to leave to get back to the office, she was satisfied that she had picked her Sophie scab enough – she knew (intimately) what Sophie looked like, how she spoke, what made her laugh. She had fleshed her out into a real person. She had poked at the kernel of guilt that had lodged inside her when Matthew moved in and made it grow. What she had done was an unforgivable thing to a real, living, breathing – worse still, nice and undeserving (although who exactly

would have been deserving, Helen couldn't now think) –
woman. She had made herself feel as bad as she could
and now she had to learn to live with it.

There was one issue she had to resolve before they
said goodbye, and it all became too complicated.

'I'm moving again, by the way,' she said, thinking on
her feet. 'The flat I'm staying in, it belongs to a friend
and, well, it's a long story but . . . she split up with her
boyfriend over the weekend and she needs to move back
in and it's just not big enough for two of us . . .'

'Oh. What a shame. Where'll you go?'

'A friend of mine in Camden's got a spare room. It's
a much nicer flat so . . .'

'I was looking forward to having a gym partner,' said
Sophie, and Helen thought that maybe she meant it.

'Sorry.'

'Well, we'll just have to go out for a drink instead,'
Sophie heard herself saying. 'How are you fixed on
Thursday? My ex-husband can babysit. You know, I don't
think I ever went out for an evening and left him looking after the kids on his own the whole time we were
married. It'll do him good.'

'Fucking hell,' laughed Helen. 'You really do need to
get a life.'

And before she knew what she was doing, she had
agreed to be in the Coal Hole in the Strand at seven
o'clock on Thursday evening.

As for Sophie, she had no idea what had made her
blurt out the drinks invitation except that she had quite
liked this woman and she'd enjoyed the last hour, thinking about something other than her own pitiful situation

and the mess that her life was in. She knew she couldn't spend all her time with just her daughters, tempting though that seemed. She needed a friend.

Back at work, Helen found Matthew hanging round the general office going over some files with Jenny. She felt nauseous when she realized that the other girls were making kissy faces behind his back and putting their thumbs up to a bemused Helen-from-Accounts through the glass of the partitioned office. She felt even worse when Helen-from-Accounts finally cottoned on to what she thought was the joke and began to join in the laughing and face-pulling. That this caused the others to explode with laughter made Helen-from-Accounts beam with acceptance. Helen didn't know what she was most annoyed at, the other woman's pathetic jokes, her stupidity or her desperation. Or maybe it was that this was the woman everyone in the office felt Matthew was most likely to be a good match with or, worse, that she would be the only one sad enough to reciprocate his advances. Matthew smiled at her, and she scowled back at him without meaning to.

Laura called her into her office and shut the door.
'Is everything OK?'
Helen froze. 'Yes, why shouldn't it be?'
'It's just you've only just got back from lunch, and I know it's not the first long lunchbreak you've had in the past couple of weeks.'
'I had to go to the dentist,' said Helen defensively.
'Again?'
Helen stared at Laura defiantly.

'Yes, again. What, you don't trust me now? You think I'm skiving off?'

'Helen, I'm not accusing you. I just wanted to say if you've got something going on or you need some time or, whatever, just tell me.'

'I'm fine.' And Helen turned on her heels and went back to her desk without another word.

Evening.

Pasta. Sofa. Wine. *Emmerdale*.

'Sophie's asked me to babysit on Thursday,' Matthew said huffily during the commercial break.

'What's wrong with that?'

'She's just doing it to irritate me.'

'Matthew, they're your kids. How can being asked to look after them for a few hours be irritating?'

'That's not what I meant. I'm looking forward to it. I just mean ... well ... she never goes out.'

'Maybe she's got a new boyfriend,' said Helen, enjoying herself.

'What?' spluttered Matthew. 'Of course she hasn't. At least, I should hope not – I mean, what would that be like for the girls, her going off with someone else so soon?'

'Not as bad as them finding out you've been with me all this time, I imagine.'

He's jealous, she thought. He still has feelings for her. And she searched right down deep inside herself to see if she minded, and she found she really didn't.

'Why shouldn't she meet someone new? You have.'

'I hope she does. Eventually,' Matthew said unconvincingly. 'I'd just be very surprised if it'd happened this quickly, that's all.'

'Then maybe she's going out on the pull. I'm sure a quickie with a stranger you've just met in a club is a great ego boost when your husband has left you for someone else.'

'OK, that's enough.'

She'd definitely touched a nerve.

'Matthew stop being so fucking po-faced about it. Sophie's allowed to go out once in twelve years, and it's none of your business any more where she's going. Just look at it as an opportunity to spend more time with the girls – you keep saying you want to.'

'You'll come with me, won't you? It'll be fun,' Matthew was saying.

'Sorry, no. I'm going out on Thursday actually. I was just about to tell you.'

'Going out where?'

'Out with Rachel. Just for a few drinks, I won't be late. At least now I know you won't just be sat in front of the TV pining for me.'

'I do love you, you know,' he said, coming over all needy.

'I know you do,' she answered, kissing the top of his head.

'And you love me, too, don't you?'

'What do you think? Let's have another bottle of wine,' she said, standing up.

14

One week later, and Helen was starting to feel like there would never be any light at the end of the tunnel, despite the fact that another Sunday with the girls had yielded these new words and phrases from Claudia:

Hi
Diet Cola
Please
Thank you

And 'history', in response to a direct question from Helen as to what was her favourite subject at school. Hardly Dorothy Parker, but it was, Helen felt, a big improvement. What's more, she'd begun to look at Claudia and Suzanne in a slightly different way following comments that Sophie had dropped about their relationship with their father. She could see that Suzanne's desperation to please him now bordered on obsessive and Claudia's 'couldn't give a shit' attitude was starting to look unconvincing. She'd wondered whether she should try and talk to Matthew about it but, frankly, it wasn't her problem.

Thursday evening had started off a bit awkwardly again and Helen couldn't really remember what she was doing there or why she had agreed to go, but a couple of vodka and tonics down, and she'd begun to feel relaxed and was thinking that, maybe, she was even having a good time.

I mustn't get pissed, she'd kept saying to herself before she left the house. My name is Eleanor, I work from home, I'm not shagging your husband. She'd waved Matthew off on his babysitting duties and then got the tube down to Charing Cross and walked up the road to the pub where she'd arranged to meet Sophie. On the way, she tried to run through areas of conversation to steer well clear of:

Divorce
Adultery
Work
Living arrangements
Anything personal
Anything else

Fuck it, she thought, I'll play it by ear.

But, well into her third large glass of wine and obviously not used to drinking or to pub measures, which meant she had pretty much consumed a whole bottle, Sophie had brought the subject round to men.

'Have you got a boyfriend?' she asked.

Oh god, thought Helen, has Eleanor got a boyfriend, I'm not sure. She thought about wheeling Carlo out again, but it all seemed too complicated a deception to keep up.

'Not at the moment, no. How about you? I mean . . . I know you're married and all that . . .'

'Was married,' said Sophie, with more than a hint of bitterness in her voice. 'He walked out a few weeks ago.'

'God, how awful.' Helen couldn't resist digging. 'Was it out of the blue?'

'I don't want to talk about it.' Sophie looked pained. 'He's got someone else.'

She took another big gulp from her glass. 'I mean, what are women like that thinking of? Making a pass at someone else's husband. There's plenty of men out there for god's sake. You know what I think? It's a power thing. It's the power of knowing they've won some kind of contest that the poor, unsuspecting wife doesn't even know she's been entered for. Or they're so desperate for a man they don't even care if they have to steal one. I should feel sorry for her.'

'Do you?' Helen was tentative.

'No! I hate her. I don't even know her and I hate her. That's what he's reduced me to.'

'And what about him?' asked Helen. 'What do you think he was thinking?'

'Oh, he'd have been flattered. He's a middle-aged man. Actually, he's a late-middle-aged man. Soon to be an old man. He'd have thought it was Christmas. To tell you the truth, I don't think he was thinking at all. At least not with his head. And he said that she threw herself at him, not that that's an excuse.'

Helen stifled an exclamation. 'He said that?'

'Yes, but then I don't know what to believe and, let's face it, even if she did, he could have said no.'

Helen couldn't contain herself. 'Seems unlikely, a younger woman – you did say she was younger, didn't you? Well, anyway – throwing herself at an older man. I mean, unless he's incredibly attractive. Is he incredibly attractive, do you think?'

Sophie smiled weakly. 'I have no idea any more to be honest. Not objectively – no, I wouldn't have thought so, no. I don't think he's irresistible to women, if that's what you mean.'

'Seems unlikely then.'

'Yes, seems unlikely.'

Helen was finding it hard to move on from this particular topic. How fucking dare he, she thought. OK so he was trying to soften the blow for his wife in some twisted logic kind of way, but to say that she, Helen, at thirty-five years old and without a doubt in her physical prime, threw herself at fifty-five-year-old well-on-the-downward-slippery-slope Matthew was just too ridiculous. He'd pursued her. She'd resisted. He'd persevered. It had all come from him at the beginning. All of it.

'Are you OK?'

Helen realized that Sophie was looking at her quizzically. She took a deep breath and forced her concentration back to the task in hand.

'I was just wondering what it must be like for you. Do you miss him?'

'Do you know what? I really don't want to talk about him. Let's have another drink.'

Helen stood up, slightly unsteady on her feet. 'I'll get it.'

And she got herself a plain tonic water and Sophie another large wine.

*

'She was drunk!' Matthew was on his high horse when he eventually got home at just past midnight.

'So what? You get drunk sometimes.' Helen had gone to bed as soon as she got in, to mull over the evening and, if she were being honest with herself, to avoid Matthew. She had found the whole thing a bit unsettling, to say the least. She'd got on with Sophie well enough, but there was something about discussing yourself with the other woman without her knowing that left a bad taste in your mouth. It was just piling one deception on top of another. And hadn't her mother always said to her that if you listened in on conversations you weren't meant to, then you were bound to hear something bad about yourself.

'You know when we first got together?' she said now to Matthew as he got undressed for bed. 'Did you think I fancied you?'

'I couldn't believe my luck.' Matthew snuggled up next to her under the duvet. 'I thought you were going to scream and slap me round the face and then go running to Human Resources. I thought I'd won the lottery.'

He started to move his right hand over Helen's stomach, thinking this line of conversation was some kind of romantic foreplay. Helen put her hand over his and stopped it from moving further down.

'You didn't think I was throwing myself at you then?' She looked directly into his slightly bemused eyes in the half-light of the bedside lamp.

Matthew laughed. 'No such luck. What's brought this on?'

'Nothing,' said Helen, turning away from him over on to her side. 'Night.'

Sophie had called Helen on her mobile next morning.

'OK, so I don't usually drink like a fourteen-year-old and throw up in the taxi on the way home – I'd just like you to know that.'

'You didn't?'

'I did. And my husband went insane because he thinks I'm setting a bad example for the girls.'

'Oh, and he's a great role model, by the sound of it.'

'Exactly.'

When Sophie put the phone down, she smiled to herself, pleased that she'd managed the requisite 'follow-up' phone call. Eleanor was easy to talk to – they had things in common, she was funny and good company and chatting with her took Sophie's mind off . . . well . . . stuff . . . for a while – and she was enjoying forging a friend-ship, really, even if she did find it exhausting. And daunting. So much easier to keep retreating home to the predictable if lonely safety of her little family to lick her wounds than to try and create a social life out of noth-ing. But, she needed to get out of the house, she needed to start putting herself back together, she couldn't spend the rest of her life just being a *mother*.

Helen had been proofing a press pack for Laura when Sophie rang. Dull interviews with the dull cast of a dull new TV series which was about to be launched. It was taking her twice as long as it should because she was watching the daily Helen-from-Accounts baiting session which was taking place in the general office as usual. Helen-from-Accounts still had no idea of the crime she was under suspicion for, let alone the hours of amusement that her new pixie hair-cut and plum-coloured lipstick was giving the other girls. She had bought a red kaftan top to alternate with her pink hoodie. Because she was on the short side and a bit plump, it made her look a bit like a post box.

Today, Annie, always the ringleader, was asking Helen-from-Accounts about her husband. Was he good-looking? ('Oh, yes,' said Helen-from-Accounts, blushing.) Was he good in bed? ('Oh, I can't answer that,' blush blush.) Was he the type to get jealous? ('Gosh, yes. He said to me only this morning, "Who are you getting all dressed up for?"' she gushed, effectively signing her own death warrant.)

'Can you keep it down over there, I'm trying to proof-read this thing,' shouted our Helen, hoping to break up the party and spare Helen-from-Accounts any more humiliation.

'Oh, don't be such a swot,' Helen-from-Accounts shouted back, looking round at Annie and Jenny for approval, like the fat twelve-year-old who shoplifts a CD in Woolworths to show the popular girls she knows how to join in.

She always gets caught.

Helen swallowed her dislike for the other woman. She was unbearable. But, thought Helen, turning back to her work, she doesn't deserve to be in this situation. It's all my doing.

'Oh, you know me,' she said, loathing herself for

joining in with the witless office banter, 'Work work work. It's just Laura'll kill me if I don't get this done by twelve, and you know what she's like when she's in a mood.' She rolled her eyes to add to the veracity of her performance.

'OK.' Annie got up from the corner of the desk she was sitting on and started to move towards reception, just as Matthew breezed in in the opposite direction. Annie stopped by the door.

'Afternoon, ladies.'

Helen cringed, willing him to walk straight through the office and out the other side, but he stopped to flick through a grey folder on Jenny's desk. She could almost feel the atmosphere thicken with anticipation, that feeling when the school bully is about to go in for the kill and everyone knows it. She decided to try a diversionary tactic.

'Annie,' she called over. 'Laura's waiting for an urgent call from Simon at Lotus. If he rings, will you put him straight through?'

But Annie had her prey in her sights.

'Matthew, don't you think Helen looks amazing today?'

Matthew looked momentarily shocked, then realized that Annie was talking not about his Helen but about dumpy little Helen-from-Accounts.

No, Matthew, Helen practically said aloud. Don't. Do. It.

Too late.

'Wow,' Matthew was saying. 'You do look incredible. That new haircut really suits you.'

Annie and Jenny snorted and spluttered and coughed. Helen-from-Accounts blushed, of course, and giggled like a love-struck adolescent. Matthew, loving all the female attention and enjoying feeling like one of the gang, continued.

'If I wasn't a married man . . .'

There was a tidal wave of laughter. Helen thought both Matthew and Helen-from-Accounts looked a little bemused by the scale of the hysteria his comments were causing, but they were smiling along gamely, Matthew no doubt thinking how he'd never lost the old magic touch with the ladies. Helen stood up.

'OK, everyone, you've really got to shut up now. I've got work to do. Go on. Fuck off.'

Matthew raised an eyebrow at her as he swaggered out towards the corridor, and a terrible realization hit her . . .

He thinks I'm jealous.

Ten minutes later, Helen had her coat on and her umbrella up and was steaming along Oxford Street trying to clear her head. It wasn't working. She knew now it was never going to work. There was no getting away from it: what she wanted was her life back and for the last four and a bit years not to have happened. Surely not too much to ask. OK, she'd settle for just a bit of it back, the bit that was Tuesday and Friday nights and the weekends when she could do whatever she liked even if in reality she rarely did anything. It was a bit like living in London: you never actually went to Madame Tussauds, but it was comforting to know it was there should you ever want to. It wasn't Matthew's fault, but she was starting to realize it had all been a big mistake. She blew her nose, stopped off at Starbucks for a double espresso and drank it on the way back to the office.

Annie had a particularly malevolent smirk on her face as Helen passed through reception on her way to the ladies before she returned to her desk.

'You missed all the fun,' she called over, but Helen couldn't be bothered to ask her what she was on about. Once in the toilets, she stopped to give herself a quick onceover in the mirror.

Sniff. A muffled noise came from behind a closed cubicle door. Helen undid her pony-tail and pulled her hair back neatly to fix it up again.

Sniff. There it was again, only this time it was followed by a distinct sob.

Helen looked round. She thought about making a quick getaway but, just as she was turning towards the door, there was another sob, and then another, and her conscience took over.

'Are you OK in there?'

Sniff sob, sob sob sniff. It was like Morse code. Helen had never been any good in situations like this, she never knew what to say and was always tempted to go with 'For Christ's sake, pull yourself together,' which was never ideal. She edged towards the cubicle.

'Do you want me to get anyone or anything? Or shall I just leave you alone?' (Please say yes.)

A mangled sentence of snot and gurgles and not many words followed. Helen thought she made out the word 'Annie', but not much more.

'Erm . . . I didn't quite get that.'

Silence.

'Who is it, by the way? This is Helen. Laura's PA. Tell me what you want me to do.'

She heard the bolt being drawn back, and the door opened to reveal a very soggy Helen-from-Accounts, new mascara running down her cheeks, plum lipstick smeared across her face, pixie hair-cut standing up on end. She let out a howl like a sick wolf and threw her arms round Helen, who stood stiffly, her own arms clamped to her sides, not knowing what to do.

'Theyallthinkimhavinganaffairwithmatthew.' Sob, sniff, howl, sniff, sob. It was like being trapped in the bathroom with the entire percussion section of the Royal Philharmonic.

'I can't understand you,' Helen said, peeling the other woman off her. 'Slow down and tell me what's going on.' But, to be honest, she knew what was coming, and her heart sank.

'The girls. Annie and Jenny. And Jamie. They all think I'm having an affair with Matthew.'

Helen took a deep breath. 'I know they do.'

'That's why they've been being nice to me. I thought they were my friends, but they just wanted to find out the gossip. What do you mean, you know they do?'

'They said . . . something.'

Helen-from-Accounts looked at her accusingly. 'You didn't believe them, did you?'

'No,' said Helen. 'I didn't believe them.'

'They cut his photo out of the company handbook and stuck it on my computer, and when I asked them why, they all started laughing and pretending to nudge me, and I knew, I just knew what they meant. And I tried to tell them it just wasn't true, but they wouldn't believe me. They said that Matthew's wife told Amelia from Human Resources that it was me he'd gone off with. But she can't have done, because it's just not true.'

'I know, I know,' said Helen, in what she thought was a soothing way, but her mind was racing. Those vicious, self-righteous bitches.

'I mean, as if I would.' The other Helen was getting into her stride. 'Look at him. I've got my Geoff – why would I look at Matthew Shallcross? He's a nice enough man but . . . well, you just wouldn't, would you?'

'No,' said Helen weakly. 'You just wouldn't.'

'You've got to help me convince them it's not true. Please, Helen. I'd just kill myself if anyone thought I was the type to go after a married man.'

'I don't really know what I can do.' Helen's head was starting to pound, and she longed to go home and forget this conversation had ever happened. But she couldn't.

'I mean it. If Geoff finds out what they're saying or . . . oh god, what if I lose my job? I'm sure they can sack you for inappropriate behaviour. Honestly, Helen, I'll kill myself, you have to help me.'

And she started sobbing helplessly again, leaning on Helen for support and dropping big wet tears on to her chest.

'OK,' Helen said, quietly. 'I'll try.'

Which was why Helen was now standing in front of Laura telling her she was giving in her notice.

'But, why?' Laura was saying. 'Is it something specific? Money? Have you got another job?'

'There's no reason.' Helen could hardly look Laura in the face.

'I just want to move on, that's all. And I'd like to go as soon as possible . . . I know I have to give a month's notice, so that's what I'm doing . . . giving it now.'

'And there's nothing I can say to persuade you to stay?'

'No.'

'I'm really sorry, Helen, honestly I am. I've come to rely on you.'

Helen managed to mutter a thanks and then got out of Laura's office as quickly as she could. When she got back to her desk, Annie was hanging round the general office, as usual, laughing with Jenny about the day's hilarious events. Helen felt sick and light-headed, like she was about to plunge over a cliff, which in a way she was. She cleared her throat.

'You've gone too far, you know, with Helen-from-Accounts.'

'Oh, come off it,' Jenny was saying. 'She deserves all she gets, shagging a married man.'

Annie joined in. 'Silly cow. Anyway, since when do you care? You don't like her any more than the rest of us.'

Helen could hear her heart beating somewhere up around her ears.

'It's just . . . it's not true, about her and Matthew, that's all.'

'How do you know that?' Annie's radar was up and working.

'Because . . . I just do.'

'You'll have to do better than that. Just because she's managed to make you feel sorry for her doesn't mean she's telling the truth. Let's face it, she must be a good liar for us not to have known what was going on.'

This was it. Armageddon. D-Day. The Apocalypse. Just walk up to the edge and jump.

'I know she's telling the truth because . . .' Helen faltered '. . . because it's me that Matthew's been seeing. I'm the one he's left his wife for. So, you see, you owe Helen-from-Accounts an apology.'

If this hadn't been the worst moment of Helen's life ever, if she hadn't been absolutely certain that nothing could ever be the same again, and not in a good way, then she would have found it hilarious. Annie and Jenny stood open-mouthed, literally open-mouthed, like two poodles with their heads out of a car window, for what seemed like a full minute. Helen shifted her weight from one foot to the other and waited for it to sink in. Annie's expression turned to stone.

'Jesus,' she said, turning to walk out, 'I always thought you were a bit of a bitch, and it turns out I'm right.'

'You are kidding, right?' Jenny was saying, incredulous. 'This is a joke.'

'Hardly,' Helen managed to mutter.

'But you let us think it was Helen-from-Accounts. In fact, you said yourself you thought it was her,' Jenny added.

'Sorry.' Helen was barely audible.

'You and Matthew?' Jenny still couldn't take it in. 'Oh my god, what about Carlo? Have you been two-timing him all this time?'

'I'm going home.' Helen was putting on her coat. 'I'll see you on Monday.'

When she walked through reception, she heard Annie telling Amelia the news. Neither woman said goodnight to Helen as she passed by.

15

On Monday, Helen thought about phoning in sick. There was no way she was going to be able to face the stares and the laughing behind her back and the in-her-face bitchy comments she knew she'd get from Annie and Jenny. Matthew seemed to think the whole thing was fine – in fact, he was irritatingly pleased it was all out in the open, whistling away to himself in the kitchen while he made coffee, but then Matthew had no idea about the viciousness of women and, more to the point, Matthew wasn't the one they were going to be laughing at. Matthew had managed to bag himself an attractive (if I say so myself, she thought) younger woman, whereas what Helen had done was waste her life on a man even pitiful Helen-from-Accounts wouldn't look at twice.

'All the other directors are jealous of me,' he'd said to her proudly the previous night after the girls had left (new words from Claudia, three: 'don't', 'be' and 'stupid' – in response to being asked whether she liked the boy band McFly).

'What, even Laura?' She couldn't keep the sarcasm out of her voice. He was trying to make her feel good, but where was the positive in being talked about like some kind of trophy fuck by a bunch of unattractive old men?

'You know what I mean.'

'I hate them all knowing, Matthew. I'm sorry but I do.

It just makes me feel . . . cheap. I feel like they're all looking at me as if they think I might give them a blow-job if they're nice to me. And what does that say about them? I mean, they've all got wives. Sad old fucks.'

'OK, OK. I was just trying to cheer you up.'

'Well, sorry, you'll have to try something else 'cos that's never going to work.'

She picked up the phone to call Rachel. The Rabbits, as Matthew had christened them, were going at it hammer and tongs upstairs, bang bang bang on the headboard, 'Oh, baby,' 'Yes, baby,' thump thump thump. Helen had worked out that their bed must be positioned right over the crack in her ceiling and now felt as if she were taking her life into her hands by sitting on her own bed while they bounced around on theirs. While she watched, the lightning-fork fracture seemed to widen before her eyes, and she tried to imagine the headline in the *Camden New Journal*:

Woman Crushed by Amorous Pair
Miserable Husband-Stealer Squashed by Overacting Lovers
Sad Near-Middle-Aged Bitch Flattened by Dull Unattractive
    Couple Having Better Sex than She Was.

She waited for the familiar scene to play itself out – 'Yes, yes, baby, baby, call me daddy' (that was a new one, top marks for invention, she thought, although slightly queasy-making), thump, bang, squeal, crescendo, silence – before she dialled.

Rachel answered, sleepy, clearly not out of bed herself yet. Helen had spent a large part of her weekend on the phone, trawling over Friday's events with her friend, so Rachel pretty much knew what was coming.

'I can't go in, I can't face them all.' Helen came straight to the point.

'Don't be stupid. If you don't go in today, then it's going to be much harder to drag yourself in there tomorrow. What are you going to do – take the whole next four weeks off sick?'

'Now there's an idea.'

'What's the worst that can happen? They laugh in your face. And behind your back. They call you a home-wrecking bitch. And a father-stealing ho. They tell you they always suspected it was you and not Helen-from-Accounts because she's too good for him and she'd never need to stoop that low . . .'

Helen was laughing despite herself. 'OK, OK you can stop now.'

'Seriously, though,' Rachel was saying. 'You hate those girls anyway, so what do you care? What do you think of Jenny? Three words.'

'Stupid vindictive cow.'

'And Annie?'

'Fucking stupid vicious vindictive sad no-life cow bitch. Cunt.'

'That's my girl. Go get 'em.'

'Did I mention that Annie was a cunt.'

'You did. And Helen, if all else fails, punch her in the mouth. What are they going to do – fire you?'

They travelled to work together for the first time, in Matthew's made-for-driving-through-the-jungle-in-a-rainstorm car, which, Helen had to admit, was better than getting the tube. Matthew turned the stereo up and they rolled the windows down, even though it was February and freezing. OK, so Magic FM in an SUV doing thirty-five down Hampstead Road wasn't exactly gangster rap in a customized Chevy bouncing along Crenshaw Boulevard, but it was fun and, for a moment, Helen felt a thrill of excitement from being out with her boyfriend, in public, like a regular couple. Then it passed and, before she knew what had happened to her, she'd started to cry. Matthew, half-way through a loud and tuneless chorus of 'Angels', did a noticeable double-take and stopped singing mid word.

'What . . . ?' he stammered. 'Are you OK?'

'Yes,' sniffed Helen, obviously not.

'Do you want to talk about it? Is it me?'

'No. Yes. Are you happy, Matthew?'

'Of course I am,' he said nervously.

'How can you be? We hardly talk to each other any more, we hardly ever have sex, the flat's way too small for the two of us, you never see your kids, your sister hates me . . .'

'We can have more sex,' he said, missing the point entirely. 'I just thought you didn't want to.'

'It's not about the sex. It's everything.'

She waited for him to be comforting, to say he understood, maybe even to say, 'You know, you're right, let's call it a day,' but instead he looked at her and his eyes flashed with irritation.

'For god's sake, Helen, grow up. This is real life. We're not playing at it any more, this is what a real relationship is like. What we had before was an unreal situation, all highs and lows. Living together is all about the day-to-day stuff, the mundane, the details. I've made the ultimate sacrifice by leaving my children so, if I can be happy with the way things are, then surely to god you can be.'

'So you keep telling me.'

Matthew nearly swerved into the bus lane as he turned to look at her again.

'Meaning?'

They'd arrived at the NCP car park across the road from the office. Now isn't the time, thought Helen, in five minutes, all eyes are going to be on us and the last thing I want is for them to think I'm unhappy, it'd be like showing a shoal of piranhas the paper cut on your finger. She looked in the mirror on the back of the sun shade and dabbed at her eyes with a tissue, trying not to disturb her waterproof mascara which had, so far, remained miraculously intact.

'Nothing. I'm just nervous about today that's all.'

Matthew pulled on the handbrake and entwined his fingers around hers.

'It'll be OK.'

As he moved in to kiss her on the cheek, she jumped, as the jarring, vaguely recognizable theme tune to *Emmerdale*, which was now her mobile ring tone, started up. She dug it out of her bag. Sophie. Shit. She pressed the red button to turn it off. Matthew looked at her curiously.

'It's just Mum. I can't face her now. I'll call her later.'

'Have you told her about us yet?' Matthew must have asked her this question twenty times in the past month.

'No, you know what she's like. Well, you don't, because of course you've never met her, but you can imagine. She reads Catherine Cookson, for god's sake. She makes teacakes. I mean, have you even seen a teacake since 1974? She collects china shepherdesses. If I told her I'd slept with *anyone*, I think she'd have a heart attack. If you want me to tell her I've shacked up with a married father-of-two, then call an ambulance first – I'm just warning you.'

Matthew laughed. 'OK, OK, but she'll have to know sometime.'

'Oooh, Matthew and Helen arriving together, now there's a surprise,' Annie smirked, as they went their separate ways at reception. 'You both look like you haven't had much sleep. I wonder why.'

'That's enough, Annie,' Matthew called jovially over his shoulder because, being one of the bosses, he could get away with it.

Helen smiled an insincere smile. 'Go fuck yourself.'

She moved on through to her desk, ignoring Jenny's hostile looks and tried to keep her head down, scrolling through her emails, but she could feel her blush rising to the tips of her ears. She played her conversation with Rachel over in her head – 'You hate them anyway, so who cares what they think of you? – but it didn't help her feel any braver. It didn't matter whether she despised these women, which, for the most part, she did, for their bitchiness and their lack of originality and the role they played in reinforcing all the stereotypes of women she hated – man-obsessed, unfunny, horoscope-believing, sport-hating, gossip-magazine-reading airheads – she could no longer look down on them, because now they knew what a fuck-up she was. It was only a matter of time before they found out how long her relationship with Matthew had been going on and they realized that, for pretty much the whole time they'd known her, she'd been lying to them. All the stories about Carlo. Oh god, Carlo. There was no way she could confess to the truth about that – that was too shaming for words. All the times they'd said anything about Matthew, good or bad, not knowing that she'd be meeting him in secret later on and so couldn't be trusted as a confidante. And, worst of all, Helen-from-Accounts. Never mind that they had taken that way too far – she'd been the one to point the finger in the first place.

I can't worry about this, she forced herself to think now. She saw Laura watching her from behind her office partition and smiled weakly. Laura stuck her head round the door.

'Helen, have you got a minute?'

Helen dragged herself from her chair and shut the door of Laura's tiny office behind her. She sat down.

'So,' Laura kicked off. 'Obviously, I've heard. You know what this place is like.'

Helen grunted a noncommittal reply. She slumped in her chair and stared at the grey prickly tiles on the floor like a teenager in to see the headmistress.

'I just wanted to say,' Laura continued, 'that if this is the reason you've handed in your notice, then I'd like you to reconsider. I know it must be awful now, but it'll all blow over. They've got the attention span of children, that lot – something else'll happen and it'll be on to the next. You could take a holiday now and just ride it out.'

'Thank you.' Helen looked up at her, genuinely grateful for the speech. Why don't I like her? she thought to herself again. Oh yes, because she's a woman and she's a director, and I'm only a secretary and I think I should have her job. Not because I'd do it any better than her, but because I'm jealous and I've made terrible decisions and I've completely fucked up my own life.

She managed a smile. 'Thank you, really. I appreciate it. But . . . it's time I left here anyway. I'm forty in a couple of months and I don't want to be a forty-year-old secretary.'

'PA.'

'Same thing. It's about time I got a career.'

'What are you going to do?'

'I have no idea. There's fuck all that I'm good at, and I feel too old to have to go somewhere and start at the bottom, even if anyone'd have me. But, I'll find something.'

'Well, I'll miss you. Really. And I'll ask around, see if I can put in a word for you somewhere.'

'Thanks. Sorry I've been such a rampaging bitch of an assistant. Better luck with the next one.'

'You know, the only reason I want you to stay is 'cos I'm terrified about who they'll make me have if you go.'

'I heard Annie wanted to move off reception.'

'OK – if you even mention this to her, then I'm not giving you a reference,' Laura laughed. 'I'm serious.'

Back at her desk and back under scrutiny, Helen looked at her watch. Lunchtime. She had survived a whole morning, and it seemed like the worst the girls had in store for her was to send her to Coventry and to throw the odd snippy remark her way. If that was as bad as it got then she could brazen it out.

Wrong.

She was putting on her coat to go out and get a solitary sandwich, which she had decided she'd eat on a bench in the square, when Helen-from-Accounts minus plum lipstick and back in her old navy suit came into the general office. Helen smiled at her and was thinking about asking whether she wanted to walk to the deli together when she realized Helen-from-Accounts had blanked her. Not just blanked her but gone over to Jenny, who was greeting her like she was a long-lost relative who had just been discovered having survived the wreck of the *Titanic*. The two girls muttered giggly mutterings and then looked over in her direction and laughed out loud. This was too much. She'd expected it from the others, but Helen-from-Accounts was taking the piss out of her. Helen-from-Accounts! She'd sacrificed herself to save that pitiful little fucker. How dare she! She glared in their direction, but they were either oblivious or else enjoying her discomfort. She heard the dumpy little pixie-haired pillar-box say something and clearly heard the word 'slut', then they both looked in her direction and laughed again. Helen felt herself colouring up once more and grabbed her bag and stormed towards the door. On the way out, she passed Annie, coat on, coming in to join the party.

'OK, girls, where are we going for lunch?'

Helen could hear her shouting above the laughter and, rather than wait for the lift and risk being there when they all came out, she went through the door to the emergency stairs and practically ran down the five flights and out into the street.

16

'Check this out,' Matthew said, producing a sheath of papers from behind his back with all the flourish of a magician with a rabbit.

'What's that?' she'd asked, reaching for them, and then her heart had sunk when she'd seen the headings on the pages. Winkworths, Frank Harris, Copping Joyce. Estate agents. Oh, fuck. OK, so they were living together already, but the *definiteness*, the *finality* of buying a place together sent a wave of panic through her. Buying together said, 'This is it, we've decided, we're together for ever,' and she didn't feel ready to say that – didn't know if she ever would, although if she admitted the truth to herself, the odds were stacking up against it. When she tried to picture herself in the future these days, that picture just didn't include Matthew. In fact, she was trying to avoid picturing her future life at all at the moment – it was too depressing.

'You're always saying the flat is too small, so I thought, what the hell.'

'But . . .' she'd said, clutching at straws, 'how can we afford it? I mean, you're still paying for your other house, obviously, and you have to give money to Sophie for the kids and I'm about to be unemployed. Unemployable probably.'

He smiled at her wryly. 'Have you got any idea how

much I earn? We can practically buy somewhere else for cash. Not a house but a big flat. Much bigger than this, at any rate. Where do you fancy? Highgate? Primrose Hill? Round here? I want to stay near the kids, but otherwise Bob's your oyster.'

She ignored her irritation at the whimsical expression. 'But I love my flat.'

'No, you don't. You said yourself, it's tiny, and it's dark, and it's damp, and the Rabbits are going to kill us in our bed one night. Plus, it's mad for you to be renting at your age.'

'At least let's wait until I get another job,' she said, thinking, that'll probably be never, 'then I can contribute. I don't want to feel like a kept woman.' This seemed to work, and they spent a quite pleasant half-hour sifting through the details he'd got anyway 'Just to see what's out there.'

'You're very nice to me,' she'd said to him as they got into bed. 'I'm sorry I'm a bit of a miserable cow to live with at the moment.'

'Tell you what, you can make it up to me,' he'd replied and moved in to kiss her. They had sex for the first time in what seemed like ages and it reminded her a bit of what things had been like before it all started to go pear-shaped. She'd been very vocal, which he'd seemed to enjoy, although, if she was honest, she had been doing it for the Rabbits' sake. When he'd fallen asleep, she'd looked at him, and he'd looked so peaceful and untormented by anxieties, so unaware of how bad things really were, that she felt achingly guilty. She'd kissed him on the forehead, glad that she'd managed to give him a nice evening for once and turned on to her side to sleep.

Helen and Sophie were back in the pub, and Helen was pushing Sophie to open up about the break-up of her marriage. She'd said no at first when Sophie had called her to arrange another evening out, but then had given in immediately when pressed. She couldn't work out if it was curiosity or some kind of masochism, she just couldn't pass up the opportunity to understand the ramifications of what she'd done from the other woman's point of view. To pick at that scab a bit more until she was able to numb the pain and allow it to start healing over. Sophie, always controlled, was resisting pouring her heart out, although she was tempted to try and dilute the enormity of the hurt she felt by sharing it. She did, however, share one piece of news with her new friend – that she had found out more about who her rival was.

'She actually works at Global. Can you believe that?'

Helen nearly choked on her vodka. She could feel the walls of the pub closing in around her. She looked around: nothing had changed, the world was carrying on as normal. Sophie was still talking.

'I mean, I knew he knew her through work, but I never thought she was someone he spent all day with. She used to be his assistant, for god's sake!'

'How do you know?' Helen managed to ask.

'Trust me, people are dying to break good news to you when things like this happen. Apparently, she just announced it in the office the other day, although Amelia said that no one's surprised, she's always been a bit up herself. No one likes her.'

Ah. Amelia from Human Resources. What a bitch, thought Helen.

Throughout the evening, Helen kept bringing the conversation back round to 'Evil Helen', as she now knew she was being perceived – quite rightly, obviously, but it still irked her to hear the things her colleagues had been saying. Other facts that Sophie had elicited from Amelia included:

Helen was rubbish at her job (this was so not true)

She flirted with all the male directors (ditto)

She had told all the girls in the office she had another boyfriend until recently ('I wonder if Matthew knows about that,' Sophie was saying)

She'd told everyone Matthew was having an affair with another woman to deflect suspicion away from herself ('Nice,' said Sophie)

She was nearly forty ('Ha!' said Sophie. 'Younger than me but not that young. She won't be able to rely on her looks for much longer')

'God, she sounds awful,' Helen found herself saying, and actually believed it for a moment, until she remembered she was talking about herself. 'Does she think it'll last, your friend?'

'Oh, Amelia's not my friend,' Sophie said. 'But she's one of those women that always want to be first with the news, so I bet she was bursting to tell me. It definitely wasn't out of concern for my wellbeing. I can't stand her actually.'

You've got good taste, Helen thought.

'And, no,' Sophie continued. 'The general perception at Global is that it won't last. They all think he'll come to his senses and realize he's made a mistake, but I doubt it. I know Matthew, he'll never admit he's wrong.'

'You never can tell,' said Helen.

'Well, that's his problem now,' Sophie replied, effectively drawing a line under the subject.

After that she wouldn't be drawn, and they drifted into the slightly less enthralling topic of Claudia's impending birthday.

'What's she like? I mean, what kind of stuff is she into?' Helen asked, thinking that she might glean a bit of useful information to use in her fight to make her Sunday afternoons bearable.

'Claudia's big love is animals. She used to want to be a vet, and I think she still does, but she can't admit it because she's in the middle of a 'can't be seen to care about anything' phase. Suzanne's the one who does well in exams. She wants to be a doctor, or at least she says she does, but I think that's because she once said so to Matthew and he's gone on about it ever since. To be honest, I think she's scared to say she wants to do anything else, because she's such a daddy's girl and she wouldn't want to let him down. She's a normal girly girl, into boy bands and make-up and pink stuff. I've never so much as known her watch *Holby* let alone take an interest in science. To be honest, I'm just grateful they're both fairly stable and not yet drug addicts or hookers or shoplifters – well, as far as I know.'

Helen laughed. 'They're what, ten and twelve?'

'Soon to be eleven and twelve. So what, they start young these days . . .'

'Do you think they want their dad back?'

'I think they'd give anything. Absolutely anything. But they're still young enough to forgive and forget. That gets much harder as you get older.'

'What do they make of Helen?' Helen was unable to leave the subject of herself alone.

'Oh, they can't stand her. Or at least that's what they tell me. By the sound of it, she makes it pretty clear she's not interested in them.'

They shared a cab home as far as Camden tube station, where Helen insisted she get out and walk the rest of the way while Sophie took the cab on up Kentish Town Road. It was such a normal, everyday thing that friends do that Helen nearly forgot who they both were and allowed Sophie to drop her off at her door, as she was trying to insist she should. Matthew wasn't there, of course – he was at the family home, babysitting the girls – and neither was his car, but it would still be a stupidly risky thing to do. What if Sophie, knowing where she lived, decided to drop round unannounced one day? No . . . it didn't bear thinking about. She picked her way past the crowds spilling out of the Electric Ballroom and replayed the evening in her head. Apart from the half-hour character assassination of herself, it had been a good evening. Strange but enjoyable. Strange, enjoyable and more than a bit reckless. She wondered if she had a deathwish.

She realized she was feeling guilty about the girls. It wasn't their fault they were caught up in the middle of this, she thought, the vodka making her uncharacteristically generous. I like Matthew, I like Sophie, there's no reason why I can't make more of an effort to get on with their offspring. In fact, she was starting to find she was growing quite fond of them, in *principle*. When Sophie talked about them, she made them sound intriguing – vulnerable, complicated, unique, all untapped potential not yet jaded by knockbacks. It was just that it was hard to equate that with the surly monosyllabic creatures who spent their Sunday afternoons glaring at her from beneath their long fringes. As she turned the corner into Jamestown Road, she vowed to try harder.

'Let's get a kitten,' said Helen, back at home, when Matthew had finished moaning about Sophie getting home late and clearly half-cut again.

'What?'

'I mean it. Let's go to Battersea Dogs Home and pick out a kitten or a cat or a dog. I don't know, let's just get an animal.'

'Has Rachel got you drunk?' he said, laughing, but Helen could see he was pleased she was in a good mood.

17

The days dragged on through the wet darkness of February with Helen forcing herself into work, sitting at her desk feigning deafness to the occasional comments thrown out by the other women and feeling genuine relief when they slipped back into their campaign of ignoring her. Matthew insisted on popping in to see her several times a day, no matter how many times she told him he was making things worse. Whenever he left again ('Bye, girls!' all round), she kept her eyes firmly fixed on her computer screen so as not to see the smirks. By Thursday, she'd taken to wearing her iPod at her desk. At lunchtime she took herself out and ate her lunch in the square round the corner, even in the rain, and it was sitting here on Friday, wet hair, soggy sandwiches, damp paperback, that she ran into Sophie. And not just Sophie, Sophie and a rather attractive man.

Helen caught sight of them a split second before they passed by her bench. She froze in shock and contemplated trying to sneak away, but it was too risky. By the time Sophie spotted her, she'd just managed to compose herself and was trying to make eating on a bench, in the freezing rain in a square just down the street from Global PR, look like the most normal event in the world.

'Hi!'

'Eleanor! What on earth are you doing sat here?'

'I . . . had a meeting in Dean Street and . . . I've got another meeting in a bit round the corner, so I thought I'd enjoy the beautiful weather.'

Luckily, both Sophie and Mr Attractive laughed. Helen took a proper look at him. Blimey, he really was nice-looking – tall, a slightly disturbing combination of dark hair and incredibly pale-blue eyes, smile lines, well built. She hated skinny men. All knees and elbows, and they always seemed to want to dress to show it off, like they were really proud of it, in stretchy tight-fit jeans that made them look like wading birds. Mind you, if anyone had asked her a few years ago if balding heads and paunches were her type, then she'd have said, 'Definitely not.' It was so long since she'd found a man even halfway fanciable that she spent just a fraction too long taking him in. Then she remembered it was rude to stare, especially at someone who might well turn out to be her new friend's new boyfriend.

It was just a momentary aberration, and it was over in a second. She knew it was just the jolt of her hormones springing back into life because she'd clapped eyes on someone half decent for the first time in god knows how long. She mentally chastised herself for even going there. She really mustn't make a habit of trying to nick men off Sophie.

'This is Sonny,' Sophie was saying, and for some reason they both laughed.

'Eleanor . . . oh, Eleanor does PR. How funny is that? Sonny's opening a restaurant in Percy Street in a couple of weeks, and I was just saying to him you should get yourself a PR person and – here you are. Give him your card.'

'I . . . er . . . I've run out, em, because of moving and

everything, you know, I'm having to get new ones printed so . . .'

'Well, I'll give him your mobile number then. You're not too busy, are you?'

Helen made a quick mental list of the pros and cons:

Pros

I'm nearly out of a job, so I could do with the money
I could do this standing on my head
This could be the start of a whole new career

Cons

I'm not a PR person
My name's not Eleanor
I can't remember what my surname is meant to be

Somehow, she decided in a split second that the pros had won and found herself saying, 'No, not at all. That'd be great. Ring me.'

And then 'Tell me about the restaurant,' she said.

'Well, it's called Verano. It's Spanish. Tapas. We import all our own ingredients. Authentic Catalan. The head chef's come over from Gaudi in Barcelona. Have you heard of it?'

'No, sorry. Have you done anything like this before?' He was so enthusiastic, it was easy to imagine him charming the press.

'I had a bistro in Richmond. Tiny. Safe. This is scaring the shit out of me, to tell you the truth.'

'I keep telling him he's crazy,' said Sophie. 'You know that statistic, nine out of ten restaurants go bust in the first year? Well, he's already had the one out of ten successful one, so it's got to be all downhill from here.'

'She's so supportive,' Sonny laughed, and Helen thought how easy and relaxed they seemed together. She was glad for her friend, although a little miffed that Sophie hadn't mentioned her new conquest in their last drunken chat. Maybe she had been seeing him before Matthew left, she thought, clutching at something that might absolve her from guilt, but she knew that infidelity wasn't Sophie's style.

She said goodbye to Sophie, who was promising to call her later in the week, and to Sonny, who was saying he'd ring that afternoon. She waited until they were out of sight before she headed back to Global, to sit at her miserable desk.

Oh god, what had she done? This was fucking insane. She'd been at Global long enough to know she could handle a small campaign in her sleep – but as Eleanor Whatshername? All her contacts, the endless editors and sub-editors and journalists she dealt with every day on Laura's behalf knew her as Helen Williamson. Maybe she could use her real name with them and her fake one with Sonny. Or she could tell him it was the PR equivalent of a stage name. Or her maiden name, although she'd never come across anyone who changed their first as well as their second name on marriage. It was a ridiculous idea. Too dangerous.

But . . . what if she pulled it off? What if she did a great campaign and he recommended her to his friends and she could set up on her own, and fuck them all at Global. No . . . because if she did a great campaign, then what he would actually do would be to recommend Eleanor Thing to his friends. Eleanor Thing would be able to set up on her own and have a thriving business and a great new career. And she wasn't Eleanor Thing. Oh god, what *had* she told Sophie her fucking surname was. She had no idea.

She went in to see Laura.

'I just wondered whether you'd had any luck – you know, if you'd heard about any jobs.'

'I have,' said Laura, handing over a Post-it with a name and number written on it in black ink. Martin Ross from Eyestorm. They were big.

'It's only secretarial, though, I'm afraid. I keep trying to tell people you're totally up to it, but they all want experience. Sorry.'

'Thanks for trying.' Helen backed out of the door. 'I'll ring him,' she said, having no intention of doing so.

The day crawled along. Helen had decided that if Sonny ever rang she would say yes. She'd do the job as Eleanor Whatever-Her-Name-Was to him and Helen Williamson to her contacts and she'd somehow find a way to smooth out the lines between the two so that by the time it was done she'd have the experience she needed to get a proper job – the proper job she should have tried to get years ago. She stared at her mobile, willing it to ring.

At five o'clock, the dull and pointless office ritual of Friday-afternoon drinks began. The routine was that a couple of bottles of champagne were cracked open, whichever of the directors were around came and hung round the general office, people necked down a quick glass and went home. It was meant to be a bonding thing. Usually, two or three of the sadder employees stayed on, drinking the dregs out of everyone else's glasses and raiding the fridge for beer, before going on to a local pub for the evening so that they had hilarious stories of their wild and exciting lives to relate to the office on Monday morning ('I was sick in someone's glass!', 'I shagged some bloke in a taxi!', 'I danced on the table in the Nelly Dean!'). Tonight, thankfully, Matthew was out at a launch, but Alan Forsyth, a partner with a well-deserved reputation for being a bit of a sleaze, was on socializing duty with Laura. The others started to drift in, Annie and Amelia among them. Helen stayed at her desk, head down, willing Laura to tell her she could leave early.

'Not having a drink, Helen?' Alan was shouting over. 'Scared you won't be able to resist me if you have a couple?'

The coven cackled.

'Pack it in, Alan,' Laura was saying, but Alan could never pass up on the chance to show off in front of an audience. Especially an audience of women.

'Not too young for you, am I?' He was finding himself so amusing, his face had gone bright purple, and Helen thought he resembled an aubergine. An overweight, sweaty, unpalatable aubergine. She willed him to have a heart attack, or a stroke at least. Nothing fatal, just something that might put him into hospital for a few weeks.

'I mean, I'm only, what, fifteen years older than you.'

OK, something fatal.

He was never going to give up, at least not while he was making the crowd laugh.

'I do have a wife and child, though. That's a real turn-on for you, isn't it?'

Helen thought about getting out her big gun. The one that would flatten Alan with one shot. The one that would let him know that the whole office was aware of his sordid email sex sessions with a woman called Felicia who was definitely not his wife. Not only aware of it, but had spent many an afternoon when Alan was away from the office reading those emails aloud to each other. Somewhere along the line, Alan seemed to have forgotten that the contents of his inbox went to his assistant, Jamie, as well as to his personal computer – Jamie, by the way, had been hired when Alan's female PA, Kristin, had complained that he had made inappropriate comments to her at the office Christmas party and then, a few drinks later, had tried to feel her up in the corridor. Of course, there had been no repercussions for Alan except that his PA had been made redundant and then, a couple of weeks later, Jamie was promoted from a runner in her place. Jamie, who was good mates with Kristin and had spent many hours listening to her complain about Alan's wandering hands, had absolutely no loyalty to his boss whatsoever and never quite got round to reminding him that his exchanges weren't, strictly speaking, confidential.

Occasionally, when one of the PAs had had a glass too many at Friday-afternoon drinks, they would throw in a quote or two – something along the lines of 'big hard cocks' or 'throbbing members', because Alan was not blessed with great originality or artfulness – and Jamie would hold his breath, hoping that his boss didn't rumble what was going on – but he never did. His supreme arrogance made him believe he was untouchable. Helen knew, though, that a direct attack would give the game away and Jamie would probably end up losing his job, while Alan would most likely get backslaps of congratulations from the other directors.

She took a deep breath and stood up and reached for her coat on the back of her chair.

'You know what, Alan, you're right. I do want to sleep with you. I'm not sure if it's your frizzy hair, your reputation, your astonishing talent or your sparkling wit, but I find you utterly irresistible.'

'Ooh, I've touched a nerve,' Alan was saying, but his laugh sounded a bit less sure of itself.

'Fuck you.'

Ignoring the collective 'oohs' of the other women, Helen stomped off towards the door. Then, with horror, she realized, just as she thought she was home and dry, that she'd forgotten her bag. For a split second she thought about leaving it, but it contained her whole life. Keys, money, mobile. Scarlet, she had to turn back and make her way through the office again, all eyes on her. She kept her head up, trying to make it look as if this double exit had been part of the plan all along.

'How dare you take the piss out of me? Don't expect a fucking reference,' Alan was spitting in her direction. Annie, Amelia and Jenny were purple with laughter.

'Oh, for fuck's sake Alan, grow up,' Helen could hear Laura saying. 'Why would she want a reference off you? She works for me.' She raised her voice so that she knew

Helen would hear. 'And I intend to give her a very good one, too.'

As Helen reached the downstairs lobby of the building, still waiting for her colour to go down, her mobile rang. It was a number she didn't recognize. She took a deep breath before answering.

'Hello.'

'Hi, is that Eleanor?'

Bingo. She felt a little light-headed when she realized who it was, and she had to force her voice to sound calm and competent.

'It is.'

'We met earlier, in Soho Square . . .'

'Yes! Hi.'

'Yeah, erm . . . I was thinking, Sophie's right, and if you think you might have time to help me out, then I was wondering whether we could meet up and talk about it.'

Helen tried to sound professional.

'Definitely. I'd love to. Name your time.'

'Well,' said Sonny, 'how about now? I'm at the restaurant, if you want to come over and see what you'll be plugging.'

Helen retraced her steps back towards the stairs and went into the ladies. I'll just check I look presentable, she thought, but then found herself completely redoing her make-up. It's important that I look good, she said half aloud as she combed her hair through, PR is all about image. But she knew she was kidding herself and she wanted Sonny to think she was attractive.

There was nothing else for it. She wanted – no, she

needed – this job, but there was something else going on and it was making her feel uncomfortable. She had to call Sophie and find out exactly what the story was with Sonny before she put herself in a situation where she might end up doing something she'd regret. She dialled. Answerphone.

Oh, fuck it, she thought. I'm an adult, I make my own choices and I am absolutely not going to do anything wrong. I just need some work.

Sonny's restaurant was undergoing the last stages of frantic renovation work. Helen let herself in and clambered over the rubble and tried not to trip over the wiring. There was clearly no electricity at the moment, and the small space was lit by a few battery-powered lamps dotted about the place. Despite the bitter cold outside, the warmth from a Calor-Gas fire gave it a cosy feel. Two men were working away, heads down, and through the layer of dust she just about recognized one of them as Sonny. He was working intently, plastering a wall, and in his old T-shirt and paint-spattered jeans, he looked the epitome of Diet-Coke man. Helen could imagine whole offices full of secretaries putting down their dictation pads and taking off their reading glasses to gather and stare at him through the window. She stood for a moment, not quite knowing what to do, and then realized *she* was staring at him again. And that the other man was staring at her staring at him.

'Can I help you?' he asked.

'Oh . . . yes . . . I'm . . . erm . . . I'm Eleanor.' She felt bizarrely nervous. Maybe it's because I'm an utter fraud, she thought, wondering if she should just back out of the door she had come in through and leg it. But Sonny had looked round at the sound of her voice and was coming over, hand outstretched, smiling.

'Eleanor. Thanks so much for coming over.' He took her hand and shook it firmly. 'So . . . this is it. What do you think?'

'It's . . . er . . .'

'It's a complete fucking state is what it is,' he said, laughing. 'But it will get finished on time if it kills me. Come through to the back and I'll show you the plans.'

An hour later, Sonny had convinced Helen that the restaurant was bound for great things and Helen had convinced Sonny that she had fantastic and original ideas for promoting it. She'd actually got so carried away with her plans for features (she knew, she just knew that Lesley David from the *Mail on Sunday* would go for a piece on Catalan specialities, and she owed her one, because she – well, Helen, not Eleanor – had got her an interview with top chef Pippa Martin when Laura was away and Pippa was refusing to do any press until her new book was ready) and promotions and a glittering launch night that she'd forgotten about her adolescent crush on Sonny. She'd invite all of Global's celebrity clients, who she had got to know over the years, to the launch. She knew the D-listers would attend any event where they stood a chance of getting in the papers, and she knew the photographers would attend any event which promised a cocktail of D-listers and free alcohol. She was just congratulating herself on how well she was handling the situation when Sonny did two things which threw her right off balance again.

He asked her out to dinner.

He asked her what her surname was.

And to deflect attention from the second, she found herself agreeing to the first.

She called Matthew from the candle-lit toilet of Sonny's restaurant. For some reason, she found herself lying to him and telling him she was meeting Rachel.

'Sophie won't . . . you know . . . mind, us going out to dinner?' she said to Sonny when she came back out, putting her phone away.

Sonny looked confused. 'Sophie? Why?'

'Well, I just thought maybe you and her . . .' She stopped when she saw that Sonny had started to laugh.

'Me and Sophie? God, no. God . . . no.'

'Oh.'

Sonny was still helpless. 'I mean . . . I love her and everything, but really . . . no. Don't worry.'

'OK.' Helen was starting to feel embarrassed. By asking him that question, she'd given away that she was interested, but she couldn't allow herself to be interested, not till she'd sorted the Matthew situation out. Try as she might, though, she couldn't bury the feeling that she was pleased he wasn't Sophie's boyfriend.

Sonny had got a grip. 'Sorry,' he was saying. 'I'm not laughing at you. It's just, it's impossible to imagine me and Sophie . . . I mean, she's lovely, but it just couldn't happen . . . God, no . . .'

Helen interrupted him, laughing. 'OK, I believe you. Let's go, shall we?'

The evening was perfect. Well, it would have been

perfect if it hadn't been for Matthew and Sophie and the fact that she wasn't really Eleanor or a real PR person. Sonny was attentive and funny. He wasn't sixty, he didn't have a family, he was uncomplicated – or at least he seemed to be. Helen knew she must be coming across as uptight, what with all the lies she was having to tell and the history she was making up for Eleanor, but he was acting like he was enjoying her company anyway. A few glasses of wine in, and she was sailing dangerously close to the wind, getting her Helens and Eleanors mixed up, and contradicting herself all over the place, but he didn't seem to notice. Everything amused him, and he made her feel like she was the most entertaining, witty person he'd ever met. For Helen, it was the ego boost to end all ego boosts – she just had to keep reminding herself that that was all it was.

At nine thirty, while they were waiting for their coffees to arrive, Sonny suddenly put his hand over hers. Helen froze. She was feeling distinctly fuzzy from all the Pinot Grigio. She looked at him, and he was looking right back at her.

Say something, she told herself.

Sonny cleared his throat. 'Eleanor . . .'

'No.' She withdrew her hand. 'Sorry, I can't do this.'

'OK.' He was looking hurt and a little bit pissed off.

'It's just, I have a boyfriend but, well, I didn't mention it before because . . . it's a bit of a complex situation.'

'I see.'

'No, you don't. I think it's over, I just haven't told him yet. God, no, that sounds awful. I'm trying to find a way to end it that'll give him the least possible pain, and that's just taking longer than I thought.'

'Eleanor, it's no big deal. I like you, but we've only just met, so it's not like I'm going to be heartbroken if you knock me back. Well, just a bit.'

He was smiling at her now; that was a good sign.

'It's probably for the best, anyway, seeing as we're going to be working together for the next few weeks. And then, once we're not working together, if it turns out you no longer have a boyfriend then, who knows, I might try again if you're very very lucky. And, of course, if I haven't met someone better in the meantime.'

'No chance,' she laughed. It was fine – it had been a moment, but it was all over, and they could still work together. They managed to make jokey conversation over their coffee and they made each other laugh, but something had gone out of the evening and they were both aware of it. A slight formality had crept back in, and Helen noticed that each of them was furiously avoiding eye contact. At one point his hand brushed hers when they both went to pick up the bill, and they jumped apart as if they'd been stung.

But when they said goodnight, he kissed her on the cheek and stayed there for just a fraction too long. Before either of them really knew what was happening – and, thinking about it afterwards, Helen really couldn't say who'd instigated it – they had manoeuvred themselves round and it had become a full-blown snog. No, not a snog she thought, that was too adolescent, too drunken and desperate and reminiscent of hen nights and Ibiza and having to ask their name in the morning, this was a kiss, grown up and loaded with meaning and things they wanted to say but couldn't. This time, though, he pulled away, embarrassed and apologetic.

'I'm really sorry. I don't know what I was thinking of.'

'It's OK,' Helen said, still reeling. 'It was . . . nice.'

But Sonny wasn't having it. 'No, no. I just promised to leave you alone till you're ready and then I do this. I never move in on other people's girlfriends. I mean, really never.'

'I'm the one with the boyfriend,' Helen said. 'I'm the one should be apologizing.'

'We won't do it again.' Sonny was moving backwards, creating a physical barrier between them.

'Definitely not,' Helen agreed.

'Well, hopefully, someday. Just not now.'

'Exactly.'

Neither of them quite knew how to end the conversation and move on, and they stood awkwardly for a few moments, their breath white in the cold air, hands rammed into their pockets to stop them making a grab for one another like two hormonal teenagers. Then Sonny pecked her on the cheek again – this time as if he were saying goodbye to his grandmother.

'Night then,' he said.

'Night,' said Helen, stepping out into the road to flag down a taxi. She waved at him as it moved off, feeling guilty about Matthew already. But she knew that the possibility was still there that something might happen in the future, and she couldn't help smiling.

Matthew, she thought, when she got back home and found him in his Calvin Klein pyjamas on the sofa, eager to hear how her night had been, is an old man. It wasn't his fault, it shouldn't necessarily have been a problem –

plenty of people had very successful and happy relationships with a massive age gap – but somehow it had become one. Up against Sonny, he suddenly seemed ridiculous. Not the powerful, suited successful man in his prime she had fallen for, but his ageing, out-of-touch, slightly needy older brother. His ageing, out-of-touch, slightly needy older brother who had a penchant for younger women, which, in any other man, she would have found sleazy. When she was fifty, he would be seventy. Was that what she wanted? To spend the rest of her life with a man who was drawing his pension?

If I really loved him, I wouldn't be thinking like this, she thought. If I really loved him, I would've told Sonny that there was no chance, that I was in a happy relationship and that I couldn't work for him after what had just happened. She had said to Sonny that it was over, that she was just waiting for the right time to tell him. And, looking at Matthew now, she was forced to acknowledge the thought which had been bubbling around in her head ever since he moved in and which she had been trying not to allow to surface – that she didn't truly love him. At least, not enough.

She just had to decide what to do about it.

18

On Saturday morning, Matthew and Helen picked out a large green-eyed tabby from the local animal shelter. They'd gone for a kitten, but there were none to be had and, anyway, the cat had almost begged them to choose him, rubbing up against the side of his cage when they walked by and rolling over and purring when they stopped to look. He was three years old and had no tragic but glamorous sob story, he just wasn't wanted. They named him Norman. Helen knew that Matthew was interpreting this act of domesticity as some kind of nesting instinct on her part. She didn't like to tell him that Norman was bait.

She had slept badly, waking often and veering between feelings of elation and guilt, about the PR job, Matthew, Sonny. Before the kiss goodnight and all the complications it had given rise to, Sonny had pressed one of his cards into her hand so that she could call him after the weekend and tell him how her plans for the campaign were going. It was hidden now, in the back pocket of her jeans, and Helen felt alternately thrilled and dismayed knowing it was there. She knew she should tell Matthew about the restaurant and her potential break, but she couldn't work her way through the tissue of lies she'd need to get there and, anyway, he'd probably get all moralistic and insist that she tell Sonny he'd hired her under false pretences. They were avoiding the subject of work pretty much now in any case, since Helen had asked Matthew whether he could put in a good word for her anywhere.

'It'd look bad, coming from me. As if I'm just saying you're good because you're my girlfriend.'

'But you've worked with me for years – it's perfectly legit that you'd give me a reference. I used to be your assistant, for god's sake.'

'Maybe in a few months, when all the gossip's died down. You could temp till then or – didn't you say Eyestorm needed someone?'

'They need a secretary. I don't want to be a secretary. Not any more.'

'Well,' Matthew said. 'You know what they say: beggars can't be choosers.'

Did he just say that? Helen was furious.

'Did you just say that? I've lost my fucking job because of you and me. Don't you feel any responsibility?'

'Oh, come on, Helly, don't be so melodramatic. You didn't have to give your notice in. There was absolutely no reason why you couldn't stay at Global.'

'You. Are. Fucking. Unbelievable. And don't call me Helly.'

She'd stormed straight out of the front door and walked round the block a couple of times, and then she'd realized she had nowhere to go, and it was starting to drizzle, so she'd gone back home again. Matthew, irritatingly, had clearly anticipated her arrival, because he had just made a large cafetière of coffee.

He'd apologized; she'd acted indifferent; he'd grovelled; she'd capitulated. Same old story.

*

Sunday morning was dull and rainy. Helen and Matthew flopped around the flat unable to summon up the energy to go down to the shop on the corner and get the newspapers. Helen made a half-hearted attempt to tidy up, knowing that critical eyes would be all over the mess later. Increasingly, Helen felt this was what her Sundays had become – a day of waiting for Matthew to pick up the girls and bring them over. A day given over to other people. She fought the temptation to sneak out with her mobile to call Sophie and casually contrive a conversation about Sonny:

So . . . how do you know Sonny?

So . . . what about Sonny? Anything I should know, not that I'm interested. Any wives, children, boyfriends knocking about? Any communicable diseases, mental health issues, religious fundamentalism?

So . . . I'm thinking about shagging Sonny one of these days. What do you reckon?

She distracted herself by making lists of publicity-grabbing ideas for the restaurant. Salsa dancers – no, too tacky; free sangria – ditto; maracas, bullfights, tortillas – what the fuck else was Spanish? Helen's only experience was a week in Ibiza five years ago, when she was already too old for it to be anything other than sad, and that was a blur of dancing, drinking, sunburn, chips and sleeping. Very authentic. Oh god, she thought, I can't do it. What would Matthew do? Or Laura? OK, forget Spain for now, think about who the restaurant is aimed at. Professionals, a young, hip, Noho crowd, business-lunchers and theatre-goers. She wrote the words in her notebook. She made another column, headed 'Positive

Attributes', and listed Barcelona chef, authentic recipes, fresh ingredients, Sonny. Then she blushed like a school-girl in the throws of her first crush and snapped the notebook shut.

'Are you OK?' Matthew was saying. 'You look hot.'

'It's just airless in here. I'm fine.'

'I'll make you a cup of tea,' he said, stroking her hair on his way past to the kitchen.

'I don't want to go. It's boring.'

Claudia sat at the kitchen table, lunch untouched in front of her, face like an undertaker's.

'Don't you want to see Dad?' Sophie was getting used to this Sunday-lunchtime ritual, but it irked her having to persuade her children to go and spend the afternoon with the woman who had ruined her marriage. Deep down, she knew that the girls were never going to think of this Helen as their new mother, but the possibility was always there that they would grow to like and even love her. That would be a good thing, Sophie tried telling herself. Whatever makes the kids happy has to be for the best. But she knew she was kidding herself. She could remember how, when she was at primary school and about seven years old, her friend April's parents had got divorced. Barely giving it a second thought, Daddy's girl April had moved in with her father and his new girlfriend and, after a couple of months, after she had been a bridesmaid at their wedding, April had begun to refer to the other woman as 'my mum'. The first time, Sophie had said to her, 'What, your real mum?', and April had explained, 'No, she's Mummy and Mandy is Mum.' Just like that,

April's mother's position as the central woman in her daughter's life had been usurped. Now there were two of them, and it seemed to Sophie that they had equal status in April's eyes. She tried to remember what had made her friend move in with her dad in the first place, when she had a mother who clearly adored her, but she couldn't, because at the time she'd just accepted it. That was April's life.

She put a dish of homemade crumble in front of Claudia; she could usually win her round with food.

'I don't mind going,' Suzanne was saying, ever obliging.

'I want to see Dad, but I don't want to see her.' Claudia wasn't budging. 'And all we'll do is sit around her smelly flat, and she gives us rubbish sandwiches and tries to talk to us about school, and it's so boring.'

Sophie smiled at her youngest daughter. She loved how difficult she was.

The doorbell rang. Matthew was bang on time, as ever – in fact, Sophie suspected he sat in the car around the corner if he was a couple of minutes early. He was trying to do this by the book. Usually, he let them know he was there, then retreated down the drive to wait for the girls but, today, when Sophie opened the door mid-goodbye, he was stood on the doorstep. She felt her heart rush up to her head and start pounding on the sides to get out.

'Oh . . . hello,' she said warily.

'How are you?' Matthew asked formally.

'Good . . . I suppose, yes . . . you?'

'Yes, yes, good.'

Christ, thought Sophie, you'd think we'd never met

before. They stood uncomfortably for a few moments while the girls looked on hopefully, as if some sort of breakthrough were about to happen.

'Well . . . anyway . . .' said Sophie, desperate to move the conversation on.

'Erm . . . I wanted to ask you about Suzanne's parents' evening. It's next week, isn't it? And I was wondering – that is, I'd like to come as usual, if that's OK.'

'Oh. Of course. I'll see you there, I guess.'

'I just didn't want it to be awkward, with the teachers and all that.'

'Matthew, of course it's going to be awkward. Everything's awkward now. But that's how it is, so we'll just have to deal with it.'

'Right.' Matthew shifted his weight, on edge. 'And I was wondering if I could pick up my golf clubs. If that's OK.'

'No, sorry.'

'No?'

'I threw them in a skip. I think that bloke from number 146 might have taken them. You could go and ask him.'

'You threw my golf clubs in a skip?' He didn't know why, but he was smiling.

'I did. Sorry.'

'And all your other stuff,' Claudia was saying. 'I helped.'

Matthew laughed. 'Well, I never get time to play anyway. Come on, girls. I'll see you at the school,' he called over his shoulder as he got into the car.

'Bye,' Sophie called after him.

'What's that smell?' Suzanne wrinkled her nose as they shut the front door behind them.

Helen came out into the hall brandishing Norman in front of her like a furry shield. 'That smell,' she said, 'is Norman. Or at least, it's Norman's litter tray.'

'Ohmygod, Ohmygod, Ohmygod,' Claudia was screaming. 'You've got a cat, let me hold him.'

Helen was transfixed by Claudia's expression. Could it be – was she smiling? It was hard to tell, having never seen her even approximate a pleasant look before but, yes, there were teeth, and the corners of her mouth had turned up into unfamiliar territory. Hallelujah, thought Helen. I win.

'Of course you can,' she said, handing Norman over. 'We got him for you, for your birthday. You can think of him as your cat.'

'I don't like cats.' Suzanne made her way down the hall to the living room.

Great.

'You do, though, don't you, Claudia? And . . . I also brought home a load of make-up samples we got given by one of our clients at work, and I thought you could have a rummage through, Suzanne, see if there's anything you want.'

'Yuk,' said Claudia, nose buried in the cat's soft back.

'Cool,' said Suzanne.

'Where did he come from?' Claudia was asking. Helen allowed herself to smile at the little girl.

'Well, we went down to the Pawprints shelter down the road and they . . .'

'What they just let you take him?'

'Yes . . .'

'They can't do that.' Claudia's smile had collapsed. 'You

could be anyone. They're meant to do home visits and check up on you first.'

'We're not anyone, are we, though, Claude?' Matthew said, trying to diffuse the bomb.

'But they don't know that. What if someone horrible went in there and just said, "Give me that dog", and they did and then they neglected it or tortured it?'

Oh, for fuck's sake, Helen thought. That didn't last long.

'You're right.' She bent down and scratched Norman behind the ears. 'That's exactly why we went there, because if they were just going to give him to anyone who asked, we figured it was better they give him to us than to someone else. Because we know we'll be nice to him. We know all the animals at Battersea or the RSPCA will go to good homes, because they'll check up, but who knows where poor old Norman could have ended up if we didn't take him?'

'It's still wrong.' Claudia wasn't backing down easily.

'I agree. But he's here now and he's all yours.'

She watched Claudia's face for a sign of her expression softening and thought she saw just a hint of it.

'And he is lovely, isn't he?'

Norman was playing his part to perfection, a big soft purring lump in Claudia's arms. She kissed his nose.

'Yes,' said Claudia. 'He is.'

Two and a half hours later, and they'd had their best afternoon to date. Suzanne was made up like a French prostitute (oh god, Sophie's going to love that, Helen thought), and Claudia was giving Helen detailed written instructions on cat care while Helen pretended she didn't already know the difference between wet and dry food and how important it was to clean out the litter tray regularly.

Back at home, Sophie waited for the inevitable moaning that followed a Sunday-afternoon visit. She opened the front door when she heard Matthew's car pull up and waved a vague greeting. Claudia shot out of the car before it had even fully stopped. She ran up the driveway.

'Ivegotacat. Ivegotacatandhesatabbyandhisnames-Normanandhesmine.'

Sophie started to say, 'You've got a what?', but the sight of her eldest girl made up like Marilyn Manson stopped her in her tracks.

'What on earth have you been doing?'

'Helen gave me loads of make-up.' Suzanne was affecting an air of thirty-year-old sophistication despite the fact she was only twelve. She looked, thought Sophie, like a clown.

'Right, good for her. Only for special occasions, though, OK. No make-up to school.'

Claudia was tugging on her arm.

'Mum, I've got a cat.'

Sophie looked towards the car, which was backing out of the gate. Matthew waved.

'Where?'

'At Dad's. Helen got it and she says he's mine.'

'You know you can't bring it home. You know I'm allergic.'

Claudia sighed impatiently. 'That's the point, stupid. He'll live with Dad and Helen, but he's mine and I get to see him every Sunday.'

'Right. Good old Helen. You like her now then, I take it?'

'No.' Claudia pulled a face. 'I still think she's a bitch, but I won't mind going round there any more.'

Sophie put her arms around her daughter. 'Great.'

But she knew there'd been a shift, and it bothered her.

19

Sometimes, when Helen couldn't sleep, she got up and wandered round the flat, switching on the TV, making coffee, reading. That had been harder since Matthew moved in because after a while she'd always hear him calling for her to come back to bed, complaining that just knowing she was up was keeping him awake. On Sunday night, though, she'd had to do something. She'd woken at one thirty, her mind immediately racing, and she knew straight away that there was no chance she was going to do anything other than lie staring at the crack in the ceiling for the rest of the night. She looked across at Matthew, deep in sleep. I could wake him up and have sex with him, she thought, that might relax me. She looked at him again: mouth open, slightly dribbly. On the other hand . . . She rolled over and got out of bed as gently as she could and tiptoed out to the hall, closing the door. The living room was dark and unwelcoming, tiny flakes of frost covered the outside of the windows. She could see her breath in front of her, so she turned up the heating, pulled on a jumper and switched on the lamp in the corner. In six hours she'd have to get up for work.

She got out her notebook and tried to concentrate, reading through the list she'd made earlier. Pitiful. Maybe she should just stick to providing the D-listers and placing some features. Stick with what you know, she thought. She allowed herself a brief second to drift off into thinking about Sonny again, then pulled herself back. For fuck's sake, what was wrong with her? OK, so a half-decent (all right, very decent) man, a very decent funny man who was her own age and had all his hair had paid some attention to her. OK, so he'd intimated that he might still be interested further down the line, once she had sorted out her tragic personal life. So what? It happened every day. But, of course, it didn't, that was the point. What if Sonny could be the next big love of her life but it all got fucked up because of Matthew? For god's sake, she thought, pull yourself together – you've barely met the man, let's not get carried away by a random pang of lust.

She looked at her watch, which was on the table, and tried to calculate how many hours it was till she could call Sonny as he'd asked and try to pretend to be having a casual work conversation. Nine thirty was too early. It'd look too keen. So was ten, for that matter, because he might think she only started work at ten and she didn't want him to think his was the first call she'd made. Ten twenty, she decided randomly. Eight hours away.

At seven, Helen woke up on the sofa, pins and needles raging down her right arm. It took her a moment to remember why she was there. She made some tea and, then, checking the bedroom door was still closed, she got out her mobile and dialled Rachel.

'What the fuck?'

'Sorry, Rach, I know it's early.'

She heard Rachel slump back down on her pillow. 'It's only Helen,' she heard her say to Neil.

'Christ, Helen, I thought I was having a heart attack. I still might. This'd better be good.'

'I've met a man. And I've got a job.'

'OK, now I'm interested. Put the kettle on,' Rachel called over her shoulder.

'It's only for a couple of weeks, but it's proper PR.'

'OK, man first. What do you mean you've met a man? You have a man.'

'I know it's insane but I think I might really like him, and he knows I've got a boyfriend, and he said he'll wait till I sort myself out and then who knows . . .'

'Is he gay?'

'No! I don't think so. He's just . . . nice. It's good that he wants to do it properly.'

'How do you know he wants to do it at all?'

'I don't. Well, I do, because he kissed me, but what if he hated it and then he was just being polite and actually he was thinking, "Thank god, she's already got a boyfriend"? Oh god, this is ridiculous.'

'I hate to be the one to say it, but what about Matthew? I thought you were trying to make a go of it.'

'I don't know if I can. Oh god, Rach, it's so fucked up. *I've* so fucked up.'

'You have to make a decision. Don't mess people around, it's not fair.'

Helen heard the thunder of the boiler starting up as the bath taps were turned on.

'Oh god, Matthew's up. Gotta go.'

She could hear Rachel saying, 'Don't do anything stupid,' as she clicked the phone off.

*

As it turned out, Helen's mind was on anything other than Sonny at twenty past ten. All hell had broken out in the general office. It transpired that Friday night's office drinks had got a bit out of hand after Helen left. Helen-from-Accounts, not used to drinking, had had one glass of champagne too many and called husband Geoff to insist he come to the Crown and Two Chairmen and meet the girls. Geoff had ordered round after round, flashing his Burtons wallet with its Friday-night fresh-out-of-the-cashpoint notes and refusing to let anyone else buy a drink. At around half past nine, they'd played a hilarious game of truth or dare and, while Geoff had taken a dare each time – going up to a very straight-looking man at the next table and asking him if he wanted a quick hand-job (no thank you), taking an empty wine glass back to the barman and demanding a fresh one because it was corked (fuck off) – Helen-from-Accounts always chose truth. Some of the facts she had let slip to the other girls included:

Geoff's pet name for her clitoris was her peanut
Helen's pet name for Geoff's penis was Sergeant Sweeney
    ('because he's always standing to attention,' she'd shouted,
    and Geoff had guffawed)
If she had to have sex with a woman, she'd choose Jenny
    ('because you're so pretty,' she slurred, in what she thought
    was a coquettish but jokey way, 'isn't she Geoff?')

By ten o'clock, as they left the pub to make their way home, Helen and Geoff could barely stand.

    'Night, then.' Geoff hugged Annie as if they were old

friends. When he'd got to Jenny, she'd clung on to his arms and, next thing Helen knew, they were kissing. Not just kissing but snogging properly, Geoff's hands running up and down her back and, at one point, Helen was sure, over her backside. Annie was watching, mouth open, the beginnings of a smirk appearing on her face. Helen-from-Accounts had grabbed her husband's arm and physically pulled him away from the other woman, who had theatrically wiped her hand over her mouth as if in distaste. As Helen pulled Geoff down the street, she could hear the two girls started to laugh. And laugh. And laugh.

To make the evening perfect, as Helen-from-Accounts stormed her way around the corner into Soho Square, Geoff following behind bemused at the change in atmosphere ('What? What have I done?'), two men who they had seen in the pub earlier came up behind them and relieved Geoff of his wallet and Helen of her burgundy leather handbag with threats of violence. Then, to top it all, Geoff was sick, mostly down himself. Helen had just about managed to find enough change in both their pockets to get the bus, and they'd sat on the top deck, not speaking, with a fug of beery old vomit from Geoff's jumper rising up around them.

Our Helen managed to piece this story together from the many different versions that were being bandied about the office because, of course, almost no one was speaking to her. The most juicy bits, she gathered from the screaming row which Helen-from-Accounts had with Jenny about four feet away from her, at about ten fifteen. Helen had her head down as usual, pretending to work while counting down the minutes till she could retrieve the little business card, which she had surreptitiously transferred this morning from the pocket of her jeans to her bag, and make the call. Through the glass wall of the accounts department, she could see a conspicuously empty chair where Helen-from-Accounts should be. She'd never been known to be late before.

At a quarter past ten, a little fat whirlwind blew through the general office and stopped beside Jenny's desk. Annie followed in behind so as not to miss the excitement.

'How could you?' Helen from-Accounts was shouting, tears already running down the two deep canyons in her cheeks which had grown over the weekend.

'Morning, Helen.' Jenny smiled at her insincerely. 'It was a great night, Friday, wasn't it? Did Geoff enjoy himself? He certainly seemed to.'

'You bitch. You bloody bitch.'

And, with that, Helen-from-Accounts launched herself, little dumpy arms and legs flailing, at the other woman. Jenny held her at arm's length, laughing as Annie chipped in, 'What, are you jealous, Helen? Do you wish she'd kissed you instead?' Jenny, Annie and a gathering of others who had come in to see what all the fuss was about were laughing themselves silly as Helen-from-Accounts, a blur of arms, legs, snot and tears, clearly a woman who had never had a fight before, continued with her pitiful attempt to make an impact.

Helen knew she should do something to intervene, but she was transfixed by the awful Jerry Springer-ness of it all. Any minute now, Geoff would come in and announce he was gay and that he was taking it up the arse from the vicar.

'You know, I'm sure I could feel Sergeant Sweeney standing to attention when Geoff was groping me,' Jenny was saying, still fending off blows with one hand. Helen-from-Accounts suddenly crumpled. She stood motionless for a brief moment, taking in her enemies and the watching bystanders, some of whom at least now had the good grace to start to look uncomfortable, then she turned and ran from the room towards the toilets. The crowd began to disperse, and Helen heard several of them muttering that things had gone a bit far. She sat shrouded in guilt. Why had she just let that happen? Half the people who worked at Global were afraid of the coven, they didn't want to risk becoming the target of one of their hate campaigns, but what the fuck did she care? She was leaving soon, she should have got in there and broken it up. She had always liked to think that she would be the person on the tube who would apprehend the mugger; now, she felt like she'd hidden behind her newspaper while a crime was committed in front of her. Annie and Jenny were still incapacitated with laughter. Helen got up and left the room.

Here we are again, she thought, as she entered the ladies and stood by the cubicle door with the familiar sob/sniff concerto going on behind it. She took a deep breath.

'Helen, it's Helen, open the door.'

Sniff. 'Go away.'

'No, not till I know you're OK.' How sad is it, she thought, that I'm the only person who's bothered to come in and check up on her, and I can't even stand the woman.

'Do you want me to get anyone? One of your friends? Do you want me to call Geoff?'

Sob, sniff, sniff. 'Geoff's staying with his mother.'

'Oh, Helen. You haven't thrown him out. Not just for that. He was slaughtered, they set him up, you've got to give him the benefit of the doubt.'

'What do you know about it? You did the same yourself, taking some poor bloody woman's husband away from her.'

Helen thought about giving up, but there was something about the other Helen's pathetic attempt at swearing that made her want to cry. She wanted to say, 'At least say "fucking", no one says "bloody" any more except on *EastEnders*.' She sat down on the floor by the sink, in for the long haul.

By the time they got back to the office, Helen was exhausted. I could never be a hostage negotiator, she thought, I'd just want to tell them to get on and kill everyone and let me go home. Have the helicopter, just shut the fuck up. Helen-from-Accounts had made her way back to her desk and seemed to be pulling herself together at least enough to get on with her work. Helen had no idea whether she was intending to call Geoff or not. She was past caring, to be honest. But the atmosphere seemed to have calmed down, and Annie and Jenny were, Helen thought hopefully, looking a little bit subdued, as if someone had told them they had gone too far.

At twelve o'clock, Laura did something she had never done before – she asked Helen to write a release to go out to reviewers with copies of a new autobiography one of the D-listers had written. Shaun Dickinson, a twenty-eight-year-old . . . what was it he did again? He was in the papers a lot but not for actually doing anything, mostly for being places (and then only when someone from Global had called ahead to make sure the press would be there), he went out with a glamour girl and together they had earned a lot of money by sharing all the intimate events in their private lives with a weekly magazine (Why we'll never get married! We're getting married! Our baby hell! His gambling addiction, her sex addiction, his drug-dealing past, her polycystic ovaries and, most recently, Our beautiful new life! featuring their recently acquired home accessorized by the magazine's design department, her new double-D breasts and their unhappy-looking Chinese adopted baby).

It was a straightforward part-biog part-hype document of the kind Matthew had regularly had her write for him, but it made Helen feel slightly panicky. She couldn't think where to start and wrote the first sentence over and over again in ever more flowery language. What if she couldn't do this any more? What if she wrote it and it was rubbish and Laura had to rewrite it herself? She tried to pull herself together – this was basic stuff, a work experience person could knock something passable together in five minutes. If she couldn't do this, then how the fuck was she going to promote the restaurant? Oh god, the restaurant. It was twenty-five past twelve, she hadn't yet called Sonny, and she'd promised him she'd be in touch before lunch to finalize the date for the launch and go over her ideas (what ideas?) for the guest list. OK, she thought, Shaun Dickinson and old fake-tits, they'll go.

She spent five minutes making a list of eleven celebrities she thought were dead certs (desperate, new single out, TV show to promote, split up from husband and wants to be seen out having a good time, desperate, desperate, desperate, record deal just cancelled, trying to get a book deal, desperate, lost sports career through drugs). Then she put her coat on and picked up her mobile; no way was she going to call from the office, she'd have to go and sit in the park. She scrabbled around in her bag for her wallet and Sonny's card. Stuffing her money in her coat pocket, she turned the card over in her fingers, looking at it for the first time. She didn't even know his full name, she thought, screwing up her face as she read the writing on it. Confused, she turned it over again, looking at the blank side, then rummaged in her bag again, checking to see if there was another, alternative card in there. Nothing. She read the words on the card in her hand again and experienced that feeling like she was going backwards on a swing: nausea, disorientation, light-headedness. She closed her eyes and then looked again, as if that might make a difference. It was no good, the name on the card still read the same:

Leo Shallcross

Matthew's son.

20

Helen sat back at her desk, turning the small white card over and over in her fingers for several minutes. She simply couldn't compute what she was seeing, she must have picked up the wrong piece of paper at home some-how and Sonny's number was . . . where? She knew she had transferred it from the pocket of her jeans to her bag in one sneaky movement, making sure that Matthew didn't see and ask her what it was. There was no way it could have got mixed up with anything else. Which could only mean one thing. Sonny was Leo, and Leo was Matthew's son by his first wife Hannah. The one he seemed to have next to no contact with. She went out into the stairwell and called Sophie.

'How's it going with Sonny?' Sophie asked after they'd exchanged pleasantries. 'He said you thought you might be able to help him out.'

'Why do you call him Sonny?' Helen asked, trying to sound casual. 'It says on his business card that his name's . . . Leo Shallcross.' She tried to make it sound as if she was reading it for the first time.

'Oh . . .' Sophie laughed '. . . it is. I just call him Sonny because he's my stepson. He's Matthew's oldest, didn't I tell you about him? And, when I first met him, there was this grown man who I was suddenly supposed to be step-mother to, so I called him it as a joke, to wind him up, and it just sort of stuck. I can't imagine calling him Leo now. Sorry, I should have told you.'

Oh fuck, thought Helen. Oh fuck, oh fuck, oh fuck.

Sophie was still talking. 'So . . . he said you got on really well and you might have time to do some stuff for him . . .'

'I'm not sure,' Helen said, desperate to get off the phone. 'Maybe – I've got a lot on at the moment is all. Anyway, didn't you say Matthew worked in PR himself, so wouldn't it make more sense if he took on the account for the restaurant? You know, discount for family and all that.'

'Stop trying to do yourself out of a job . . .'

Helen cut her off. 'Listen, Sophie, I have to go, I've got a deadline.'

'Are we still on for Wednesday night?' Sophie was saying.

'Yes, fine. I'll see you there.' Helen punched the phone off before Sophie could say goodbye.

Oh fuck, oh fuck, oh fuck.

She tried to picture Matthew as he would have been at thirty-eight. Would he have looked like Leo? They had those same fucking bright blue eyes – why hadn't she noticed? But, then, Leo was darker – of course he was darker, Matthew had gone grey already – and Leo didn't have the Shallcross nose. His was narrower, straighter – Paul Newman to Matthew's Dustin Hoffman. Oh god, I've kissed my boyfriend's son, she thought, and forgetting that Leo was way closer in age to her than Matthew was, she decided that that made her a child molester, or some kind of pervert anyway. There was bound to be a name for it. Matthew had changed his nappies (well, probably not, knowing Matthew, but anyway), and now she was practically having sex with him. As far as Matthew was concerned, there was no one in the world it would have been worse for her to have kissed – well, Suzanne or Claudia maybe, or his mother. But, given she was a heterosexual woman who had missed out on the whole bi-curious thing, then surely Leo was the worst. His dad maybe, if he had one, but even that wouldn't have been as bad. Oh god, she was like one of those teachers you saw on the news who ended up in prison pregnant by a fifteen-year-old boy in their English class who they'd forced themselves on at break.

She sat down on the top step, trying to figure out what to do. In fact, she thought, there isn't even anything to figure out. I can't do the job, I can't see him again, end of story. I have to ring him now and tell him I'm too busy. That's the end of it, and that's the end of my shot at getting something on my CV. She walked back through to her desk to find his number but Laura was there, rooting through the piles of paper.

'This is good,' she said, holding up the half-written release.

'I haven't finished it yet,' Helen answered defensively.

'I know, I'm just saying, what you've done so far is good. I'll need it in the next ten minutes or so though.'

'No problem.' Helen took the early draft back from her and sat down at her computer. She'd just finish this before she made the call.

Ten minutes later, she was in Laura's office, waiting as her boss read over the final version of the press release.

'Great,' Laura said. 'I don't need to change anything.'

'No problem,' said Helen, turning to go.

'Oh,' said Laura, 'one other thing. Sandra Hepburn wants us to come up with a stunt – something to get her maximum coverage on the weekend before the Ace Awards nominations are announced. You know the kind of thing – think Gail Porter on the side of Big Ben. I'm struggling, so if you have any ideas . . .'

'Why are you asking me?' Helen said suspiciously. What was it with Laura all of a sudden?

'I'm asking everybody,' Laura said calmly.

'I'll have a think,' said Helen, backing out. It was one o'clock: she really must phone Sonny. Leo. She must phone Leo.

Back at her desk, she could see that her inbox had one new message. Ignore it, she told herself. Ring Leo and then look at it, but it was an irresistible potential way to avoid making the call for another five minutes. I'll just see who it's from, she thought, then I'll call. She clicked on the message, which was under the unfamiliar name Helen Sweeney. Helen-from-Accounts – of course it was, from-Accounts not being her real surname, surprisingly enough. To tell the truth, she couldn't really care less what the message had to say, but she read it anyway to kill a bit more time.

Dear Helen (it said)

I wanted to say thank you for being so nice to me this morning. I know we haven't always been the best of friends (we're still not, Helen thought to herself, don't kid yourself), *and I want to apologize if I've ever been anything other than generous towards you. I've been thinking about what you said about me and Geoff, and I've decided I'm going to ring him this evening and sort everything out. Thanks again.*

Helen peered over the top of her computer and could see the other Helen smiling inanely at her. She smiled back, baring her teeth, then looked at her watch – five past one. OK, hopefully Leo would be having some kind of business lunch and his phone would be turned off and she could just leave a message ('Sorry, something's come up,' or 'There's been a death in my family' – no, too drastic – how about 'One of my regular clients has got in a bit of trouble and I need to try and keep it out of the papers, so I've promised him I'll concentrate on him, and nothing but him, for a few days. His life . . . no . . . his marriage depends on it'? Yes, that'd do. Throw in a few hints that the fictional client was someone very important. Promise to call Leo in a week or so's time when it was all sorted, to see how he was getting on, and then forget she'd ever met him. Perfect. It was a shame, but it was so, so much better that she distanced herself from him now than further down the line when who knew what might have happened. She thought briefly of his hand on top of hers across the restaurant table and then pushed that thought from her mind.

Back out in the stairwell, she dialled his number and then crossed her fingers waiting for the answerphone to kick in. Shit, it was ringing. She was about to hang up – he'd get a missed call, he'd know she'd tried him, then she'd just keep her phone switched off for the rest of the day, and the evening, and tomorrow – when he answered breathlessly.

'Eleanor! I was just thinking about you. How's it going?'

'Er ... OK ... but ...'

She tried to remember her prepared script.

'Erm ...'

'In fact,' Leo was saying, 'I've been thinking about you all weekend. I know I shouldn't say that, I mean, I know we're not going to talk about stuff like that until your situation's different, if it ever is, I mean, I'm not assuming. God, I'm rambling. Sorry.'

'It's OK. Listen, Sonny, I mean, Leo. Should I call you Leo now? Anyway, something's come up.'

And she told him the excuse she had concocted, although, she thought later, she'd elaborated too much, adding in class A drugs and illegal payments and rumours of homosexuality.

Leo sounded devastated – as much for the fact that he wouldn't be seeing her on a regular basis as that she wouldn't be doing his PR for him. He could get another PR.

'I'm really sorry, I know I've wasted your time and everything ...'

'No, Eleanor, listen, it's OK, I understand. I'm just disappointed, that's all. I thought you'd do a great job and we'd get to see more of each other ...'

'Sorry, Leo, really I am. I hope you get someone good. And I hope the restaurant's a huge success, I'm sure it will be.'

'Maybe we could go for a drink ... sometime ...' he was saying.

'No. I don't think so. It's just . . . it's difficult at the moment. I'm a bit, you know, a bit busy. Oh god, I have to go, the *News of the World* is on the other line.'

'How do you know?'

'How do I know what?'

'How d'you know it's the *News of the World* if you haven't answered it yet?'

'Because they said they'd call me back and my other line's ringing so it must be them.'

'I can't hear it.'

'Flashing, it's flashing. Ringing's just what you say, isn't it? You'd never say, "I have to go, my other line's flashing."'

'Wouldn't you?'

'No, it'd sound stupid – "My phone's flashing."'

'If you say so. OK, well, you'd better go then. Don't want to keep the *News of the World* waiting. Bye, Eleanor.'

Oh shit.

'Bye, I'll call you in a week or so, see how you're getting on.'

'Yes, you do that,' Leo said, without conviction, and put the phone down.

Fuck.

Well, Helen thought, still sitting on the top step, that's well and truly blown that. But then, it was well and truly blown anyway, because Sonny wasn't Sonny, handsome young restaurateur with no baggage, he was Leo, son of Matthew, her married boyfriend, and she wasn't Eleanor Whatsherface, PR, she was Helen Williamson, secretary, girlfriend of Leo's married father. So what if Leo had taken offence and probably never wanted to speak to her again – it was for the best. She'd just have to write it off as a meaningless ego boost that never had a chance of going any further. She just wished she hadn't liked him so much. And he hadn't been so good-looking. And funny. And considerate.

She went back to her desk, skipping lunch, and tried to concentrate on coming up with ideas for Laura. Fucking Laura getting me to do her fucking job for her, she thought, conveniently forgetting all the times she had moaned because no one seemed to be interested in what she had to offer.

OK, Sandra Hepburn. Famous for taking her clothes off, would do anything to get in the papers. Literally anything. But it was hard these days to think of anything so extreme that it would guarantee you column inches, because the tabloids were full of young women who had 'forgotten' to wear any knickers when they put on their mini skirt and went out and climbed a ladder. Probably the most outrageous stunt Sandra could pull would be to put on a knee-length dress and go to church. Tragedy always sold. If Sandra could pull out an aborted baby or a cancerous lump or a dying loved one, that would do it, but Helen had a feeling she'd already told all of those stories 'exclusively' in the past. She could have a liaison. Helen quickly ran through all of Global's male clients to see if any of them was looking for a quick publicity boost. Or one of the women – although the part-time-lesbian market had been a bit saturated of late. Come on, Helen said to herself, you're always claiming you have great ideas, where are they? But she couldn't focus on anything except Leo's monotone, 'Yes, you do that,' and the click of the phone cutting off. She wanted to ring him back and say,

'No, you don't understand, I really really really fancy you, but you see I'm the woman who stole your dad away from your stepmum, so it's all a bit complicated' or 'Let's run away together and never tell anyone where we are, especially our families' or even just a pathetic 'Can we be friends?' Although that would be pointless, because, of course, they couldn't.

She jumped as her mobile rang. It had to be him. Maybe he was ringing to say that he knew all about who she really was but it didn't matter because he was besotted with her anyway, and as soon as she'd resolved the situation with his dad and Sophie, he'd whisk her away for a new life, or even a long weekend. She scrabbled under the papers on her desk to find her phone. Rachel. Helen decided she couldn't face talking to her friend, she'd let it go to answerphone.

'Do you know your phone's ringing,' Jenny said archly from the other side of the office.

'No,' said Helen, mobile in hand, mock innocent. 'Is it?'

'Tell me about Leo,' she said to Matthew in the car on the way home. His expression clouded.

'What's to tell?' he said miserably. 'I know that he despises me for leaving Sophie.'

'Why, though?' Helen was genuinely intrigued. 'She's not his mother.'

'No, but he gets on well with her. When he first met her he tried to warn her off me, told her I was bound to do the same thing to her as I did to Hannah. And of course he was proved right. I've barely heard from him in the last few years – mostly, I'd hear his news through Sophie.'

'You must miss him,' Helen said, thinking, I know I do, already.

'Every few months he drops in unannounced and stays for dinner.'

Helen blanched. 'Does he know where you're living now?'

'Oh, yes, I've told him, so you never know . . .'

'Lovely,' said Helen, feeling sick.

That evening she fell asleep on the sofa and dreamed that Sandra Hepburn had stripped naked at the opening of Verano, thus giving both herself and Leo's restaurant some much-needed publicity. Not a bad idea, she thought, when she woke up. I'm sure Sandra would be up for it. She fed Norman and sat down on the kitchen floor beside him, scratching between his ears while he ate.

Sophie was examining herself in the mirror in the harsh light of the bathroom in a way she had rarely done since she got married – back view, side view. She wanted Matthew to think she looked good. Not because she cared if he thought she was attractive any more, she told herself half-convincingly, but because she didn't want him to compare her unfavourably to Helen, she didn't want him to think he'd won the top prize at the raffle. Not just that, but she didn't want Suzanne's teachers to be whispering behind her back, saying it was no surprise he felt he needed to look for something better. Not that she had any evidence they would; it was just deserted-wife paranoia.

Leo was coming over to babysit his little sisters, which meant that she would get a chance to ask him about Eleanor. He'd sounded a bit down on the phone, and she didn't seem to be doing his PR for him any more, which Sophie hoped didn't bode badly – in her head, she had already paired off her new friend and her stepson. She wasn't given to matchmaking, especially with family, because it inevitably ended in disaster, but there had been an undeniable spark between them when they'd met and she'd always hoped Leo would end up with someone she'd get along with. It was a tenuous thing on paper, a relationship with an ex-stepchild, but Sophie had thought of Leo as family for fifteen years and dreaded him meeting a woman who wouldn't understand what that meant to them both. Not that Leo had been out with that many women since she'd known him, not for more than a few dates anyway. He took the whole idea of relationships very seriously, probably as a reaction to his father's complete lack of respect for them.

Suzanne and Claudia were hysterical at the prospect of spending the evening with their older brother, and Suzanne had plastered herself in the make-up Helen had given her in order to look more grown-up. Leo did a mock double-take when he saw her.

'My, but who's this delightful young lady,' he said in his best Leslie Phillips voice, and Suzanne screeched with laughter and blushed at the same time.

'That's Suzanne, stupid,' said Claudia, missing the point.

'So,' said Sophie, leading Leo into the lounge, 'what's going on with Eleanor?'

'Nothing.'

'I know that look. Remember, I'm your mother – sort of. Come on.'

Leo sighed. 'I kissed her.'

'Hold on a minute,' Sophie jumped in. 'I thought she was just doing PR for the restaurant.'

'I kissed her and then she said she has a boyfriend that she's in the last death throes with. So, I said, fine, I'm not about to mess up your relationship. I'll wait for a bit, if it turns out you and he go your separate ways, then maybe we can get together then.'

Sophie had gone very quiet. Leo carried on with his story.

'So, she seemed really up for it, then, next thing I know, she's calling me saying she can't do the job, and that's that, basically. What? What are you looking at me like that for?'

'I don't know if I should say this to you really, but I guess it's best you know the truth . . . Eleanor hasn't got a boyfriend. Trust me, we talk about those things.'

Leo was looking like he'd taken a punch to the stomach.

'So she was just making one up as an excuse. Christ, I feel stupid. I thought she liked me, I thought she was as torn as I was. She certainly didn't pull back straight away. Fucking hell, why didn't she just say, "Sorry, I'm not interested"? And, more to the point, why all the stuff about them being about to split up?'

'I don't know. I'm sure she had her reasons,' Sophie said uncertainly.

'Nice friend you've got there,' Leo said bitterly. 'Anyway, forget it. I just need to concentrate on the opening right now. Any suggestions?'

'Well, there are hundreds of PR firms to choose from but . . . and I know you'll shout me down . . . why don't you ask your father? You know he'd be thrilled to help you out.'

'Why do you care?'

'Because much as I think he's a complete fucking shit right now, he's still my daughters' father and I'd hate for them to lose touch with him the way you have. He's never going to change, Leo. In a few years he'll dump this Helen for someone even younger – I hope so anyway, does that make me a bitch? – and he'll keep doing it for as long as he can get away with it, but you shouldn't let it affect your relationship with him. You only get one father, and all that bollocks. OK, speech over.'

'I'll think about it,' said Leo defensively.

Forty minutes later, and Sophie was running late, having not been able to find a parking space in the school playground, which was doubling up as a car park for the night. So when she reached the assembly hall, she was red-faced and breathless, with little beads of sweat running down her forehead. She spotted Matthew holding a place in the queue for Mrs Mason, Suzanne's form teacher.

'Oh, thank god, you're here already,' she panted at him. 'You look . . .'

'What, sweaty? Exhausted? Purple? What?'

'I was going to say "Nice."'

'Oh, right. Good.'

Mrs Mason was a large unhealthy-looking woman with black-rimmed glasses and breasts that rested heavily on her protruding stomach. She looked as if the expression 'sack of potatoes' had been coined with her in mind. Sophie and Matthew edged forward in the queue, both of them struggling to think of a way to start a conversation with the other.

'How are the girls?' attempted Matthew.

'Fine, yes, fine,' said Sophie, trying and failing to dredge up an interesting anecdote.

They shuffled on a few paces as another couple moved on to start the rounds of the subject teachers.

'I saw Leo today.'

'Really. Is he OK?'

'Yes, he's fine.'

This is going well, she thought, although, truthfully, compared to many recently separated couples who couldn't even stand to be in the same room as each other, it wasn't actually going too badly.

'How are your family?' she offered up.

'Good, thank you.'

Silence.

'Oh . . . Claudia's very happy about the cat.'

'Yes. I can't take the credit, though, that was Helen's idea,' he said, and that killed the scintillating conversation stone-dead.

'I'm worried she's putting herself under too much pressure,' Mrs Mason said, leaning forward on her elbows, her big saggy chest resting behind like two bags of shopping. 'She's only twelve, she needs to balance up her school work with other things. Putting it bluntly, she doesn't seem to have many friends.'

'But you must be pleased with her grades?' Matthew looked confused.

'Of course, her test scores were exceptional,' Mrs Mason was saying. 'But the development of a child her age isn't all about exam results. Social skills and character are just as important.'

'But . . .' Matthew was blustering '. . . she just happens to be good academically. What, is that frowned on now?'

Sophie felt her exasperation growing. Why couldn't he just listen to what was being said to them. 'Matthew, you know you have unrealistic expectations of her. You've never let her forget she once said she wanted to be a doctor.'

'What, so this is all my fault? Whatever "this" is. Personally, I don't see what the problem is . . .'

Mrs Mason cut in. 'She spends all her break-times studying, she never goes out and plays and, to be honest with you, I don't think that's healthy.'

Sophie stopped glaring at Matthew and turned her attention to the teacher.

'I didn't know that.'

Matthew looked deflated. 'What does she do that for?'

'Why didn't you tell us this before?' Sophie was aware that the couple behind were listening in and felt like she had been publicly unmasked as a bad parent. She thought of all the times she had scoffed smugly when a distraught mother on *Trisha* claimed not to have realized that her child was taking drugs, and she considered turning round and saying, 'Stop looking so superior, she's about to tell you your son's on crack.' She knew that Suzanne struggled more than she let on to keep her title as the cleverest, but not that it was a daily obsession, and she felt devastated that she had somehow failed her daughter.

'Because it's got much worse lately. I was going to write to you if you hadn't come in tonight. I know there are problems at home . . .'

She paused to allow them to jump in and contradict her, but Sophie and Matthew looked at the floor like two surveyors whose attention had been gripped by a nasty bit of subsidence.

'. . . and it could be that she's trying to make sure she gets your attention.' Mrs Mason was fixing her look on Matthew.

'Are you a qualified psychiatrist now?' he said childishly.

'Matthew . . .' Sophie said quietly.

'Well, what is this? Am I on trial all of a sudden?'

'You're overreacting, this isn't about you. Mrs Mason . . .'

'Leanne.'

'. . . Leanne's got a point. No one's saying it's your fault, it's just the situation we're in . . .'

'But I'm the one who left, right? I'm the guilty one because I'm the one who broke up the happy home.'

The couple behind were practically leaning forward now, they were straining so hard to hear every detail. Sophie shot them a filthy look, then lowered her voice.

'You're being ridiculous. We both need to think about what to do if Suzanne thinks we're only going to notice she's there if she gets top marks. I've tried to tell you before, we put too much pressure on her by constantly going on at her about how clever she is.'

'I do, you mean.'

Sophie couldn't believe he was capable of being so selfish. Actually – no, she could.

'OK, yes – *you* do. It's all you ever say about her – "This is Suzanne, she's the clever one, she's going to be a doctor." She probably thinks it's the only thing about her that's important.'

'Don't you dare make this my fault.' Matthew had raised his voice again. 'Just because I've left, that doesn't make me a bad father.'

Sophie looked round at the man and woman behind, who weren't even attempting to pretend they weren't listening now.

'Can I help you?' she asked, smiling in a slightly maniacal way. The couple looked away, shame-faced. 'No, really,' Sophie carried on. 'Feel free to join in.'

'Maybe we should set up a meeting to discuss this further,' Mrs Mason was saying. 'In private.'

'Good idea,' said Sophie standing up and practically dragging Matthew up with her. 'I'll call you tomorrow.' 'Why don't you follow us out?' she said to the couple behind. 'I'd hate for you to miss anything.'

They pushed their way through the crowd and out into the playground, Sophie's face scarlet with embarrassment. When they rounded a corner out of sight of the large windows of the assembly hall, she turned on Matthew, furious.

'How dare you?'

'Oh, I see, this *is* all my fault . . .'

'How dare you embarrass me like that in front of all those people . . . more to the point, all those people who are the parents of Suzanne's friends. And her teacher. And, most importantly, how dare you make this all about you and not your daughter. Grow up, Matthew. The whole fucking world doesn't revolve around you.'

'She was trying to say I'm a bad parent,' he spat. 'What the fuck does she know? I'd bet my life she's a spinster, with only a couple of cats for company.'

'This isn't about you!' Sophie realized she was shouting, and turned the volume down. 'This is so fucking typical. Someone's trying to tell us that Suzanne might have a problem, and all you can do is think about yourself . . .'

'Because everyone's trying to make out I'm to blame . . .'

'SHUT UP. SHUT UP. SHUT UP.'

Matthew was stunned into silence. Sophie carried on.

'OK, so what do you want me to say? Yes, it *is* all your fault. You've spent years praising her when she does well in exams and telling everyone how clever she is and, then, one day, you just up and leave us without any warning, and now she thinks it's because she didn't try hard enough. It doesn't take a psychologist to work it out. But it's my fault, too, because I didn't spot how bad it'd got.'

'I thought praising her was good. I wanted her to feel proud of herself.'

His voice caught, and Sophie realized with unease that he was crying. She softened her voice to a more gentle tone.

'Of course, it's good, but isn't the whole point that you have to praise her for the effort, not the results? So if she comes bottom but she's worked hard, then that's as good as coming top. That's kind of obvious, isn't it?'

Matthew nodded, sniffing hard. Sophie could see tears on his cheeks and had to resist the urge to wipe them away. He was like a child sometimes.

'I thought it just came naturally to her.'

'Well, now we know. And, to be honest, if it did, then that would be all the more reason to make a fuss of her about something else instead. Praising someone for being naturally clever is like praising them for being pretty. Like praising them for being lucky in the lottery.'

'She must hate me. I'm a shit father.'

'Oh, Matthew, for god's sake. You know damn well she wants your approval because she adores you. Just start giving her encouragement about something she's rubbish at. Don't mention exams. It'll all be fine. I'll talk to her too. OK?'

She looked at him, and he seemed to have pulled himself together a bit, but then his face contorted and he let out a noise that sounded like a police siren starting up.

'I miss them so much.'

Sophie patted his arm comfortingly, but at the same time she was filled with irritation. This situation was all of his own making.

'That was the choice you made,' she said, trying to make her voice sound as unjudgemental as she possibly could. She waited for him to snap back at her, but all the fight seemed to have left him.

'They hate coming over at the weekends, I can tell. And Helen hates it, too. I mean, she tolerates it, but I know she'd rather I took them somewhere else.'

Sophie was stung by this – how dare that woman not welcome her children? – but she wasn't going to let Matthew off too lightly.

'You didn't have to leave, that's the bottom line. And however much we try to protect them from it, the girls will always think you chose her over them.' (And me, she thought, but she forced herself not to say it.)

'I've fucked it up again, haven't I? I've fucked up being a father again.' He was sobbing now, and parents who were crossing the playground on their way to their cars were looking over to see what the drama was. Sophie didn't want to kick Matthew when he was down, but she couldn't help herself.

'Like I said, that was your choice. You had a family who loved you, but it wasn't enough. You can't have it all, Matthew, no one can.'

'I'll make it up to them,' he was saying.

'Just don't try and buy them, OK? No more cats and make-up and god knows what. What they want is your time and attention and approval. And, to be honest, Helen's probably right, you probably should take them somewhere else, because you can't force them into a relationship with her yet, it's too soon.'

He nodded pitifully, wiping his eyes on his sleeve like a toddler. 'OK.'

'Where's your car?' Sophie said. 'You should get home.'

21

'So . . . Sandra Hepburn,' Laura was saying at the weekly ideas meeting. 'Any thoughts?'

'How about a few "opportunistic" shots of her out shopping with the girls, but she's forgotten to put her knickers on?' Alan offered up. 'You know the sort of thing, short skirt, windy day . . .'

'Are you offering to be the photographer?' asked Helen, who was there taking notes. Alan glared at her.

'Let's face it,' Laura was saying. 'It wouldn't be anything we haven't all seen before. No, I think we have to try and show a different side to her.'

'High-profile date?' someone else chipped in. 'Simon Fairbrother's got a new series coming out, he could use the publicity.'

'Or Annabel de Souza? Lesbian's very big right now.'

Fucking hell, thought Helen, these people are paid three times as much as me and their best suggestions are the ones I rejected straight off. She nearly jumped as she became aware that Laura was saying her name.

'Mmm?'

'I just wondered if you'd had a chance to come up with anything?'

Helen realized that six pairs of critical eyes had turned on her, as the people who thought of themselves as the most creative in the company – in fact, that was what they were paid for – tried to disguise their complete lack of interest in anything she might have to say. She also realized that she had completely forgotten all about Sandra Hepburn.

'Erm . . .'

Oh, shit. Think, quick.

'No . . . sorry.'

She blushed a furious red but then, thankfully, the spotlight had gone off her as quickly as it had arrived and Laura was asking everyone to keep thinking. Fuck, she thought. Fuck.

But the worst wasn't over. Moving on to another topic, Laura announced to the meeting that they had a new client. Leo Shallcross, Matthew's son, was opening a new restaurant and needed a publicity drive and a launch organizing. Matthew, Laura explained, felt it would be more appropriate for someone other than himself to handle Leo's business, which would be short-term and low-paying (Matthew had insisted he be given a special rate) but was one of those favours they all had to pull every now and then.

'I'll get Helen to collate all the information and get it to you this afternoon. Is that OK, Helen?' Laura asked.

But Helen was staring fixedly at the table, all the colour draining from her face. She felt sick. This couldn't be happening. What would it mean? That he would be coming to the office for meetings? That as Laura's PA she would be expected to set up those meetings and – oh, fuck – attend them and take notes? And then what? It was too awful to contemplate the way her life would fall apart if Leo found out who she really was. Fuck, she wished she had holiday she could take. Or maybe she should just walk out now? What could they do except not pay her? Or give her a reference? She'd never be able to explain it to Matthew. OK, she'd just have to keep one step ahead of the game, call in sick whenever she knew he was due to come in. She felt exhausted just thinking about it. This was too much.

'Are you all right?' Laura was asking her.

'Yes. Fine,' she said quietly.

After the meeting, Laura touched her arm, thinking she was still upset about the Sandra Hepburn thing.

'Sorry,' she said. 'I didn't mean to put you on the spot like that.'

'It's OK,' Helen said miserably. 'I should've had something ready.'

'Why? You saw everyone else's ideas – none of them had an original thought, and that's their job.'

Helen went through to the company's tiny kitchen, to make herself some toast and to hide for five minutes while she calmed down, and found Matthew in there, hovering around the kettle. He liked to appear egalitarian and make tea for himself and Jenny once in a while, and this morning he was making a particular deal of being in an all's-right-with-the-world mood because he and Helen had had a blazing row the previous night when he got home from the parents' evening. He was whistling to himself, one of Helen's pet hates, and as she banged her bread into the toaster, she convinced herself that he was doing it just to annoy her.

He had returned from the school early, in a very odd

mood. He was sullen and quiet and, when Helen had tried to push him as to what was wrong, he had told her he didn't want her to be there when Suzanne and Claudia came at the weekend. 'But this is my flat,' she'd said, and he'd got angry and loud and accused her of not caring about his relationship with his children. They'd gone to bed, got up and driven to work not speaking, and she still hadn't got to the bottom of what it had all been about. Now she was furious that he hadn't mentioned Leo and his restaurant to her, although she honestly couldn't think of a good reason why he should have or, truthfully, what she could have done if he had.

'Can you stop doing that?' she said, tight-lipped, as he whistled an approximation of the *Dam Busters* theme. She decided to go back to her desk, despite the many notices on the wall warning people that unwatched toasters caused fires. Helen had often wondered who made these signs, which appeared overnight – 'Your mother doesn't work here, so please clear up after yourself,' 'Please do not leave dirty dishes in the sink,' and her personal favourite, 'The cleaners are not paid to do your washing-up.' She'd always hoped to catch someone in the act of putting one up, just so she could ask them exactly what the cleaners *were* paid for, given they came in every day and the place always seemed to be a mess. She sat down and pushed some papers around her desk, then got up again and headed back to where Matthew was.

'Why didn't you tell me we were taking on Leo's PR?' she asked him accusingly.

Matthew looked taken aback.

'Because we weren't speaking to each other,' he said

calmly. 'He only called me this morning. Can I ask why you're so bothered?'

She hated him when he was like this, super calm and rational, when she knew all he was trying to do was score points.

'Because . . . I felt stupid in the ideas meeting not knowing anything about it when everyone knows – you know – about you and me.'

'Well, I hardly felt it was important, given the circumstances.'

'Well . . . it was,' Helen said sulkily.

'Your toast is burning,' Matthew said, infuriatingly, looking over her shoulder.

'Oh, fuck the toast,' Helen turned and stomped out of the kitchen.

'Grow up, Helen,' Matthew called after her, loudly enough for anyone passing to hear.

Back at her computer, she found another email from Helen-from-Accounts. She read the first line, which seemed to be the beginning of a blow-by-blow account of her phone call to Geoff the previous evening. Helen closed it again – too . . . what? . . . tired, preoccupied, uninterested, to read the whole thing. Jenny and Annie were finding themselves hilarious, loudly offering each other a bag of peanuts, so that Helen-from-Accounts could hear, even through the glass partition.

'Peanut, Annie?'

'No, thank you, I'd prefer a carrot. Ha ha.'

'Really, I would have thought you'd like a bit of dry-roasting.'

They fell about laughing at their own wittiness. That's not even a joke, thought Helen, you might as well just say, 'Clitoris? No, I prefer penises, thanks. Really, I thought you'd like to be shagged up both ends by a gang of footballers.' It made no sense, but Jenny and Annie were creased up, and Jamie was smirking, too.

I'm going to go insane in this place, Helen thought. I'm going to get an AK47 and mow them all down and laugh while I'm doing it. She noticed a pile of papers Laura had put on her desk. There was a note on the front which read, 'Here are the relevant details for the Leo Shallcross launch. Please organize them into a document and distribute to the team. Also, could you call Leo and arrange for him to come in. Thanks.' She'd known it was coming, but this was the final straw. It was too much, this fucking ridiculous situation she'd got herself into. I can't cope with this, she thought, I just can't. She tried to breathe deeply to calm herself down, but she could feel her mouth trembling, and before she could get up and escape to the toilets for some privacy, tears started to well up in the corners of her eyes. She dabbed at her cheeks, trying to stop the flow before anyone noticed. The last thing she wanted was to let this lot see that she was crying – it would be like an antelope telling a pride of lions about its broken leg. Asking them to sign its cast. It was no good, though, tears were falling, her nose was starting to run. She didn't even have a tissue to hide behind. There was nothing she could do except get up and rush through the office head down in the hope that no one would see her.

'Oh, no,' she heard Jenny calling as she left. 'Matthew hasn't dumped you, has he?'

'Maybe he's found someone even younger,' Annie was saying, and they both cracked up.

Once in the toilets, she locked herself in a cubicle, sat down on the lid and gave in to crying. Proper, big shoulder-heaving sobs which she had no control over. Helen rarely cried. Almost never, in fact, and it was invariably out of frustration rather than sadness. Now, she couldn't stop.

She heard the outer door squeaking open, and she held her breath so as to make no noise. The last thing she wanted was anyone trying to comfort her, and she knew without a doubt that Helen-from-Accounts was the only person who would bother to try. Sure enough, she heard the other Helen's voice saying her name. How fucking ridiculous and humiliating that their roles had been reversed in this way. She stayed absolutely silent. Helen-from-Accounts was playing exactly the 'I'm not leaving till you come out' card that she had played herself. Trying hard to remain quiet, she slowly lifted her feet up off the floor and balanced with her knees held in her arms. She sat perfectly still till her back started to ache and then, just as she'd had enough, she heard the outer door open and close again. Poor old Helen-from-Accounts – at least she'd tried. Helen realized gratefully that in concentrating all her efforts on remaining hidden, she'd stopped crying.

She sat there for a moment or two until she was sure she wasn't going to start again, and then she gingerly opened the door and peeked round to make sure she was alone. While she washed her face in cold water, she tried to decide what to do. She could sneak home sick, but all that would do would be to delay the inevitable. She decided to try to appeal to Laura's sympathetic side – she'd explain that it was too awkward for her to get in touch with Leo herself, given that she was the woman who was shagging his dad. She'd happily type up his stuff and take the minutes at the ideas meeting, but she didn't want to have to meet him or attend any events where he was likely to be.

'But you've got to meet him some time,' Laura said, when Helen had said her piece, after reapplying her make-up and walking through the general office with her head held high, ignoring Jenny's raised eyebrows and Annie's fake smile.

'Maybe that's why Matthew suggested I handle it, so that the two of you could spend some time together?'

'He just wasn't thinking, more like,' Helen said nervously. She wondered if she should try and turn on the tears, but she felt all cried out and, anyway, Laura would most likely respect her more if she stayed calm.

'The thing is, Laura,' she said. 'Matthew wants to rush things, and I want to do everything properly, give his family a chance to meet me on their own terms whenever they feel the time is right. Honestly, it just feels really wrong . . .'

'OK, OK,' Laura said eventually. 'Just do that document and I'll get Jenny to call him.'

'Thank you, thank you, thank you.' Helen felt like hugging her. 'Honestly, I really appreciate this.'

'Maybe you should tell Matthew how you feel, though. It'll save arguments down the line.'

'Yes, I know. I will. And thanks again. And sorry for, you know, being a pain.'

'We need to talk,' Helen said to Matthew as they banged pots around in the kitchen, barely speaking except to say, 'Can you pass me the frying pan?' or 'Have you got the bread knife?' after a silent drive home. She had thought about it all afternoon, and she knew what she had to say.

'Matthew,' she said.

Matthew, still sulking, scarcely acknowledged her and carried on chopping up vegetables. Helen put down the cloth she was holding.

'This just isn't working.'

He didn't look round, but she could see that he'd frozen, knife in hand, waiting for whatever was going to come next. She took a deep breath. Here goes.

'I want us to split up.'

He still didn't say anything, just stood there rooted to the spot.

'Did you hear what I said? I want us to split up. I'm not happy, you're not happy, your kids aren't happy. I'm sorry, I wish it could have been different, but it's doing my head in . . .'

He turned towards her slowly. He looked devastated.

'What? Because we have one little row, you want to end it? Just like that?'

'It's nothing to do with us having an argument,' she said. 'I just can't handle it all – everyone's disapproval, feeling like a home-wrecker.'

'I'm sorry, OK, for what I said about you not being

here on Sunday when the girls come. I didn't mean it, I was just worried about Suzanne . . .'

'I've just said, this is nothing to do with that. It's a much bigger problem than one disagreement. It's just not how I ever imagined it. I'm not happy.'

'We both have to make sacrifices, we always knew that. You can't expect things to be perfect right away. We both have to adjust.'

Helen resisted the temptation to say, 'But I didn't choose to adjust, you just showed up out of the blue one night and I had to go along with it.' Instead she said, 'I want my life back.'

'What life?' said Matthew, not aggressively but genuinely curious. 'We've been together more than four years, I am your life.'

'OK, then, I want a new life. One that doesn't involve other people's ex-wives and children and people laughing behind my back . . .'

'Oh, so that's it,' he said, entirely missing the point. 'You're ashamed of me because I'm so much older than you, you think people are taking the piss . . .'

'That's so not the point but, now you mention it, yes, they are.' Helen looked at his crestfallen face. 'Sorry. Sorry. Forget I said that. Like I say, that's not the point.'

'So what is the point? That you don't like the fact that I have an ex-wife – who, I should say, is being incredibly accommodating and mature about this whole thing and who you have had to have absolutely no dealings with whatsoever – or children, who you see once a week for three hours and who, as I said last night, you don't have to see at all if you don't want to. At least not for a while.'

'Matthew, there's no point us fighting about it. It's over. That's it, end of story.'

'You don't love me?'

'I don't think I do, no. Sorry.'

'But you said you did. All those times. You begged me to leave Sophie and move in with you. Do you really think I would have done that if I hadn't been absolutely sure it was what you wanted?'

'I know. I'm sorry.'

Matthew was working himself up.

'Jesus Christ, Helen, I ruined my kids' childhood so that I could be with you, because I thought that was what you wanted.'

'It was. Once. But it isn't any more.'

'You can't just change your mind like that. We're not children, this is real life, serious stuff. We've messed up people's lives. You can't just go, "Actually, I made a mistake."'

'I'm sorry, I have to.'

'No, Helen, no. Please don't do this to me. Please.'

She had known, of course, that he would do this, that he'd fall apart, whether because he really loved her or because he couldn't face the humiliation of having to admit to the world that he'd been deluded, and she had told herself that she had to remain resolute and just get through it without wavering. But the sight of him begging, the fact that this was so clearly the last thing he ever expected, the tears on his face, unsettled her.

'Please don't. Please,' he said, grabbing hold of her arm. 'I'm too old to start again. I couldn't cope. I'm telling you, I'd do something stupid.'

She was struggling to recognize the powerful, rational man who had always been so in charge of their relationship in this pitiful, sobbing wreck. Oh god, she thought, *I*'ve done this to him. She tried to stand rigid and unmoved as he pawed at her, completely floored by what she'd just said, but it was hopeless. Fuck it – she didn't have the strength to stand up to him. She began to stroke his head, and he realized there had been a sea change and threw himself on her, arms round her neck.

She knew she should tell him to get off her and pack his bags. She couldn't.

'It's OK,' she said. 'It'll be OK.'

22

Helen was dreading meeting Sophie on Wednesday evening. She knew that Leo would have talked to her – about the fact that she couldn't handle his contract, if nothing else – and she knew she'd have to explain herself somehow. She thought about cancelling, but with Rachel watching videos at home with Neil and a Chinese take-away, not to go would mean spending yet another evening on the sofa with Matthew, something she just couldn't face. Besides, the masochistic side of her was desperate to hear exactly what Leo had said.

She'd passed the day in a kind of trance. She was living a nightmare, and what made it worse was that it was a nightmare of her own making and one which seemed to have no obvious end. She had been so close. She had got as far as telling Matthew that it was over, that she didn't love him after all. If she could just have held her ground for a few minutes more – but maybe the fact that she couldn't meant that she was kinder than she thought. Great – it's taken all this to realize I'm quite a nice person. Hallelujah. Give me a medal and let me get back to being my usual hard-edged self, kicking sand in children's faces, treading on puppies' tails and able to dump a boyfriend I no longer feel anything for. She toyed with the idea of running away again, but what good would that do? She'd have nowhere to live, no money, no job.

Laura had warned her that Leo was coming into the office the next day for a preliminary meeting. Twelve thirty. She'd asked to be able to take an early lunch, and Laura had reluctantly agreed. She had half-expected to hear from him – she couldn't imagine on what pretext – but it upset her that he'd been put off so easily, even though it would have made her life far more difficult if he hadn't. Oh, well, she told herself, it obviously wasn't a big deal to him, I shouldn't flatter myself that it was. All the same, it irked her.

The office was quiet. The Helen-from-Accounts *versus* the coven war had died down or at least was in a lull, and Helen was getting used to being more or less ignored by her co-workers. Every now and then, an odd comment was thrown her way, but they were getting bored now. There was still a flurry of hysteria every time Matthew visited the general office, but he remained oblivious and carried on flirting clumsily with all the girls and taking their laughter as encouragement. Two and a half more weeks to go, and they could all go fuck themselves, she thought, looking round and realizing there was no one there she would miss.

To take her mind off the train wreck that passed for her life, she tried to concentrate on the Sandra Hepburn problem. Sandra was hoping for a nomination in the 'Most Fanciable Female' category at the Ace Awards, having no discernible talent to speak of, but it was a field that spawned fierce competition. She needed to do something to make herself stand out from the crowd of pretty but pointless girls. Helen made a list.

Sandra's plus points:

Tits

She chewed on her pencil and tried but failed to think of anything else. So, she started another sheet of paper headed, 'Negatives', and began to write:

No talent
No career
Unpopular
Ugly

Great start, she thought. Then she scribbled out 'ugly' and replaced it with 'unattractive'.

She tried to analyse Sandra's problem, making notes as she went. The way she saw it, the main competition would be young actresses from soaps and the odd pop-singer. There were hundreds of good-looking girls around. The trouble with Sandra, if one were to be brutally honest, was that she was neither good-looking nor was she blessed with a stunning personality. She was just a girl who had large breasts and liked to show them off along with any other bits of her that conveniently dropped out when there were photographers around. If she didn't, then no one would ever notice her, because there was nothing to notice. Her desperation was what made her famous, but it was the worst kind of fame. She was despised by women and laughed at by men who made a lot of mantelpiece and fire comments while they shared round pictures of her as 'Whoops!' her straps came undone and 'Oh my god, I was so embarrassed,' her chest was on show again. Sandra liked to describe herself as a model, by which she meant she had done several full-frontal spreads in one of the more downmarket porn mags, legs akimbo, no money for airbrushing, accompanied by the thoughts of Chairman Hepburn – 'I'd love to have a threesome with two other hot babes' or 'I'm a four-times-a-night girl.' Basically, she was just a big cliché eking a living out of not very much.

Since Helen had been at Global, scores of these girls had passed through on the client list. You could smell the ambition on them, but in a way they were a PR company's dream, because they would do anything and everything to get in the papers. It always turned sour in the end, though, when the next one came along and the public turned its attention to them. Then there would be months of angry phone calls ('What am I paying you for?'). Then the tears ('Please, please. What else am I going to do?') until, finally, they were put out of their misery and never heard from again. Sandra was approaching the end of her shelf life, but Helen had a soft spot for her – she was always polite, never lost her temper and was completely honest about the lengths to which she would go to avoid having to get a real job. The sum total of her ambition was to be famous and popular. So far she'd achieved only the first.

Helen realized with surprise that the past fifteen minutes had flown by and that she was actually enjoying herself. She had always wanted to have a job she could get totally absorbed in, had always envied those people like Matthew who said the days motored by, they were so engaged by what they were doing. She started to drift off into her usual self-pitying 'I should've been a contender' thought process but pulled herself back just in time. Concentrate, she thought.

OK, so, Sandra was never going to win a nomination in a fair fight. She'd become a kind of national joke and even if anyone out there did fancy her, they'd be hard pressed to admit it for fear of people laughing in their face. So, Global's job, Helen scribbled on her notepad, was to remarket her as someone it was OK to find attractive. They had a couple of weeks in which to get people saying, 'Actually . . . when you look at her closely, she's not bad.' She couldn't sing, she couldn't act, she could barely speak, for god's sake. The only thing she had was her looks, well, to be honest, her looks from the neck down, and even they were nothing to write home about but, still, they could work on giving her model claims some kind of legitimacy. After all, if the papers said often enough that she was a model, then people would start to believe it, however unlikely it seemed. So, they had to get her an upmarket modelling shoot. Clearly, no photographer was ever going to be interested in taking pictures of her with her clothes on, it would draw too much attention to her face. And none of the chic magazines would touch her with a fork. Unless, that is . . .

Helen smiled to herself. She loved this feeling, when you systematically trawled through the problems and came up with a solution. It was like being a detective – you just looked at all the clues and up popped the answer. One phone call later, and she was ready to go in and present her idea to Laura, but when she stood up and turned away from her desk, she nearly walked straight into Helen-from-Accounts, who was loitering nervously behind her. Helen forced a smile.

'You all right?'

'Yes,' said Helen-from-Accounts nervously, 'but I was wondering if you wanted to come and have lunch with me, if you're free.'

Helen's heart sank. Her mood, which had lightened considerably over the past half-hour, dropped down to the carpet again. She immediately scrabbled around on the floor of her brain for an excuse.

'Oh, Helen, I'd love to, but . . . I have to go and speak to Laura, it's important, and this is the only time she's got all day . . .'

'Listen, if you don't want to, just say so,' Helen-from-Accounts was saying, 'but Laura's gone out for a sandwich with Matthew, I just saw them.'

'Oh!' Helen's face fell, and she tried to pick it up and rearrange it into something happy, with a reasonable degree of success.

'She must've forgotten to tell me. Great! I'll meet you downstairs in two minutes, I just need to use the ladies,' she said, anxious that the others didn't see the two of them – the office pariahs – leaving together.

'That is genius.'

Laura sat down behind her desk, smiling at Helen. 'No, really, it's fucking genius. And she'll love it.'

Helen's idea was beautifully simple. She knew that if the papers referred to Sandra as a model often enough, then people would start to believe it. She'd seen enough Global press releases which referred to a client's new girlfriend as a 'former model', when, in fact, all she had ever done was a shoot for a catalogue aged fifteen or a catwalk show for the local department store when she was eight.

The tabloids always picked up on it. It was obviously too late with Sandra to start claiming some kind of glamorous past, but what if they could issue a statement saying she had gone away on a modelling assignment with a photographer from *Vogue*? What if they could leak some of the pictures – ones from a suitable distance, of course, to avoid showing up too many of Sandra's faults, but clearly showing it as a fashion not a porn shoot? OK, so *Vogue* were never going to print the pictures – in fact, they wouldn't even know about it. OK, so the photographer, Ben Demano, was a Global client who had just got out of rehab and was struggling to get anyone to take a risk on hiring him in case he went off the rails again. OK, so Sandra would be paying for the privilege of being photographed by him. But, they'd both win – Sandra would get her positive publicity, and Ben would get his money and also his name in the paper to show his ex-employers that he was not only still alive but functioning. They'd be vague about the date for publication and, by the time anyone realized that the photos were never going to be printed within a mile of a top fashion magazine, the awards would be over and it wouldn't matter. All it needed was for Sandra to agree to cough up £3,000, the price of Ben's soul.

'She'll jump at it, I know she will,' Laura was saying. 'Well done, honestly – really well done.'

For the rest of the day, Helen's mood swung between elation for her pitch having gone down so well – Laura had called Sandra, who didn't bat an eyelid at the amount of money she was being asked to pay out, although god knows where she was going to get it (probably another full frontal, Helen thought) – and despair at the mess she'd got herself into. Throwing herself into her work like that had reminded her that she really needed to start applying for jobs, but she didn't have the heart. She'd temp for a bit and just see what was around.

Sophie was already there when Helen arrived at the wine bar near Russell Square tube station. Helen had stopped questioning why she was meeting her ex-rival for drinks and a chat, it had simply become part of her routine. Something she looked forward to, even. And, when she did allow herself to wonder what on earth she was doing, she buried the thought quickly, because the truth was, she had no idea. They greeted each other pleasantly enough, but Helen could tell Sophie was not quite herself and, in fact, as soon as they'd ordered drinks, Sophie came straight to the point.

'I just need to get this out of the way,' she said ominously. 'I'm sure you've got your reasons, but why did you tell Leo you've got a boyfriend?'

Helen had been expecting a conversation about why she was no longer doing Leo's PR, but not this. She had to think fast.

'Erm . . . because I do, sort of. Well, not really, it's over, and I've told him that, but he won't accept it. I totally consider myself single – that's why I never told you about him – but it's too messy a situation to expect anyone else to get involved in. Certainly not anyone I like.'

Relief showed on Sophie's face. She accepted what Helen was telling her immediately, because that was Sophie, she took everyone at face value and always wanted to think the best of those she was fond of – which, of course, sometimes backfired.

'I knew that you weren't just messing him around. Oh god, Eleanor, I hope I didn't make things worse by telling him I thought you were single, but I was just so surprised when he told me what you'd said . . .'

'It's OK,' Helen said, feeling miserable. 'It wouldn't make any difference anyway. Until I sort myself out, I think I should just keep out of Leo's way. So that we don't start getting close – you know.'

'So is that why you can't do the work for him? Or are you genuinely too busy?'

'I just don't think we should put ourselves in a potentially tricky situation. So, yes, that was a lie, I'm afraid. But I thought it was less messy that way. I'm really sorry if I've upset him . . . or if I've put you in an awkward situation . . .'

'I really care about Leo, that's the thing,' said Sophie. 'And I'd love to see him happy in a relationship – especially with someone I could be friends with – but I've got to stop trying to pair him off. Listen, I'll tell him, you know, that the boyfriend thing is true. Just so he doesn't think badly of you . . .'

'Thanks.' This should have made Helen feel better, but it didn't. What difference did it make if Leo liked or hated her, she could never have a relationship with him now.

'So,' Sophie was saying, 'tell me about this man. What's his name? What's he like?'

Oh fuck. Oh god. Oh fuck.

'I hate talking about it, to be honest,' said Helen unconvincingly.

'Well, I've gathered that. Does he live with you?'

'Erm . . . sort of. I'd like him to leave.'

How the fuck did this become about me? Helen thought, frantically trying to come up with a way to steer the conversation on to another topic.

'God,' Sophie was still enthralled. 'Can't you just throw his stuff out on the street and change the locks?'

'I wish. But I can't. He's done nothing wrong, I just don't . . . want to be with him any more. It's not his fault.'

'You're too nice,' Sophie said, completely unaware of the irony of her words.

'So, what's up with you?' said Helen, in an attempt to change the subject. She tried to remember whether Sophie had mentioned the parents' evening coming up last time she'd seen her but decided not to risk it. As it happened, it didn't matter, because it was the first thing Sophie told her about.

'What, this Helen actually said she hated the girls going over there?' Helen was incredulous. The fucker. Painting her as the bad guy (yes, yes, yes, she was, she knew that, but still), just so he could get some sympathy.

'Well, that's what he implied. I mean, fair enough, it's tough to get to know someone else's kids but even so . . . To be honest, though, I'll be glad if they don't see her for a while. I get the feeling she's trying to buy them, and it makes me nervous – what if she succeeds?'

'Maybe she's not very experienced with kids. You know, sometimes people aren't quite sure what to do for the best – not that I'm trying to defend her,' said Helen, who was doing just that.

248

'Well, anyway, now I don't know what's going to happen. He'll have to take them to the zoo or something.'

'What, every week?'

'I don't know . . . the park, then.'

'Why don't you let him visit them at yours?' Helen could see it now, long afternoons stretched out in front of the TV, peace and quiet and no more sullen pre-teenage sulks.

'No way,' said Sophie, shattering Helen's daydream. 'I don't want to have to go out every Sunday afternoon for the next ten years.'

'You don't have to. Listen, surely it's better for the kids if they can see the two of you, together, not at each other's throats . . .'

'But we would be . . . it's too soon.'

'You said yourself you were getting on better – it's only one afternoon a week. What's the alternative?'

'That my children get brought up in McDonald's or by a wicked stepmother who hates them,' Sophie said reluctantly. 'Maybe you're right. We don't have to do it every time, I guess – maybe I'll try it this Sunday and see how it goes. I can always hide in the kitchen if he's getting on my nerves.'

'Maybe he'll see what he's missing and start wishing he'd never left.'

'Well, tough,' Sophie said. 'Want another drink?'

Later, when Sophie had had a couple more glasses of wine, she said, 'Leo really likes you, you know. Do you think maybe you'll call him once you get rid of old what's his name? What is his name?'

'Erm . . . Carlo,' Helen said, thinking, here we go again. 'I don't know, I don't want to think about it, to be honest. Not yet.'

'Well, I hope you do. Really. By the way,' Sophie continued, 'I persuaded him to let Matthew's firm do his PR. I don't know why I feel the need to make sure that things turn out OK for Matthew – why do I care if he and Leo patch up their relationship or not?'

'You probably still care about him.'

'I do not!'

'You must do, you can't just turn it off like that.'

'Prick,' said Sophie vehemently.

Two more glasses down the line, Sophie got into a maudlin phase.

'You're right, I do have feelings for him. I miss him,' she said, her eyes getting teary. 'Not him so much, not now, but I miss being a family and having someone to share stuff with. And I miss thinking I have a perfect life and that I'm happy. That's what I really hate, the fact that I was deluded all those years. I thought we were happy, but we weren't.'

'I'm sorry.' Helen slurred slightly, sailing dangerously close to the wind, stricken with guilt seeing her friend like this, all because of her – well, and Matthew, too – in fact, he was the one who owed Sophie loyalty and respect, but she was the third party. Undeniably, Helen was the outsider who had breezed in and ruined their marriage, although, god knows, Matthew was capable of that on his own. Helen was under no illusions that, if she had turned him down, he would have gone off with the next available attractive woman who came along. In fact, she knew that she hadn't been the first woman to threaten Matthew and Sophie's marriage. He had told her that, before they got together, when Sophie had first told him she was pregnant with Suzanne, he'd had a brief fling with a woman he'd met at his gym. It was the thought of Sophie's body blowing up to unrecognizable proportions, he'd told Helen (as if that were an acceptable explanation), that made him turn to the super-toned personal trainer he'd booked for a few one-on-one sessions. It had only lasted a couple of weeks, and then the trainer – Helen couldn't remember her name – had found out that his wife was pregnant and knocked him back. Matthew had seemed bemused by this, Helen remembered. She remembered, too, uncomfortably, that at the time she'd laughed at his story, because she hated the idea of his wife and it thrilled her to think that he treated her with such utter disrespect. Now, it felt to her that she owed it to Sophie to come clean about everything. The alcohol convinced her that it was the right thing to do and that, once Sophie had got over the initial shock, Helen could express her remorse and Sophie would forgive her and all would be well.

'I'm really, really sorry . . .' she started again. Luckily, Sophie was too self-absorbed to even pause for breath in her monologue.

'I thought he loved me, but he didn't,' she was saying, finding that now she had started to open up it was difficult to close the floodgates. 'I used to look at our friends and think, I know your marriage isn't as good as ours, I know you resent him or you're cheating or you're thinking of leaving. I was smug . . .'

'Really, though . . .' Helen was still trying.

'I want it all to be like it was,' Sophie said, sniffing. 'I want to go back to the four of us being a family. I can't start again at my age, with two kids. This is it, I'm on my own for the rest of my life.'

'No. No, that won't happen . . .' Helen took a deep breath. 'Sophie . . .'

Sophie interrupted her.

'That fucking whore. That fucking stupid cow. Honestly, if I ever meet her, I'll kill her. Really, though. I can't wait. She's fucking pond life. The fucking scum of the fucking earth.' Sophie paused for breath and noticed that Helen had gone a bit quiet. 'Oh god, I'm drunk, I've come over all Old Kent Road, haven't I? I'll shut up. Really. Sorry.'

Later still, when they were both slurring and had drunk the best part of a bottle and a half each, Sophie said, 'There's another reason I wanted Leo to use Global so much, you know. I wasn't just trying to be nice.'

'Eh?' said Helen incoherently

'He'll get to meet that Helen bitch and he can tell me what she's really like. I've asked him to get a good look at her. Bitch.'

'Fucking bitch,' Helen agreed, too drunk to be worried.

And later still, 'I want him to come home,' Sophie sobbed as they said goodnight. 'I really do. I want him to come home.'

At three o'clock in the morning Helen woke with a fuzzy head, and the full impact of what Sophie had said hit her

– 'I want him to come home.' That was it – the perfect plan. She knew that her friend would never admit what she had just said when sober, but she also knew that deep down she must have meant it. If Matthew and Sophie got back together, she would get her life back. Matthew wouldn't have the humiliation of being dumped by the woman he'd given up everything for – indeed, he'd be the one feeling bad that he'd let Helen down – and Sophie would have her family back together.

'Excellent,' thought Helen. 'I'm a fucking genius.'

She just had to work out a way to make it happen without Sophie or Matthew finding out what she was trying to do.

23

Helen peered out from under the covers at nine o'clock, half an hour after the alarm had gone off. Matthew was standing at the end of the bed with a cup in his hand, Norman was yowling for his breakfast.

'I've brought you some tea,' Matthew was saying.

'Thank you,' she tried to say, but it came out as 'Ang yer.' Her head hurt, and she knew without looking that she'd gone to bed with all her make-up on. She realized with alarm that she couldn't remember arriving home last night – she knew she'd got into a taxi after saying goodbye to Sophie, but after that everything was a blank – god knows what she might have said to Matthew. He seemed happy enough, though, smiling at her indulgently as he waited for her to get out of bed. He was still overflowing with gratitude for her about-turn the other night, threatening to stifle her with his appreciation.

'Sick,' she managed to say.

'I'll get you a Resolve.'

Matthew, thankfully, left the room, and Helen managed to feel her way across to the door and out into the bathroom, like a blind woman. Once there, she flinched when she saw her mascara-streaked face in the mirror and stepped straight into the shower, letting the water fall directly on to the top of her head. She didn't even have the strength to add shampoo. All she wanted was to get back into her bed and sleep through the day, but she knew that today was one day she couldn't phone in sick – because today was the day of Leo's meeting and Laura would never believe she'd stayed away for any other reason. What had she been thinking of? She had to keep her wits about her when she was with Sophie. What if she had just confessed the whole stupid plan? She liked her, that was the problem, so she felt comfortable hanging out in the pub and drinking with her. She wanted her to be happy, she realized. In fact, she hated the thought that she was investing so much in a friendship which was destined to end abruptly in a few weeks' time. She loved Rachel, but she was enjoying having someone else, someone a bit older, with different preoccupations and worries, to spend time with. Her isolation at work and Rachel's increasing reliance on Neil had left her feeling battered and lonely. She had no one to talk to, she thought self-pityingly. She needed another friend, and Sophie was definitely a friend she would choose if she could. She felt her stomach heave, and she threw up into the toilet bowl. Matthew was knocking on the door.

'Are you all right in there? Do you want me to call Laura and tell her you won't be in?'

Helen slid back the bolt on the door.

'I'm OK,' she managed to say.

She didn't know when she had started to lock herself in when she used the bathroom, but now it was habit. She didn't want Matthew walking in on her most private moments. She had never been one of those women who had been happy to use the toilet in front of their partner, talking about what was for dinner while they hoicked down their knickers. It was important, she felt, to keep some mystique, even when the relationship was so patently disintegrating. But the step from closing the door to bolting it was a recent one, and one of not insignificant symbolism. She was putting the barriers up.

She spent the morning counting down the hours till lunchtime, drinking glass after glass of water and making two more visits to the ladies to throw up. She'd received a text from Sophie which said, 'Not again. What are you trying to do to me?', which had made her laugh and lessened her spiritual hangover somewhat – it was always a major relief to discover you hadn't been the only one who'd made a fool of yourself. At ten past twelve she'd stuck her head round the glass wall of Laura's office to tell her she was on her way out for her long lunch.

'Are you not even interested to get a look at him?' Laura had asked.

'No,' Helen said firmly. 'I'll be back at two.'

She walked down to Oxford Circus and killed half an hour mooching round Top Shop. She couldn't spend any money because she was about to be unemployed, so the fun of having time to spend checking out the shops was limited. She started to make her way back down towards the office, unsure what to do with herself, and then, before she really realized what she was doing, she found herself in Charlotte Street, seconds away from Verano. I could just walk past it, she thought. She checked her watch – five to one: Leo would definitely be in his meeting now, so it couldn't hurt to have a look, see how it was progressing. She walked down Percy Street on the opposite side of the road, trying to look casual, and threw a glance over at the restaurant as if it was the most natural thing in the world. The inside still looked like a bombsite, with bits of plasterboard leaning up against the wall and tables and chairs stacked in one corner, but the outside was finished, with a tiny patio area with a foot-high wall around it, just big enough for two tables of two. Fairy-lights hung from beside the upstairs window to the tree that grew by the side of the road and laurel bushes in aged-down terracotta pots already stood by the front door. The windows were folded back to open the inside on to the street, and a space heater mounted above them was blasting heat out into the cold afternoon, presumably to keep the lone workman she could see inside from freezing. Even though the place was a mess, it looked like somewhere she'd like to sit out on a warm night.

At five past one she arrived at the café where she had arranged to meet Rachel for a sandwich, feet aching from walking round and round to kill time. They hadn't seen each other for weeks, Helen realized, hadn't had a night out since . . . well, she couldn't remember. Rachel was already sitting at a table in the window, half a coffee down.

'Jesus, you look awful,' she said, as Helen took her coat off. 'Are you OK?'

'Hangover,' Helen explained. 'I was out with Sophie.'

'OK, I want all the details. First, though, I've got some news . . .' She left a dramatic pause. 'Me and Neil are getting married . . .'

'Oh my god, Rach . . . oh god . . . that's brilliant, I'm so happy for you . . .'

'Not for ages, next year probably. Look . . .'

She waved her left hand around, and a small, tasteful stone glittered on her third finger.

'It's beautiful,' Helen said, and then realized she was crying. Again. Rachel was looking at her, dumbstruck.

'Sorry . . . god . . . I shouldn't have told you . . .'

'No! I'm really pleased for you, honestly.'

'Oh god. I'm so stupid.'

'No, Rachel. I mean it, I'm thrilled. I just, I don't know what's wrong with me . . . it's just my life's so . . . shit. I've messed everything up. Oh fuck, I'm turning into one of those crying women.' She managed a laugh. 'Those women we hate. And now I've ruined your big announcement.'

'I should've thought, I should've known my news would upset you, what with all that's going on,' Rachel was saying.

'No!'

Neil was a nice man. He'd make Rachel happy. OK, so a few months ago she might have been eaten up with jealousy that Rachel clearly now had everything. Now, she was so wrapped up in how wrong her own life was going, she couldn't be bothered to compare herself with anyone else. What's the point in competing in a race you can never win? She had no interest in getting married herself, that impulse was long past. No, what she wanted was the complete opposite, she wanted to be single, to be free to be on her own or to play the field or to do whatever she wanted. Part of her was worried that Rachel would suddenly come over all maternal and, next thing you knew, she'd be having babies, and then that truly would be

258

Helen's last real friend gone down the swanee, but that really wasn't why she was crying. She was crying because her own life had now gone so far awry that she couldn't imagine what she might have to do to set it back on the right path. She was crying because she was miserable and she wanted to indulge herself, and because Rachel was the only person she could talk to about it because Rachel was the only person who knew. And thinking that made her cry even more, because soon she might not even have Rachel.

Helen filled Rachel in on everything that had happened since they'd last spoken and her newly hatched plan for putting it all right, still feeling guilty that she'd ruined her friend's big moment. When she got to the part about Leo being Matthew's son, Rachel laughed out loud.

'So, what?' Rachel said incredulously a few minutes later, when Helen had finished telling her about the previous night. 'You're really friends with Sophie now?'

Helen nodded. 'Kind of.'

'But you know you can't be? You're not who she thinks you are. You ruined her life,' she added, spelling it out.

'I know, I know. Oh fuck, this is all so fucked up. But it helps in a way, don't you see? Because I genuinely want her to be able to have her old life back. Or at least what she thought her old life was.'

'And is that what *she* wants, do you think?'

'Of course. OK, so she thinks Matthew's a bastard now, but she'd get over it.'

'Helen, don't end up messing up her life even more by accident.'

'Like how?'

'I have no idea, but just don't get too involved with her. Just do what you need to do and get out.'

'When did you get to be so fucking wise about everything?' Helen asked, irritated.

'I think I read that last bit in an Andy McNab novel,' Rachel laughed. 'Besides, I'm soon to be an old married woman, I'm meant to be wise.'

Helen smiled at her. 'I am really happy for you. Honestly.'

'Well, you have to help me plan it all. I'm relying on you.'

'Of course I will.' She looked at her watch. 'Fuck, I'd better go. Do I look OK? I mean, do I look like I've spent most of my lunch-hour crying?'

'Well, you've got mascara half-way down your cheeks, but you could just be a Cure fan.'

Helen began frantically to wipe the skin under her eyes with her finger.

'And your eyes are a bit pink. Like . . . you've got hayfever.'

'In February? Oh fuck it, I don't care what they all think of me anyway, it'll give them something to gossip about.'

They left the money on the table to cover their sandwiches and coffees and turned to go out, just as the front door opened. Helen froze as she recognized the man walking in as Leo. She put her head down, hoping he wouldn't recognize her, but then she heard his familiar voice saying her name. Or one of them anyway.

'Eleanor?'

Rachel, oblivious, carried on burbling about whatever

it was she was burbling about. Helen kicked her on the ankle.

'Leo. Hi.'

Thank god it was Rachel, who knew about the deception, that she was with and not someone else. Matthew? It didn't even bear thinking about.

'What are you doing here?' she managed to say.

'I've been for a meeting up the road, at Global – you know, my father's company. Are you OK? You look . . . awful.'

'Thanks . . . oh, this is Rachel, my friend. Rach, this is Leo . . .'

'Oh . . .' said Rachel knowingly. 'Hello.'

Rachel and Leo shook hands, and then they all stood there for a moment unsure what to do next. Rachel suddenly made a move.

'Well, I should go . . . I'm sure you've got stuff . . . you know . . . to talk about. Nice to meet you,' she said, as she almost made a run for the door. 'I'll call you later, Hel . . . Eleanor . . .'

'I should go too,' Helen was saying, although she didn't move.

'Sorry, I didn't mean you looked awful. I just meant you looked upset.'

'I'm fine,' Helen said. 'Really. So . . . you went with your father after all?'

'Kind of,' Leo was saying. 'I'd rather you were doing it, though.'

'Listen . . . I'm sorry, you know, about all that . . .'

'It's OK,' he interrupted. 'Sophie explained all about Carlo. It's fine, honestly. I'd still like to think that we could go out for a drink one day, you know, once it's all sorted out . . .'

'Me, too,' said Helen genuinely, trying not to throw herself at him. She could feel her face going red and then remembered the mascara and began to rub at her eyes again, she hoped, subtly. Fucking typical to bump into the first man she'd fancied in years when she looked like this.

'Tell you what, once I've sorted my life out, I promise I'll ring you and explain the whole story, and then you can decide whether you still want to go for a drink with me.'

'I guarantee I will,' he said, and more than anything in the world she wanted to lean over and kiss him.

'We'll see,' she said, thinking, 'You definitely won't, you'll hate me.'

'Listen, I'm late,' she started to move past him towards the door. 'I have to go.'

Leo touched her on the arm as she passed and leaned in as if to kiss her on the cheek, then thought better of it.

'Bye then.'

'Yeah, bye. By the way, do I really look like shit?'

'Yes,' he laughed, 'but in a good way.'

Back in the general office, she had to listen to Jenny and Annie banging on and on about how good-looking Matthew's son was and how he had obviously got all the good genes. 'Matthew's first wife must have been very beautiful,' Jenny was saying, looking over at Helen for a reaction. Helen had cleaned herself up in the ladies on the way up, and now she was mascara-free but still red-eyed, so she kept her head down and pretended she couldn't hear. No such luck that she would get away with that though . . .

'He was asking about you,' Jenny shouted over. 'Wanted to know which one was the slut that his dad had gone off with.'

'Of course he was,' Helen said sarcastically, knowing that Leo would never stoop that low.

'Well, you'll have to meet him next week anyway. He's coming in again to finalize the plans for the launch.'

'When?' Helen's heart nearly stopped.

'Wouldn't you like to know?' Jenny said, smirking at her.

24

Matthew had arranged an evening out with Amanda and Edwin on Friday. An attempt, he said, to start integrating Helen into his family. And although she had protested and said it was too soon and that she had already made an unfavourable impression on his mother and Louisa, he'd insisted, and Helen couldn't say what she was really thinking, which was, 'This is all a waste of time because we're not going to be together for much longer.'

She had spent the day preoccupied with trying to establish when exactly Leo was going to be coming into the office again. She'd asked Laura, who had been vague – 'Oh, I can't remember, some time in the next few days, I think' – and she'd skirted round the issue with Jenny again, who'd immediately spotted what she was up to and laughed in her face. Every time she heard the lift doors open, she jumped as if he might be arriving at any second. There was no point trying to look at Jenny's computer, because she locked it every time she as much as went to get a Diet Coke out of the fridge, and she religiously changed her password every week to stop people logging on in her absence. Helen had often wondered what exactly it was she had to hide. It would be in Laura's diary, which Helen attempted to keep up-to-date but which was currently in the bottom of her boss's handbag somewhere in her office. Laura had never been able to get to grips with Microsoft Outlook, so they had long ago given up trying to keep her diary on the computer.

It had been impossible to concentrate on anything. Helen had made the final arrangements with the photographer for Sandra Hepburn and had managed to book the flights – the shoot was to take place on a Greek island – in the wrong name. At one o'clock, when both Laura and Jenny were out at lunch, she went into Laura's office, sat at her computer, composed an email which simply said, 'Jenny, can you email me back when we scheduled the next Leo Shallcross meeting asap,' and sent it. The reply would come to her as well as Laura, and she'd just have to find a way to delete it from Laura's computer before she noticed something was up. Sure enough, as soon as Jenny got back, a reply popped up – Monday ten thirty – and five minutes later, Helen went back into Laura's still empty office and deleted both her sent email and the reply. It was so childish – Jenny would know that her reply to Laura would go to Helen, too, but she couldn't ignore Laura's request and she'd still feel she'd won a victory if she never actually answered Helen's question directly. Helen relaxed – as long as she could keep one step ahead of the game it'd all be OK.

At eight thirty, Helen and Matthew were sitting at their favourite table in the window of the Italian trattoria round the corner from Helen's flat, waiting for Amanda and Edwin to arrive. Amanda was the elder of Matthew's two sisters, married to ultra-conservative alcoholic Edwin. Helen had decided to drink only water with dinner in an attempt to get on Amanda's good side. She didn't know why she cared, but it felt important to her that at least one member of his family might say, 'Oh what a shame, she was lovely,' when they found out he had deserted her and gone back to his wife. It wouldn't happen, of course.

Matthew had tried to reassure her that Amanda wouldn't judge her in the way that Louisa had, because she didn't empathize with Sophie in the way that Louisa did, but Helen now knew enough about the Shallcross family to know that they all suffered from the same superiority complex which allowed them always to believe they were right and everyone else was wrong. It had something to do with growing up wealthy, Helen believed – it made you think you were better than everyone else. They were that middling sort of rich – the sort who could send their children to public schools without batting an eyelid at their bank statements and whose cleaner spoke in RP but who couldn't afford a chauffeur or a yacht. She couldn't remember what their father had done for a living – something dry and colourless, underwriting maybe. Their mother had never worked, of course. Both the girls had 'married well', which meant they had landed men with enough money for them to overlook the drinking and the forays into wife-beating. They had called their children Enid Blyton soppy-posh-child names like Jocasta and Molly and India and Jemima which guaranteed they'd be beaten up if they went to the local comprehensive, which, of course, they never would. Thinking about it, Matthew had done quite well with the more down-to-earth Suzanne and Claudia, which Helen gave Sophie credit for choosing. And Leo, of course, although I'm not thinking about him, Helen thought, thinking about him now.

Her thoughts were interrupted by a waft of cloying perfume that nearly made her gag as a blur of lipstick and Hermès accessories swooped down on Matthew. Someone – Amanda presumably – engulfed Matthew in a theatrical hug. Helen sized her up. It was clear that Amanda had won the gene lottery over Louisa – she had the kind of fair-haired, pale-grey-blue-eyed, pink-skinned good looks that a certain kind of Englishman seemed to like, nothing too threatening, very feminine, looks which Helen always felt blended into the background, so perfect were they in their blandness. But at least she had been spared the somewhat overpowering Shallcross nose, which on Matthew looked manly and distinguished but which gave Louisa a slight hatchet-faced look which perfectly suited her personality. There was no sign of a man who might be Edwin.

'Edwin sends his apologies. He's unwell,' Amanda said half-convincingly, which Helen read as, 'He's drunk in a ditch somewhere.'

Matthew pulled out a chair for his sister to sit in, help-ing her out of her dark wool coat first. 'This is Helen,' he said, waving an arm in her direction as if he were present-ing an exhibit at the County Show. Helen stuck her hand out politely, and Amanda reluctantly flopped her own into it, limp and damp, like a lettuce leaf. Clearly, hand-shaking was too coarse for her refined sensibilities. Like Louisa, she barely gave Helen a glance and engaged her brother in a conversation about mutual acquaintances which was designed to exclude her. Helen drew patterns on the table-cloth with her fork and tried not to let her irritation show.

'What is it with your fucking family?' Helen hissed at Matthew when Amanda went off to the 'little girls' room', as she nauseatingly put it. 'It's like they're programmed to be rude.'

'She was the same with Sophie,' Matthew said, as if that were any consolation. 'It's nothing personal.'

To give him credit, Matthew tried valiantly to include Helen in the conversation, but she had precious little to say about the Countryside Alliance (well, not much that didn't include a lot of swearing anyway) and absolutely nothing to contribute to an exchange about the merits of Cheltenham Ladies College versus Roedean, so she concentrated hard on her rack of lamb, as if she were carrying out a complicated liver transplant. By the time she had finished eating, the other two had barely made a dent in their entrées. Helen stifled a yawn.

'I always thought Sophie spent far too much time at work and not enough with the children,' Amanda was saying. Helen waited for Matthew to put up a defence, but the silence hung there. He's probably not listening to her either, boring old bitch, Helen thought.

'You told me Sophie always took the girls to school and was there when they got home,' Helen jumped in, feeling the need to defend her friend and also to remind Matthew of her positive qualities.

'Did I?' He looked confused, and quite rightly, because of course he had never said anything positive to Helen about Sophie for fear he might get his head bitten off. Helen nodded encouragingly.

'Well, actually, Helen's right,' Matthew turned to Amanda. 'Sophie working never affected the girls at all. Well, not in a bad way.'

'It doesn't seem right to me, that's all I'm saying.

Children need their mother's full attention. She's no good to them if her head's full of stocks and bonds and what she's going to wear to the office in the morning.'

Matthew sat like a rabbit in the headlights, unsure what he was allowed to say in his ex-wife's defence.

'Actually,' Helen stepped in again, 'I think it's much healthier for children if they're not the whole focus of their mother's life. And you liked it, too, didn't you, Matthew, having a wife who was successful in her own right? It's attractive, isn't it?'

'Erm . . .' said Matthew, terrified of putting his foot in it. 'Erm . . .'

'Well, I think it is. There's nothing sexier than an independent career woman who's also maternal and a fantastic mother. Isn't that right, Matthew?'

Helen smiled at him broadly, and he muttered something that might be in the affirmative but that couldn't be held against him in court. Amanda placed her knife and fork side by side on her plate neatly and decisively.

'Well, I disagree.' The tone said, 'This subject is now closed,' and Helen knew not to push her luck by trying to keep it going.

'Dessert?' asked Matthew, and Amanda declined with a small shake of her head. 'Just coffee, please.'

On Saturday morning Helen walked down to the shop on the corner, ostensibly to get the newspapers, but more as a cover to call Sophie to give her a pep talk before Matthew's visit the following afternoon.

'Let him see what he's missing out on,' she said. 'Put on your most flattering clothes and do your make-up –

269

no slobbing round in sweatpants. Make him go home feeling like he's made the wrong decision. Honestly, it'll make you feel good about yourself.'

'Are you sure you don't mind me going over there?' Matthew had said to her the night before on their way home from the restaurant.

'Why should I?' Helen had replied, thinking that if she cared for him at all, she would have been distraught at the thought of him spending a cosy family afternoon with his ex wife.

Matthew seemed almost disappointed that she wasn't exhibiting even the slightest signs of jealousy. 'I mean, Sophie probably won't even be there.'

'I told you, I'm not worried if she is.' Helen was bored of this conversation already. 'They're your children, after all, you have to see them. And if Sophie doesn't want them around me for a while, then I respect that.'

'God, I love that you're so rational,' he said, kissing her, and Helen thought, 'Oh fuck, maybe I'm playing this all wrong.'

'Well, don't go getting too cosy with her, will you?' she said, thinking that maybe she should be playing the needy woman a bit more in order to drive him back into Sophie's arms. 'I mean, I will be upset if you all start playing happy families.'

'No chance of that,' Matthew had said, laughing.

On Sunday she made sure Matthew wore the brown trousers and stripy Paul Smith shirt that made him look his youngest and slimmest.

'I want her to see that living with me is doing you good,' she said, combing his hair back over his balding spot.

Sophie, meanwhile, was trying to take her friend Eleanor's advice on board, but it felt wrong to be paying so much attention to what she looked like for an afternoon to be spent hanging around her own home. She did want Matthew to think she was coping fine without him, that much was true, but what if he thought she'd made an effort because she was trying to attract him back? God, that would be too humiliating. Eventually, it was the girls who took charge of the situation when they came in and saw her putting on an old pair of tracksuit bottoms she wore to do the gardening.

'You're not wearing those.' Suzanne looked horrified.

'Why not?' Sophie had asked, knowing what the answer would be.

'Because Dad's coming,' Suzanne said, as if stating the obvious.

'Your father's not going to be worried about what I look like . . . not any more.'

'But that's the whole point.' Suzanne was nearly crying. 'If you look like rubbish, he won't notice you at all.'

'God,' Claudia chipped in. 'You are so fucking stupid sometimes, Suzanne.'

'Claudia . . .' Sophie started to chastise her daughter, but Suzanne was carrying on.

'And then he'll just go back to her and think she looks better than you. And then . . .' She looked at her younger sister, knowing exactly what button to push '. . . And then he'll stay with her for ever and we'll spend the rest of our lives having to go over there and be nice to her and only seeing Dad on Sunday afternoons.'

Claudia looked panic-stricken. 'Mum, get changed.'

'Please, Mum. Please.' Suzanne threw herself on the bed dramatically. Claudia started to search frantically through Sophie's wardrobe, throwing clothes out in the direction of her mother.

'Here, wear this. Or this.'

Sophie picked the dresses off the floor and laughed. One was a floor-length black number she had worn to a Christmas party at work once when the men were in black tie and she was a couple of sizes smaller, and the other was a low-cut red slip that you could only get away with in the afternoon if you were sitting in a shop window in Amsterdam.

'I'm not dressing up like I'm trying to pick him up at a nightclub. Here, I'll compromise . . .'

She picked out a flowery knee-length skirt which she knew was flattering and a red fitted T-shirt. Hardly February, but as long as she stayed indoors with the heating on she'd be OK.

'Happy?' She looked at the girls, who nodded.

'Put some make-up on though,' Suzanne added.

'You can help me,' Sophie said, knowing Suzanne would love that. 'Not too much though.'

By ten to three she had just had time to wipe off the blusher and heavy foundation Suzanne had caked her in and replace it with a look she hoped was healthy and youthful. Suzanne would notice, of course, but she'd worry about that later. She tried to decide what she should be doing when Matthew arrived. She felt bizarrely nervous, as if he were coming to pick her up for a date, and she wanted to find just the right balance of friendliness and casual indifference. Cooking would make her look too homely, like the middle-aged housewife he had decided to get away from. Watching TV, too slovenly – he'd always looked down on people who idled away their afternoons watching mindless programmes. Reading? It might look as if she'd just grabbed a book as he arrived in order to look occupied, which would, of course, be the truth, but anyway. Likewise listening to music. She settled on painting, an occupation which she'd taken up and abandoned again several times over the years. He had always admired her work whenever he'd seen it. She rushed around trying to find the long-abandoned canvases and brushes. She came across a half-finished picture in the cupboard under the stairs which wasn't half bad and slopped some fresh paint on to it to make it look like a recent effort. She put newspaper down on the big pine kitchen table and made a creative mess on top, complete with paint-covered rags and splotches of water-colour – carefully chosen not to stain – on the wooden floor. Then she added a tiny, authentic-looking, and, she thought, rather fetching in a Felicity Kendall sort of a way, streak on her carefully made-up cheek and sat down to await his arrival.

At three o'clock precisely she heard the door bell ring and Claudia and Suzanne rush to answer it. She picked up a brush and dabbed away at a corner of her painting, fixing her face into an expression of concentration.

Claudia burst through the door first, leading Matthew by the hand.

'Dad's here.'

She stopped dead at the sight of the mess and Sophie at the centre of it.

'What are you doing?' she demanded.

'Painting,' Sophie said, as if that was the most natural thing in the world. 'Hello, Matthew.'

'Why?' Claudia asked.

'Because I enjoy it.' Sophie was colouring up. 'I often paint.'

'No, you don't. Ow.'

Claudia was rubbing her shin where Suzanne had kicked her, she hoped surreptitiously.

'What did you do that for, you fucking silly bitch?'

'Mum,' Suzanne was saying. 'She swore at me.'

'Well, you kicked me.'

'No I didn't.'

Claudia looked outraged.

'You did. When I said Mum doesn't usually do painting you kicked me. Ow. Mum, she did it again.'

Sophie was scarlet. She looked up and saw that Matthew was smiling – no, smirking, it seemed to her – in a way which said he knew that what Claudia was saying was right, that she was just pretending to be immersed in her painting to impress him.

'Well . . . I've just taken it up again recently,' she said unconvincingly, starting to clear up and accidentally wiping a streak of ochre through her freshly blow-dried hair.

'Actually, your mum used to paint all the time,' Matthew

274

was saying. 'But probably when you were at school, so you just didn't realize.'

Sophie smiled at him weakly, grateful that he'd stepped in but irritated that he clearly felt she needed him to get her off the hook with her own children. She felt ridiculous. What was she doing, sitting there in a summer outfit looking like she was going out for the evening? She felt like she had felt when she was fourteen years old and Mark Richardson, the coolest, best-looking boy in the lower sixth who she had had a crush on for ever, had come over to her parents' house. He had first noticed her at a party given by his parents which her Mum and Dad had dragged her along to, she being too young to say no, unlike her brother, who, at a year older, was deemed grown-up enough to stay home on his own. It had turned out they were both fans of Patti Smith – Sophie because she had taken to reading the *NME* in an effort to appear grown-up and sophisticated and it had told her she should be – and Sophie had mentioned that she had asked for and been given the new album, *Horses*, for her birthday a few weeks before. He was saving up for the LP himself, Mark had said, from his wages as a Saturday boy in WH Smith. As he left for the Red Lion, he asked Sophie where exactly she lived. 'I'll pop round tomorrow about seven,' he'd said, giving her a smile to die for.

She'd tidied her room and swapped her Snoopy poster for pictures of Deep Purple and Genesis she'd cut out of magazines. She'd burned joss sticks and hidden her toy rabbit, which she still always slept with, in a drawer. At four o'clock she'd started to get ready, trying on five different outfits and eventually settling on a faded pair of jeans with triangle inserts of floral material with a scoop-neck top and a pair of blue cork wedges. She put in a pair of beaded dangly earrings and wound strings of coloured beads around her wrists for bracelets. She was ready by six and then sat in her room playing cool-sounding songs loudly on her stereo. Seven o'clock came and went. Then five past. Her mum came in and said, 'Boys', and rolled her eyes. At eleven minutes past seven the doorbell rang and her heart lurched. She'd tottered down the stairs nervously, to find Mark, sitting in the kitchen with both her mum and her dad, who were doing their best to ruin Sophie's life by making banal small talk with him. He jumped up when he saw her.

'Hi,' she'd said shyly.

'Do you want a cup of tea, Mark?' her mum was saying, and Sophie wanted to hit her. This was a boy who spent his evenings at the Red Lion drinking beer – what'd he want a cup of tea for?

'Can I just get the LP?' he'd said, still smiling. 'Only Kev and Julian are waiting for me in the car.'

Sophie had felt faint. 'LP?'

'*Horses*,' he'd said. 'You said you'd lend it to me.'

She could feel her parents' eyes on her, but she couldn't bring herself to look up to meet them. Her face was burning, and she could feel tears welling up in her eyes.

'Did I?' she'd said faintly. She couldn't remember if she had or not.

'That's why I'm here. I said I'd come over, pick it up.'

As she ran upstairs, she'd heard a car horn toot impatiently. Obviously, Kev and Julian were desperate for a pint. She grabbed the album off the stereo and put it into its sleeve, not even worrying if she was getting fingerprints all over it. She just wanted him out of there as quickly as possible.

'Here.' She tried to smile.

'Brilliant, thanks. I'll tape it and then give it back.' He was already moving towards the front door. Sophie didn't even wait until she heard the porch door shut. Flushed and humiliated, she ran straight up the stairs towards her room.

'Soph—' she heard her mother calling.

'Don't!' Sophie shouted, slamming herself into the bedroom. She'd changed and taken off her make-up and got into bed.

Of course, Mark had never returned her record or, in fact, ever bothered to talk to her again.

After that, she'd approached anything which sounded like a proposition with extreme cynicism. If a boy asked whether he might see her on the weekend, she'd ask 'Why?' or 'What do you want?' If she managed to establish that they were in fact interested in her rather than her possessions, she'd still greet them in her oldest jeans and T-shirt, no make-up on, terrified of being accused of having made an effort. One upside of the Mark episode, at least, was that her parents never again hung around to meet the boys who occasionally braved the lack of encouragement to come round. In fact, Sophie discovered that if she'd wanted – if she'd been that kind of girl – she could have locked herself and her pursuer in her bedroom all evening and done god knows what without fear of her mum popping in with cups of tea. But that wasn't what she wanted at all. Wary of ever again seeming like the eager one, she became the opposite, a girl with a reputation of being hard to get. It was a reputation she became proud of and which led to her hanging on to her virginity until she got to university, despite all of her friends succumbing years before.

By the time she had met Matthew, she was coming out of the second serious relationship of her adult life. She was enjoying being on her own, feeling inclined for the first time to 'put it about a bit', as her mother would have said. She knew she wanted children one day, she'd always known it, and she knew that more than anything she wanted a relationship of equals where she could relax and not be constantly assessing how she thought she felt or whether she was allowing herself to be too open. What she'd certainly never imagined she wanted was to settle down with a married man with a grown-up son.

Now, sitting at the kitchen table formerly known as hers and Matthew's, she knew she looked like she was trying too hard again. She had wanted to make him think she was in control and over him, but she'd ended up looking like she was trying to lure him back. Thankfully, Matthew had taken the girls off to the living room to play the Xbox and she was free to sink back into her chair and fight off the tears of humiliation that were welling up. She picked up the cordless phone and took it outside into the back garden despite the rain.

Helen was reading a book, lying on the living-room couch, when her mobile rang.

'Hi, Sophie, what's wrong?'

She knew it must be something to do with Matthew,

who she was hoping was at that very moment realizing that he never wanted to leave his beautiful house and family again.

'Oh god, it's a disaster,' Sophie was saying. 'I think he thinks I'm trying to impress him because I'm all dressed up, and I thought I was acting casual but I went over the top and now he thinks he's made me all flustered. Which he has but not for the reasons he thinks.'

She was babbling.

Oh good, thought Helen.

'Oh shit,' said Eleanor. 'I'm sure he doesn't. I'll bet you anything he's nervous as well. He's probably just relieved you're not throwing stuff at him. Anyway, how about him? I bet he's made an effort,' she added, knowing full well that she had forced him to.

'Actually, he does look pretty smart. Not in the casual stuff he usually slobs around in at the weekends.'

'See,' said Helen/Eleanor. 'Imagine if you looked like shit and he was all dressed up, he'd be at a real psychological advantage. You've done the right thing, you just have to keep it up. Don't let him see he's rattled you, go back in and show him how calm and in control you are. You can do it.'

'OK.' Sophie sounded more confident. Just then, Norman pushed his face up against Helen's arm and meowed impatiently.

'I didn't know you had a cat.' Sophie had heard him.

'Oh, yes, have I never mentioned him?'

Oh for fuck's sake, she thought, now I have to remember that Eleanor has a cat.

'What's his name?'

'Erm . . .' Helen looked round her flat for inspiration '. . . Cushion.'

'Cushion?'

'Yes. He's fat, he looks like a big furry cushion. Sophie, why are we talking about my cat when you've got an ex-husband to go and show off to?'

Sophie checked herself in the hall mirror, practised a confident smile, then burst *faux* confidently into the living room.

'Anybody want a drink?' she smiled, looking a bit unhinged.

'Shh,' said Suzanne, who seemed to be in the middle of a drugs deal.

'Kill that hooker,' Claudia shouted, trying to take the handset off her. 'She's trying to get away with your crack. Shoot her, for fuck's sake. Quick.' Sophie thought that, if she'd been asked, this probably would have been on the list of the top ten sentences she never thought a ten-year-old daughter of hers would say. Matthew rolled his eyes at Sophie inclusively. Her smile softened into something more natural. He stood up.

'I'll have a cup of tea,' he said, stretching. 'If that's OK.'

Matthew followed Sophie out to the kitchen, getting out the tea bags while she filled the kettle, like two people who had shared a kitchen for fifteen years which, of course, they had.

'Do you think they should be playing that?' Sophie asked him, as he rooted around in the cupboard over the sink for mugs.

'They're from a broken home, they're destined to be drug-addicted criminals anyway, so they might as well learn how to do it properly. You never know when a prostitute might run off with your stash and you need to be equipped to deal with it.'

Sophie laughed. 'I was going to teach them all that myself. Just not for a couple of years.'

'I'll take it off them if you want,' he was saying. 'It's just they've been on at me for years to let them play and, as a part-time dad, aren't I now meant to indulge them every Sunday with things you wouldn't approve of, thereby rendering your authority useless and ensuring my place as the favourite parent?'

'Just maybe not every week, eh? I don't want social services coming round.'

There was a bit of an awkward silence while they waited for the kettle to boil, but Matthew didn't seem in any hurry to go back into the other room. In fact, he sat down at the kitchen table, seemingly completely at home. Seeing him there made Sophie's stomach turn over. It could be a snapshot from a couple of months ago, an ordinary couple sitting round and chatting while their children played in the next room. Anyone looking in would have thought how nice that they still made the effort to look good for one another and to spend time, just the two of them, talking over their week. For a moment she felt like she wanted to throw herself at him and beg him to come back – she could learn to pretend it had never happened. Then, as quickly as that thought had come, it was replaced by the memory of what he had done to her and the girls and she felt sick with the realization that in a couple of hours he would go home to Helen and the new life he had chosen. She took a deep breath, taking her time finding the milk and the sugar bowl, which had not been used since Matthew had left. Eleanor was right, she had to show him that he hadn't destroyed her. The only real revenge she could take was to show him what he had left behind in the hope that a part of him would wish he hadn't. If he started to regret what he had done, then a part of him might start to feel a fraction as bad as he had made her feel by leaving, and – maybe it was petty, but it was only human nature – there was some satisfaction to be had in that.

By the time she sat down with him, she had recovered her composure enough to tell him about the post-parents' evening fallout with Suzanne who, having been told that no one expected her to come top of the class any more, seemed to have abandoned school work altogether and was now talking of becoming a beautician.

'She already told me,' Matthew said. 'God, I hope she grows out of it.'

'She will. I give it a couple of weeks, and then she'll settle back down. She's just pushing us to see if we really mean it.'

'I knew we should have called her Shirley. Or Kylie.'

'Don't go on at her about it, Matthew. If you do, it'll make her want it even more.'

Sophie heard Claudia shouting from the other room for Matthew to go and play Scrabble.

'Want to play?' he said. 'The girls would love it.'

By the time Matthew left, slightly after his allotted time of six o'clock, Sophie felt like they had crossed over into a whole other relationship. One where they could be civilized and spend time together with their children. One which Helen could never understand or be a part of because she and Matthew had a history that was undeniable. She could see that a tiny part of him felt reluctant to leave, to go back to what Claudia had gleefully told her was 'a dingy shit-hole', and she felt like she'd scored a point against Helen. Just one, but it felt good. Her life might never be able to go back to what it was, but that felt more bearable if she knew that Matthew wasn't living a dream life somewhere else. Immature maybe, but true nevertheless.

Helen was pacing by the time Matthew got home. She'd thought about ringing Sophie to see how it had gone, but she couldn't be sure he would have left, and she didn't think she could carry off a performance as Eleanor knowing that Matthew was hovering in the background somewhere. She was wearing her least flattering pyjama bottoms and a shapeless fleece with a food stain down the front. She'd washed her hair and left it to dry naturally so that it frizzed. She knew that Matthew would still have a picture in his head of Sophie looking her best.

'How did it go?' She pounced on him as soon as she heard the front door open.

'Good,' he said enigmatically. 'Yes, it went well. Oh,' he said over his shoulder as he went through to the bathroom. 'Sophie suggested we do the same next week, if that's OK?'

Hallelujah, she thought.

'Fine by me,' she said, trying to sound a little put out.

25

The opening of Verano was happening the following Friday night. The invitations were due to come back this morning, Monday, and preliminary yeses had been given over the phone by twelve of the thirty-five D-listers Global had so far invited. That was a respectable enough figure to lure some paparazzi, especially as Shaun Dickinson and his surgically enhanced ex were bringing their new partners ('Our break-up!', 'My three-in-a-bed romp!', 'Poisoned by my implants!', 'I'm engaged again!' being some of the headlines which had appeared in the weekly glossies in the last few days), and the press had been promised that it would be ex-girl-band member Kellie Shearling's first night out since she had left rehab for 'depression' apparently brought about by no longer making enough money to fund her rather more secret cocaine and alcohol addiction.

It was hardly going to be a glittering affair, and Helen couldn't help thinking that Leo didn't quite know what he was letting himself in for, but it would generate publicity, and that could only be a good thing, even if it wasn't the sort of publicity he would have envisioned for his beautiful, tasteful restaurant. They had so far not managed to place any features, and Helen was resisting the temptation to pick up the phone herself to call Lesley David at the *Mail on Sunday* and cash in her favour. This was nothing to do with her any more – it was far less complicated if she just kept out of it. Leo was coming in this morning to go over the final details for Friday evening, hence Helen was spending the early part of the day sitting in a café on Old Compton Street reading the papers.

At eleven fifteen she called Helen-from-Accounts.

'Helen Sweeney,' Helen-from-Accounts answered in an annoying sing-song voice.

'It's Helen. Has Matthew's son left yet?'

'Yes . . . just.'

'Great. Thanks. Bye.'

Helen cut off the call before Helen-from-Accounts tried to engage her in conversation. She was in the office by eleven thirty. She called Sandra Hepburn to check that she was ready for her trip the following day.

'I've got a massive spot on my chin,' Sandra said. 'And carpet burns on my knees.'

'It'll be fine,' Helen reassured her, thinking she must talk to Ben about airbrushing. She read through the press release she'd drawn up about Sandra's modelling assignment and thought she'd done a good job of implying that it was for *Vogue* without ever actually saying so. She took it through to get Laura's approval before she sent it out and found Laura looking a little flushed and distracted.

'Helen. Perfect. Sit down. I want to talk to you.'

Helen did as she was told. 'Are you OK?'

'Fantastic. Listen, I've handed my notice in. I'm leaving Global.'

Helen stared at her, unsure of what to say.

'I'm setting up on my own,' Laura continued. 'I've

been planning it for ages, but I couldn't say anything till I'd got my finances in place. I have to give three months' notice, but I actually told the other directors a while ago so I'm starting to sound out clients. Contractually, I'm not allowed to approach anyone on Global's list but, to be honest, I'm not sure I'd want to. I'm done with the D-listers. I'm going upmarket – fielding offers for people instead of trying to create celebrities. Patrick Fletcher and Anna Wyndham have already said yes,' she added, naming two of the British film industry's current favourites.

'Wow,' Helen said, trying to disguise her jealousy. She realized that she was genuinely pleased for Laura but that didn't wipe out the overriding feeling of envy that she was also experiencing.

'Congratulations.'

'Oh,' Laura said, picking up the lack of enthusiasm in Helen's expression. 'I forgot the main bit.' She paused for dramatic effect. 'I want you to come with me.'

Helen raised her eyebrows, trying to look interested. There were worse things than continuing to be Laura's secretary. Laura was still talking excitedly.

'Not as my PA but as a junior account manager. I know you're up to it.'

Helen suddenly felt dizzy. 'Are you serious?'

'Of course,' Laura laughed. 'It won't be like here – I mean, it'll just be me and you, an assistant and an accounts person to start off with, and you won't be on any more money than you are here for a while but, you know, you can have clients of your own . . .'

'Oh my god.'

The truth of what was happening was dawning on Helen. 'Is this definite? I mean . . . oh my god.'

'What do you reckon?' Laura asked her. 'Are you interested?'

Helen let out a noise somewhere between a laugh and a squeal. 'Of course I'm interested. Thank you. Really, thanks.'

'I thought you could start setting up the office as soon as you leave here. Well, after you've had a holiday. And then I'll join you in a month or so.'

Helen resisted the temptation to hug her. She couldn't stop smiling. 'Thank you again. Honestly.'

Helen sought out Matthew, something she had rarely done at work since he'd moved in with her.

'Did you know?' she asked.

'I did,' he said. 'And it's no more than you deserve. You'll be brilliant.'

She felt like she ought to be cross with him for keeping secrets from her, but nothing could puncture her good mood, and he seemed so genuinely delighted and excited for her that she put her arms around his neck and kissed him, in full view of Jenny who had come in with a letter for him to sign.

Back at her desk, her head was buzzing. Laura had asked her to keep it a secret from the other girls for the next few days, which wasn't going to be a problem, given that nobody was really speaking to her, but she found herself smiling at them whenever they came anywhere near her, which unsettled them, and when she realized that, she did it some more.

'What are you looking so happy about?' Annie said eventually.

'Nothing.' Helen couldn't help her smile getting even wider.

'Stop smiling like an idiot then.'

'Sorry, can't.'

When Laura went out for lunch Helen shut herself in her office and called Rachel with her news. Rachel, who had been Helen's closest friend and confidante for the past ten years and who had heard her moan about her thwarted ambitions countless times, was thrilled for all of thirty seconds, and then went into a long monologue about place settings and tiaras. Helen feigned interest for as long as she could but, actually, it irritated her beyond belief that her friend could be so self-obsessed. On Rachel and Helen's list of 'Women we hate', there had been not only women who steal other women's husbands (Helen, obviously, these days) and posh women, but also women who put their boyfriends before their friends and women who bore you to death with stories about their wedding and/or babies. The full list in fact read:

Women who steal other women's husbands (Helen)

Women who put their boyfriends before their friends (Rachel)

Women who bore you to death with stories about their wedding and/or babies (Rachel)

Posh women

Fat women who go on about how little they eat

Women who have their tits out all the time (with a subsection of women who substitute big tits for personalities)

Tits-on-a-stick (jealousy alone put that very rare breed of women who were both slim and naturally big-chested beyond the age of twenty-five on the list because, Helen and Rachel were convinced, all well-endowed women had fat in the post which would arrive with their cards on their twenty-sixth birthday)

Fat women who brag about their large breasts (in fact, breasts in general could have taken up a whole page of the list, as could fat women, but they had decided to draw the line)

Women who like Dido

Women who like Bridget Jones

Women who are like Bridget Jones

Sophie

Women who go on about how much they love shoes (subsection – women who think *Sex and the City* is real life)

Women who obsess about chocolate

Women who ask you what your sign is

Jennifer (neither of them could remember who Jennifer was, but they had agreed to leave her on because they must've had a good reason for adding her to the list once)

Thin women who make a big fuss because they've fattened up to a size ten

Cry-baby women (arguably Helen these days, but anyway)

Women who say 'pants' or 'wicked' or 'fierce' (or whatever the catchphrase of the day is)

Women who talk in little-girl voices

Women who tell you they're mad (unless they are actually clinically insane)

Anyone who refers to themselves or anyone else as a yummy mummy

Girly girls

Women who refer to their periods as 'women's problems'

Women who think you're interested in their IVF treatment

Broody women

Women who've had therapy

Women who fish for compliments ('I look so fat today,' pause
to give you time to say, 'No! You're tiny')

Women who refer to their boyfriends as their 'fella'

Laura (recently crossed out by Helen)

Women who wear suspenders. Or basques. Or anything else
they've read in one of their boyfriends' lads mags is
supposed to be sexy

Women who try too hard (see above)

Women who wear flowers in their hair/pashminas/black bras
with white tops/court shoes

Mothers who work part-time and expect the whole world to
revolve around their commitments ('Oh, I'll have to change
my day next week, Sam's nursery's closed for redecoration')

Women who breastfeed in public

Women who are still breastfeeding when their children are old
enough to ask for it.

OK, so Helen might be guilty of a major crime on the
list, but Rachel was now culpable on two counts and probably would soon be ticking off a few more.

Helen cut the call short, promising to spend some time
over the next few weekends visiting potential wedding
venues. She thought about asking if Rachel was up for a
drink later in the week, but she knew she wouldn't be –
or if she was it would be on the proviso that Neil came
too – not that that was a bad thing in itself, Neil was
good company, but it wasn't the same. Helen didn't feel

she could talk about the Matthew problem with Neil chipping in every so often that he thought Matthew was a 'nice guy' and when were they all going to go out again. She knew that Sophie, under different circumstances, would indulge her, but of course Sophie thought she was a successful publicist already, so she couldn't share her news with her. Still, she wanted to hear the details of yesterday afternoon, so she called her anyway, reminding herself not to let anything slip about her own situation.

'Honestly,' Sophie said when Helen pressed her, 'it was great. The girls loved it, we got on, no arguments. You were right, you know. I felt in control – well, once I got over the painting thing anyway, and I think that however happy he thinks he is with that bitch, he must've gone back thinking he was missing out on his family. I hope so anyway.'

'Well, you have to keep it up,' Helen said in reply, trying to ignore the irrational twinge of jealousy that she was feeling. She should be pleased – and she was – but it wasn't the world's greatest ego boost to know that he could slip back into his old life so easily. 'Make him suffer.'

'I will. Thanks, by the way,' Sophie was saying, 'for all your advice and stuff. I really appreciate it.'

Helen decided to leave work early, walking out while Jamie was reading aloud the latest instalment from Alan's emails (detailing an evening at a hotel which had taken place recently) to the general office. She headed home to find that Matthew had beaten her to it and was in the middle of dressing the front room so it looked like, Helen thought, a brothel at Christmas. Coloured scarves were draped over the table lamps – she was sure she could smell burning – and candles teetered precariously on the bookshelves. The table was laid for dinner for two and a bottle of champagne sat in an ice bucket in the middle. Helen looked at her watch – it was only half past five. She could hear Matthew humming away to himself in the shower, and she knew she'd ruined some kind of big surprise or other, so she didn't even take her coat off but, loath as she was to leave the death trap her flat seemed to have become, with the lethal combinations of not only scarves and naked lightbulbs but candles and an inquisitive cat, she turned round and walked out the front door. Then she unlocked the door again, went straight back in, picked Norman up and, despite his protests, shut him in the kitchen.

She left for a second time and walked up the steps to the street trying to decide how to kill an hour. She was tempted to go to the cinema and return hours later, feigning innocence and pretending to be mortified that she'd missed whatever he had in mind. Oh god, she couldn't face an intimate dinner for two. It was very sweet of him to have bothered, of course it was, but all she wanted to do was relax with the TV. She felt as if they had hardly anything to say to each other these days and certainly not enough to fill, what, four hours, before he'd come over all soppy and start trying to edge her into bed. They'd managed to avoid sex now for a good few weeks, and that suited her just fine. She felt sick at the idea of him pawing at her – something she'd enjoyed for years – and not because there was anything really wrong with him or he was a bad lover, quite the opposite. It was just that he was Matthew.

She walked through the rush-hour pedestrians return-
ing home from the tube, down on to the high street, and
mooched around the shops, which took all of ten minutes,
so she sat on a bench outside the KFC shivering in her
inadequate coat. At half past six she started to trudge
back towards the flat, rehearsing her shocked and
delighted reaction in her head. Matthew was hovering in
the hall when she let herself in, like a nervous party host-
ess, looking so eager and excited about his big secret that
she didn't find it too hard to indulge him a bit.

'What?' she said. 'What's going on?'

Matthew indicated the living room with a flamboyant
wave of his hand.

'Da da.'

Helen went on through. The candles were burnt down
to stumps, and she could see one of the coloured scarves
had been discarded and was lying on the chair with a
suspicious looking black ring in the middle. The burning
smell, which had got worse, had been joined by a delicious curry aroma.

'Wow, Matthew, what is this?'

'Celebration dinner,' he said proudly. 'In honour of
your new job.'

'You've cooked?'

'Well, I ordered a takeaway.'

'It looks amazing in here. Thank you so much.'

It *was* sweet that he'd gone to all this trouble for her.
Three or four months ago, she would have been blown
away, would have bored Rachel to death with every detail.
Today, she was just about managing to look grateful.

'Have a glass of champagne.'

Matthew lifted up the bottle, which was by now sitting in a pool of water, and poured her a glass. She drank it back in two swigs and held her glass out for another.

Two hours later, they had finally finished eating, and Helen was trying to decide which was the lesser of two evils – claim tiredness and go to bed, knowing that Matthew would be expecting payback, or try to stay up until he was falling asleep himself and have to sit through maybe another three hours of stilted conversation. To be fair, they'd managed to pass the time pleasantly enough, bitching about work and speculating on Helen's future career, but she was struggling to think what topics they could cover next. Maybe she should bring Sophie up again and point out a few more of her good points.

'Oh,' she heard Matthew saying. 'I heard from Leo.'

Helen's stomach lurched into her mouth.

'He's looking forward to meeting you on Friday.'

'He's . . . what?' She wasn't sure she'd heard right.

'At the launch. I told him I'd like to bring you, and he said he's looking forward to it. I think Sophie's going to be there, but that's OK, isn't it? I mean, I feel like every-one's behaving like an adult now, so I'm sure she'll be fine about seeing you.'

Helen was in a blind panic.

'No.'

'No what?'

'It's too soon. To meet them all. I can't.'

'Don't be ridiculous. Of course you can.'

'No, Matthew, I can't.' She felt like she was near to tears.

'Tell you what. I'll find out what time Sophie's going to be there, and we'll go later. I don't know what you're worried about, though, she won't behave badly, she's not that sort of woman.'

'No, I can't go at all. I can't meet Leo. Not yet.' Uncontrollable tears were now falling down Helen's cheeks. This was hell.

'Anyway,' she tried desperately. 'I'm busy Friday.'

'Doing what.'

'Seeing Rachel.'

'You're seeing her tomorrow.' Matthew was, of course, unaware that Helen was, in fact, planning to spend her Tuesday evening with his ex-wife to be.

'She's getting married, Matthew,' Helen said, as if that should explain everything. When he looked blank, she carried on. 'I'm helping her with the plans. I'm her best woman or whatever the fuck it's called. I've promised.'

'Oh, for fuck's sake, cancel it. This is my family, Helen. You know what my relationship with Leo is like. It's a miracle he even invited me and, what, I'm going to say, 'Sorry we can't come, we've got something better to do'?

'Of course you've got to go. But, I'm not coming with you. I'm sorry.'

'Helen, there is no way that I'm going to tell Leo that you've turned down his generous offer to meet you.'

'Stop being so fucking pompous. Leo doesn't really want me there. He's just being polite, and it is very nice of him, but it's too soon for me, OK? End of story. Just tell him I had other plans.'

'You're just being ridiculous. You're coming with me and that's it.'

'Well, I'm not.'

'Helen, grow up. I've already heard from the girls in the office that you make a point of going out whenever he has to come in. I put it down to you being worried that he might pick a fight with you, but now that I'm telling you he wants to meet you, that he's actively seeking to get to know you, you're still saying you won't do it. I mean, what's going on?'

'Nothing. I'm just not ready. I'm not coming and you can't force me to, OK? You're not my father, Matthew. You can't ground me if I won't do as you say. I'm not coming, get over it.'

'You're acting like a teenager.'

'No, I'm acting like a thirty-nine-year-old woman who can make her own decisions, it's just you're acting like an old man who thinks everyone should do what he tells them. And do you know why that is? Because I *am* a thirty-nine-year-old woman and you *are* an old man.'

Matthew stood up from the table. 'I'm going to bed.'

'It's ten to nine.'

'I'm still going to bed.'

'Fine, I'll sleep out here.'

'You do that.' He slammed the bedroom door behind him.

'Prick,' Helen shouted, wanting to have the last word.

Five minutes later, Matthew's head appeared round the door of the living room again. 'You're putting no fucking effort into this relationship,' he barked at her.

'Go on, say it, you gave up everything for me. Well, I didn't ask you to.'

'Yes, you did.' He raised his voice to a shout. 'Yes, you fucking did.'

He retreated again.

'Oh, fuck off,' Helen called after him.

Five seconds later he was back. 'One evening. Just one fucking evening to help me support my son. Is that too much to ask?'

'Yes. I'm sorry, but it is,' Helen said, lying down on the sofa and pulling a throw up over her head.

26

Helen sat in Museum Tavern across from the British Museum robotically stirring a plastic stick round in a Bloody Mary. Sophie was late. Not just her usual ten minutes late but half an hour now. Helen had tried to call her, but her mobile was going straight to answerphone, and knowing that Matthew would be at the house to babysit the girls made her nervous about trying her there. She nursed her drink and looked up to glare at a man who was looking at her curiously from another table. He whispered something to his two male companions, and they all turned to stare. Helen thought about shouting, 'I'm not a prostitute, I'm just waiting for my friend,' but instead she coloured under their scrutiny and looked down at a bar mat which she pretended had suddenly caught her attention. She wished she had a magazine or a book – reading said, 'I am a respectable woman and I have a legitimate reason for sitting alone in this pub.' Just drinking alone, however, apparently said, 'I'm anyone's for the price of a vodka.' She looked at her watch; she'd give it five more minutes.

In fact, Helen had been sitting in the pub on her own for just over an hour because she hadn't been able to face going home first, knowing that the detritus of the previous evening's meal would still be all over the living room. She was fucked if she knew why she should clear it up – the meal had been Matthew's idea, and as far as she was concerned, he had started the argument which ended it prematurely. And, anyway, though she hadn't intended them to fall out, now that they had, it suited her plan, so she was in no rush to make it up with him.

Matthew had once said to her that Sophie was passive-aggressive.

'She wears you down, bit by bit, and somehow she always ends up getting her own way. I much prefer a big argument,' he'd said. 'Blow everything up and clear the air.' Judging by his sulky behaviour today when their paths had crossed in the office, he had been lying. Or maybe what he meant was, 'I prefer a big argument if I win it,' she thought bitterly. God, he was annoying.

Three minutes and fifty odd seconds after she last looked and having suffered several raised eyebrows and at least one wink from the men she now realized were Dutch businessmen, Helen looked at her watch again and decided to call it a day. She was putting her bag across her chest when her mobile rang. Finally. She checked the caller ID just before she answered, although she pretty much knew it was Sophie, and discovered that it wasn't – it was a number she didn't recognize.

'Hello.'

A man's voice answered. She wasn't sure whether it was the fact that the voice was familiar or the fact that he called her Eleanor that gave it away first. It was Leo. She tried, and failed, to sound nonchalant at being caught off guard like this.

'How have you been?' he was saying, like it was the most natural thing in the world for him to call.

'Good, yes. Busy, of course. How was your launch?' she asked, knowing full well that it hadn't happened yet.

'That's why I'm ringing. It's on Friday. I thought you might like to come along, see how it's turned out. Not like a date or anything . . . when I say "you", I mean "you and your boyfriend". You are still with your boyfriend, aren't you?'

He must still be interested in her – why else would he call? She felt a rush of . . . what? Lust probably. She suppressed the desire to say, 'No, I'm all yours if you still want me.'

'Erm . . . yes. We're trying to make a go of it, you know.' God, if only he knew how far that was from the truth. She could have sworn she detected a hint of disappointment in his voice.

'Well, like I say, bring him. Honestly, I'd love for you to be there, then I can show off at being the big restaurateur and know you'll be looking at poor old Carlos and wishing you were single. Although now I'm the new Gordon Ramsay I'm not sure I'd be interested in a humble little PR woman like you any more.'

Helen laughed. 'It's Carlo not Carlos. And I'm really sorry, but I have plans on Friday night already.' She was thinking fast. 'One of my clients has a play opening.'

Leo sounded doubtful. 'Right.'

'Her name's . . . Rachel . . . er . . .' She looked around. The Dutch businessmen were still checking her out, convinced she was a call girl.

'Ho. Rachel Ho.'

'Rachel Ho?'

'She's Chinese. Half Chinese. Her father. She's only just

out of drama school and, you know, she needs all the support she can get. Honestly, I would have loved to otherwise . . .'

She trailed off as the door opened and a breathless Sophie burst in.

'We *can* just be friends, you know. We're adults,' Leo was saying. 'But if you don't want to come, that's fine . . .'

'I have to go, Sophie's here. Sorry. And thanks again, for the invitation – I mean it – but we really can't come.' She hung up before he could protest. Shit, now he'd think she was being curt, although, truthfully, what did it matter if he did?

'Sorry, sorry,' Sophie wheezed before Helen could say anything. She had obviously been running.

'I rushed out of the house so fast I forgot my phone, so I couldn't call and tell you I was on my way. I'm really sorry. Have you been here hours?'

She noticed Helen's bag over her shoulder.

'Oh god, you were leaving.'

'It's fine,' Helen reassured her. 'Calm down and I'll get you a drink.'

'It was Matthew,' Sophie said, and Helen sat down again, drink forgotten.

'He was in a bit of a state, and he wanted to talk. He and Helen have had a big fight apparently.'

Helen gulped. 'What about, did he tell you?'

'Helen's refusing to go to Leo's opening. Can you believe it? Says she doesn't want to meet any more of his family.'

'Maybe she's afraid you'll be there.'

'Well, I will, but so what. I was quite looking forward

301

to getting a look at her, to be honest. And it's not like I'm going to cause a scene and ruin Leo's night. That reminds me, he wants to invite you along.'

'I know, that was him on the phone just then. But I'm busy on Friday.' She stood up. 'White wine?'

'So, I think the scales are finally falling off his eyes,' Sophie said once they had their drinks.

'Why?' Helen was aching with curiosity. 'What else did he tell you?'

'That their relationship has changed. That he feels like she's not interested in him now she's got him. Christ knows why he thinks he can come to me for sympathy.'

'Because he knows you'll give it to him. Which is good. It shows you're getting over him if you can listen to him bang on about the intimate details of his new life without getting hysterical.'

'He did tell me quite intimate things, actually. Like they have no sex life any more. None.'

'None?'

'Apparently not. Serves him right. Actually, that's not fair – I found myself feeling sorry for him. I mean, how does he do that? He can behave in the most appalling way and yet he always ends up getting all the sympathy.'

Helen's mind was still on other things. 'What, he said, literally no sex?'

Sophie nodded. 'She's just not interested any more, he said. That didn't take long.'

Helen thought of the sympathy shag she had bestowed upon Matthew only three weeks ago or was it four? She loathed having sex with him now, but every now and again she went along with it, because she felt it was unfair on him if she didn't. She put on a good performance – there was no way he would know she was just going through the motions. But now, if he was going to go around telling people he wasn't getting any, she just wouldn't bother again.

Sophie was immersed in her own train of thought. 'Why would you do that? Split up a family and then freeze the man out. It doesn't make any sense, unless it was all a game to her and she just wanted to have the satisfaction of knowing she'd won. I mean, what a bitch.'

'Maybe she did really want him but now she's changed her mind.' As usual, Helen couldn't help but try and defend herself. 'Maybe she's gone off him. It happens.'

'But you can't just go off someone when they've uprooted their whole life for you. I mean, you just can't.'

'I guess it's out of your control,' Helen was saying. 'I'm sure she didn't plan it.'

'And why wouldn't she go and meet Leo, when it means so much to Matthew? She sounds like a right cow.'

'Well, that's a given,' Helen laughed.

'Sophie,' Helen said a couple of minutes later, while Matthew and Helen were still the main topic of conversation. 'The other night you said you thought you wanted him back. Did you mean it?'

'I never said that,' Sophie protested, but she coloured up enough to give herself away. Helen laughed again.

'You did.'

'I must've had too much to drink. Of course I don't

want him back.' Sophie reddened even more. 'Let's change the subject.'

While Sophie was at the bar, Helen checked her messages for a penitent one from Matthew, which, of course, wasn't there.

'Helen!'

She froze.

'I thought it was you.'

Oh god. Oh god. Oh god.

She half looked up. Sophie was still at the other end of the bar, redundantly flapping a ten-pound note at the barman. Helen smiled at Kristin, Alan's ex-assistant, who was standing beside her.

'Kristin. Hi,' she said weakly, thinking, 'Please go away.'

'How are you?' Kristin made as if to sit down.

'I'm great. Listen, someone's sitting there.'

'Oh, I know,' Kristin said, getting comfortable. 'I'll move when she comes back. How's Global? Alan got any new slappers?'

Helen was watching over her shoulder: Sophie was chatting to the man behind the bar as he served her.

'I don't really know, to be honest.'

'I know, by the way,' Kristin leaned in conspiratorially, 'about you and Matthew Shallcross. Jamie told me. He seemed to think it was a really big deal, but I said good on her if that's what she wants. Shame about his wife and kids and all that but . . .'

Helen could see Sophie moving back towards her with the drinks, looking puzzled to see someone sitting in her seat. She could see Kristin's mouth still opening and shutting, but the pressure buzzing in her ears was drowning out the words. She wanted to hit her with a spade to stop her talking. She wanted to die.

'Kristin –' She stopped the other woman in mid sentence. 'Sorry. It's just, my friend, she's had some really bad news. She's ill, really ill. Terminal. And she needs to talk to me, before she dies, you know, about what's going to happen to her kids and stuff so . . .'

Sophie was about three feet away.

'Oh god. I'm sorry.' Kristin got up from the table. 'I'll leave you to it. Ring me sometime, OK?'

Sophie put the drinks on the table.

'Hi,' she smiled at Kristin. 'Don't get up, I can find another stool. I'm Sophie, by the way.'

Kristin looked at Sophie's outstretched hand as if it were covered in leprous sores. She took it weakly.

'Kristin. Erm . . . no, I'm with my friends. I have to go. You look great, by the way.' She looked at Sophie with something that was meant to resemble admiration. 'Really.'

Sophie looked bemused. 'Thank you.'

Kristin looked at Helen. 'Bye then.'

'I'll ring you.'

'Who's she?' Sophie asked, as soon as she was gone.

Helen was just beginning to breathe again. 'Oh . . . just someone I used to work with once. Years ago. I hardly know her really.'

Helen got home before Matthew, who, she had no doubt, was filling Sophie's head with yet more horror stories about her before he returned. She hoped so anyway. She cleared up exactly half of the dirty dishes as quickly as she could and then got into bed and turned out the lights so she could pretend to be asleep. About ten minutes later, she heard the front door open and close and then Matthew clattering about, presumably finishing off the job she had started. She lay with her eyes closed, waiting for him to come in, but as the minutes went on, she realized that he was intending to spend the night on the sofa, as she had last night. For some reason, that made her red with anger, and she considered getting up again and having it out with him. She lay back down – what was the point, after all, the end was definitely in sight, she just had to wait it out.

The following morning Matthew had left for work by the time Helen got up at seven forty-five. The kitchen was clean apart from one curry-stained bowl which he had left on the side like a challenge. She decided to ignore it.

27

By the time Friday came around, Helen and Matthew had reached something approaching civility in their exchanges. He was still angry about Leo's launch and hadn't lost an opportunity to make what he thought were subtle digs about it. She was feeling guilty and so countered every one of those digs with what she thought was a conciliatory but noncommittal mumble. When they had first started speaking properly again, on about Wednesday, he had risked kicking the whole thing off for a second time by repeating the invitation. Prepared, this time, Helen had refused to be drawn and had stuck to her story that she was seeing Rachel. It had been tense for a while but, in the cold light of day, neither one was prepared to go into all-out battle. So, Matthew had accepted her excuse but not forgotten his anger about it, as was only too apparent from the odd barbed comment that slipped out.

Helen was on a high – Sandra Hepburn had returned from Kos, and some promising 'candid' pictures had been leaked to the Sunday papers. Helen was confident that at least a couple would run the story on their gossip pages. Best of all, Laura had told her that she no longer had to keep her new job a secret, so at Friday-night drinks, Helen had come up with a sure-fire way of letting the coven know without having to speak to them directly, which involved sharing her good news with Helen-from-Accounts in a low voice. Helen-from-Accounts then squealed with excitement and said, 'Congratulations,' so loudly that Jenny had been forced to ask her what she was going on about. The stony-faced lack of enthusiasm for her good fortune had given Helen a warm glow.

Matthew had decided to go straight to the restaurant after work, despite the fact that the launch didn't begin till eight. He'd got it into his head that he could help Leo set things up, which was probably a terrible idea, but at least it meant Helen could go straight home and not have to pretend to be getting ready to go anywhere herself. Of course, there was a possibility that Leo and Matthew would have a fight, and he would come home early and catch her lounging on the sofa in her pyjamas, but she decided it was a risk she was prepared to take. Naturally, she had called Rachel and told her that if Matthew ever asked, they had spent the evening together.

'Fine,' Rachel had replied, and then immediately followed it with, 'Do you think solid silver or antique bone handles for the cutlery?'

'I have to go,' Helen had said quickly, putting the phone down. Bone handles? What had happened to her friend? She'd turned into some kind of mimsy Victorian lady since announcing she was getting married. She'd started to use words like corsage and stays and bodice. She found napkins fascinating and could spend an hour weighing up the virtues of different kinds of name cards to go on the table settings. Pictures of veils could cause her to faint with excitement. Helen picked up the phone and dialled Rachel's number again.

'Didn't they have to kill animals to make the bone handles?'

'Or people, I'm not sure. But it was years ago. No one's killing anything to make cutlery out of now, don't worry.'

'Go for solid silver,' Helen told her. 'Bye.'

She dug out her copy of the 'Women we hate' list and added 'Women who have a personality transplant/bypass when they get engaged'. After it, she added, '(Rachel)'.

Sophie, Claudia and Suzanne arrived at Percy Street at ten to eight, and the first thing they saw when they rounded the corner from Rathbone Place were the strings of lights from the windows to the tops of the trees and the glow of the space heaters on the front patio. Verano looked stunning. The deep-red walls and rows of flickering candles in coloured jars threw a warm glow out into the street and made it almost impossible to walk past on a bitterly cold February evening like this. Inside, Leo and Matthew – who seemed to be on civil, almost amiable terms – were busy seeing to the finishing touches – in fact, Matthew seemed to have a paintbrush in his hand. Laura was running through the final guest list with a man they'd hired for the night to stand on the door. They were expecting fifty guests, eighteen of them 'celebrities', although they were notoriously unreliable. The chef had prepared tapas, which the waiters were going to circulate on trays, and there was a fridge full of high-quality champagne (and some cheaper stuff to open later when people's tastebuds had got a little less discerning). Leo had managed to persuade a few friends and family to arrive on the dot of eight so that, if any of the promised D-listers did turn up, they wouldn't take one look and keep moving. He looked pathetically grateful when he saw his ex-stepmother to be and his half-sisters there so early.

Matthew handed Sophie a glass of champagne and the girls an orange juice each and pronounced a toast to Leo and the restaurant, and they all raised their glasses. Sophie looked round the group: this was real twenty-first century dysfunctional happy families – a separated couple, stepchild, half-brother and sisters – all it needed now was for Hannah and Helen to show up to complete the picture, but Hannah was away diving – her latest in a series of new passions since her husband had abandoned her all those years ago – and Helen, of course, had refused to come.

Leo had wanted his mother to be at his big night and was somewhat aggravated when she had announced she was going away, but there was no denying it made the evening less complicated. Just as he resented Helen's non-appearance but at the same time was grateful for it.

By twenty past eight the restaurant was filling up and, despite the fact that none of the promised celebrities had yet shown up, Leo instructed the waiters to begin circulating with the first of the tapas – tiny bite-sized portions of Verano's starter menu, delicious anchovies and chorizo and tiny rings of chilli-fried squid. A couple of paparazzi had arrived and were mooching about outside rubbing their hands together to keep warm. At eight thirty there was a sudden flash of bulbs and Shaun Dickinson burst through the doors with a large-breasted blonde following close behind. By ten o'clock a couple of soap stars, a reality-game-show loser, Sandra Hepburn and Shaun's ex, complete with new footballer boyfriend, had also come through the doors. Most only stayed for half an hour, sampled the food and declared it delicious, knocked back three or four glasses of champagne and then moved on to try and be photographed somewhere else, but the paparazzi got what they wanted. Suzanne and Claudia collected autographs they could show off to their friends about on Monday, and Leo took advance bookings for the following week.

Matthew, Sophie and the girls had gravitated towards each other early in the evening and stayed that way, sitting at a table in the corner watching the evening unfold and bursting with pride for Leo. Sophie knew she was getting curious looks from the representatives from Global, Laura included, but she decided that the only thing she could do was keep her dignity and her distance and not let it ruin her evening. The girls, watching their parents sitting together drinking and chatting, were almost hysterical with happiness.

'How are things with Helen?' Sophie managed to ask after a couple of glasses.

'Better, thanks. At least I think so – I still couldn't persuade her to come.'

'Good,' Claudia chipped in.

Jenny breezed over. 'Going well, isn't it?' She sat down and turned to Sophie, *faux* innocent smile on her face.

'Hi, you must be Sophie. We've spoken on the phone before. I'm Jenny, Matthew's assistant.'

Sophie tried to smile at her, feeling humiliated that this young girl must know all her personal business.

'I've been helping Laura organize this,' Jenny was saying

disingenuously, 'because, you know, it was Helen's job really, but she didn't want to have anything to do with it. Sad that, isn't it, you'd think she'd want to get to know Matthew's family. Still . . .' she said, conspiratorially lowering her voice so Matthew couldn't hear '. . . she's a bitch, but I'm sure you know that. We all hate her in the office for what she's done.'

Sophie had no idea how to respond. She ought to have taken some comfort from the knowledge that her rival was not liked, but she wanted this girl to go away and leave her alone. She looked pleadingly at Matthew who, thankfully, hadn't forgotten how to pick up her secret signals.

'Jenny, I think you should go and help Laura keep the guests happy. We don't want them leaving too quickly, it won't look good.'

Jenny reluctantly dragged herself out of her chair. 'Bye, Sophie. Great to meet you at last.'

'Sorry about her – she's a bit of a cow,' Matthew said once Jenny had gone.

'You've got great taste in assistants.' Sophie managed a smile, which he reciprocated gratefully.

By eleven the evening was beginning to wind down. Sandra, the last of the D-listers to leave, rather the worse for free booze and on the arm of a man she hadn't arrived with but who may have been one of the waiters, set off another round of flashbulbs as she left, and then the paparazzi went as stealthily as they'd arrived, on to the next event. Laura had come over to Matthew and declared the evening a major success. Sophie had felt as if Laura was avoiding her, probably embarrassed that it was her assistant who had stolen Sophie's husband, so she made a big effort to smile expansively in her direction and Laura returned the gesture with a look of relief but also, Sophie felt, guilt. Oh god, she thought, please don't let her be another one of Matthew's conquests. A cloud briefly settled over their table, but Leo swept it away when, having seen off the rest of the guests, he strode over with a fresh bottle of champagne and began a victorious debrief of the evening. The girls were dead on their feet, but Sophie stayed for one last glass to toast his success before bundling them into a taxi home.

Helen heard Matthew bumping into the hall table at about one o'clock – at least, she assumed it was him and not a burglar, but she was too tired to check. Let him steal Matthew's toy cars – what did she care? Then she heard another crash and an 'Oh fuck' and knew it was definitely Matthew, a bit the worse for wear.

'How'd it go?' she asked sleepily when he eventually stumbled into the bedroom and turned on the overhead light, causing her to squint.

'Fantastic,' he slurred. 'A triumph. You should have been there.'

She ignored the sarcasm. 'Was Leo pleased? Did he think it went well? Did he enjoy it?' OK, stop asking him questions about Leo. Next it would be, 'Did he look nice?' or 'Did he look like he was pining for someone called Eleanor?' She changed tack.

'Did any of the celebs turn up?'

'Great turn-out. Shaun, Janice, Sandra . . .'

'Sandra was there?' For some reason, this made Helen nervous. 'She did behave, didn't she? Did you keep an eye on her?'

'Hardly my job.'

He managed to register her disapproving expression. 'Don't worry, she was fine.'

He flopped into bed, socks still on, and turned on to his side, breathing heavily almost immediately, asleep within seconds. Helen sighed and got out of bed to turn off the light.

On Saturday morning Helen was up early and out to the shop to get the tabloids. She was looking for Sandra's modelling story, of course, but just as eager to see if Leo's launch had got any coverage. She knew there was no chance he would be in any of the pictures, if indeed there were any, but, in that way that when you're fourteen you want to keep walking past the house of the boy you fancy even though you know he's away on holiday with his mum and dad, she just wanted to catch a glimpse of something that was connected to him. She started flicking impatiently through one of the papers as she walked along the street. Nothing. Letting herself into the flat, she sat down on the sofa and began hastily skimming the next one. On page five, there was a picture of Sandra. But it wasn't the picture she'd been hoping for. There was no headline in the 'Sandra's a Model Girl' vein. The picture was taken outside Verano – she recognized the laurel bush in its pot by the door and the wrought-iron table and chairs. There was no mention of the restaurant by name, or of Leo, because the focus of the piece was on Sandra. Sandra who was hanging on to the arm of an unnamed man Helen had never seen before; Sandra who had a food stain on her seethrough white top; Sandra who was cocking her leg at the paparazzi like a publicity-hungry spaniel to show them she was wearing no underwear. The paper had pixillated the offending area to protect her modesty. The headline read 'Put It Away, Love.'

Helen broke into a cold sweat. She checked the other two papers – both had gone with the same picture and the captions, 'Thong Gone' and 'Sandra's No Cover Girl'. There was no mention of Verano anywhere, no one had gone with the pictures of the other D-listers arriving or leaving and, of course, why would anyone use the 'candid' modelling shots when they had these. She tried to tell herself that the Sundays might pick up her *Vogue* story, but she knew there was no chance now.

Matthew flinched when she dropped the papers on the end of the bed.

'It's a fucking disaster.' She showed him one article after another, holding them up to his face as he lay there.

'You know, this wouldn't have happened if you'd come,' he said helpfully.

She lay down on the bed, defeated. 'I know, I know.'

But Matthew wasn't done. 'So now Leo will think I couldn't handle his campaign. Great.'

'I'm sorry. But it wasn't me who invited Sandra. I didn't know she was going to be there.'

'True. But let's face it, Helen, if you hadn't refused to have anything to do with Leo's PR, you could have checked who was on the guest list and, failing that, if you hadn't refused to come last night, you could have kept an eye on Sandra when she did turn up. Stopped her drinking, sent her home.'

Defensiveness was getting the better of Helen. 'Laura was there. She should have sorted Sandra out.'

'True, but Laura was in charge last night. She had enough on her plate. And, anyway, she'd given the responsibility for Sandra's story to you.'

'Fucking Jenny must've invited her. She knew I was expecting the story to go in this weekend. She must've done it hoping to stitch mc up.'

Matthew lay back on the pillow. 'Don't be so melodramatic. And do you know what? I can't be bothered to worry about Sandra. It's far more important to me that we've let Leo down. Shit, I'd better ring him.'

Leo, as it turned out, was not overly concerned by the lack of coverage, because bookings were stacking up and he knew the word of mouth would be positive. He was actually relieved that the restaurant had not been named in conjunction with Sandra's flashing and couldn't quite understand why his father was being so overly apologetic.

Laura, on the other hand, was spitting. Helen's phone practically exploded when she answered her boss's call.

'You've seen the papers, I take it?' Laura sounded unlike Helen had ever heard her before, both icy and boiling with anger at the same time, if such a thing were possible. Helen took a deep breath and waited for the worst.

'There's no chance she'll get her nomination now. Absolutely no fucking chance. Jesus, what a disaster.'

There was a brief pause, and Helen, feeling like she was obliged to say something, offered up, 'I'm sorry.'

Laura wasn't listening. 'I mean, being drunk, falling over, that would have been bad enough, but we might have overcome it. But showing her bits. Oh god.'

It crossed Helen's mind to say, 'Look, you can take back your offer of a job. I'll understand,' but all she could manage was, 'I'm sorry,' again, followed by, 'I'm really sorry.'

Laura had finally taken a breath. 'What are you sorry for? It's not your fault.'

'It is, of course it is. If I hadn't refused to work on Leo's account. Or even if I'd have come last night . . .'

Laura interrupted her. 'But, you weren't working on it, that's the point. Maybe you should have been but you weren't, and I accepted that. No . . .' She paused. '. . . It's that bitch Jenny. Sandra's name wasn't on the list last time I checked it, so she must have invited her herself, knowing that every time she goes near free booze, she makes a fool of herself. I didn't even realize Sandra was there until about ten o'clock, by which time she was already half-cut. I told Jenny to keep an eye on her, take her out the back door, put her in a taxi home. Fucking hell. I should've done it myself.'

'But it's still my fault, don't you see . . . it's because she hates me so much. She wanted Sandra to fuck up so I'd look bad.'

'Stop making this all about you. Of course she did it to get at you, but Sandra's my client so she's made me look bad as well, and she's not going to get away with it. I phoned you for a moan about *her*, not to tell you off.'

The relief which washed over Helen was almost tangible. She sat down at the kitchen table and forced herself to breathe normally. 'So, what are you going to do?'

Laura breathed in sharply. 'Well, if I find out she invited Sandra, then I'm going to take it up with the other directors. Global can't trust someone who behaves like that.'

Almost as soon as Helen hung up, her mobile rang again. Sandra. Thankfully, the caller ID had told her this because otherwise she never would have guessed from the high-pitched wail that came at her down the phone. It was like being called by a distraught dolphin.

'You've seen the papers then?'

She thought she heard Sandra say the words, 'my minge,' amid the crying. Part of her wanted to tell Sandra off for being so fucking stupid: why did she accept the invitation, knowing that there would be paparazzi there and that she had a positive story waiting to go into the papers; if she had to go, why couldn't she stay sober (silly question) or at least put some knickers on. She was her own worst enemy but, truthfully, she was too stupid and desperate to know any better. Jenny wasn't.

'Sandra, calm down.'

'Eeeeee.' A noise came back like Flipper trying to alert her to someone in danger.

'Listen, just lie low today. Don't answer your phone unless you know who it is. Don't go out, OK? There's still a couple of weeks till the nominations are announced, we'll think of something,' she said, knowing there was absolutely no chance.

She took the sound which followed as an agreement.

'Sandra, who invited you last night? I mean, I didn't know you were going to be there.'

It was Jenny. Helen managed to decipher enough to establish that Jenny had called Sandra just after her return from Kos and told her that Laura thought it would be a good idea if she showed her face at the launch. What's more, Jenny had refilled her glass several times and persuaded her from leaving when Sandra had had a pang of responsibility at around nine o'clock. That was the last thing she remembered. The waiter – for he had indeed turned out to be one of Leo's employees – had thankfully slept on the couch and had been very attentive this morning, bringing her Resolve and making her a fry-up. He hadn't seemed offended at all when she had asked him who the fuck he was.

'Look, you never know . . .' Helen knew she didn't sound convincing '. . . One of the Sundays might still run the Kos piece and then we'll capitalize on it like mad. Don't feel too bad, OK?'

Helen was desperate to run straight into the bedroom and crow to Matthew that it *was* his precious assistant who had fucked the whole evening up, but she knew he'd just think she was being hysterical. Anyway, better to leave it to Laura to deliver the bad news – let the grown-ups fight it out.

28

Matthew was feeling utterly at home drinking tea in Sophie's big, welcoming kitchen. This is modern living, he thought. This is being an adult. Sitting having a civilized conversation with your ex-wife before spending the afternoon with your children. He took a big sip, contented. OK, so things were a bit rocky with Helen, but it was just one of those phases relationships go through. She was having a tough time adjusting, having to get used to being painted a marriage-wrecker, losing her job, nervous about her new one. It'd calm down.

'I want to see Norman,' Claudia demanded when he was saying goodbye.

'Well, come over to the flat next week.' Matthew looked over at Sophie for approval, and she nodded, 'I'm sure Helen'd love that.'

'I don't want to see Helen. I just want to see Norman. You said he was my cat and if he's my cat, what's the point if I can't see him?'

'How about I run you over there now? You can play with him for ten minutes, then I'll bring you back. How's that sound?'

'Can I, Mum? Please.'

'Go on then. Really, only ten minutes, though, Matthew, before you bring her back again. She's got school tomorrow.' She looked at her other daughter. 'Do you want to go, Suzanne?'

Suzanne had warmed to Helen more than Claudia, but she was in no rush to see any more of her than necessity dictated. However, she would never pass up the chance to spend ten more minutes with her father. She weighed it up.

'OK.'

'Ten minutes,' Sophie called after them as they left.

Helen was lounging in the bath, face mask on, contemplating her last week at work. She wondered if anyone would buy her a leaving gift – unlikely, she thought, under the circumstances. She wasn't having a party, obviously, but Friday-night drinks would be held in her honour, and the few people who could still look her in the eye would come and stand round awkwardly for half an hour or so and have a glass of champagne. The Sunday papers had, of course, all failed to pick up on the 'Sandra Hepburn – Model' story and, indeed, most of them had reprinted the spaniel picture but, having reported her conversation with Sandra back to Laura, she knew that Jenny was in for a shit week and that gave her a warm feeling. She ducked her head under the water to wash the mask off as she heard the front door open. When she emerged, she could hear the unmistakable voice of Claudia saying, 'Oh good, she's not here,' as she ran round the flat, presumably in pursuit of Norman. She hauled herself out of the bath miserably, wrapped a towel around her and stuck her head out into the hall, pretending not to have heard Claudia's remark.

'Oh, hi. I wondered who that was. Hi, girls, this is a nice surprise.'

Claudia, who was brushing the cat furiously, in a way that implied he had been neglected since her last visit, ignored her. Clearly, now she got to spend her Sundays at home seeing her father on her own territory, she no longer felt she had to bother.

'Great. Well, shall I put the kettle on?'

'We're only staying a few minutes so Claude can see the cat. I'm just going to have a shower, then I'm running her back again.'

Helen could see that Matthew was willing her to be nice, but she wanted to grab on to his leg and plead with him not to leave her alone with the children. They scared her, these girls.

'You ought to be a vet.' Helen was watching Claudia expertly clipping Norman's claws, although he was so placid, he probably would have let next-door's Rottweiler do it. Claudia kept her head down, ignoring the remark, seemingly intent on her task. Suzanne gazed at her fingernails, impassive as ever. Helen felt an unexpected jolt of guilt – it wasn't right that they had had to get caught up in her and Matthew's mess. She didn't know why she'd been surprised that they hated her – of course they did, she'd broken up their family. She could hear Matthew singing cheerfully over the noise of the shower, clearly in no real hurry. She took a deep breath.

'Listen, girls. I might not get another chance to say this, but I want you to know I'm really sorry. For everything. For what I've done to you and what I've done to your mum.' She looked up and saw that Suzanne was looking back at her and even Claudia had momentarily stopped what she was doing, although when she saw that Helen had noticed, she turned quickly back to the cat.

'I'm not proud of myself,' Helen continued, her voice cracking nervously. She didn't know why it was suddenly so important she apologize to the children, but she realized, at least, that it was for their sake rather than hers. 'And neither is your dad. But I want you to know it was more my fault than his. I pushed him into leaving home and I really shouldn't have done that. I know he misses you like crazy. All of you.'

Helen had never seen herself as someone who would fall on her sword, but it felt good. So what if she was reinforcing the stereotype that women were all evil temptresses and men were hapless martyrs to their hormones? It would ease Matthew's passage back into the family and that had to be a good thing.

'I don't think I can compete with that, to be honest.'

'What do you mean?' Claudia was eyeing her suspiciously.

'Nothing, really. I just wanted you to know that your dad really loves you both and that I think everything'll be OK in the end.'

'How?' Suzanne sounded hopeful.

'Erm . . .' This was starting to get awkward. She couldn't tell them her plans, obviously, and she certainly didn't want them to start asking their father what was going on. In the other room she could hear Matthew's mobile ring and him answering it.

'Things have a way of working out, that's all I meant.'

'OK,' Suzanne said trustingly, half-smiling at her.

'And there's nothing wrong with wanting to be a beautician. It's a good job. And don't let anyone tell you otherwise,' Helen added for good measure, just as Matthew came in, holding his phone and looking pale.

'It's my mother,' he said quietly. 'She's had a heart attack.'

Matthew had looked so lost and devastated that her heart had gone out to him and she'd gone over and put her arms round him, rubbing his back. She had no doubt that his mother was a hateful old harridan the same as – in fact the reason for – the rest of his family, but she was still his mother and he was still her only son. Within minutes he had packed an overnight bag and called his answerphone at work to leave a message for Jenny that he probably wouldn't be in for a couple of days.

'You will come with me, won't you?' He looked at her pleadingly.

She weighed it up quickly. Verano had opened for its first night of proper business last night, so there was no way Leo would be making a mercy dash to his grandmother's side. And, anyway, Sophie had told her he wasn't that fond of Matthew's family (what good taste, Helen thought, and then pushed the thought from her mind). Sophie had the girls, who had to be at school tomorrow and she, too, had never been overly keen on her mother-in-law, so Helen figured she was safe to go and, even though she was dreading it, she was pleased that she could give Matthew a bit of support. It might make up for her no-show on Friday night and at least ease the atmosphere between them.

'Of course I will.' She stroked his arm and he looked so grateful she thought he might cry.

'I'll just have to drop the girls back.'

Shit, Claudia and Suzanne. Of course. It would be fine – it was dark, she'd wait in the car, there would be no way Sophie would spot her. Matthew went out into the hall to bully Claudia – who was still holding the cat in her arms – into her coat. Helen wrapped a big scarf round her neck and half-way up her face and then pulled a mohair cloche hat low down on her head. Thank god it was February.

'You look like a spy,' Matthew said teasingly when she met him at the front door.

'It's cold out there.'

Sophie's – and Matthew's, of course, on paper – house was, as Helen knew only too well, a mere ten-minute drive away. It was as beautiful as she remembered it, lights burning in the windows behind coloured drapes giving it a dolls' house look. Matthew indicated to turn into the small drive at the front.

'No! Don't,' Helen almost shouted. 'I don't think I should go in there. Park it up on the street.'

She could practically hear Claudia rolling her eyes, but Matthew did as he was told and pulled over directly opposite the house.

'Bye, girls,' Helen said cheerfully.

'Bye,' Claudia grunted, the first time she'd ever bothered to say it as, usually, she figured that the end of the visit meant she could forget about having to be polite for another week or so.

'Bye, Helen.' Suzanne leaned over to the front seat and gave Helen something which may have been a hug. Helen patted her arm affectionately. It felt like a major victory. Forget the war – she was happy just to have won this tiny battle. Nelson would have been fucked if his opposition had been two sulky adolescent girls. She watched as Matthew took Claudia's hand and crossed the road, going up to the front door to tell Sophie what had happened. She sat slumped down in her seat, her view partially obscured by a tree on the other side of the road. It was all over in a couple of minutes – Sophie didn't even look over, and Matthew was on his way back down the drive.

'Helen's in the car,' Claudia told her mother as she was closing the front door.

'Is she?' Sophie was seized by curiosity. She pulled the door open before it had fully shut and took a couple of steps out into the drive, peering into the darkness. She just caught sight of Matthew's tail lights as he pulled away.

'Shit, I wanted to see what she looked like.'

'She looks a bit like you,' Claudia called over her shoulder as she ran up the stairs.

Matthew and Helen arrived in Bath about two and a half hours later and headed straight for the Malmesbury Private Hospital, where Amanda and Louisa were already sitting beside their mother's bed. Sheila was unconscious, hooked up to a ventilator and wired to a selection of machines that beeped at different intervals. Oh shit, she's going to die, Helen thought, looking at the pale, waxy-skinned elderly woman in the bed who, she thought, resembled a velociraptor. Hospitals made her feel uneasy at the best of times, but being this close to someone who seemed to be hovering between life and death made her positively panicky. This was real – one of those major events that defined adulthood. It made her relationship troubles seem inconsequential, and she knew she had become ridiculously self-involved. She took a deep breath, wanting to be able to keep it together for Matthew's sake. He had fallen on his sisters tearfully and then sat in the chair closest to his mother's head and was holding her hand. Helen hung back awkwardly in the doorway. Neither Amanda nor Louisa had acknowledged her presence, and Matthew was understandably too preoccupied to worry about her. She stood for what seemed like an age and then decided to go and find the cafeteria and get some coffees.

Once there, the best thing to do seemed to be to sit at a table in the corner drinking hers and let the family have some private time. The cafeteria was overflowing with people who, it seemed to Helen, looked alternately shell-shocked or relieved, people whose loved ones were worse or better than they had feared. She drank her coffee slowly, stirring the plastic spoon round and round to kill time. After twenty minutes she had stretched it out for as long as she could, so she queued up again and bought three more cups to take upstairs. She panicked a bit around the sugar and then stuffed six sachets into the pocket of her jeans along with six little milk cartons and three stirrers.

When she stepped out of the lift on the second floor, she knew that something was wrong because Matthew,

Amanda and Louisa were huddled in the corridor and doctors were running in and out of Sheila's room. Helen hovered awkwardly with her coffees, unsure whether or not to ask what was happening, and then one of the cardboard cups started to burn through her hand. She looked around hurriedly for somewhere to put them down, and then the other hand began to burn and she bent quickly to try and set them down on the floor, but the pain made her flinch and she dropped all three from about waist height, splattering hot coffee across the polished floor.

'Shit. Fuck. Sorry.'

Matthew, Amanda and Louisa all turned to look at her in silence. Helen was on the floor now, dabbing at the liquid with an inadequate tissue and was about to apologize again when one of the doctors came out of Sheila's room, walking this time, and they all turned their attention to him. The kindly looking doctor walked them down the corridor a few paces as if to say, 'Let's move away from the madwoman.' The whole scene played out in front of her like a silent film, and it was obvious what the story was. Louisa buckled and clasped on to Matthew's arm for support. He put his arms round her and his other sister, drawing them close to him. The doctor touched each of them gently on the arm and walked away, on to his next job. Helen didn't know what to do with herself; there was something about other people's grief that was so exposing, so personal, that she felt she shouldn't be looking, but she was also rooted to the spot by concern for Matthew. She considered going over and joining their group hug, but she knew she wouldn't be welcome, and even when she knew they were suffering, she couldn't handle the hypocrisy of pretending she could give a fuck about how Amanda and Louisa felt. She felt bad for anyone who lost their mother, of course she did, but that didn't mean it was appropriate to comfort them. Or that they would allow her to. The decision was finally made for her when the trio, without so much as a glance in her direction, shuffled into the small sideroom to say their goodbyes. Helen was left standing in the empty corridor with no option but to wait it out and see what was expected of her.

Half an hour later they were saying goodbye in the car park.

'I'll call you about the arrangements,' Amanda said to Matthew as she kissed him on the cheek.

'Bye,' Helen shouted over, but no reply came.

Jenny was being hauled over the coals. Helen could tell this even though Laura's door was shut and she couldn't hear what was being said. The body language said it all – Laura was sat bolt upright at her desk, leaning forward, all but wagging her finger. Jenny was slouched in a chair opposite. Matthew wasn't in there – although he had come to work despite his bereavement – and Helen guessed that Laura was making it clear to Jenny that her punishment would be severe without actually telling her exactly what it would be. Sadly, there was no way she could sack Matthew's PA without his agreement.

Matthew had sat up late into the night, crying occasionally but mostly staring into the distance, and Helen had stayed with him, although she knew there wasn't anything she could do to make him feel any better. This morning he was stoic again and into brusque work mode. Helen knew the issue of the funeral was looming, but she couldn't face raising it herself yet. She needed to come up with a plan.

Ten minutes later, Jenny emerged from Laura's office slightly pink around the eyelids but staring defiantly at Helen as if to say, 'I know you're loving this, but I'm not going to let them get to me.' Helen knew it was a bluff – what Jenny had done was too serious not to merit proper repercussions. She had effectively ruined two campaigns for two paying clients who had put their faith in Global. OK, so Leo had been given a cut-price rate, but that wasn't the point and, anyway, he was Matthew's son, and Helen knew that that fact alone was going to make them treat her actions seriously. As for Sandra – poor Sandra had blown any chance she had of redemption in the eyes of the public. There was no chance of that nomination now – she had reached her sixteenth minute, and there was nothing she could do about it. There was an argument to say that this was her own fault, that had Jenny not invited her, she would have gone out somewhere else and got drunk and made a fool of herself. But the point was she hadn't. Jenny had told her that Laura wanted her there, had plied her with drink, had failed to provide her with an exit plan and had left her to hang herself in public. Helen smirked back at Jenny. Got you.

Later that afternoon Matthew shut himself away with Laura, and then with Jenny and, next thing, Jenny was packing up the contents of her drawer into a cardboard box, Annie and Jamie at her side like two mourners at a funeral. Helen was desperate to know what had happened, but she knew she couldn't ask. She emailed Helen-from-Accounts.

'What's going on?'

She got a reply almost immediately.

'She's being moved to IT to be a general assistant. Typing up memos for the computer boys. I feel quite sorry for her.'

'I don't,' Helen typed in reply.

Just before the end of the day, Jenny stopped by Helen's desk on her way out with her third boxload. 'He tried it on with me, too, you know.' She smiled malevolently at Helen.

'By "he", I take it you're referring to Matthew?'

'About three years ago. Took me out to lunch and held my hand and told me I was beautiful. I turned him down, of course. God, can you imagine? Gross.'

Helen thought. Three years ago she had had her pregnancy scare. She looked at Jenny, long dark hair tied back in a ponytail. Yes, it figured.

'Bye, Jenny,' she smiled disconcertingly. 'Have fun in the basement.'

'Jenny told me you made a pass at her once,' Helen said to Matthew later that evening, just to see how he'd get out of it.

'She said *that*! No way. God, that's her revenge for being demoted, can't you see?'

'If you say so.'

He took hold of her arm, turning her to face him.

'Helen, I haven't always been a saint, I know that's true.

The fact that I was married when we got together should tell you that. Maybe I did try it on with her once, I honestly can't remember. And if I did, I'm really really sorry. But that would have been before I realized exactly how much you mean to me. I've changed. You know that.'

There it was again. That thing that Matthew had – charm? disingenuousness? naivety? She didn't know what it was, but it got him off the hook time and time again. He had a habit of pulling it out of the bag just at the point when you thought you'd had enough, and waving it in your face. It was the fact that he always believed it himself that made it so utterly winning. She knew she should hate him, but she just couldn't. He didn't have a malicious bone in his body; he was just weak. She felt pity for him – it must be awful to be so spineless, so emotionally immature, so reluctant to admit you were growing older. Soon he would become an object of ridicule – a creepy old man still trying to lure young women into bed. Hurt as she was, she felt she wanted to protect him from himself, from his own worst instincts. Sophie would be a match for him now. She'd toughened up, she wouldn't take any of his shit. She'd keep him in line, and he would probably thank her for it.

29

The prospect of Sheila's funeral was sending Helen into a cold sweat. There was no way she could go. Sophie had already told her on the phone that Matthew had called her and asked her to be there.

'Oh, really,' Helen had responded, intrigued.

As if that wasn't bad enough, Leo was also planning on going, according to Sophie. She didn't see how she could just state she didn't want to go, as she had with Leo's launch. This was her boyfriend's mother's funeral, for Christ's sake; he was entitled to expect her support. Illness was the only answer. A sudden bout of violent food-poisoning coming on in the morning before they were about to leave ought to do it. Something tangible and unquestionable like being sick. Matthew would never fall for claims of a bad headache or a temperature; she needed to present him with something he couldn't argue with. Helen was no actress, so she planned her sickness with military precision. It was important that she and Matthew ate different things the night before – she would order a takeaway and let him choose first. Then, on the morning, she would get up early and put on a little pale make-up, drink a cup of salt water and then make herself throw up loudly in the bathroom. It shouldn't be hard – she'd stick her fingers down her throat or something. If all else failed, she'd just make the noise and hope for the best. The real thing would be better, though, that telltale aroma in the bathroom, the giveaway sheet of sweat on the forehead – then he'd never think she was putting it on. The church was booked for Thursday afternoon at two, with sandwiches and drinks in Amanda and Edwin's house nearby afterwards. Matthew had booked a B&B just up the road, despite Amanda's house having four spare bedrooms, thinking, rightly as it happened, that Amanda would not welcome Helen.

Helen had suggested – knowing that she wouldn't be there – that it might be nice to stay in the same hotel as the kids. Matthew had been by turns suspicious, then nervous, then delighted. Once Helen had convinced him that she had no intention of flaunting her personal victory in Sophie's face, he had taken her suggestion as proof that she was ready to move their relationship on a stage. She told him she missed seeing the girls, and because he wanted to believe her, he did. And so Matthew had duly asked Sophie where they were intending to stay, so that he could inquire about a room there too.

'Helen's coming,' Sophie said to her over a glass of wine in the pub on Tuesday night. 'I finally get to meet her.'

'How do you feel?'

'Sick. Angry. Dying of curiosity. Nervous. I'm already worrying about what I'm going to wear and when to get my hair done. I mean, is that any way to be thinking about your mother-in-law's funeral?'

Helen laughed. Sophie continued.

'She'll be looking at me, feeling all superior, wanting

me to be frumpy and housewifey, and I'm not going to give her the satisfaction. I'm going to look drop-dead gorgeous.'

'I'm sure Matthew's mother would appreciate the effort.'

Sophie paused. 'He wants us all to stay in the same hotel, you know.'

Helen pretended to splutter her drink and made too good a job of it, causing the bubbles to go up her nose. She coughed. 'Why?'

'He thinks it would be a good idea, for the children, you know, that we all show we can get along.'

'And can you, do you think?'

'I doubt it. I told him I'd think about it but, to be honest, I know what I think already – it's a terrible idea. I get to be humiliated not just at the funeral but overnight as well. Great.'

'I don't know.' Helen seemed to be mulling over the idea. 'Isn't it worse for her? You and Matthew are getting along well these days. The girls will be delighted the whole family's there together. She'll feel like an outsider. Plus . . .' she took a deep breath '. . . the fact that Matthew doesn't want to spend time with her alone down there tells me he's not feeling so great about the decision he made. She'll be furious.'

'I suppose I've got to meet her sometime,' Sophie sighed.

'And it might as well be when she's at a disadvantage. Think about it – she'll have his whole family looking at her disapprovingly all day, and then you there in the evening. It's hysterical.'

'More than anything, I want to get a look at her close up.'

'Maybe you'll like her,' Helen said. 'Imagine that.'

The office felt much calmer without Jenny. Annie had less reason to hang around, and Jamie on his own was harmless enough. They still all met up for lunch, Jenny throwing malicious looks in Helen's direction whenever she came up to their floor, but it felt like their power had been curtailed. Matthew was being looked after by a temp – a pleasant fifty-something woman who just kept her head down and got on with it. Helen-from-Accounts had taken to coming and hanging round the general office at lunchtimes without fear of being taken the piss out of, except by Helen, who did it with a certain amount of affection. She had managed to forgive Geoff completely for his indiscretion and was as nauseatingly in love as ever. Whenever Helen mentioned that Friday was her last day, she looked crushed for a few moments, like a five-year-old who's been told to mime in the school choir because they can't sing, before she remembered not to be selfish, and then she would gush to Helen about how thrilled she was for her.

On Wednesday evening Helen told Matthew they were having a takeaway because there was no food in the fridge. They decided on Indian.

'I'll have a chicken danzak, pilau rice, a peshwari naan and a sag daal,' Matthew said, without even looking at the menu.

'Mmm . . . I think I'll have a prawn balti.' Prawns were always good for blaming a bad stomach on.

'Actually,' Matthew was saying, picking up the phone, 'that sounds good. I'm changing my order. I'll have the same as you, no rice, two naan.'

Fuck, thought Helen.

'Hold on! I haven't had a chicken tikka masala for ages. I'm going to have that.'

'Sure?'

'Sure.'

'This chicken tastes funny.' Helen pulled a face. 'I hope it's OK.' She poured herself another glass of wine when he wasn't looking and knocked it back.

'Don't eat it then. Here.' He handed over his plate, still half full. 'Have mine, I've had enough anyway.'

'No, no, I'm sure it's fine really.' She pushed his plate away and carried on stuffing large forkfuls of the chicken into her mouth.

'We've got a big day tomorrow, you don't want to risk making yourself ill,' he said annoyingly, guaranteeing that he would be able to tell her he told her so when the time came.

They had planned to get up at nine, so at ten to Helen made a few moaning noises and rubbed her stomach.

'I don't feel too good,' she said, making sure he was awake to hear her performance.

She clutched her stomach and mock staggered to the kitchen, where she drank a disgusting salt-water concoction, and then into the bathroom, where she leaned over the toilet bowl and started to dry heave noisily. She was feeling distinctly queasy from a combination of the hot curry and the salt, and she managed to throw up a little – enough to induce a pallor and a cold sweat. She looked in the mirror – she resembled Linda Blair in *The Exorcist* – perfect, no need for make-up. She waited a moment for Matthew to come and knock on the door asking if she was OK. Nothing. She opened the door a little further and repeated the performance, this time feeling genuinely overwhelmed as the wine and the curry sauce and the salt all got their revenge. She upped the noise to a level not even Matthew could sleep through.

'Jesus. What's going on?' she heard through her groaning. Bingo.

Matthew was standing in the doorway, concerned. She wiped her mouth and turned to look at him, a clammy sheen covering her white skin. The stench of vomit and curry was making her eyes water, so god knew what effect it must be having on him. Helen lay down dramatically on the cold tiled floor. She knew it would pass, but at the moment she felt like she was about to die, and she knew, from the way she looked, there could be no doubting her sincerity. Matthew leaned over her and flushed the toilet, peering in at the orangey-brown mess inside.

'I told you not to eat that fucking curry. Jesus, Helen, today of all days. Have a bath, you'll feel better when you clean yourself up.'

And he walked out, shutting the door behind him.

Helen lay there for a moment, stunned. Was that it? Have a bath and you'll feel better? No 'Oh, my poor darling, are you OK'? No 'Go back to bed and don't even think about coming to the funeral'? She pulled herself up to her feet. She had to act fast before she started to look too healthy again.

Matthew was in the kitchen making tea, whistling tunelessly to himself.

'I think I need to go back to bed.' Helen grasped her stomach and then faked a retch, clutching her hand to her mouth.

'We have to leave in an hour.'

'Matthew, I'm ill.' She was sure he was being deliberately obtuse.

'You'll start feeling better now it's all out of your system. Tell you what, go and lie down for half an hour and then I'll run you a bath. You can put your make-up on in the car,' he said magnanimously. This was a disaster.

'I'm going to be sick.' Helen gagged again and rushed into the bathroom, shutting the door behind her and making loud hurling noises into the toilet bowl. Her head was starting to throb with the effort of the performance. She stood up, looking into the mirror again. Jesus. Pale sweaty skin, hair on end, panda eyes where the residue of yesterday's mascara had run on to her cheeks. She looked like a woman who had reached rock bottom, and maybe she had. This plan had to work, there was simply no alternative, and she could see the desperation oozing out of her reflection. Goodbye, dignity. Goodbye, self-respect. One more noisy dry heave, and she was done. She splashed cold water on to her face before she came out again.

'I don't think I can go.'

'Of course you can. We can stop on the way if you think you need to be sick.'

There was nothing for it but to run to the bathroom and repeat the whole charade again, only this time, when she'd done, she looked up and there was Matthew standing beside her.

'See,' he smiled at her. 'You've stopped bringing anything up already. You'll probably have a few stomach cramps and some false alarms but the worst is definitely over.'

'Matthew, I feel like death.' Oops, slightly inappropriate today of all days, she thought. 'It's true, I might've stopped being sick, but I guarantee you any minute now it'll start coming out the other end.'

Matthew looked slightly nauseous and she thought she'd got him, but it wasn't going to be that easy.

'Take some kaolin, lie in bed for . . .' he looked at his watch '. . . twenty-five minutes. We can stop on the way. By the time we get to the church, you'll feel fine.'

'No. I can't go. You don't know how bad I feel.'

'You're being ridiculous. It's a bit of food-poisoning . . .'

'How the fuck can you tell me how I feel?' Helen was panicking. Not only was it out of the question that she attend the service and come face to face with Sophie and Leo, but this was a perfect opportunity for Matthew and Sophie to spend some time together and get a bit closer.

'I feel like shit, OK?' Oh god, she hadn't meant it to be like this. In her fantasy, when Matthew saw how ill she was, he would insist that she mustn't think about coming to the funeral. She would protest how much she wanted to go. He would kiss her and say he knew she wanted to be there to support him but it was out of the question. She had never meant for them to have a fight – today, especially. She genuinely wanted to put her arms round him and tell him she hoped it wasn't too awful and that he'd feel better once it was all over, but now she couldn't risk letting him think she was giving in. 'I'm sorry about the funeral, I really am, but I'm going back to bed and staying there.'

'I told you not to finish that chicken.'

She couldn't resist rising to the bait. 'Oh, so it's my fault now? I deliberately gave myself food-poisoning to get out of going to your mother's memorial service?'

'Well, it's fucking convenient.' She would have sworn he stamped his foot petulantly.

'You'll have your whole family there, OK? I'm really sorry, but I have to go and lie down. Come and say good-bye before you leave.'

Half an hour later, she heard the front door slam shut.

Sophie arrived at the church ten minutes before the service was due to begin. There was drizzle in the air and she had to decide whether to go inside the little fifteenth-century stone church and risk bumping into either of the sisters before it was absolutely necessary or to hover among the graves out of sight of everyone and risk her hair frizzing up. In the end she put up her umbrella and found a side porch which seemed like a safe place to hide. She was feeling pathetically nervous about meeting Helen, and the anxiety was making her feel light-headed. She hadn't been able to eat before the two-hour drive, and she was regretting that now, swaying slightly and wondering if she might faint or whether the palpitations she could feel in her chest were actually a heart attack in the offing. The girls had run inside and were no doubt now being fussed over by their aunts. Sophie was checking her make-up in a small hand-bag mirror when, out of the corner of her eye, she recognized Matthew's slightly loping walk over behind some trees. She jumped like she'd been caught having a sneaky cigarette by her teacher and snapped the mirror shut, shoving it into her coat pocket. She must have missed Helen walking in front of him, or else she was still in the car, because Matthew seemed to be alone. Head down, hands in his pockets, he looked miserable. Well, it was his mother's funeral, after all, so he was hardly going to arrive blowing a whistle and letting off party poppers, but he looked beaten down. Older than she thought he'd been looking recently. He made his way straight into the vestibule, and Sophie decided to wait a couple more minutes for him to parade Helen around before she went in and got a look at her. That way, she could hang around on the periphery and, hopefully, observe her for a few minutes before the inevitable introduction took place. Ideally, the service would just be starting and she could delay the meeting until afterwards. She wished the girls were out here with her, she needed moral support.

Two minutes later, she checked herself out in the mirror again and decided she had to bite the bullet and get it over with before her hair got any damper and, more importantly of course, she had to walk into Sheila's memorial part way through. Stepping into the small outer room of the church, she realized everyone had gone on through and seated themselves, waiting for the organ to strike up. As she walked up the aisle, she could feel all eyes on her – at least that's what it felt like, although, in reality, the church was packed with Sheila's many friends from the village, who had no idea who she was – and she felt herself blush as she was forced to walk further and further forward to find a space to sit. She looked around frantically for Suzanne and Claudia and saw them beckoning furiously for her to come and join them. Relieved, she edged her way along the row and then noticed Matthew sitting on the other side of Suzanne. A moment of sheer panic nearly caused her to fall over, and she steadied herself on the wooden railing, then forced herself to look up again and saw that he was seated at the end of the pew. Where was Helen? She looked at the row behind and saw only old ladies, hats on, ready for a good cry, and Leo doling out hankies. She smiled a hello at him. Claudia was tugging at her sleeve.

'Where have you been?' she whined.

'Outside.' Sophie sat down and whispered to her daughter. 'Where's Helen?'

'Oh, she's not here,' Claudia replied loudly, and Sophie coloured, unable to look up and meet Matthew in the eye. 'She's got food-poisoning.'

Sophie felt overwhelmed with relief, disappointment and embarrassment all at once.

'Oh, what a shame,' she said unconvincingly, forcing herself to smile at Matthew just as, luckily, the first strains of a hymn, mangled out of all recognition by the elderly organist, struck up. Within seconds, the whole church was in tears, including Sophie, who had never been her mother-in-law's greatest fan.

As soon as the service was over, a long convoy – minus Leo, who made a noisy exit, having the perfect excuse to rush back to London to check that the restaurant was still in one piece – snaked its way to Amanda and Edwin's mock Tudor barn for 'nibbles' and, Sophie was hoping, alcohol. Suzanne and Claudia, who had been inconsolable during the eulogy, had cheered up considerably the minute the final chord of the final tune had been played and had begged to travel in Matthew's car, leaving Sophie to follow on her own. As she was doing up her seatbelt, Leo ran over and leaned through the driver's window.

'So, do you think she even exists or what?'

'Helen?'

Leo nodded, smiling.

'I think I'd feel even worse if he'd had to make up a girlfriend to get rid of me.'

'Tell you what I think – I think she's scared to show her face. And so she should be.'

'I appreciate it, Leo, but the truth is she only did what I did to your mum. I'm as bad as her. I've been thinking about that a lot lately.'

'Yeah, but you're lovely and she's a bitch, that's the difference.' He kissed her on the cheek and Sophie couldn't help laughing.

'Maybe she really is ill.'

'Maybe she's got another man on the side already and she just wants Dad out the way for the night.' He smiled wickedly.

'Or she's genuinely got food-poisoning.'

'Or she's so unattractive she can't bear the thought of us all seeing her.'

Sophie squeezed his hand. 'Bye, Leo.'

*

344

In a stroke of extraordinary pretension, Amanda had hired caterers to make canapés and sausage rolls for the guests. Two waiters in uniform wandered, bored, from group to group, trying to press duck pâté spread over hard little toasts on to old women whose teeth weren't their own and children who were complaining about the lack of cheese sandwiches and salt and vinegar crisps. Sophie bit her tongue when Amanda and then Louisa told her how delighted they were that she had come, and how brave she was being and that she was, of course, still family, because she was, after all, the mother of their nieces. She looked around desperately for anything that approximated a drink, but Amanda had clearly decided that Edwin and alcohol didn't mix, and the waiters seemed to be serving only coffee and orange juice. She looked at her watch – half past three – there was no way she could leave before six without being rude. She decided to kill ten minutes by walking round the garden, despite the weather, and immediately found Matthew at her side.

'Sneaking off to the pub? 'Cos if you are, I'm coming with you.'

'Your sisters would come after me with a shotgun. It's almost worth risking it though.'

'Luckily, I was anticipating this, so I've got a bottle of vodka in the car. Care to join me?'

'Lovely.'

Once Matthew had reappeared with his litre of Absolut and gone round the mourners, adding it to their orange juices, things lightened up considerably. Edwin, after a couple of sips, decided that his wife was being unreasonable and broke the lock on the under-the-stairs cupboard where she had hidden his supplies. Amanda remained stony-faced as he doled out whisky and red wine, drinking two himself for every one he poured. By four thirty, the afternoon felt like a proper wake, with Sheila's bridge partners telling endless unfunny anecdotes and Louisa at one point bursting into tears because she believed she had always been her mother's least favourite child (she was right, in fact, and Sheila had occasionally said so). The children, slightly tainted by memories of the last drunken family gathering they had attended, took themselves out into the garden before things got out of hand.

Helen had so far spent the day lounging around the flat. It was a glorious feeling to know she had the place to herself until tomorrow, no Matthew to get on her nerves, an evening of total indulgence before her last ever day at Global. She wondered how he was coping down in Bath, still feeling bad that he'd left on such a sour note. Earlier in the afternoon, she had picked up the phone, tempted to call him on his mobile just to check that he was OK, but she'd decided that the resentment he was feeling, though unfortunate, might work in her favour. She was being cruel to be kind, as it were. He might think she was being heartless now, but if thinking that pushed him closer to Sophie, then he'd be grateful in the end. And, of course, the more unfeeling he thought she was being, the easier it would be for him to leave her, so they would both win. She allowed herself to feel optimistic for once – things were turning round. Slowly, more like a tanker than a speedboat, but changing direction nevertheless.

She was both looking forward to and dreading the next day. She knew there'd be no party, no great fuss, but there would be the agonizing embarrassment of Friday-night drinks in her honour. Probably no one would come, which would be fine, preferable even. She could just wait till a respectable hour, pick up her boxes and leave. There was no reason she would ever have to see Annie or Jenny again in her life. She felt bad about Sandra – poor, miserable Sandra, whose only hopes of redemption had been dashed – she knew she was her only champion and that, once she and Laura had gone, Global would probably drop her as a hopeless case. The Ace Award nominations were announced tomorrow – obviously, Sandra didn't have a hope in hell. Helen knew she should ring her, check she was OK, but she couldn't face it. She turned on the TV and lay on the sofa. Bliss. She wondered whether she and Matthew would get into a custody battle over Norman once this was all over, and then remembered that Sophie was allergic. Claudia would be gutted, but, then again, you lose a cat, you gain a father, that must be a good deal. She looked at her watch – twenty-five past four – hopefully Matthew and Sophie were bonding away merrily down in Bath. She realized she was bored. She longed to phone Rachel, to kill an hour talking about nothing, but she couldn't face being taken step by step through the intricate differences between kinds of typeface for the invitations. She fell asleep.

Sophie, Matthew and the girls were eating dinner at the hotel, having finally escaped from Amanda and Edwin's at about seven o'clock, leaving behind an impending, alcohol-fuelled bust-up. The restaurant of the hotel was effectively someone's living room with four tables nestling intimately in the middle. Ambitious three-course meals were cooked by the owner, and her husband waited the tables. Tonight it was just the four of them, and to Sophie it felt bizarrely like they were having a cosy evening at home. Matthew had driven them all over because, after three glasses of vodka, she didn't feel she should be driving and she had left her car in Amanda's driveway for collection tomorrow. Matthew's relief that the funeral was out of the way was palpable. Never very comfortable at big family gatherings, this one had been made much worse by Sheila's drunken old cronies giving him a hard time for splitting up his family. It was hard to conduct a fair argument with a half-cut eighty-year-old especially when all you wanted to say was, 'It's none of your fucking business, actually.' Now they were on safe ground, he had lightened up visibly and was knocking back big glasses of Pinot Grigio and telling stories to make the girls laugh.

'How's Helen feeling?' Sophie asked when there was a lull in the conversation, assuming that Matthew would have called her when he went to dump his bag in his room.

'I haven't spoken to her,' he said, and then, seeing Sophie's puzzled expression, he added hastily, 'I don't want to disturb her if she's sleeping.' Which, Sophie thought, was interesting.

By half past nine, Sophie had taken Suzanne and Claudia up to their room to bed, despite their protestations.

'Come back down and have another drink,' Matthew

had said to her and, because she was enjoying herself, she'd agreed, so now she was sitting back downstairs beside the open fire, swilling a large brandy around an even larger glass. Matthew's mood had shifted slightly somewhere during the last glass from jolly to maudlin, and he had gone into quiet mode. Sophie looked up and caught him staring at her.

'Are you OK?'

'I might have made a mistake.'

Sophie's expression said that she was unsure how to take this, and he carried on.

'With Helen. I think I might have made the wrong decision.' His voice was wavering.

Sophie sighed. 'What's happened?'

'I should never have left you. I should have stayed. I miss you and the girls.'

'If you're really not happy, then you have to do something about it. Now, before you get married or . . .' she struggled to say it '. . . have more kids that end up getting dragged into a break-up.'

'You feel the same, don't you? You'd like us all to be a family again?'

'Matthew, if you want to leave Helen, then you have to leave Helen, but don't do it because you think I might take you back.'

'But would you ever, do you think?'

'Is that really what you want?'

He nodded miserably. 'I think so.'

Sophie wished her head wasn't so fogged with alcohol. Was he really saying this, that he wanted her back, that he wanted to start again? She had no idea how that made her feel. Elated that she had won the battle against Helen, angry that he thought she would just drop everything and accept him back after all he'd done to her, sad that it could never be the same again anyway, incensed that he would just drop this on her with no build-up when he knew they'd both had a few too many. She shook her head to try and clear her thoughts.

'We can't talk about this now. It's not fair. Do whatever you need to do with Helen, and then we'll see what happens.'

'You're not saying "no" then?'

She almost laughed at the pitiful way he looked at her. 'I'm not saying anything. OK?'

'OK.' He placed his hand over hers, and she was too tired and drained to move hers away.

'Matthew, can I ask you something? I want you to be totally honest with me, OK? I want you to tell me the truth.'

'I will.'

'How long have you been seeing Helen? I just need to know.'

Sophie didn't notice Matthew's brief hesitation or the slight panic that fluttered across his face.

'About six months before . . . you know . . . I moved out.'

'So, when we went on holiday to Italy you were . . .'

'Yes, sorry.'

She nodded sadly. 'I enjoyed that holiday.'

'So did I . . . it wasn't . . . you know . . . like I didn't want to be with you when I was with you. I wasn't sitting there thinking "I wish I was with Helen."'

'Six months. That's the same as me and you . . . with Hannah,' sighed Sophie. 'At least it wasn't years. I'd hate to think our marriage had been a sham for years.'

Matthew gulped his brandy, looking down. 'No, it wasn't years.'

'Will you sleep in my room?' he asked when they were in the corridor on their way to bed. 'Not, like that, you know. Not unless you want to, of course.' He raised an eyebrow at her, smiling. 'Actually, I'd just like to know you were there.'

'I can't. I think I want to, but I can't. We'd regret it, even if we didn't do anything. At least, I would.'

'Can I kiss you goodnight?'

'No, Matthew.'

'I am your husband.' He tried his best drunken twinkle. Sophie laughed.

''Night.'

Despite the amount she'd drunk, Sophie barely slept. Her head was buzzing with everything that had happened. There was no way she could have seen this coming. She had thought they were edging their way towards a civilized twenty-first-century split which would ensure that their children suffered the minimum of mental trauma. She didn't like it, but she was getting used to it. She didn't know if she could trust Matthew, she didn't even know if she wanted him any more, but when she really thought about what was troubling her most at the moment, it was the fear that he would wake up tomorrow and regret what he had said.

30

Helen woke at six with a dry mouth. She felt about on her bedside table for a glass of water and, not finding one, she dragged herself out of bed and through to the kitchen to get one. She threw back a whole glassful and then poured another. On the way back to the bedroom, she picked up her mobile and switched it on, sure there would be a message from Matthew. It was unlike him that he hadn't phoned the flat to see how she was, even though he was angry with her. Her voicemail alert beeped – there he was – and she put the phone to her ear.

'You have seven new messages,' the robotic voice told her. Oh shit. He must've been trying and trying, getting more and more annoyed that she'd switched her phone off when she moved from the sofa to the bed. Well, too bad, he should have tried the home number, it's not as if he didn't know where she was. She pressed a key to listen to the first message. It was a woman, a voice she at first didn't recognize because it was slurring, and the woman was crying and babbling incoherently. And then she realized that it was Sandra.

'It's all shit,' Helen could just make out. 'My life's shit.'

She pressed to move on to the next message. Sandra again. 'Where are you?'

Three, four and five were similar: 'Where the fuck are you? I need you.'

Helen was anxious. She moved on to number six.

'There's no point. There's absolutely no fucking point. I'm a big joke. A big fat ugly fucking joke. Well, fuck it.'

Helen could just make out the rattle of what sounded like a bottle of pills underneath Sandra's crying. She scrabbled through a pile of papers on the desk in the living room, looking for a list of client addresses while she listened to message number seven. Nothing but laboured breathing and the occasional half-hearted sob. The message was timed at ten past four. Two hours ago.

Helen was out and in a taxi on her way to, where was it? . . . she looked down at the list again, Sandra lived in Shepherd's Bush . . . within five minutes. She had called an ambulance, slightly hysterical, giving them far too much detail about the distressing phone messages, when all she should have been giving them was the address. She couldn't understand why Sandra would have chosen to unburden herself to her of all people, they barely knew each other. Oh god, she couldn't cope with this on her own. She knew Matthew would be asleep and that he was annoyed with her anyway, but she couldn't think who else to call, she needed someone.

Matthew was, indeed, fast asleep, and sounded sleepy and irritated at the same time when he answered his mobile.

'What time is it?'

'It's Sandra, she's taken an overdose. She left me all these messages. I'm going over there. Shit, I'm really scared.' She was babbling.

Suddenly Matthew was wide awake. 'Helen, calm down. Tell me what's happened.'

Somehow she managed to find a coherent path through what had occurred so far, and she had barely finished when Matthew told her he was leaving straight away to come back up to London. Despite the fact that it would take him two hours and, god knows, it'd probably all be over by then, the thought that he was on his way calmed her immediately. He'd know what to do.

'Did you give her real name to the emergency services,' he was saying, already in work mode.

'Of course,' she replied realizing immediately that that had been the wrong thing to do.

'OK, I need to think about how best we handle this. Meanwhile, Helen, if you get there before the ambulance, wait outside. Don't go in on your own.'

'Really?'

'You can't do anything for her anyway. She's either OK or she's . . . not. I don't want you to have to go through that, OK?'

'OK.'

'Call me when you get there.'

Matthew thought about leaving a note for Sophie before he left, but he didn't know what to say. If he was honest with himself, he was glad to have an excuse to leave before she was up. He could remember every word of their conversation last night, and he had meant it. He was glad it had been said, and he wouldn't take any of it back, but without the alcohol to give him courage he felt embarrassed at the thought of seeing her, he wouldn't know how to act around her now he'd put his cards on the table. He left a message with the receptionist to tell Mrs Shallcross that he'd been called away for work.

He'd deal with Sandra first, and then sort out his personal life.

It would have been obvious which was Sandra's flat, even without the ambulance outside, because of the pink feathery curtains in the window and the twinkle of the fairy-lights behind them. Helen threw a tenner at the driver and ran up the steps to the front door just as it opened and two men in paramedic uniforms came out. They seemed remarkably cheerful, considering, and Helen would have sworn that one of them was carrying a signed photograph. Helen stopped in front of them.

'Is she . . . ?'

'False alarm,' the man holding the picture said.

'False alarm?' Helen was incredulous.

'Was it you who called us?'

Helen nodded.

'Next time, check your facts, love. She's fine.'

Helen pushed the flat door open and wandered in, confused. Sitting on the sofa in a pink dressing-gown and fluffy mules was a very not-dead Sandra, and holding her hand was a man who looked vaguely familiar. Oh yes, it was the waiter from the opening night of Verano. The one who had been pictured leaving with Sandra in the shot that had ruined her chances. Guido or Julio or something. Sandra blinked up at her.

'What are you doing here?'

'You called me, remember?' Helen couldn't believe what she was hearing.

Sandra looked at Guido/Julio, who shrugged.

'I called all sorts of people. Sorry. I was desperate.'

Helen balanced on the arm of a chair. 'So what happened? I don't understand.'

'Well, I was very drunk and unhappy, and I kind of remember taking the pills. Then, the next thing I know, Giovanni was here, and I was being sick, and then I felt fine. Sorry. I feel really stupid.' She blinked up at Helen, her mascara streaked down under her eyes like a sad panda.

Giovanni smiled. 'I broke down the door. I must've got here just after she swallowed them, 'cos I stuck my finger down her throat and they all came up. All of them.'

Helen was momentarily thrown by the fact that his accent was more Romford than Rome.

'The ambulance men said she'll have no ill effects because the pills weren't in her system long enough. Imagine what might have happened if I hadn't got here when I did.' He stroked Sandra's hand fondly.

'Yes, imagine. Well, Sandra, if you're sure you're OK, I'll leave you to it. Do you need anything?' Helen was backing out of the room.

'Giovanni'll look after me,' Sandra said coyly.

As she closed the front door behind her, Helen bumped into another young woman running up the steps.

'Does Sandra Hepburn live here?' She was sweating quite heavily.

'Yes. She's fine.'

'Is she? Shit, I called an ambulance as soon as I got her messages.'

'Go on in and see her if you want, I'm sure she'd be pleased.'

'What? No, god, I hardly know her. I've done her nails a couple of times, that's all. I'm surprised it was me she called actually.'

Helen could hear the sirens approaching as she walked round the corner looking for a taxi.

Sophie was woken by a banging on her door and Claudia's voice shouting over it. 'Mum. Mum, let us in.'

Convinced that something must be seriously wrong, Sophie jumped out of bed and ran to let her daughters in.

'Dad's gone home,' Suzanne said miserably. 'He told the woman on the desk that he had to go back to work.'

Sophie was stung. The girls were looking at her expectantly. 'Oh, right. Well, I'm sure it must've been something important.'

So that was it. He'd woken up regretting all the things he'd said to her and, in typical Matthew style, he'd run away rather than face the consequences. She felt ridiculous and foolish for having been taken in by him. The bottom line was he'd seen an opportunity and tried to take it. He hadn't changed.

Matthew was already on the M4 when Helen called to tell him the panic was over. He was thinking about Sophie and the look on her face when he'd told her how he felt.

31

Helen had left for her last day at work before Matthew even got home. She felt exhausted, the irritation she was feeling with Sandra outweighing the relief that she was OK. Matthew had phoned asking her to tell his temporary assistant, Marilyn, that he would be in this morning after all, but when she reached the general office, Annie and Jenny were hanging around, laughing about some unfunny thing or other with Jamie, so she went straight to her computer, hoping they wouldn't spot her, and sent Marilyn an email instead. She'd only been there a few minutes when Helen-from-Accounts appeared at her side holding a small, wrapped gift.

Oh god, thought Helen, not now.

Annie turned. 'Aaah, look, she's bought Helen a leaving present.'

All eyes turned to look at Helen-from-Accounts, who blushed.

'Do you think it's a packet of peanuts?' Jenny shouted, and they all fell about laughing at how hilarious they were. Helen rolled her eyes at Helen-from-Accounts as if to say, 'What a bunch of twats,' but Helen-from-Accounts had come over all teary-eyed and threw the present on to the desk before running out in the direction of the toilets.

Great, Helen thought. Here we go again. She picked up the small box and followed reluctantly.

'Jenny'll be getting jealous if you and Helen-from-

Accounts keep on going to the toilets together,' Annie called after her, and they all doubled up again.

Helen went through the usual rigmarole to coax Helen-from-Accounts out of the cubicle.

'You have to toughen up,' she said, when the other woman had finally stopped snivelling. 'They only do it because they know they'll get this reaction.'

'I can't help it.' Sniff. 'You're the only nice person that works here.' Sniff. 'Apart from Matthew, of course,' she added hastily, in case Helen – who couldn't care less – got offended. 'And now you're leaving.'

She started sobbing noisily again, and Helen patted her on the arm half-heartedly.

'Thank you for my present.' She started opening the little package, anything to distract the other Helen and shut her up. Inside was a gold necklace with 'Helen' spelled out in italics across the front. It was a carbon copy of the one which bobbed around on the throat of Helen-from-Accounts. It was hideous.

'It's beautiful, thank you. Really,' she managed to say. 'And I bet it's the only present I get today. It's really thoughtful of you.'

'I'm going to miss you so much,' Helen-from-Accounts wailed, and she threw her arms round Helen, her head reaching somewhere around Helen's chest. They stood like this for a few moments, Helen rigid as a broom handle, until she felt it was OK to break away and gently push the other woman off her. There was a small damp patch on her shirt in exactly the right place so she looked like she was lactating.

'You'll be fine, honestly. Just ignore them.'

'Will you keep in touch?'

'Yes,' said Helen, unable to imagine a single instance in which she might. 'Of course.'

The day dragged by endlessly. Matthew had said very little on the phone about how the funeral had gone, except that he had drunk a few too many brandies afterwards and had a bit of a sore head. Sophie's phone had been switched off all morning, and Helen was beginning to think that she wasn't making any progress with her plan when her mobile suddenly jumped into life and Sophie was on the other end.

'Where have you been? I've been calling you all morning.' Helen tried not to sound too impatient.

'I turned my phone off. I was trying to avoid Matthew, not that he's been trying to call me, as it turns out, or at least if he has, he hasn't left a message. Listen, I have to talk to you. Can you meet me tonight?'

Something must have happened. 'Definitely.'

'I don't want to ask Matthew to babysit, so do you want to come over to mine? You can meet the girls, not that that's much of a draw, I have to admit.'

Shit. 'Oh, fuck, I've just remembered I've got something on this evening. How about lunch? I've got meetings in Soho, but if you were around . . .'

'I'll meet you at the Stock Pot at one.'

'He asked me to sleep with him.' Sophie sat back, waiting for the full impact of her statement to take effect. 'And I nearly said yes.'

Helen tried to take in what Sophie was saying to her. She had hoped that a night away would push Matthew and Sophie closer together, but she hadn't quite anticipated this. Her immediate reaction was one of anger. Matthew, who was always declaring his overwhelming love for her, was away for one night, and he had asked someone else to go to bed with him. For fuck's sake, what was wrong with this man, was he incapable of being faithful to anyone? Almost immediately, though, while Sophie was filling her in on the details, her mood switched – this was fantastic. If Sophie would only say yes, she'd be off the hook, she'd have her life back.

'So why did you turn him down?'

'I really wanted to do it. In fact, I couldn't believe how much I wanted to. But I decided that if anything is going to happen, then I want to do it right this time. However much I hate Helen, I wasn't going to do to her what I did to Hannah. Anyway, I'm just relieved now that I did say no. I would have made a right fool of myself.'

Helen's stomach turned nervously. 'Why?'

'Because it was obviously just the drink talking. He snuck away before I even woke up this morning, left a message with reception about being called away for work or something, but what could have been that important? I mean, at six o'clock in the morning? And if it was genuine, then why hasn't he tried to call me since?'

Fucking hell, Matthew.

'Maybe whatever emergency he got called back for has kept him busy all morning.'

'There was no emergency.'

'Well, maybe he had a crisis of conscience. Felt bad about

it all and came home to dump Helen before things went too far with you. Like you said, to do things right this time.'

Sophie pushed her plate away, her food hardly touched. 'That's what I want to believe, but I just don't. It still doesn't explain why he hasn't called.'

Helen wanted to find Matthew and scream at him, 'This is your one chance of happiness, so don't blow it, because I'm not going to be around for much longer.' He was such a flake, so completely incapable of making an adult choice for himself.

'So you have decided you want him back then?' she asked tentatively.

Sophie took a long breath. 'Yes. I think so. At least I did last night. I couldn't sleep, I just kept thinking about him and what to do and I decided I should give him a second chance. Because I think he really means it. Or, I did. Now I don't know what to think, but I am not going to let him fuck me around again, I'll tell you that much. Am I being stupid?'

'Look, don't assume the worst, just wait and see what happens before you decide to write him off.'

Sophie looked tearful. 'I can't go through it all again. I really can't.'

They paid up and walked down towards Charing Cross Road, Helen pretending she had a meeting in Shaftesbury Avenue and wondering how far Sophie was going to accompany her before she had to go into a random building and wait there for five minutes before she dared come out again. As they crossed Cambridge Circus, she spotted Jamie coming the other way and stared steadfastly at the ground, willing him not to spot her.

'All right, Helen,' he called as he passed.

'Helen?' Sophie looked confused.

'He always gets my name wrong. Drives me fucking mad. First time I met him I told him my name was Eleanor and he obviously misheard it as Helen, and that's what he's called me ever since.' Oh god, she thought, please get me out of this. And even though she didn't believe in him, he did. Sophie's mobile rang and she dug it out of her pocket, looking to see who was calling.

'It's Matthew. Shit, what shall I do?'

'Answer it. I'll leave you to it.' Helen gestured vaguely up the road to imply she would keep walking. Sophie grabbed her arm.

'No, wait. I need the moral support.'

She pressed a button on the phone. 'Hi, Matthew.'

Helen shuffled awkwardly from one foot to the other. It was uncomfortable enough that she was listening to one end of her friend's intimate phone call, but the fact that that friend was talking to her own boyfriend who was calling clandestinely to discuss leaving her made it positively surreal. She tried to gauge what the gist was from Sophie's noncommittal answers.

'Mmm-hmm . . . I see . . . oh dear . . . I'm not sure . . . oh god, I don't know . . . OK . . . OK . . . OK . . . OK.'

OK what, for fuck's sake?

'OK . . . eight o'clock then . . . OK . . . bye.'

'Well?' Helen could hardly wait to find out what had been said.

'Apparently one of their clients tried to commit suicide, which, I suppose, does constitute an emergency. And he's been busy trying to deal with the fall-out all morning, make sure it doesn't go in the papers.'

Liar, thought Helen. The story had never got to the papers because Sandra hadn't been taken to hospital. Helen had made sure of it herself, phoning round the tabloids to gauge whether they'd got wind of anything and doing a good job of persuading the one who had that it was just a malicious rumour.

'And?'

'He's coming over tonight to talk about things. God, Eleanor, I feel really shaky. Am I doing the right thing?'

'Definitely. If it's what you want, then it's the right thing.'

'Shit, I need to get a hair appointment. I've got to run.' She kissed Helen on the cheek. 'Thanks for everything.'

'Good luck,' Helen said as Sophie hurried down towards Covent Garden. 'Call me and let me know what happens.'

She turned back towards Soho, feeling about a stone lighter. It was nearly over. Sophie would have her husband back, Matthew wouldn't end up alone, and she would. It was perfect. There was just a tiny shadow of unease in her – she could barely feel it and she had no idea why it was there, so she pushed it away. It was time to celebrate.

At five o'clock Laura appeared with a bottle of champagne and a cake. It was a pitiful turn-out – Laura, Helen-from-Accounts, Jamie, Matthew's new assistant and a couple of the IT boys who would turn up to anything if there was the promise of free alcohol. Annie made a big show of sitting out on reception and refused to take a glass of champagne with her. Matthew popped in briefly between meetings and, as he left, he touched Helen's arm and said quietly, 'I'm really sorry, I've got to work this evening. I forgot to tell you, I promised to go and see Danny Petersen's show.'

Danny was opening as the fourth replacement for the John Travolta role in a tour of *Grease* at an out-of-town theatre. Helen was tempted to say, 'Why don't I come with you?' just to see Matthew panic, but instead she said, 'Oh, poor you,' and smiled benignly at him.

'I'll be home late because I'll have to stay and have a drink with him, and then I'll be getting back from Guildford,' he added, pushing his luck.

'No worries,' she said thinking, 'Fuck, he's a really good liar.'

He kissed her discreetly on the cheek and she heard a squeal of revulsion from the reception area. Oh, fuck them, she thought, and turned Matthew's face round to hers and kissed him full on the mouth. Behind his back, she stuck two fingers up in the general direction of Annie and waggled them around. She heard Helen-from-Accounts and Laura laughing. When she broke off, Matthew looked surprised and . . . what? Guilty? It wasn't an emotion he experienced often, and he looked unsure how to handle it. She pushed him towards the door.

'Have a good time,' she called after him.

By quarter to six there was only Laura, Jamie and Helen-from-Accounts left, the IT boys having escaped down to the pub and Matthew's assistant having gone home to her husband. They downed their drinks half-heartedly, and Helen wondered what was the earliest she could say she was going home without looking ungrateful. A couple of the other directors popped their heads round the door to say goodbye, claiming to be too busy to stay for a drink and, then, rather unexpectedly, Alan came striding in. Doing his best to avoid even looking at Helen, he walked purposefully over to Jamie and handed him a few sheets of paper.

'I need that typed up before the end of the day.'

Jamie very deliberately looked at his watch and raised his eyebrows, and Alan turned to leave.

'Not staying for a drink, Alan?' Helen asked *faux* sweetly.

'No, thank you.' He kept on walking.

'Oh, hold on,' she continued. 'I've got something for you. To say thank you, you know, for being so supportive.' She held out a plain white envelope.

Alan turned suspiciously. He walked a few steps back and took it from her hand.

'Go on, open it now.'

He ran his finger along the inside of the flap, tearing the paper, and pulled out a single white piece of A4. As he scoured it, his face turned a bright, furious red, his lips tight with anger. Screwing the paper up into a ball, he turned and walked out of the room without saying a word.

'Bye, Alan,' Helen called merrily.

'What on earth . . . ?' Jamie started to say. Helen interrupted.

'It's OK, I made sure it was from long before your time, and I printed it off his computer, not yours, so he's not going to blame you.'

366

Back in his office, Alan smoothed out the crumpled sheet of paper and reread what was on it. It was a print-out of an email he had sent to Felicia, the woman who was most definitely not his wife, along with her reply. It read, 'I can't stop thinking about your luscious lips around my old man. I just had to knock one out in the toilets. Ax.'

And she had replied, 'Not long now, big boy. See you at the hotel at six for two hours of fun. Fxx.'

Alan sat down at his desk, sweat building up on his forehead. That fucking bitch Kristin, she must have shown everyone his private emails. At least Jamie was a man – he'd understand, he could be trusted.

In the general office Jamie had just promised to forward on any particularly juicy emails between Alan and Felicia to Helen's new computer, and because Laura and Helen-from-Accounts had only just found out about Alan's penchant for cyber sex, he had agreed to send them on to them as well.

The afternoon was winding down. Helen could see Annie hovering, wanting to come in and get her coat so she could go home but not wanting to be forced into saying goodbye, and she was almost tempted to open another bottle just to fuck her off, but instead she started to put the last few of her things into a box, indicating to the others that it was time to go. When she looked up from her packing, Helen-from-Accounts' little fat face had gone all pink again and tears were forming at the corners of her eyes. Her mouth had crumpled like a teething baby's. She tried to smile at Helen and failed.

Oh god.

Once again, Helen had to resist the urge to punch her.

'I just have to say goodbye to Laura before she goes.'

Laura had gone into her office to get her coat and bag. Helen followed her in and shut the door.

'You know you said there'd just be me, you, a secretary and an accounts person?'

Laura looked at her quizzically.

'Well, do you know who that accounts person is going to be yet, because Helen's never going to cope if she stays here?'

'Don't worry, I already thought of it. I'm going to ask her next week.'

'Is there any way you could do it now, because she's doing my fucking head in.'

Laura laughed. 'OK.'

Five minutes later, as Helen was putting her coat on, she heard a pig-in-an-abattoir squeal from Laura's office and smiled to herself. Shit, she thought, I'd better get out before she comes and thanks me. She practically ran out into reception, clutching her box. Annie and Jenny were huddled round the front desk. They looked away theatrically as she passed.

'Bye, cunts,' Helen shouted cheerfully as the lift doors closed. When the lift reached the ground floor, she pressed to go straight back up to the second again.

'I meant to say, "Bye, sad no-life, unattractive, witless cunts."' She waved as the doors closed for the second time, leaving Annie and Jenny staring after her open-mouthed, each trying to think of a suitable comeback.

32

Sophie was drinking Diet Coke and, though she'd offered Matthew a glass of wine, he'd opted for coffee. Neither of them was taking any chances this time. They had sat opposite each other, either side of the kitchen table, as if they needed to put a physical barrier between them, something solid to stop them doing anything foolish. At one point, Sophie's ankle grazed the table leg and she jumped, thinking she had touched Matthew, then laughed when she realized how foolish she must have looked. Matthew tried to hold her gaze, but she flicked her eyes down to the table. An awkward silence hung heavy in the air. Then –

'I want to come back.'

Sophie had guessed – hoped and dreaded by turns – that this was coming. She'd rehearsed what she might say in reply, planned whether to make him work for it or to throw herself on him and accept gracefully or to turn him down flat. What she hadn't managed to do was to decide which of those options she would pick when the time came. Now he'd said it, she sat staring at her glass on the table in front of her, her mind racing. She longed to be part of a whole family again and, for all his many faults, she missed Matthew's company and their shared history. No one else would ever be able to understand and equal her love for her daughters. No one else could (or would want to) reminisce with her about the minute details of their childhood. But was that enough to base a relationship on? History? Basically, did it come down to a fear of being alone? No, she decided, she'd got over that fear, she knew she could cope on her own now. There was no way she was going to put herself and the girls through the trauma of being let down again. If she was going to take him back, things had to be different – *he* had to be different – this time. She forced herself to look up and meet his gaze.

'How do I know things would be better this time?'

'I've changed. I'll prove it to you.'

'But you tried to get me into bed while you were still with Helen. How's that you changing?'

Matthew took her hand across the table. 'I was drunk. I was desperate. I want you back so much. But I do want to do it the right way this time. And I'm going to tell her . . . that it's all over.'

Sophie knew she should be firmer with him, insist that he finish with Helen regardless of whether or not she would agree to take him back. Make him do that first before she would even discuss it with him, to prove that he was serious, but she was scared of losing the moment, scared that he would change his mind if she made things difficult for him.

'Matthew, I can't go through what we just went through again. Not ever. Don't do this to me if you don't think you truly mean it.'

'I do. God, Sophie I really do.' Matthew was close to tears. 'I'd never expect you to take me back after what I did, but if you do . . . god, I'd never do anything wrong ever again. I promise you that.'

'And you have to be honest with me. Really, really honest.'

'I will.'

'And no more working late or squash or whatever, because it's going to take me a while to trust you again.'

She had used the present tense – it's going to take me a while – not 'It would take me a while,' as if it was still speculative, as if it might not happen at all, but 'It's', as if she had made up her mind. It hung in the air between them.

'Anything.'

'I feel uncomfortable, them all knowing at Global and . . . her still working there with you.'

'She's left – Helen. She's gone with Laura.'

Ah, Sophie thought, so that's why Laura could barely look me in the eye at the restaurant opening.

'But I've thought about it anyway. I can set up on my own, scale things down, work less hours. Maybe work from home a couple of days a week.'

Sophie placed her other hand on top of his. 'You deceived me for six months Matthew. *Six months*. That's a long time. I have to know that that deception is over and that it'll never happen again.'

'I promise,' he said, and a tear rolled off his face and on to her hand.

They sat in the big kitchen, talking and drinking tea and Diet Coke, until past midnight. The girls had come in to say goodnight, dragging themselves away from the Xbox half an hour after their prescribed bedtime because Sophie and Matthew had forgotten all about them.

'What are you doing?' Claudia had said, pulling a face. 'You're holding Mum's hand.'

Sophie was grateful that she had just said to Matthew that they shouldn't get the girls' hopes up until everything was finalized, because she knew that he was dying to jump up and hug them and make a big statement about the fact that he was coming home to be with them again and they were all going to live happily ever after. There was a tiny nagging feeling deep down inside her that told her to tread carefully. Not to go issuing a statement just yet. It's natural, it's self-preservation, she thought. There's nothing wrong, I just need to protect myself.

'Of course we're holding hands, we like each other.' Matthew, Sophie realized, was looking slightly unhinged with the emotion of it all.

'And you look like you've been crying. Gross.'

By the time Matthew left for home, they had decided that he would break the bad news to Helen the following day, and that once that was done, he would stay in a hotel for a week, for what Sophie described as a 'cooling-off period', before he returned home. Matthew had pushed to be allowed to move back in straight away, but Sophie was adamant.

'I want to know one relationship is completely over before the other begins. Just for once.'

He had agreed reluctantly, knowing that he had to play things her way for a while. When he left to go back to Camden, they had hugged each other but agreed not to kiss.

'It's not fair on Helen,' Sophie had said, wondering when she had become so reasonable.

*

Helen had spent the evening home alone, bored out of her mind with her own company. There was no one – literally no one – she could call up for a drink. Apart from Sophie, that is, and obviously that was out of the question this evening. Rachel had been taken by the domestic-bliss body-snatchers, and even though Helen thought about calling her to see what she was up to, she quickly decided there was no point. Besides, Rachel hadn't called her since their slightly snippy conversation about cutlery, and Helen didn't see why she should be the one to make the first move. After all, she wasn't the one who'd changed. Ten years as best friends, speaking several times a day, and then, overnight, they had nothing in common. If she didn't have Sophie, then that thought would be almost unbearable. But, of course, she knew that soon there would be no Sophie either, because she was confident that Matthew was on his way back to his family and, as soon as that happened, she would have to break off all contact. Tell Sophie she was moving away or something, and then never return her calls. Leave them to repair their broken marriage and herself to her new single life. She had a new job – well, a career now – and she would soon have her freedom back. She'd just have to do without friends for a while. Her liberty would come at a price, but it was a price she had decided was worth paying, although, when she thought about the endless evenings with nothing to do and the lack of anyone to share her thoughts with, she felt like crying. Fuck this, she was never meant to get to *like* Sophie. Befriending her was an accident, a mistake, a ridiculous French farce turn of events.

She tried to wait up for Matthew, but the hours

dragged and, when the clock moved past midnight, she decided to throw in the towel and go to bed, secure in the knowledge that it must be going well or he wouldn't be out this late. When he finally got home, just before one, she was sound asleep, and he crept around the room so as not to wake her. He felt elated. He was being given a second chance with a woman who loved him. His family would forgive him, his friends would drift back one by one, he could go back to a normal, comfortable life, and he would try – really try – to make it work this time. But when he looked at Helen sleeping peacefully, her head thrown back on the pillow and one arm flung across the whole width of the big double bed, he felt overcome with guilt again. He had no idea how his life had become so complicated. He would just have to tell her straight in the morning, put her out of her misery quickly. He tried to rehearse ways to break it to her gently:

I've made a mistake.

It's not you, it's me.

I've fallen back in love with my ex-wife (maybe not).

It's for your own sake – when you're my age, I'll be eighty, what sort of a life is that to look forward to? Yes, he thought, drifting off to sleep. That was a good one.

'OK.'

'OK?'

'OK.'

'I tell you I want to break up, and you just say OK?'

'Well, what do you want me to say? Good? Me, too?'

Matthew was stunned. He had woken at seven and spent two and a half hours gearing himself up to this moment, which he'd attempted to soften by bringing Helen tea in bed.

'Don't you want to know why?'

'Let me see, Danny Petersen's performance in *Grease* was so moving you've decided you're gay.'

'Don't be so facetious.'

Helen stretched. 'How was Danny's performance, by the way?'

'Good. Fine. Can we get back to the point? The thing is, Helen, I've been thinking, I'm twenty years older than you . . .'

He stopped when Helen laid her hand on his arm. 'Listen, we both know it hasn't been going well. I've tried to end it myself before, but you wouldn't have it. Now, I don't need a big explanation from you about why you've changed your mind, it's fine, we both agree finally. It's the right decision, Matthew. Don't feel bad.'

He knew he should be relieved that she'd taken it so well, but it riled him that she didn't seem to care at all.

'Don't look so irritated. What, you'd rather I was heart-broken? You'd rather I sat here saying you'd ruined my life?'

Upstairs, the Rabbits were getting into their stride. 'Oh, baby. Yes, baby. Yes. Yes. Yes.' The headboard thundered against the wall.

'I just can't believe that what we've been through means nothing to you. That you can be so flip about us breaking up, that's all.'

'Jesus Christ. Listen to yourself. Look, you want to

break up. So do I, as it happens. Everyone's happy. Claudia and Suzanne will be delighted.'

'This has nothing to do with Sophie and the girls,' he said defensively.

'I didn't say it did.' Helen couldn't hide her smile. 'I just said they'd be pleased. Have you told them yet?'

She noticed he couldn't look her in the eye. 'Of course not. This is about you and me.'

The Rabbit crescendo was rising. All the old favourites were coming out, including, 'Call me Daddy,' which had become a regular fixture. Then, just as Mrs Rabbit was shouting another, 'Yes, yes,' another voice, unmistakably female, joined in with an orgasmic squeal of, 'Oh Daddy. Fuck me, Daddy.' Helen looked at Matthew.

'I don't fucking believe it. He's got two of them up there.'

Matthew rolled his eyes. 'Forget about them. We're having an important conversation here.'

'What the fuck is it? I mean, is it pheromones or something, because it's certainly not his looks or his sparkling personality?'

'Helen . . .'

'Doesn't that bother you? Aren't you curious at all?'

'Helen, for fuck's sake. Have you been listening to what I've been saying to you?'

'You want to split up. It's nothing to do with Sophie.'

Matthew sighed and got up from the bed. 'Is this some kind of joke to you?'

Helen forced herself to turn her attention back to him. 'I hope you'll be happy. Whatever you decide to do.' She noticed him looking at her sceptically. 'I mean it.'

So that was it. Four years of her life, four years of fighting for her man and passing up other opportunities and allowing friendships to slide and her self-esteem to follow. And it had all come to what? To a feeling of relief that it was finally over and a wave of regret that she had thrown away so much time and energy on what had been – all along, it had turned out – a lost cause. She felt deflated – but it was the wasted years, the time she would never get back, that depressed her, not the thought of a life without Matthew.

When Helen got out of bed, Matthew was packing a suit-case in the living room.

'Where will you go?'

'A hotel for a few days, till I sort myself out.'

'Good for you.'

Then she felt bad that he looked a bit pathetic, a grown man trying to cram all his possessions into two cases and a couple of hold-alls.

'You don't have to move out straight away, you know. You can stay here till you decide where you want to go.'

He smiled at her gratefully and with genuine warmth. 'No. Thank you, but I want to make a clean break. I think it's best.'

Partly because it felt awkward to watch him packing up, and partly because she wanted desperately to call Sophie and hear her version of the story, Helen decided to go for a walk to kill a couple of hours. She reached the top of the steps from the basement just as the Rabbits came out of the front door along with another, rather beautiful, young woman. Helen realized that she was staring with an expression that must look very like disgust at the idea that they had somehow managed to lure this girl into their bed. She jolted herself out of it and said hello.

'Oh, this is my sister,' Mrs Rabbit said, indicating the other woman. 'She's staying with us for a few days.'

Jesus Christ.

Helen opened and shut her mouth, but nothing came out. Mr Rabbit jumped in.

'Actually, we were wondering whether you'd like to come up for a drink one night. You know what London's like, you live above someone for years, and you never really get to know them.' He snorted a laugh that was meant to be friendly but came out more Dr Crippen than Dr Phil. 'Not properly anyway.'

Oh god.

Helen decided to ignore the invitation.

'Erm . . . your bed . . . I was wondering if you could move it. It's over a big crack in the ceiling, you see, and I'm afraid you'll all come tumbling down on top of me one night. Well, not all of you, of course. Just . . . ' she indicated the two Rabbits '. . . you two obviously. Well, anyway, thanks.'

She moved off down the path without waiting for a reply, waving over her shoulder as she did so. Fucking great – now she'd have to move. One of the greatest things about London was the fact that no one ever spoke to each other, because the minute they did you'd realize that they were fucking insane and you had no choice but to get as far away from them as possible. She walked round the corner to the scrubby patch of green beside the lock that passed itself off as a towpath, ignoring the group of young men, hoods up, openly selling cannabis, and called Sophie's number.

'So?'

'Oh god, Eleanor, he wants to come back, and I've said yes. At least, I sort of have, I've told him he's got to finish with Helen first and move out, and then we can try and start again. Have I done the right thing? Oh god.'

Helen laughed. 'Calm down. Tell me all about it.'

'I think he's really changed. And then I think am I just being a sucker and Helen's thrown him out and he needs somewhere to go or something. But I don't think so. I think he's for real.'

'Slow down.'

'Sorry. Sorry. I'm just, I'm all over the place. How are you?'

'I'm fine. Just tell me how it went.'

'He seems different. He said that he'll leave Global and set up on his own so he can spend more time at home.'

'Wow,' said Helen, who knew that, for Matthew, work was everything. Maybe he really had changed. For her friend's sake, she hoped so.

'And he was honest with me. Probably for the first time ever. He told me he'd been seeing her for six months before he moved out.'

Helen felt her elation dissipate. 'Really? Six months?'

'I know – it's awful, isn't it? I'm trying not to think about all the things we did in that time. All the excuses he made when he was home late or whatever. Mind you, he was always home late, so I didn't notice anything different. But . . . I think that's a big step, him telling me the truth, because he knew it'd upset me, but honesty won – and I appreciate that.'

'Six months?' Helen was still trying to take this in.

'Exactly the same as me and him with Hannah,' Sophie said sadly.

'That's a coincidence.'

'I feel bad about Hannah. I can't believe I cared so little about her at the time.'

'I'm sure she's happy. It's been a long time.'

They arranged to meet for a drink on Monday night, which, Helen knew, would have to be the last time. After that, Eleanor was dead, without even a surname to put on her gravestone. Helen sat on a bench wondering what to do next, feeling utterly deflated. This ought to have been a great cause for celebration, the day she'd been waiting for for the past two months. She had her life back. At least, she didn't, because she didn't want her old life back – what she had was the chance of a new life. She had herself back. So why did she feel like crying?

33

Matthew had moved out by the end of Saturday, checking himself into god knows where with his cases and hold-alls. Helen had happily agreed to let him come back and pick up the rest of his things later on – some of which were still in boxes from his last move. She had never really made him feel at home in her flat, she thought, with a tinge of guilt. In the end, there had been no battle over Norman, who sat, oblivious, on the sofa while Matthew packed up around him, because, of course, Matthew knew he was going back to Sophie, and Sophie was allergic. The flat felt twice the size, even with some of his things remaining, and Helen felt a prickle of pleasure at having her own space back. No more toy cars or felt slippers. No more Sunday afternoons nervously awaiting the return of Suzanne and Claudia. Hopefully, Matthew had learned a few things and was going to be a better father now that he had had to acknowledge that Suzanne wasn't a genius, she was just an ordinary girl who was a bit too eager to please, and now that Claudia was free to come top in exams without fear of stealing her sister's thunder. The weekend stretched out before her and on into the following week, and she had nothing – literally nothing – to do. Well, she would enjoy it, she was determined she would. She would pamper herself and do all those things she never had time for before her new job started in two weeks' time – if only she could remember what those things were.

On Sunday she slept in until midday with Norman – previously banned from the bedroom at night-time – stretched out beside her. It felt right to be on her own. Scary, but right. She would build her life up slowly, piece by piece, and this time she would make no mistakes, she would make sure everything was right, work, friends, home and, maybe, eventually, a boyfriend – but this time, one who definitely didn't belong to someone else. She would never do that to another woman again. She would start with her career – she'd been given a chance and she intended to put her heart and soul into making the most of it. Everything else could wait.

She briefly thought about Matthew and Sophie. Six months, he had said, and Sophie had believed him. Helen wished she didn't know that he had lied to her so soon.

The only thing she did on Monday was to call Sandra to break the news she had forgotten to give her on Friday, that she had failed to get a nomination at the Ace Awards. She knew that it would come as no surprise and she knew that Sandra had probably found out for herself by now, but it felt like a loose end, and she wanted to do the professional thing and pass on the news herself. Sandra sounded surprisingly bubbly when she answered the phone.

'Oh, fantastic,' she said, when Helen asked her how she was feeling, apparently having forgotten her suicide attempt of three days ago.

'Oh, well,' she said, when Helen told her the bad news about the awards.

'Sandra, what's going on?' Helen asked, confused.

'I'm giving up showbusiness. I'm going to stop trying to be a celebrity, which, let's face it, I should have done a long time ago. And I'm going to go and live in Italy with Giovanni and have babies and milk goats or whatever it is they do.'

'Giovanni?'

'You know Giovanni. From that restaurant. Anyway, it turns out he's only been over here for a couple of weeks – he lives in Siena now, even though his mum and dad are in Clacton – and he was temping as a waiter to pay for his trip. He had no idea who I am. I mean it, no idea. He'd never heard of me, never seen my picture in the paper – well, till the day after that do, you know. But he still looked after me and took me home and didn't try and sleep with me. And now he does know who I am he doesn't care. And I'm so happy.'

'Listen, I'm really really pleased for you. I think it's great. A fairytale.'

'Thanks . . . sorry, who is this again?'

Helen smiled. Sandra might be giving up celebrity, but it didn't seem as if she was going to be any less self-obsessed. 'It's Helen.'

'Oh, Helen, sorry. You've always been really nice to me, thanks.'

'Good luck,' Helen said as she ended the call. God knows Giovanni could turn out to be a wife-beater or a drunk or a cross-dresser, Sandra barely knew him, but she sounded so happy and, Helen thought, she deserved a bit of happiness.

*

Sitting at a corner table in the Lamb in Lamb's Conduit Street, Helen tried not to think about the fact that she would never see Sophie again. She had thought about telling her tonight that she was moving away, but she couldn't face the goodbyes and had decided to go for the coward's way out – be unavailable for the next couple of weeks, take longer and longer to return calls and then, once Sophie had begun to tire of her flakiness, announce she was going away. She wanted tonight to be fun, and she wanted to hear all the details of Sophie and Matthew's reconciliation. Had she seen him since he had moved out? Had he told her that Helen had wanted the break-up as much as him? Had she slept with him yet?

The pub was packed with office workers out for a quick one before they set off on their journeys home, all hoping to avoid the evening rush hour on the tube. Helen was sitting in the quieter back room near an open fire, jealously guarding the empty chair opposite her. Christ knew how long it would be before she got to go out for a drink in a pub again – it wasn't something she could – or would want to – do on her own. Pubs required friends and, currently, she had none. Or boyfriends – ditto. Maybe she and Laura could be friends once they started working together, stop off for the odd drink to talk about work and find they had things in common to chat about. It was a definite possibility – three months ago she'd hated the woman, now she was genuinely fond of her – at this rate, she'd be in love with her by Easter. Or Helen-from-Accounts? No, that didn't bear thinking about. She took another long sip of her vodka and cranberry. Piece by piece, career first, and then she would worry about her lack of a personal life. She just had to keep reminding herself that that was the plan.

Sophie was ten minutes late, as always. Helen had adjusted her mental clock so that an arrangement to meet Sophie at six thirty actually meant twenty to seven. She looked at her watch – six forty-two – Sophie was two minutes late. Right on cue, Helen saw her friend pushing through the crowd, looking flustered as if she'd been rushing, but also unmistakably flushed with something other than the stress of fighting her way through the rush-hour crowds. Helen had never seen anyone glowing before, but Sophie was doing a pretty good impression of it. She stood up and hugged her. Sophie shook her wet umbrella, put it on the floor underneath the table and sat down.

'You look . . . amazing.' Helen gave her an exaggerated look, up and down.

'I feel great. I've made the right decision, I know I have.'

'So, has he done it? He's broken it off?'

'He has. He's staying in a hotel round the corner from us. Do you know what's insane? That I felt sorry for Helen. He told me that she begged him to stay, used all kinds of emotional blackmail, but that he knew he was doing the right thing.'

Helen bit her tongue. She'd just about got over caring for her own sake that Matthew always felt the need to paint her as the weak, desperate one, but the fact that he was still doing this now while at the same time promising Sophie that he had changed was *so* infuriating.

'Really? I thought you'd got the impression that she was losing interest anyway. Didn't he say . . . ?'

'Well, apparently not. Anyway, I'm not going to lose any sleep feeling bad about her. She obviously didn't feel bad about me those whole six months . . .'

'Obviously.'

'And it's over. He's promised never to have any contact with her again.'

Helen could feel her anger rising on her friend's behalf. Fucking hell, that man was incapable of telling the truth.

'Don't they have things to sort out? I mean, he moved out pretty quickly . . . all his stuff?'

'In storage.'

'Right. Well . . . good for him.' She couldn't get involved, couldn't worry about this, it wasn't her problem any more. Sophie had got him back, which was what she wanted. It was up to her whether or not to fall for his bullshit again. But Helen could see why she had. He was so plausible, so vulnerable, so fucking manipulative. How did he keep getting away with this? The answer was simple. Because women – like herself – allowed him to. They *enabled* him. She thought about coming clean with Sophie, saying, 'I'm her, I'm Helen,' and then exposing all his lies, but the whole idea was too terrifying, she wouldn't know where to start. Sophie would probably think she was playing some kind of sick joke, or she'd just attack her – hadn't she once said that she wanted to kill her rival? There was no point getting involved. She would just have a couple of drinks, say goodnight and leave them to it. She'd done her bit, she'd done what she had set out to do, she'd put the world to rights – now it was up to them. If Sophie was stupid enough to allow him to walk all over her again, then that was her problem.

'I'll get us a drink.' Helen stood up. 'What do you want?'

And then Sophie said something which made Helen's knees buckle and the room start to swim in front of her eyes.

'Oh, wait for Matthew to get here. He'll be here any minute.'

She thought she must have misheard.

'Mmm?'

'Matthew, he's just parking the car, and then he's going to pop in and say hello. He gave me a lift down, and I wanted him to meet my friend. He'll only stay for one, because he's got to pick up the girls from their friends . . .'

Helen didn't hear the rest of what Sophie said because all the blood from her head had rushed down to her feet and she was having to concentrate on not falling over. She sank back down on to her stool again.

'Oh. Great,' she said weakly.

She tried to think straight. She had to get out before he arrived. She could feign illness, but that might take too long, with Sophie fussing over her before she could make her escape. Fuck it. She was never going to see Sophie again anyway, so she would just pretend she was going to use the toilet and then simply walk out. It would be a mystery, but at least they would never know the truth or, if they did work it out, then she would never have to be confronted by it.

She stood up again, legs shaking and picked up her bag. Her coat she would have to leave behind.

'I'm just going to the ladies,' she said and turned round to find herself looking straight at Matthew. His expression was a mixture of anger, confusion and fear.

'Helen?'

She was trapped. She thought about making a run for it, but she would have had to push Matthew out of the way. Sophie was looking at them, bemused.

'Matthew, this is Eleanor, my friend I was telling you about.' She looked from one to the other. 'Do you two know each other?'

Helen stood there dumbstruck, looking at the ground. There was nothing she could do to save herself here.

'Eleanor?' Matthew was saying. 'This is Helen.'

Helen couldn't look at Sophie's face.

'I don't understand,' Sophie said quietly. 'Eleanor, what's going on?'

'What the fuck have you been doing?' Matthew growled.

The truth was starting to dawn on Sophie. 'You're not . . . ?'

'I can explain,' Helen muttered.

Matthew practically pushed her down into a chair in the corner. She was trapped, one of them on either side and the table in front of her. A few other drinkers were looking in her direction, fascinated by the drama. Her eyes filled with tears.

'Go ahead,' he said tersely.

Helen looked up at Sophie for the first time, and her expression floored her. All of the glow had left her, she looked confused and vulnerable, not wanting to take in what she was being told.

'I'm sorry.'

'I'm waiting.' Matthew ignored her apology. Helen took a deep breath and looked at Sophie.

'You were never meant to know.'

'What is this, some kind of fucking game?' Matthew interrupted.

'I felt bad about what I'd done. I realized I didn't want Matthew any more and I felt awful that he'd given up his family.' She looked up and saw Sophie staring fixedly at her. 'I thought I could try and help you get back together. Put things right.'

'You made up this whole thing? You . . . engineered our friendship to try and fuck with my life even more? I confided in you. I told you . . . things. Christ, you fucking bitch.'

Sophie had raised her voice, and the people on the other tables were riveted.

'No. No . . . making friends with you, that was never meant to happen. I just wanted to see what you were like, because I was feeling so guilty about what had happened, and then I fell over, and then . . . well . . . then I got to like you. You were my friend. And I wanted to try and put things right.'

'Whatever it is you're trying to do, it won't work. I want Sophie back, and there's nothing you can do to get in the way of that.' Matthew was practically spitting.

'That's what I'm trying to say. I want you and Sophie to get back together.' She turned to look at him. 'I don't want you, Matthew. When you turned up on my doorstep, I thought we could try and make a go of it. But we couldn't. And then I realized I didn't want you any more, but you were so pathetic I couldn't just throw you out. I thought . . . well, I know now it was a stupid idea . . .'

'Pathetic? You begged me. Begged me to leave Sophie. And now, just because I don't want you any more, you're trying to ruin things for us. I should never have got involved with you. Sophie's right, you're a bitch.' He put his hand territorially over Sophie's.

Helen met Sophie's hostile gaze.

'It's true. I did beg him to leave you. Over and over again. For how long was it, Matthew?'

Matthew flushed a furious red.

'Six months,' Sophie said coolly.

'And let's not forget the other three and a half years,' Helen added quietly, turning to stare Matthew down.

'Don't listen to her.'

'Four years, Sophie. That's how long we were together. And I'm not proud of that. Believe me, it sickens me. And I'm not telling you that because I want to hurt you, I'm telling you that because you need to know he's still lying to you. He's never going to change.'

'She's the one who's lying,' Matthew insisted, but Sophie was looking at Helen intently. Neither woman looked at him.

'Remember that time you thought Claudia had meningitis and you couldn't get hold of him because his phone was turned off? She must have been, what, eight at the time? That's because he was with me. Or the time you were meant to go on holiday to France and Matthew cancelled at the last minute? My fault, I'm afraid. I'd just had an abortion and I threatened to tell you if he didn't stay and look after me. Trust me, I'm *really* not proud of that.'

'Fuck you.' Sophie nearly spat in her face.

'You're too good for him, Sophie. Don't do it.'

'Fuck off. Just fuck off.'

'I'm going.' She stood up, and Matthew moved his legs to let her pass.

'Oh, and his stuff.' Helen turned back to Sophie. 'It's not in storage, it's at my flat.'

'That's not true.' Matthew glared at her.

Helen was still looking at Sophie. 'Sophie, I'm really really sorry. For everything. I was a bitch for the last four years, but I've been trying to make up for it. I know you won't believe me, but it's true. I've really valued our friendship and I'm really going to miss you.' She felt a tear escape down her cheek. 'I know you're never going to believe that but it's true.'

'Please go. I don't want to listen to you any more.'

'I know. Just . . . I know it's none of my business . . . but I care about you, I really do. Just think hard before you take him back. He's still lying to you, Sophie. He's incapable of behaving any other way.'

'Matthew and I are getting back together, and there's nothing you can do about it,' Sophie half-called after her as she left.

'You came on to my son? You came on to my fucking son?'

Helen banged the phone down. She didn't know why she'd answered it, she'd known it would be him, no one else ever called on the home number. She wiped her eyes, poured herself another glass of wine and lay back down on the sofa feeling – temporarily – all cried out. She didn't know why this hurt so much, she never had to see either Sophie or Matthew again, so what difference did it make if they knew what she'd been doing? What difference did it make if they hated her?

It was the fact that she had been so close – she'd been home and dry, everyone had got what they wanted, she would be thought of sympathetically as poor old Helen who had been stupid enough to think that Matthew could give up Sophie for her, she could move on knowing she had done a good thing. Now, she felt dirty, like a criminal, like a pervert who had insidiously oiled her way into other people's lives for her own ends. Of course they didn't understand that she'd been acting with their own interests at heart – Why would they? It was insane – even she didn't understand it.

In desperation, she called Rachel, knowing it was pointless, they could never get their old intimacy back.

'Bali or Mauritius?' Rachel sounded chirpy, clearly she hadn't even noticed that their friendship was on the rocks.

'I don't know. Rachel, it's all fucked up,' she sobbed loudly.

'Jesus, Helen, what's up?'

Helen couldn't get the words out. When she tried, a sort of gurgle drowned out what she was trying to say.

'Stay where you are. I'm coming over.'

'Will you?' Helen felt pathetically grateful.

'Of course. Shit. I can't, I've got someone coming round about flowers at eight. And then we're going away for a couple of days first thing – to look at venues,' she added, slightly sheepishly.

'Never mind,' Helen managed to say.

'Tell me about it now – I've got five minutes and then I could call you back later, once the bouquet person's gone.'

'Don't worry. I'll talk to you soon, Rach.'

'No . . . wait . . .' Rachel started to say, but Helen had cut the call short.

34

The next few weeks passed in a kind of haze. Helen felt numb, as if she was observing things through a thick fog rather than participating. She couldn't decide what she was more depressed about, the fact that Sophie had now thrown away her life on a man who would – inevitably – fuck her over again in the future, or the fact that she, Helen, had orchestrated the whole thing. She had spent the rest of the week, before she started her new job, painstakingly packing up the rest of Matthew's belongings, which were now stacked up in the hall. She was beginning to think that he was never going to come and get them, but she couldn't bring herself to throw them away, nor was she about to call him and ask him what he wanted her to do with them. She had endured two days of angry phone calls from him before she had decided to unplug the phone and leave it unplugged. She only answered her mobile to Laura and her mum – and Rachel if she ever got around to calling, but she never did. Well, she would make a decision about his belongings when she moved – she had given in her notice at the flat and was half-heartedly looking for new places, although there was something about being told again – at nearly forty – that you weren't allowed to keep a pet or that you mustn't hammer a nail into the wall to hang a picture, that she was finding utterly soul-destroying.

There was no getting away from it – she missed Sophie. She had known she would, of course, and she thought she had prepared herself for it, comforting herself that she was doing the right thing by her friend. It was bizarre that someone she had known for such a relatively short time should leave such a big gap in her life. Bigger than the loss of Rachel, her confidante of ten years, or at least it felt that way at the moment. Maybe it was because she knew that Rachel would drift back once the wedding hysteria had died down, although their friendship could never be the same – because Helen now knew she couldn't count on her to be there regardless. Or maybe it was because she realized there was only one person she wanted to call right now to share her troubles with – and she was never going to be able to speak to that person again.

The first couple of weeks at her new job were lonely, setting up the office in Marshall Street on her own, sitting by a phone that rarely rang. She knew she should be out hustling for new clients, but at the moment it took all her energy to drag herself home on the tube for *Emmerdale*, pasta, wine and then bed. When Laura joined her on week four and their assistant Rhona shortly after, she started to feel like she was waking up, and work became a friendly alternative to being home alone. It was still a few weeks before Helen-from-Accounts would arrive with her hilarious postcards of anthropomorphized kittens and coffee mugs adorned with witty sayings. Helen knew she would be wanting to put up posters in the kitchen about washing up after yourself before too long, and she had already decided to have a quiet word asking her not to bother.

Occasionally, Laura and Helen went to the pub after work, which broke up the week, although they were still at the stage where they mostly talked about business and, though they got on, hadn't yet found much common ground elsewhere. Sometimes Laura accidentally mentioned Matthew, who was still, apparently, at Global, with no signs that he was intending to leave to spend more time with his family. Of course not, Helen thought bitterly, he's got her where he wants her now, why should he?

As a favour to Sandra, Helen placed a 'Sandra turns her back on celebrity' piece because, although Sandra had chosen to bow out quietly, she hadn't chosen to bow out *that* quietly, and that led to several follow-up stories about how Sandra had really been a good girl at heart, looking for love all along. Before she saw it coming, Sandra was signing a contract for a reality TV show following her first steps in her new life in Italy, and Helen had agreed to take on all her PR. Walking with a demurely dressed Sandra through Soho after leaving a press conference to announce the commission, about two months after the night that she spent a lot of time trying not to think about, Helen stopped dead as she saw a familiar figure. Up ahead of them was Matthew, striding along with that overconfident walk he had when things were going his way, and walking next to him, holding his hand while she struggled to keep up, was a woman. A woman who wasn't Sophie.

'Jesus,' Helen found herself saying out loud.

'What? What is it?' Sandra strained to see what Helen was looking at.

Matthew and the woman – who, though attractive and

with the requisite long brown hair tied back in a loose ponytail, was most definitely in her fifties, which was unusually appropriate for Matthew – stopped outside Global, where they kissed, on the lips, in full view of the world.

'Isn't that Matthew?' Sandra said, starting to wave. Helen grabbed her flailing arm.

'No . . . I don't want him to see me with you. He might be upset . . . you know . . . that you left Global and went with me,' she said, knowing full well that Global had dropped Sandra weeks ago.

Matthew went up the steps and into the building, and the woman turned back the way she had come and walked straight past Helen and Sandra, who were still rooted to the spot. She smiled vaguely as she passed them in that way people sometimes do at strangers, and Helen thought she looked . . . *nice*. She didn't look like a homewrecker, she looked like someone's slightly glamorous but homely aunt. Like someone who would look after you when you had the flu while still remembering to put on her lipstick.

It was unbelievable. No, wait, it was all too credible given Matthew's history. Maybe a bit sooner than she'd expected, but inevitable just the same. Matthew was incapable of sticking with one woman at a time, he lived his whole life terrified that the grass was greener somewhere else or that somewhere there was a party he ought to get himself an invite to. He'd conned Sophie into taking him back, and now he was doing this to her . . . and it was all Helen's fault.

Helen hugged Sandra goodbye and wished her luck for filming, which started in two days' time with a scene in which – it had already been decided – Sandra would make a spontaneous decision to throw out all her skimpy outfits, which weren't going to suit her new life and personality. She walked back round to the office – the 'Carson PR' sign still gleaming bronze outside – and shut herself in her own small room. She had no idea what to do. This was none of her business. This was *so* none of her business, but she couldn't bear to sit back and let Sophie have her life ruined all over again. Shit, why did she have to see him? Why did she care? She was sitting with her head in her hands, staring at the top of her cluttered desk, when Laura came in and Helen found herself confiding the whole story to her.

'Don't get involved.'

'I can't just let him get away with it.'

'I mean it, don't get involved. What good can it do?'

'I can get her to see what he's really like before they get too serious again. I don't know.'

'My guess is they're serious already. Leave it alone.'

'Oh god.' Helen laid her head down on top of a pile of papers. 'Oh god. Oh god. Oh god.'

At six o'clock she persuaded Rhona to go to the pub for a quick one, where she downed three large glasses of wine while she listened to the twenty-three-year-old assistant's sweet but inane ramblings about the merits of Usher *versus* James Blunt. By the time she got home, she knew she was pissed, and she knew it was a bad idea, but she sat down with another glass anyway and punched Sophie's mobile number into her phone. If she answered, Helen would hang up – she couldn't face another fight and, besides, Matthew might be there listening in to the other end of the call. If it went to answerphone, she would leave a message – saying what, she hadn't quite decided, she realized, as she heard the ring tone change to indicate the call was going on to voicemail and then Sophie's voice telling her to leave a message.

'Erm . . . god . . . Sophie, it's . . . erm . . . Eleanor, well, Helen . . . you know . . . me. Oh shit, this is such a bad idea. Erm . . . I'm not calling to apologize again because I know you don't want to hear it, and I know you hate me at the moment.' At this point she sniffed loudly and a drunken tear rolled down her cheek and landed on the sleeve of her jumper. She dabbed at it with her spare hand.

'Anyway. I have to tell you something and . . . please hear me out, don't hang up . . . I'm not doing this out of any kind of revenge or anything other than that I feel bad that I pushed you back towards Matthew and now he's screwing someone else behind your back. Again. Shit, that's what I've got to tell you – I saw him with another woman and I'm not imagining things, he was definitely *with* her, if you know what I mean. I don't know about the screwing bit, but I'm guessing . . . knowing Matthew. I want you to know what he's like – that he hasn't changed, and you shouldn't let yourself get dragged through all that again. You're too good for him. Way, way too good for him. And . . . I'm going now. Thanks for listening. If you did. Sorry. Bye.'

She pressed the red button to cut the call off and then immediately dialled again.

'It's me again . . . if you get this call first, then don't

listen to the other one. I can't remember what order they play them back to you in. But, if you do, don't listen. Ignore it. Oh . . . and if you've already listened, then sorry. Bye.'

Oh fuck, she thought once she'd hung up, I didn't say who it was that time, which means she'll definitely listen to the other call, just to find out. She considered ringing for a third time, but even in a slight alcoholic haze, she could see that that would be stupid and would turn the whole thing into even more of a Ray Cooney farce than it already was. It was fifty fifty; Sophie would either hear the bad news or she wouldn't. It was out of Helen's hands.

She woke up in the early morning, clothes on, TV blaring, lying on the sofa still in her shoes. Her mobile phone lay on the floor beside her. Oh shit, she thought. What the fuck did I do that for? She switched it off, half-stumbled to the bedroom, took off her top layers and crawled into bed hoping to sleep some more. She found herself thinking about Leo, though, something she didn't allow herself to do very often. How had he felt when he heard the news that the woman he'd kissed was his father's girlfriend? His potential new stepmother. That must've been a good day, like walking on to the set of *Jerry Springer*, the only one who doesn't know why he's there about to be humiliated. And how about the fact that she had talked to him about her disastrous relationship that she was trying to get herself out of? With his father, he must now realize. Oh, and the small fact of her lying to him about her name, her job, pretty much everything. Except the fact that she fancied him, Helen thought. That bit was true.

35

Spring moved into early summer, and Helen waited for a response from Sophie, jumping every time she heard her phone ring, but there was nothing. Either she never listened to the message or she had decided to ignore it. Helen didn't know what kind of response she was expecting – anger, probably – but after she got over the relief that it was looking like she'd got away with it, she began to feel cheated. How could Sophie just turn a blind eye to a piece of news like that? What was wrong with her?

Helen knew that the gossip machine must have gone into motion, that everyone she knew must know that Matthew had gone back to his wife, although the sympathetic looks she often got from mutual acquaintances made her think – gratefully – that Matthew must have kept the whole Helen/Eleanor saga to himself and was allowing her to play the victim, which suited her just fine. Helen-from-Accounts had mentioned tentatively one day that Geoff had a friend who might be a good match for Helen, and Helen had wondered (aloud as it happened, although she hadn't meant to) whether suicide might be a better option.

One morning, Helen arrived for work and found Laura, Helen-from-Accounts and Rhona standing round a large messy-looking chocolate cake with 'Happy 40th,

Helen,' written on the top in squiggly writing. She was late, and they'd clearly given up waiting for her and were having a conversation about *EastEnders*, so she had to cough to let them know that she was there so that they could launch into a painful version of 'Happy Birthday'. Helen had been trying to forget about her big day, and she didn't know whether to laugh or cry for a moment, but when she thought about the fact that these three women were the only people in the world who had remembered her birthday – not her mum and dad, not Rachel, not any of her other friends who she saw once a year – she opted for crying, which brought the singing to an abrupt end.

'I made the cake myself,' Helen-from-Accounts said, which made Helen cry even more.

To make matters worse, they had bought her a gift – a very tasteful bracelet, which Helen guessed (rightly) that Laura had chosen – and they went out for lunch to the local dim sum restaurant and drank Tiger beer and went back to the office late and slightly giggly. Helen felt both awkward and flattered about the fuss the others were making, and tried not to think about how depressing it was that the sum total of her forty years amounted to this random little bunch of people she had ended up working with. At the end of the day, they tried to persuade her to let them take her down the pub, but she knew they were only doing it because they felt they should, and that they all had lives they wanted to get home to and, besides, the beer from lunchtime had given her a headache, so she claimed other plans and went back to her flat.

*

She was putting some pasta into a saucepan when the doorbell rang. She had long since stopped expecting Matthew to come back for his things but, even so, the jarring croak of the bell made her stomach lurch and her heart start to pound. She felt sick with nerves as she half-crept to the front door to peep through the spyhole. A flickering light – a candle maybe – seemed to be burning outside her door against a white background, like a benign version of a Ku Klux Klan ritual. There didn't appear to be a face attached, or at least none she could see. She could just tiptoe back down the hall and hide under her duvet until they went away, but curiosity and the fact that she felt pathetically grateful that someone – even if it was someone who hated her and was likely to throw petrol over her and use the candle to light it – had remembered her birthday combined to overcome her nervousness, and she turned the key in the lock, putting the chain on first.

The white cardboard box – for she now saw that's what it was – contained a large cream and fresh fruit birthday cake with one lit candle sticking out of the centre. As the door scraped open on the mat, the box was lowered, and Helen saw Sophie looking – rather blankly – over the top of it.

'Happy birthday,' she said, in a voice that was impossible to read. 'It is your birthday, isn't it?'

Helen was thrown. She had often imagined a fraught and anger-filled meeting with Sophie one day and, in her lowest moments, had comforted herself with a well-crafted – and deeply unlikely – fantasy in which her former friend came round to say she forgave her for everything and they somehow picked up exactly where they had left off before it all went wrong (only with Helen being Helen and not Eleanor, of course). But this Sophie didn't seem to have read either of those scripts and was now standing awkwardly on the doorstep, cake in hand, looking like she didn't know what to do next. The fact that she'd brought the cake, though – and lit the candle in quite a festive way – that surely had to be a good thing. Unless it was poisoned, of course.

'God. Thanks.' Helen blustered. 'I can't believe you remembered.' And then, realizing she had to do something to break the stalemate, 'Do you want to come in?'

'OK. Just for a minute.'

Helen led the way down the corridor wishing she'd tidied up at any point in the past month.

'So,' Sophie was saying, looking round, 'this is where Matthew was living.'

'Erm . . . yes.'

There was what seemed to both women an endless silence. 'Have you come to pick up his things?' Helen said eventually.

Sophie didn't answer her question. 'I got your message.'

'Oh . . . I was drunk. I'm sorry. I really wasn't trying to make trouble . . .' She ran out of steam.

'It's OK, I know all about her – Alexandra – I've known for a while.'

'Right.' Helen realized Sophie was still holding the box and took it from her. 'It's a lovely cake.'

'Isn't it?'

'I'll get us a drink. You will stay for a drink, won't you?'

She opened a bottle of Pinot Grigio and poured two large glasses, then went back through to the living room and sat on the chair opposite the sofa where Sophie was now sitting. What the fuck was going on? She took a deep breath.

'Sophie. Don't get me wrong, it's great to see you, but I don't understand. Last time we saw each other – well . . . let's just say I wasn't expecting you to remember my birthday.'

Sophie took a long sip of her wine. 'To be honest, I don't really know what I'm doing here. I felt bad knowing it was your birthday and knowing you might be sitting here on your own . . .'

'Because I have no friends . . .'

'. . . because you have no friends. Understandably.' She half-smiled. 'And I wanted you to know something, just because . . . well, I just wanted you to know.' She breathed in deeply, looking at Helen over her glass. 'Matthew and I aren't together.'

'Oh. Right . . . Alexandra.'

'No. Alexandra came later. She's very recent, actually, they met at some kind of divorcee meeting. She's nice, I like her, but it's early days and it might be too much to hope he'll stick with someone who's his own age.'

'She *looked* nice.' Helen had no idea where this conversation was leading.

'I hated you that evening,' Sophie carried on. 'You have no idea how I felt, having to take all that in – about you, about Matthew.'

Helen was looking intently at a spot of dirt on the coffee table. 'I'm sorry.'

'But I knew you were telling the truth about the fact that he was still lying to me. I thought you were telling me because you wanted him back for yourself . . .'

Helen snorted despite herself.

'. . . and then I realized it didn't even matter if that was the reason, the fact was, he hadn't changed and he was probably never going to. So I told him I wasn't going to take him back.'

'How did he take it?'

'Cried, shouted, blamed it all on you. At one point, he was definitely considering asking you if he could come back here, though – he hates being on his own.'

'Shit, I really messed everything up. If it wasn't for me, you wouldn't even have got close to him again. I should've just told him that night when he turned up on my doorstep that it was wrong, that I didn't want him. Saved us all a lot of trouble.'

'You should've never fucked my husband in the first place.'

'That too. I'm sorry.'

'I haven't come here to try and give you a hard time. I just thought you deserved to know, that's all. How it all turned out.' Her voice softened. 'I know you were worried about me. At least, that's what I gathered from those drunken messages.'

She put her glass on the table and stood up. Helen suddenly felt more than anything in the world that she wanted to keep Sophie there long enough for them to patch up their friendship properly.

'Don't go. Please. Have another glass of wine.' But Sophie was putting her coat on.

'I don't think I should. It feels . . . weird. I don't even know what to call you.'

'What about the cake? At least help me eat it. You can't bring me a whole cake and then leave me to it.'

'Oh,' said Sophie. 'I meant to say. The cake, it was Leo's idea.'

'Leo's?'

'He made it.'

'For me?'

'No, for someone else. Of course for you.'

Helen felt a lump rise in her throat. 'How is he?'

Sophie looked at her tentatively, and then lowered her voice to soften the blow. 'He got married.'

So that was it, the end of that particular fantasy Helen had somehow allowed herself to indulge in where Leo came knocking on her door telling her he couldn't live without her and, so what if she had been shagging his dad only a couple of months ago, he loved her. 'He got married? Who to?'

Sophie laughed. 'Oh, sorry, did I say he got married? I meant to say he got a new car. Of course he hasn't got married.'

Helen managed a laugh. 'How could you do that to me? I mean . . . obviously I've done much worse to you . . .' she added, feeling as if she had to keep apologizing for her behaviour. Sophie interrupted her, still smiling.

'I'd rather we didn't keep bringing it up, to be honest.'

'So, truthfully, how is he?'

'He's good. He said to say hello.'

'He did? And he made me a cake?'

'It's taken a while for him to get used to the idea that

his father was Carlo – that *he* was the reason you didn't get together. There wasn't a real Carlo as well, was there? I get so confused . . .'

'No!' Helen was indignant, and then remembered she had no right to be. 'Honestly.'

'Because if you ever get involved with Leo I for one would kill you if you messed him around.'

If she ever got involved with Leo? Had Sophie really just said that?

'Erm . . . do you think that's possible, that we might ever . . . ?' The question hung in the air between them.

'Elean . . . Helen, we have to take this one very small step at a time. Who knows what might happen further down the line, but we have to all agree that it's nothing but the truth from now on.'

Further down the line? That implied they were going to see each other again. That there might be a future for their friendship. And who knew what else.

'Of course.'

'To be honest, I don't want to hear anything more about you and Matthew, but I do need to know who's Helen and who's Eleanor, if you know what I mean. I don't even know if I know who you are. All I do know is that I miss whoever I thought was my friend and I'd like to see if I can get that back.'

'Me too.' Helen was near tears.

'So I thought maybe we could go for a drink, start again, and see how we get on.'

'Really? Yes. Please.' Don't beg, she thought. 'That'd be great.'

'But you have to promise me you won't get in touch

with Leo till I say it's OK. Not a thing – not even to say thanks for the cake, because I know what he's like . . . I don't want you anywhere near him till I know I can really trust you. OK?'

To Helen, this felt like the most reasonable request she'd ever heard.

'OK,' she said, starting to smile. 'I promise.'

They stood in the living room, slightly awkwardly, for a moment, neither quite knowing what the next step should be. Did they make a date to go out for a drink? Did they leave it and Helen be left like a lovesick teenager, waiting anxiously for Sophie to call her? There was a blast of cool evening air as the cat flap swung open and Norman breezed in from the small back yard, shaking the length of his body huffily to dry himself. It had started to rain outside.

'Oh, is this Cushion?' Sophie asked, and then looked as if she was about to sneeze. Helen grabbed him up and bundled him into the kitchen, shutting the door behind him.

Helen sighed. 'Actually, his name is Norman.'

'Right. Of course it is.' Sophie's tone betrayed a tiny streak of irritation. 'Claudia's cat.'

Helen grabbed a pile of photographs from a small table in the corner. 'I've been keeping these for her, as a record of how he's doing. Look,' she said, brandishing one of the pictures in front of Sophie, 'he caught his first mouse. I was going to send them to her . . . one day . . . but I didn't know . . . well, you know . . .' She ran out of steam. She knew that Norman coming in had just reminded Sophie that everything about her was a lie, that she couldn't even assume the tiny, insignificant details she thought she knew were true.

'Well, anyway . . .'

Sophie took the photographs from her and put them in her bag. 'She'll love them, thanks.'

Helen inhaled deeply. 'And obviously, I'm not a successful PR either. Not yet, anyway.'

'I gathered that,' Sophie said. But she smiled when she said it.

'I'll tell you what,' she continued, starting to take off her coat again. Helen held her breath. 'I will have another glass of wine. And you can start to tell me who you really are.'